THE
GREATEST
Evil

ALSO BY
WILLIAM X. KIENZLE

The Rosary Murders

Death Wears a Red Hat

Mind Over Murder

Assault With Intent

Shadow of Death

Kill and Tell

Sudden Death

Deadline for a Critic

Deathbed

Marked for Murder

Eminence

Masquerade

Chameleon

Body Count

Dead Wrong

Bishop as Pawn

Call No Man Father

Requiem for Moses

The Man Who Loved God

THE
GREATEST
Evil

WILLIAM X. KIENZLE

Andrews McMeel
Publishing

Kansas City

www.andrewsmcmeel.com

98 99 00 01 / RDH 10 9 8 7 6 5 4 3 2 1

Library of Congress Cataloging-in-Publication Data

Kienzle, WIlliam X.
The greatest evil / William X. Kienzle.
      p.   cm.
ISBN 0-8362-5206-3 (hardcover)

1. Koesler, Robert (Fictitious character)—Fiction.
2. Catholic Church—Michigan—Detroit—Clergy—Fiction.
3. Detroit (Mich.)—Fiction. I. Title.
PS3561.I35G74 1998
813'.54—dc21   97-37738
CIP

CREDITS
Editor: Donna Martin
Associate Editor: Matt Lombardi
Production: Chuck Harper
Production Editor: Polly Blair
Book Design: Edward D. King
Jacket Design: George Diggs
Composition: Hillside Studio, Inc.
Printing and Binding: R.R. Donnelley & Sons Company
Harrisonburg Division

ATTENTION: SCHOOLS AND BUSINESSES
Andrews McMeel books are available at quantity discounts
with bulk purchase for educational, business, or sales promotional use.
For information, please write to Special Sales Department,
Andrews McMeel Publishing, 4520 Main Street,
Kansas City, Missouri 64111.

For Javan

My wife

and

collaborator

Acknowledgments

Renée DeRoche, Director of Camp Operations, St. Vincent de Paul Society, Detroit

Inga Eccles, Organist

Sister Bernadelle Grimm, R.S.M., Pastoral Care Department, Mercy Hospital, Detroit (retired)

The Reverend Anthony Kosnik, S.T.D., J.C.B., Professor of Ethics, Marygrove College, Detroit

Thomas J. Petinga, Jr., D.O., FACEP, Chief of Emergency Services, St. Joseph Mercy Hospital, Pontiac

Arthur Schaffran, Director of Substance Abuse Services, Beyer Hospital (retired)

Werner U. Spitz, M.D., Professor of Forensic Pathology, Wayne State University

Mary Helen Wegrzynowicz, Lay Procurator Advocate, Archdiocese of Detroit

With special thanks to the reference staff of the Detroit Public Library and to Pete Fierle, Information Services Manager, Pro Football Hall of Fame, Canton, Ohio

Any technical error is the author's

In memory of the Reverend William C. Cunningham

THE
GREATEST
Evil

1

1953

It was the middle of July, but Bob Koesler was shivering.

He tugged at his sweatshirt. Still it did not cover his swim trunks. He pulled the bulky towel more tightly about his neck. That didn't help; the towel was wet. He hugged himself as he shifted from one foot to the other. There was no getting away from it: He was freezing.

He probably would get out of this alive. But he didn't have to like it.

His discomfort was by no means unique. This was the ninth consecutive summer he'd been a counselor at Camp Ozanam.

O-Z, as it was more casually known, was financed and run by the St. Vincent de Paul Society. Catholic parishes affiliated with S.V.deP. were given tickets to distribute to financially distressed boys. The only expenditure for each camper for the entire two weeks' stay—there were five such tours each summer—was the five-dollar round-trip discount bus fare from Detroit.

O-Z was located some thirty miles north of Port Huron. It helps to know that Michigan is mitten-shaped. The camp sat just south of the thumb's knuckle. The western border was U.S. 25, the extension of Gratiot Avenue, which began in downtown Detroit.

Its eastern border was mighty Lake Huron. And that is where Bob Koesler was at the moment: shivering atop a diving tower in Lake Huron about thirty-five yards from the shore.

No diving would be permitted today; the water was too rough. Near gale force winds blew from the north. Ordinarily frigid, the water this day was only relatively bearable. Thus counselors having beach or even water duty were less tested. The genuine torture was reserved for the poor wretches on the towers: They had to swim to their stations.

Which Koesler had done. After all these summers at camp, the maneuver was well practiced: He wrapped towel and sweatshirt around his left arm, then sidestroked, with his right arm and the scissors kick.

Once safely atop the tower, the lifeguard would dry himself, then use the towel and sweatshirt for as much warmth as they would afford. But the combination of water and wind-chill factor regularly challenged the counselor's immune system.

A casual observer—or trained philosopher—might ask why: Why program a swim in such challenging conditions?

Answers might range from, Because the lake is there; or, Such challenges make men (or kill in the attempt); or, Because a consensus—to swim or not to swim—could not be arrived at.

Probably the last reason came closest to a truer explanation. If the campers—all two hundred of them—were assembled on the beach and not one of them wanted to enter that threatening water, undoubtedly the swim would be canceled. But with two hundred boys, there were always a few who were impervious to cold water. And if those foolhardy souls chose to swim, then counselors would necessarily play lifeguard.

Safety, especially water safety, was given high priority at camp. The swimming perimeters were clearly defined. Each swimmer was assigned a buddy who had to stay nearby; each was responsible for the other. Periodic buddy checks took place: At the head beachman's signal, each and every camper in the water had to stand silently holding his buddy's hand aloft.

Koesler had played lifeguard so many times the routine was now automatic. Perhaps that was a contributing reason why he did nothing but watch as a developing situation called for action.

Due to the weather, few boys were in the water this morning. But a solitary lad was trying to swim out to Koesler's post. He was supposed to have a buddy in order to even enter the swim area. But no kid was within the prescribed proximity. Where was his buddy? In trouble?

That question, however, did not even occur to Bob Koesler; he was too interested in what was happening to the camper who was trying to reach his platform.

This lad, fighting his way through the water, arms flailing, legs thrashing, head turning from side to side with mouth and nostrils held above water level, was not a class swimmer under the best of circumstances. And these were nowhere near the best of circumstances. As the waves washed over him, the dogged boy continued his flailing struggle. And, as might be expected, in his attempts to gulp down air, he instead swallowed water. And then, also to be expected, he panicked.

Koesler watched as the boy repeatedly disappeared beneath the waves—where, presumably, he bounced off the lake bottom—broke the surface, coughed, momentarily gulped air, then disappeared and eventually reappeared again . . . but always a little nearer the tower.

What was remarkable—and memorable—was the fact that throughout this episode, not once did it occur to Koesler that he should go get the boy.

Such an action was, after all, Koesler's responsibility. A swimmer was in trouble. Koesler should have blown his whistle—the signal for just such an emergency as this. The swim would have been halted and immediate steps taken to help the camper. This would involve Koesler's dropping towel and sweatshirt and diving into the water.

Of course he'd have to do that at the end of the swim period in any case. But this was not the end. If he dove in now, he would, after rescuing the kid, have to climb back on the tower. Once again he would have to battle the renewed wet cold. And, after all, the camper was making progress: With each submerging, the lad was getting nearer the tower.

As luck—or the power of prayer—had it, the swimmer reached the tower, somewhat the worse for a near-death experience. At which point Koesler spotted the missing buddy: He was swimming—much more easily than his pal—toward the tower.

With the two youngsters now hanging on to the platform, Koesler crouched down and assured them that it would be much easier going in to shore than it had been coming out.

In time, the two pushed off and made their way with, instead of against, the waves.

Only then did Koesler reflect on what had just happened.

That, he concluded was *dumb*. In time—and particularly because it had ended well, it would be funny. But for now he was guilty of an insensitive and derelict reaction to a potentially dangerous emergency.

Of course, he told himself, he had not taken his eyes off the swimmer. If there had been an immediate problem, the lifeguard would have acted at once. Nevertheless, he should have been in the water, supporting the youngster.

The two buddies made it to shore without further incident. For them there were no aftereffects. Not so for Koesler, who was left with a troubled conscience. But he had little time to mull over his actions: A whistle sounded, short and sharp. It emanated not from the head beachman's tower on shore, but from a nearby tower in the water.

Koesler turned to see fellow counselor Pat McNiff dive. Without hesitation, Koesler dropped towel and sweatshirt and dove in the general direction McNiff had taken.

A few strokes and a couple of thrusting kicks brought Koesler to the side of a camper who was almost literally scared stiff. Koesler was joined by McNiff and Vince Delvecchio, the third counselor on tower duty.

The water, at this point, was some five-and-a-half-feet deep. Since Koesler and Delvecchio were a few inches over six feet tall, the two were able to stand on the bottom and, allowing for the waves to wash over them, still support the camper, who was frightened but otherwise unharmed.

McNiff, considerably shorter than the other two, was treading water. Suddenly the light dawned. "Are you guys standing on the bottom?" There was rancor in McNiff's tone.

"Uh-huh," Koesler and Delvecchio chorused.

"Shit!" McNiff turned and swam back to his tower, there to brood over a cruel fate, not to mention genetic codes, that decreed each individual's height and build.

Still awash with guilt over his recent selfish reaction, Koesler volunteered to carry the camper to shore. For either of the two tall counselors, it was only a short walk. Delvecchio nodded and Koesler carried out the uneventful rescue.

The Present

Father Zachary Tully chuckled. "So that's the way you got to meet one of Detroit's auxiliary bishops . . . over a drowning kid?"

"You mean," Father Robert Koesler said, "something like, 'I'll carry this kid to shore and . . . uh, by the way: Just who are you?' No, nothing like that . . . although if Vince Delvecchio hadn't been a counselor at Ozanam, I doubt that I would have gotten to know him well—or at all."

"You *were* in the seminary together?"

"Yes, of course. But Vince was five years behind me. Which meant that I was in college when he was in high school. When he was in college I was in Theology. And by the time he got to Theology, I was ordained a priest. You know how that goes, Zack: In the seminary in the good old days you got to know who the guys ahead of you were, but you weren't as likely to know the guys younger than you—especially if you're looking at a time frame of five years or so."

"I suppose . . ." Tully mused. "Except that in a Josephite seminary it wasn't that difficult to know just about everybody. There weren't that many of us."

Zachary Tully had been ordained a Catholic priest in a religious community known as the Josephites. Basically, the order staffed parishes that served Afro-Americans.

Tully's father was Afro, his mother Caucasian. Aside from a few so-called black characteristics, he could easily have passed for white.

He had come to Detroit almost a year ago. Ostensibly his mission had been to deliver an award to an outstanding Catholic layman who had been extremely generous to the Josephites.

Parenthetically he had parish-sat St. Joseph's downtown so that Koesler could take a most rare vacation. And, as luck would have it, Father Tully had become involved in a homicide investigation.

More important to Father Tully than his official presentation assignment, his substitution for Koesler, and even his participation in solving a murder, was his meeting with a half-brother when neither had previously known of the other's existence.

Lieutenant Alonzo "Zoo" Tully shared a father with Zachary Tully. They had different mothers. Alonzo's mother—black—became a single parent when his father suddenly and simply left Detroit, his job in an auto factory, and abandoned his family.

The senior Tully had settled in Baltimore, where he met and married the woman—white—who would become Zachary's mother. She in turn became a single parent when her husband died shortly after Zachary's birth.

Zoo's mother was Baptist. The denomination held no relevancy for Zoo. For as long as he could remember, he had been absorbed with police work. This single-minded dedication had cost him a wife and five children, as well as a live-in relationship.

He was now in his second marriage. Anne Marie, his present wife, was Catholic. And, until his brother Zachary appeared on the scene, Anne Marie had been Zoo's principal link to Catholicism.

That changed radically with Father Tully's arrival in Detroit.

Zachary's mother and her family were staunch Catholics. They saw to it that the now fatherless Zachary was steeped in this faith.

As a result, it was quite natural that Zachary was attracted to the priesthood. Indeed, Zachary was as dedicated to his priesthood as was Zoo to his homicide squad.

Before leaving on his mission to Detroit, Zachary—whose mother was now dead—was told by his aunt about his brother.

Where Zachary had been intrigued by the relationship, Zoo was incredulous. As a boyhood Baptist and an adult irreligious, it was a radical shock for Zoo to learn that not only did he have a hitherto unknown brother but, notably, that this brother was a Catholic priest.

However, Father Tully had quickly been absorbed into Zoo's family life.

Having carried out his mission, helped solve the homicide case, and bonded with his half-brother and sister-in-law, Father Zachary Tully had prepared—a bit reluctantly—to return to his Dallas parish—despite everyone's urgings to stay.

In this, Father Koesler had been particularly persuasive. He announced that he was about to retire. He offered the pastorate of St. Joseph's to Zachary. Of course, that appointment was not Father Koesler's to give. But he was confident that he could convince Cardinal Boyle, Detroit's archbishop, to make the assignment.

The Josephites granted Father Tully a leave of absence from his religious order. The Detroit archdiocese welcomed him and conferred on him faculties that empowered him canonically to exercise his priesthood in Detroit.

So it came to pass that Father Koesler now was on the brink of retirement. Father Tully was about to take over as pastor of Old St. Joe's, though the assignment was not yet official.

Several testimonials had been given by various individuals and groups in observance of this retirement. Koesler had been deeply touched. But on each such occasion he had assured his friends as well as former and present parishioners that he would always be available to them. His priesthood by no means was about to end; it would merely take on a different form. Since he would no longer be responsible for the nitty-gritty of parochial life, he would be even more accessible.

But on this balmy thirty-first day of July 1998, Koesler would host the final retirement party.

Father Tully of course would co-host. He had been living in the rectory for the past few weeks. By a happy good fortune, Zoo and Anne Marie Tully's home was within walking distance of St. Joe's rectory.

In addition to the two priests, present at tonight's party would be Zoo Tully and Anne Marie, Inspector Walter Koznicki and his wife Wanda, and auxiliary bishop Vincent Delvecchio.

Walt Koznicki had for a record number of years headed the Detroit Police Department's Homicide Division. Since Father Koesler had helped solve a series of murders of nuns and priests many years ago, Koznicki and Koesler had become fast friends.

There was no essential reason for Bishop Delvecchio's presence. But he and Koesler, though disagreeing with some frequency, had nevertheless been friends for a long while. And, in keeping with that friendship, they had composed a ceremony over the delivery of the Cardinal's document giving Koesler Senior Priest status.

As yet it was early. Koesler and Father Tully were alone in the vast rectory. The caterers would arrive later.

Meanwhile, Father Tully was pumping Koesler for as complete a backgrounding as possible into the thought processes, values, and theological bent of Bishop Delvecchio. After all, Father Tully would be expected to deal with Delvecchio rather than with Cardinal Boyle. Routinely, the auxiliary bishops were the court of first appeal. The court of final appeal was the Cardinal—who was much happier when disputes and questions were settled without his involvement.

2

"I'm Johnny-Come-Lately on this scene," Father Tully said. "Of course, I've been a priest for twenty-one years, so the oils of ordination are pretty dry by now. But I've been in Detroit only a few weeks—even counting the time I relieved you last year. All the other Detroit priests know their way around. As far as Detroit is concerned, I might as well be newly ordained— especially when it comes to Bishop Delvecchio. And he's already on my case. So far, all you've told me about him is that you and he rescued a kid at a summer camp."

Father Koesler laughed and ran both hands over his freshly shaved face. "Well, there you are, Zack. Ask me what time it is and I'll tell you how to make a watch.

"Seriously . . . there's a method in this madness: Vince has the reputation of being rather conservative."

"Does he ever!"

They both laughed.

"Well," Koesler said, "it was not always thus. I think—I really think the best way of telling you all you need to know about Vince Delvecchio is with a few anecdotes. And I'm starting at Camp Ozanam because that's where I first got to know him. I'm aware that all you can gather about him from what I've told you is that he can swim. But trust me: A couple more stories and we'll have a good foundation."

"Okay." Tully shifted in the upholstered chair to a position of greater comfort. "Fire away."

After a moment's thought, Koesler asked, "When you were a kid, did you ever go to camp . . . I mean far enough away from home so you were stuck there for a week or two?"

Tully smiled. "You're kidding. Summer was spent on the streets of Baltimore—literally. Street ball and cement hockey were our games. The only thing I had going for me was that I could pass. And I wasn't telling any of the white kids I played with that I was black."

"Gotcha. But if you had been from a poor—or relatively poor—family in Detroit and your Catholic parish had a unit of the St. Vincent de Paul Society, you might have qualified for Camp Ozanam—or Camp Stapleton if you were a girl.

"The minimum age for O-Z was twelve . . . or so the regulations said. But S.V.deP. councils sent much younger kids; some of our campers were only seven or eight. Their extreme youth, plus the fact that some kids simply missed home, inevitably caused an epidemic of homesickness, especially in the early days of the two-week stay.

"Each counselor had his own way of handling homesick kids—increasingly mechanical, as the season wore on. Like: 'Shut up and do what you should be doing now!'

"At this point, I must tell you, in all the summers I was there, I don't think a single kid made it home before the scheduled bus return. Oh, it wasn't that hard getting started: The camp was right on U.S. 25. And many's the kid who tried it. But we had lots of checks through the day. And if someone did make a break for it, a bunch of counselors would hop in Old Betsy, the camp Model-A, and sure enough we'd find a kid with his thumb out. And after a brief chase, we'd catch him and drag him back to camp so he could enjoy his vacation."

Father Tully was smiling, but the look in his eyes said, When do we get to Delvecchio?

"You're probably wondering when I'm going to get to Vince . . ."

Still smiling, Tully nodded vigorously.

1953

There wasn't a cloud in the sky. The heat was crushingly intense. It was early August. A fresh batch of campers had descended on Ozanam just two days before. Time enough for them to discover that Lake Huron was still formidably frigid, there was plenty of discipline, the air was friendlier to lungs than Detroit's smog, in most cases camp food was not like home, and with all these complaints there was no momma to wipe away a tear.

At the same time, the staff was stagnating. This was the beginning of the fourth trip of the season. So far, over six hundred boys had spent their two weeks at camp. And there was still a fifth trip to come.

Each summer, this period was known as the Fourth Trip Jitters.

Among those suffering from homesickness was one lad determined to do something about it. But what? He had heard from boys who had been at this camp in previous seasons that there was no escape.

The truth was that the overwhelming majority of campers were having the time of their lives. But this fact served only to intensify the misery of those who pined for home. Tommy had to get out of here!

He wiped away his tears with the back of his hand, sat on his bunk— it was early afternoon rest period—and pondered.

Among the more impressive aspects of this camp was how very Catholic it was. This fascinated Tommy. The campers attended Mass daily. Daily! At home, Tommy's family did well if they went to Mass a single day other than Christmas and Easter.

Then there was the grotto.

Just across the long footbridge over a deep ravine, tucked away in the woods, was an idyllic grove. Statues of Mary, the Blessed Mother, and of Ste. Bernadette Soubirous made claim that this was a sacred spot. It was Camp Ozanam's extremely humble response to the famed and miraculous grotto in Lourdes, France.

O-Z's grotto boasted no crutches, braces, or wheelchairs discarded by cured clients. Its statues lacked here a nose, there some toes and fingers. But the grotto was a place where campers and counselors gathered periodically to pray.

Tommy thought long about that poor grotto until a plan formed.

He approached the bed where counselor Vincent Delvecchio, having found a rare moment of quiet, was trying to nap.

"Counselor . . ." Tommy stage-whispered.

Delvecchio forced one eyelid up. "Go back to bed."

"But, Counselor, I gotta talk to you."

"Talk to me when we aren't sleeping."

"It's an emergency."

"You gotta go to the bathroom? Go ahead. Just get outta my dream."

"No, it ain't that. I gotta talk to you . . . outside."

Delvecchio groaned and eased himself off the bed. He led little

Tommy out of the tent and tried to stay in the shade. If Vince could not nap, he would at least try to stay as cool as possible. "Okay, what's the emergency?"

"Well . . ."

"Come on! Come on!"

"Well . . ." Tommy's lower lip was trembling. ". . . after lunch I went over to the grotto—"

"After lunch?! Why in the world would you do that?"

"I wanted to pray."

"Nice. But why the grotto? We're trying to tell you you can pray anywhere. Besides, if you want to pray, we've got the chapel right here on our side of the ravine. Why go to the grotto—no, never mind! Maybe we can salvage some of this rest period. Forget why you went to the grotto. Say you just felt you were called to the grotto . . . okay?"

"Yeah . . . I was called to the grotto. A voice inside me told me to go to the grotto."

Kid's got a pretty good imagination, thought Delvecchio.

"Anyway, I went to the grotto and I was just standin' there . . . you know, lookin' at the Blessed Mother . . . when, all of a sudden, I saw her!"

"Saw her? You mean you saw her statue? What's so odd about that?"

"No," Tommy insisted, "it wasn't the statue. It was like she stepped out of the statue. I had . . . a vision!" He spoke in a reverential whisper.

"A vision," Vincent repeated. "You sure?"

"Oh yes. A vision. A vision of the Blessed Mother!"

Not knowing exactly how to react, Delvecchio postponed reaction. "Okay, then what?"

"She spoke to me."

"Uh-huh. What did she say?"

"She told me to go home!"

It was all Delvecchio could manage to keep from erupting in laughter. He relished the prospect of telling the other counselors all about Tommy's "vision." But what to do now? "She told you to go home, eh?"

"Yes. That's right." Tommy was very proud of himself. He had carried this off better than he could have hoped.

"Tell you what: Let's go back there . . . just you and me."

"What for?" There was uncertainty in Tommy's voice.

"Let's just do it. Trust me." In reality, Delvecchio had no idea what should happen next.

The two—the long and short of it—walked hand in hand across the bridge and into the grotto. The other campers and counselors were all in their cabins or tents. Only Tommy and Vincent were out and about.

Wordlessly, counselor and camper stood before the statue of Mary. They remained motionless for a couple of minutes that seemed like hours to the young lad.

Finally, Vincent spoke. "I think I see her."

"You do?" Wonderment in Tommy's voice.

"Yes . . . yes . . . I see her. She's saying something. She says . . . she says you gotta stay here!"

Tears trickled down Tommy's cheeks.

What could he do? It was his vision against the counselor's.

Tommy would never forget the day the Blessed Mother failed him.

The Present

Father Tully grinned. "Pretty inventive—on both parts. You think that excuse for going home was unique?"

"As far as my experience and everything I've heard—yes. Coming right out of the blue like that, I'd say Delvecchio's reaction was . . . maybe inspired. And funny," Koesler added.

"But it doesn't sound like the kind of guy I've heard and heard about," Tully said. "It's like Dr. Jekyll and Mr. Hyde. Are you sure counselor Vinnie eventually became Bishop Delvecchio? It doesn't add up.

"You did say the two of you were friends . . ."

"We were. I think we are. We don't see each other very often, but our friendship goes back such a long way—" Koesler stopped to figure. "Forty-five years!"

"Wow!"

"Just to make sure we're not building straw horses: What sorts of things have you heard about Vince?"

"Oh"—Tully leaned forward—"I guess the usual things you hear about most bishops: that he's for whatever the Vatican wants—and against anything that disturbs the Vatican. A company man. Matter of fact, most of the guys seem to wonder how he got to be an auxiliary to Cardinal Boyle."

"Well," Koesler said, "our Cardinal is not a crashing liberal."

"He's got a reputation that would lead one to believe that he is."

"I know. His talent is to tolerate people whose opinion he doesn't share. Which is part of the reason we have Bishop Delvecchio as our auxiliary."

"Oh? This I haven't heard."

"Scuttlebutt, mostly . . . that and clerical gossip have it that Vince wasn't even on the list Boyle sent to Rome as bishop material. Word has it that Rome thought Detroit was slipping out of their control. And they guessed correctly that Detroit, in the person of Cardinal Boyle, would not challenge them.

"And by the same token that Boyle tolerates the more aggressive of liberals here—and we've got them!—so he will tolerate somebody like Vince. It doesn't mean that 'anything goes' in Detroit; there are limits on both sides. And Boyle will step on toes if he's pushed or shoved.

"Actually, Detroit is neither liberal nor conservative . . . just sort of 'open.' And that, in this day and age, is enough for me."

"And me," Tully said. "But, in the meantime, I've got to deal with Delvecchio. He's my area auxiliary. I'm trying to get to know what makes him tick. And I figured you'd know as well or better than anyone."

Koesler didn't speak for a moment. "I'd like to help you, Zack," he said finally, "but I wouldn't want you to think that Vince and I are the best of friends. Lots of people are closer to him than I . . ." He paused. "Now that I think of it, all those who are closer to him are priests. Over the years, he's separated himself from the laity. And yet . . . I don't think he would be considered 'a priest's priest.'"

"Well," Tully said, "maybe I'm getting ahead of this briefing. You said you had a few things—anecdotes—to tell me."

Koesler smiled. "Oh, there are more than a few. These stories of our time at the summer camp are meant to sort of set the scene. I thought it might be helpful if you got to know what Vince was like as a young man—a seminarian a few years from ordination."

"I'll try not to get ahead of the game." Tully smiled. "Okay, Counselor: Tell me a story."

3

"Are you even old enough to remember the Requiem Mass?" Father Koesler regarded his successor dubiously.

Father Tully snorted. "You mean the black vestments and the interminable *Dies Irae* and that? You mean the kind of Mass almost every priest used to say almost every day, Monday through Saturday?" Tully nodded. "I grew up with it as an altar boy and it was still around a little while after Vatican II. So, yeah, I remember the Requiem Mass."

Catholic laity regularly ask that Masses be offered for their intention. And nine times out of ten—or even more often—the intention is a prayer for a deceased person. For centuries, the Mass offered for a deceased person was the Requiem, with its foreboding music and scary language. And, of course, the actual funeral liturgy was the Requiem, with additional chants at the beginning and end.

Gradually, after the Second Vatican Council, the Requiem disappeared as the Church chose to emphasize the joy and fulfillment of heaven, rather than the sorrow of death. Few parishes even kept black vestments. Few choirs remembered the solemn chants.

Thus Koesler's questioning Father Tully's memory of the Requiem was not capricious.

"Okay," Koesler said. "Well, at camp, fortunately, the chaplain tried to keep down the number of Requiem Masses. Most of the campers gave every indication that they were pretty well bored with daily Mass. The repetition of the Requiem would only have intensified the monotony."

Tully seemed puzzled. "But what happened to all those Mass intentions for the dead?"

"There weren't all that many. The camp chaplain was on the priest faculty of the minor seminary—Sacred Heart."

"So?"

"So, he just did parish work on the weekends during the school year. He didn't have access to Mass intentions or their stipends."

"Compared with the other Detroit priests, your chaplain comes out as a poor relation."

"Not really. Most of the faculty went out every morning—or as often as they wished—and picked up the stipends for the scheduled Masses they offered. The point is, Zack, that at camp we had an occasional Requiem, but not as regularly as in the parishes."

"What does this have to do with Delvecchio?"

"Just this: Over all those summers we were at Camp Ozanam, I was the organist and choir director."

"You play the organ?"

"Not very well." Koesler smiled. "Ozanam couldn't afford E. Power Biggs. There was an old pump organ in the chapel. That was our Casavant—just like the grotto with its broken noses, missing toes and fingers, was our Lourdes.

"The thing is that Vince also played the piano—and thus qualified on our pump organ. This—nineteen fifty-three—was my last summer at camp—no matter what happened. Either I would drop out of the seminary or I would be ordained. Of course, I was ordained in June of 'fifty-four. My camping days were over.

"And before that summer of 'fifty-three ended, I wanted to pass the baton to Vince. So we kind of relieved each other by the week. I introduced him to the kind of music we used, and he got the practice he needed to go from piano to organ.

"Well, one morning toward the middle of June, Vince directed and accompanied the gang in his first Requiem Mass. Afterward, when I could talk to him privately after breakfast . . ."

1953

"Vinnie . . . hey, Vinnie, wait up."

Bob Koesler trotted to the side of Vince Delvecchio and joined him in walking to the cabin side of the ravine. "What've you got this morning?"

"I'm supposed to take squads two and five for boxing instructions." Delvecchio snickered. "It'd be nice if I knew what I was supposed to do."

"Nobody took you through boxing instructions?"

"Uh-uh. I just looked at the bulletin board this morning, and there I was: taking two and five. I guess I'm supposed to teach them how to box. I don't think they meant making boxes for packing things."

Koesler threw an arm over Delvecchio's shoulder. "Congratulations! The way I hear it, that's pretty much how we're expected to function once we're ordained."

"What?"

"Ex officio," Koesler explained. "From what I've heard, we'll find little use for a lot of what we learn in the seminary. I mean, we're not expected to put down Manichaeanism or refute Jansenism. We're supposed to count and bank the weekly collection. And teach catechism—even though we're not qualified as teachers. Everything is ex officio.

"But boxing: That's an entirely different can of worms. You could get killed!"

"That thought crossed my mind." Delvecchio stopped walking, turned to Koesler, and grinned. "Some of those guys are bigger than I am."

"You've got something going for you."

"I'd really appreciate knowing what."

"The kids probably think you're an expert at the manly art of self-defense."

"Excuse me, but how does that help me not get my block knocked off?"

"You must've seen some amateur or professional boxing matches someplace down the line."

"A few."

"A few," Koesler repeated. "Just enough to carry this off, I think."

"You *think!*"

"Show the kids footwork. That's a big part of boxing . . . at least I seem to have read that. You know how to dance?"

"I'm a seminarian."

"I know. But you have a sister, don't you?"

"Yeah. But I never danced with her. And they're sure as hell not teaching it in the seminary. Unless . . . at St. John's . . . ?"

"No, no. I've got only one more year at St. John's—and I'm pretty sure the record of keeping seminarians away from girls will remain unblemished.

"Okay . . ." Koesler thought for a moment. "Here's what you do: You ask the kids if anybody knows anything about footwork in the ring—"

"And if somebody volunteers, I let him teach everybody whatever he knows."

"Exactly."

"And if there aren't any volunteers?"

"You're still in business. If nobody knows anything, make it up as you go along. Just keep moving. Try like hell to remember what you've seen in the movies or whatever."

"And after footwork?"

"Try to make it last."

"For an hour and a half?"

Koesler tended to agree that might be stretching things. "Maybe then you could do a little shtick on the role of hands and arms as instruments of self-protection."

"You mean, put the gloves on?"

Koesler shook his head decisively. "No! Under no circumstances do you get in the ring with anyone. Some of our darlings may be itching to take out their frustrations on the staff. Not necessarily you . . . but you would make an interesting target in a boxing ring with the gloves on. Just offhand, who do you think the kids would be rooting for?"

Without answering, Delvecchio turned and headed on. Koesler walked along with him.

"So," Delvecchio said finally, "what I do is I fake it for as long as possible. And if, after I do everything I can, there's still time to kill . . ."

Koesler pulled at his lower lip. "You might match the kids according to height and weight and let 'em go at each other for a minute or two."

"Yeah, but given that I haven't actually taught them a damn thing, isn't it likely they could hurt each other?"

"Haven't you seen the gloves we use?"

"No. I didn't have any reason to look for them."

"Well, when you go to the property room, I guarantee you'll be impressed with the gloves. I think the camp got them brand-new about thirty or forty years ago. Unless you know how to tuck the excess padding under your fingers and make the surface taut, it's like having a pillow fight."

"Okay. Thanks, Bob." Delvecchio stopped and lifted his eyes heavenward. "I'll let you know how it all comes out," he said as he turned back to Koesler. "But if something goes wrong with the advice you so generously gave me, look me up in the infirmary."

Koesler chuckled. He took a fresh look at Delvecchio. Vince resembled Murphy's Law animated. If something could go wrong with him in a boxing ring, it would. At six foot two or three, he had plenty of height, but he was rail-thin. In a year, when he would graduate from Sacred Heart to St. John's Seminary, the food would take a sharp turn for the better and he probably would fill out. Meanwhile, height alone would not help him survive in the ring.

Delvecchio needed prayer.

And this reminded Koesler of the reason he wanted to talk with Vince. It had nothing whatever to do with the squared circle. "But teaching boxing isn't what I wanted to talk to you about."

"I was wondering . . ." Delvecchio's look was open but puzzled.

"It was about Mass this morning."

"Really? Was I bad? I'm still trying to master a legato touch. You don't have to worry very much with the piano."

"No, it isn't the legato; you're doing all right with that."

"I'm just lucky I don't have to mess with pedals. I don't think I could coordinate the whole thing . . . not unless I had a lot more time to practice."

"It's not the organ work," Koesler said. "Or, well, actually, it's the *amount* of organ work."

"Huh?"

"This morning we had a Requiem Mass."

"Yeah, I know. Are you upset 'cause I put half the *Dies Irae* in a monosyllabic monotone? If the whole thing is chanted the way it's written, it takes all day."

"No, it isn't that. This is your first Requiem. You probably aren't aware of the rubric for a Requiem High Mass. The organist is allowed to play only—*only*—to accompany the singing. You're strictly limited to accompaniment alone. This is only a word for the future. I'm sure you didn't know that rule; very few people do."

"I knew it."

"It's probably one of the least known rubrics in— What?"

"I know you're not supposed to play the organ except to accompany the singing. In a Requiem High Mass."

For a few seconds, Koesler was speechless.

"You knew?" he asked finally.

"Yeah, I knew. I pay attention in Father Flynn's chant class. I thought he knew what he was talking about from the first day. One of the first things he told us was that if we got ordained, and, inevitably, we were to sing a high Mass—starting with our first Solemn High Mass the day after we are ordained—the rubric in the missal is not going to read, 'Can the priest sing?' or, 'Is it safe to let the priest sing?'; it just says, 'The priest sings.'"

"But"—Koesler's tone was one of disbelief—"you knew about playing the organ during a Requiem Mass . . ."

"Uh-huh. Just like I said. I knew."

"Then why, if I may ask, were you playing it when there wasn't any singing?"

Delvecchio shrugged. "But I only played it during Communion time."

"The rubric doesn't say, 'The organ may be played for accompaniment only—with the exception of Communion time.'"

Delvecchio was beginning to be ambivalent. He did not appreciate being quizzed as if he were a child. On the other hand, he admired Bob Koesler in many ways.

"Look, Bob: For a lot of these kids the novelty of going to Mass every day wears off pretty quick. They pay better attention to what's going on as long as there's something going on. Even in a Requiem Mass there's something to focus on most of the time. Except for Communion—it takes one priest a long time to give Communion to roughly two hundred people. And while that's going on, the only sound is feet shuffling down the aisle. It's tough for the counselors to keep the kids in line. I think it helps if the organ is going . . . don't you? I mean, don't you, really?"

Koesler exhaled in frustration. "The point is not that organ sounds can soothe the savage camper. I tend to agree with you that it does. But the point is, the rule directs that there should be no music played at a Requiem High Mass except to accompany singing. The rubric makes no exception. That's the point."

"'The guys who made up that rule were never counselors at a boys' camp!" Delvecchio was becoming heated.

Koesler reflected that heat. "I happen to be music director here. And I say we keep that and all other rubrics in our liturgies."

"Well, for Pete's sake, Bob, I didn't know we were dealing with the greatest evil, the unforgivable sin."

Koesler turned in disgust and walked away. After a few steps, he turned his head and, while continuing to walk, said, "On second thought, Vince, maybe you ought to get in the ring with one of the campers . . . one of the *big* campers."

4

The Present

Father Koesler was blushing ever so slightly. At this stage in life, in retrospect, he considered the argument between Delvecchio and himself childish. Especially on his part. And it embarrassed him not only to recall the incident but especially to confess it to Tully.

But Father Tully was chuckling. "I'd have to agree with Delvecchio: Fooling with the organ during a Requiem Mass probably isn't the ultimate sin of despair."

"Especially," Koesler agreed, "when you consider today's liturgies: There's virtually no distinction between 'high' or sung, and 'low' or spoken. But there still are rubrics."

"Not many. And particularly guys my age and younger aren't uptight about adapting the liturgy to the occasion." Tully sat back in his chair, reflecting on the drastic changes in liturgy that followed Vatican Council II.

"I can remember quite vividly," Tully said, "how tight everything was then: hands extended, facing each other at shoulder position and distance. The whispered words. The directed gestures. Nothing, absolutely nothing, was left to chance or choice.

"Oh, not that there weren't priests who veered from the rubrics. But most of them were just playing out their own idiosyncracies. Every single thing that went on in the Mass of yesterday was spelled out in precise detail."

Koesler nodded. "I'm getting thirsty. What would you say to some iced tea?"

"Iced tea?" Tully thought for a moment. "Did you make it, Bob?" He remembered all too well a couple of cups of coffee brewed by Father Koesler. They had been indescribably unpotable.

Koesler smiled. He was aware that his guests hardly ever finished a cup of his coffee. His tea, however, did not live in like infamy. "Mary O'Connor made the tea, Zack. Want some?"

"Sure." Tully had learned quickly that Mary O'Connor could be trusted to run the whole parish, not to mention make a beverage or snack. He found it unfortunate that Mary was going to follow Koesler into retirement.

Father Robert Koesler had met Mary when he was named pastor of St. Anselm's in a Detroit suburb almost thirty years before. She had been parish secretary for his predecessor. Mary and Koesler were eminently compatible.

Mary would have long since retired, but she had determined to stay with it as long as her priest-friend did.

Father Tully well knew that finding anyone the equal of Mary would be to stumble across perfection. At least Mary had agreed to stay on until a successor could be found.

The two priests went to the large kitchen where their paragon was busily preparing for the arrival of the caterers. She poured the tea as they exchanged small talk. The priests, glasses in hand, then returned to the living room.

Tully rattled the ice cubes, coaxing them to melt.

Koesler stood at the window, his back to Tully, and contemplated the impressive buildings, many of which had been erected since his arrival at the old parish.

"By the way," Koesler said, without turning, "I believe you said Bishop Delvecchio was giving you a difficult time?"

"I'll say!"

"What's the trouble?"

"He keeps bugging me about taking the Profession of Faith and the Oath of Fidelity."

Koesler turned to face the other priest. "Profession of Faith and Oath of Fidelity? Oh, yeah; I think I remember now. When we became pastors, we were supposed to take the ancient Oath Against Modernism— which was a very poor relic of the nineteenth century. It was like promising to remember dinosaurs. Then this new thing came into effect. How long's it been? Something like nineteen eighty-nine, wasn't it? I didn't pay much attention 'cause I was sure this would be my final pastorate and I never would be expected to deal with them. So, forgive me: Are they a real problem?"

Tully nodded. "They're a real problem. I guess," he added after a moment, "it depends on how seriously you take them. The good bishop was kind enough to send me copies. Want to hear some of the more ear-catching parts?" At Koesler's nod, Tully rose and walked to the file cabinet in one corner of the living room.

Koesler felt a sudden twinge. It wasn't Tully's file cabinet; it was *his*, Koesler's!

For an instant, he forgot that he had emptied the cabinet of his effects several days ago—part of his gradual leavetaking of Old St. Joseph's. Little by little he was gathering his things.

He found the process more wrenching than he had anticipated. Fortunately, the rectory had lots of room for storage, as boxes multiplied like coat hangers in a closet. All this because Koesler had not yet made a firm decision as to where he would live in retirement.

There was time.

Tully fingered through papers in the top drawer, found what he wanted, and returned to his chair. "I suppose we can start with the Profession of Faith. It's by far the more familiar. That's 'cause the main body of the Profession, as you probably know, is simply the Nicene Creed.

"Now I've got no problem believing in God—Father, Son, and Holy Spirit. And no problem with the Resurrection, forgiveness of sin, and eternal life. As I said, that, pretty nearly, is the Creed. But somebody in Rome tacked on an addendum. Get this: '*With firm faith, I believe as well everything contained in God's word, written or handed down in tradition and proposed by the Church—whether in solemn judgment or in the ordinary and universal magisterium as divinely revealed and calling for faith.*'

"That's not all," Tully continued. "*I also firmly accept and hold each and every thing that is proposed by that same Church definitively with regard to teaching concerning faith or morals.*

"What is more, I adhere with religious submission of will and intellect to the teachings which either the Roman Pontiff or the college of bishops enunciate when they exercise the authentic magisterium even if they proclaim those teachings in an act that is not definitive."

Tully lowered the paper and looked at Koesler. "How about that!"

Koesler shook his head. "Doesn't leave much room, does it?"

Tully rose and began pacing slowly. "According to that statement, there isn't any practical distinction between infallibility and the ordinary teaching office of the Church.

". . . whether in solemn judgment or in the ordinary and universal magisterium . . ." he repeated slowly.

"To be perfectly frank, Bob, I don't think this document is being very fair toward the Church. What sort of institution will not leave a margin for error? And, since the framers of this Profession believe that this stuff is part of the deposit of faith—that it goes right back to the beginning of Christianity—it covers things like usury—condemning money lending—and Galileo—and earth being the center of the universe—and evolution—and on and on.

"And it also includes today's concerns: like women priests, a married priesthood, birth control . . . etcetera, etcetera, etcetera." He shook his head. "The Church has reconsidered . . . and it will have to reconsider again.

"But what are we supposed to do?" Tully raised his hands in a gesture of frustration. "Form our faith and morals along with the Church and then change our minds with the Church? And do we do all this whether the teaching is infallible or not? What's the point of having infallibility"—he threw up his hands again—"what does infallibility stand for, if we're not going to make a practical distinction between ordinary and infallible teaching? I suppose the antonym of 'infallible' is 'fallible.' But the way this document is written, the Church has two ways to be right! And no way to be wrong!"

A feeling of relief permeated Koesler's mind. He understood and could sympathize with much of Tully's argument. But, bottom line, it was not Father Koesler who would be asked to make this Profession of Faith. Regardless, he would not shy from helping Father Tully make up his mind what to do. The important thing was that Tully be the one to decide the response to this demand.

But, Koesler recalled, there were *two* documents that required a new pastor's external assent. "What about the other statement . . . the Oath of Fidelity?"

Tully again picked up the paper from which he had read. "There's more, all right. But to my mind the damage was done by the Profession of Faith."

The rectory was now in shadow. Tully switched on the lamp next to his chair. "I'll just read you the salient parts.

"*In carrying out my charge, which is committed to me in the name of the Church, I shall preserve the deposit of faith in its entirety, hand it on faithfully and make it shine forth. As a result, whatsoever teachings are contrary I shall shun.*

"*I shall follow and foster the common discipline of the whole Church and shall look after the observance of all ecclesiastical laws, especially those which are contained in the Code of Canon Law.*'

"And finally, '*With Christian obedience I shall associate myself with what is expressed by the holy shepherds as authentic doctors and teachers of the faith or established by them as the Church's rulers . . .*'"

Tully let the document flutter to the floor as he looked up dejectedly at Koesler.

"That's it?" Koesler asked.

Tully was surprised. "That's not enough?"

"Oh, it's enough, all right." Koesler took a chair opposite Tully.

"To tell the truth, Bob, this bothers me more than I've let on. And we're getting closer all the time to the point of no return."

"How's that?"

"I take it that when you accept that document making you a Senior Priest"—here, Tully did a better-than-passing imitation of Delvecchio's voice. "'We do not speak of *retirement* from the priesthood'"—now he returned to his own voice. "in effect you will be a Senior Priest. In effect, you will retire, too."

Koesler laughed at the mimicry. "I don't get the impression that it works all that automatically. I mean, it's not like Australian tag team—

where one wrestler tags his partner and then takes over the match. There's probably a little room to breathe.

"But, yes, I don't think they expect me to linger here for months—or even weeks."

"Okay, so it's not tonight. But sometime very soon, I'm going to be face to face with a Profession of Faith and an Oath of Fidelity. And, frankly, Bob, I don't know what I'm going to do. But it sure looks as if the ball is in my court."

There was silence as both priests considered the situation.

"This is awkward, isn't it?" Koesler said finally.

"You betcha!" Tully confirmed.

"Your appointment should be published soon in the *Detroit Catholic*. And of course the parishioners here have been informed for at least several weeks. Most of them are familiar with you from your stay last year." Koesler paused. "These papers—the Profession and Oath—they are the only problem facing us?"

"Absolutely. I mean, I prayed over this move for months before deciding to come here. I really loved the folks in Dallas. It was painful to leave them. And that option is closed since the Josephites have already named my successor. I can't go back to Dallas."

"I hesitate to ask," Koesler said, "but do you have anyplace to go?"

"What?"

"This requirement isn't just for Detroit. It's Canon Law. Wouldn't you run into the Profession and Oath no matter where you went?"

Tully smiled, but without warmth. "I'd bet my bottom dollar I'd have no problem finding a Josephite superior who would take a benevolent approach to this canonical demand."

Koesler was silent briefly. He looked at Tully with genuine sympathy. "Have you given any thought to refusing this parish and returning to the Josephites?"

"Sure. But it's a kind of Catch-22. I want to be a part of my brother's life. He's the only close family I have. This is a good parish with lots of exciting possibilities. The more I want it, the more ominous those oaths are.

"It comes down to this, Bob: Just what sort of person is Delvecchio?

Is it possible to negotiate with him? Can he bend? What might make him sort of lenient? Is there a chance? Is there any hope?"

Koesler lowered his head, then turned to gaze out the window.

"I know, Bob, you can't make my decision for me," Tully said after a minute. "And I don't expect you to. But to come to a fully informed conclusion, I need reliable backgrounding, dependable information. I've got to know if I have a chance with this guy.

"And I've got to say, Bob, that those stories you told me about Delvecchio were more confusing than anything else. Based on them alone, Delvecchio comes across as a crashing liberal with a quick wit. As a matter of fact, the villain of those pieces is you: You not conscious of your duty as a lifeguard, you insisting on the letter of a ridiculous rule.

"While Delvecchio is inventive and imaginative. Somebody who recognizes a ridiculous law when he sees one." Tully tried to smile, but couldn't quite muster one. "What's up?"

Until having this conversation, Koesler had been chiefly concerned with his own immediate future.

Of course he would have to find a place to live. Senior Priests were expected to move from the parish they were currently serving. An ultimate destiny was theirs to find and establish. The thinking was that if a retiring priest remained in his current parish, parishioners would still seek him out for advice, consultation, and/or support, rather than properly looking to his replacement.

Thus, moving away was intended as beneficial to the retiring priest as well as his successor.

In addition to arranging for a new home—no small consideration in any case—Koesler was becoming intrigued with the thought of a new lifestyle. What would it be? Certainly far different from anything he had experienced to date. There were so many avenues. Many Seniors helped out with weekend ministries at one or at several parishes. That way the priest could keep his hand in. It was also a source of supplementary income—for many, the sole such source.

And there were other avenues. By the age of retirement, priests had made so many acquaintances, formed so many friendships, established so many second families. There would be time now to enjoy these relationships. There would be time now to be of greater presence and service to them.

These and many similar speculations had occupied Koesler in recent weeks.

Now, leaning on the wealth of his experience, Koesler was able to detect the turmoil churning deep in Tully. The younger priest had kept his inner conflict hidden. But as the time for a decision loomed, Tully was near to panicking.

Koesler wanted to help. And it was clear what form that help would be. From his experience, he could provide almost exactly what Tully wanted and needed: accurate information on what made Bishop Delvecchio tick.

"Okay . . ." Koesler settled more deeply into his chair. "I think I know what you want. And I think I can give it to you.

"The stories I just told accurately described two young men as they were when they were—one about twenty-four, the other about nineteen. They were different from each other then; they are different from each other now. Somewhere along the way, they passed each other on a bridge, so to speak."

Koesler fell silent. Tully did not intrude.

"It's funny," Koesler at length continued, "in all these years I've met so many people. They weave a pattern in my life. Now that I look back on my relationship with Vince Delvecchio, I see our paths have crossed many times. But I've never considered him in any . . . distinct way. Now that I think of him, of our contacts in an unbroken story, I'm not sure exactly what I'll find."

Koesler took a deep breath. "To begin with, our ages were against our ever getting to know each other well. That he was five years younger argued against any kind of familiarity, let alone friendship per se."

"Because," Tully contributed, "you were in college when he was in high school. And you were in Theology when he was in college."

"Right. But mostly the separation between college and Theology. High school and college were in one gigantic building complex— Sacred Heart Seminary. Whereas the final four years were at St. John's

Seminary in Plymouth. During my final four years, I wouldn't even have seen Vince if it hadn't been for camp.

"See, Zack, in the mid-fifties there were three Catholic boys' camps that hired seminarians exclusively: Sancta Maria for wealthier campers; CYO for those who could afford to pay, but not on the level of Sancta Maria; and Ozanam, intended for kids from poorer families.

"Counselors around my age were rather fiercely committed to our individual camps. After all, counselors at any of these camps spent practically the entire year with each other: September to June in school and June through August at camp. Even Christmas and Easter vacations frequently were times to go to movies together or, one way or another, to be in each other's company.

"That's the way it was with Vince and me and the other counselors at Ozanam. There was this bond . . . not as strong as that between counselors who were also classmates, but a bond nonetheless—"

"It would be a good idea for me to pay attention to this camp thing, wouldn't it?"

"Yeah, it would. But you should remember that in recent years, although the camps are still functioning, they're no longer staffed by seminarians."

"Because there aren't that many seminarians anymore . . . right?"

"Exactly." Koesler did not merely look at, he studied his watch. "Well, we've got a lot of territory to cover, but we should have enough time.

"What I want to do, I think, is to relate certain incidents that involved Vince and me . . . incidents that I hope will help you understand things that happened to Vince and helped shape him into what he is today.

"You want a background on Vince. I'm going to try to give you just that: I'm going to try to paint a picture as well as I can of how Bishop Delvecchio developed and changed over the years."

5

"**My last summe**r as a counselor was wonderful. My last year in the seminary was glorious. Mostly because I knew that the priesthood was within my grasp. And that was all I ever wanted to be . . ." Father Koesler leaned back in his chair, eyes half closed as he recalled his Golden Year.

"June fifth, nineteen fifty-four . . ." Koesler smiled in memory. "I was ordained. Then we had a short vacation before we got our first parochial assignments. About the time we were moving into our parishes, seminarians in high school, college, and Theology were going back to school.

"So I was sent to St. William's on Detroit's east side—on Outer Drive near Gratiot.

"Just an aside, Zack: That neighborhood was solid upper middle-class. If anybody had predicted that some day that parish would close and the buildings be sold, he'd have been committed to an asylum. But a few years ago it *did* close.

"It was amazing: Here I was, twenty-five, and everybody calling me 'Father.' I had so much to learn. But what am I saying? You had the same experience—only somewhat later than mine."

Father Tully was grinning. "I sure did. Except that my first assignment—we called them 'missions'—was hundreds of miles from home."

"That's right: You were a missionary. Funny: I still tend to think of missionaries as 'foreign'—like in Maryknoll.

"Anyway," Koesler continued, "I—we—had to get out of our textbooks and deal with people. People who came to us for instruction, answers, forgiveness, help . . . food. And the odd thing about it was that in most cases we could deliver. Sometimes the answers weren't right at my fingertips. But I could—and I did—rely on the books on the shelves behind me. If I didn't know the answer to anything that anybody threw at me, I was certain I could find it in one or another of those books.

"Did you have that experience, Zack?"

Tully shook his head. "Bob, you said you started out in an upper-middle-class neighborhood. With the exception of my previous short stay at St. Joe's, this will be the first upper-middle-class parish I've ever worked. By and large, Josephites live poor with the poor. We were a long, long way from splitting ecclesiastical hairs with prospective converts. But I suppose hardly anybody is doing that anymore . . . no matter what the parish's financial standing is."

"True enough," Koesler agreed. "Just about everything has changed. I wonder if the guys today when they're starting out in the priesthood make the same mistakes we did . . ."

"Mistakes?"

"Uh-huh. Books were our world in the seminary. But after ordination, when we started as priests, we were dealing with flesh-and-blood people. It was one thing to be taught the 'evil' of birth control . . . and to get the latest word on 'rhythm' that would solve the whole problem. And it was another thing to counsel and absolve good people for whom 'rhythm' meant nothing on a practical basis. They were avoiding artificial birth control because it was a 'mortal sin.' They depended on an undependable system. And they were hyperpopulating the parish every nine months or so. Their marriages were under incredible stress. And we had the cold answers in the books on our shelves."

Koesler slipped into the meditative replay of those memories.

Faithful Catholics of that era had their faith tested by moral directives that had little to do with the reality of their lives.

In the silence, Father Tully reflected on how different had been his priestly experience. Family planning had meant something contrastingly different for his average parishioner. The poor had children or not, depending on the consensus of a married couple. And that decision had nothing to do with a calendar or theology. There were problems—lots of big problems. Generally, family planning was not one of them. Food, clothing, shelter, employment—these were crises constantly gnawing at Tully and his parishioners.

Father Koesler had not had to confront any of these challenges. Nor had Bishop Delvecchio. And it was the mind of Delvecchio that Tully wanted to investigate. Thus, what Koesler had to say was of major importance to Tully.

"At any rate," Koesler broke the silence, "I was entering the real world—or what passed for us as the real world. I spent the first several months pretty much bewildered by a new routine—a new way of life. Only slowly getting accustomed to dealing with people—people with problems. People who looked to me for solutions, support. And I was slowly learning that all the answers weren't in those books.

"Meanwhile, Vince Delvecchio spent his summer at camp. After this season, he would enter St. John's Seminary. Those impressive buildings were only five years old at that time. Everything even smelled new. It was September nineteen fifty-four . . ."

1954

Visiting Sunday.

The first Sunday of each month was Visiting Sunday at St. John's Seminary.

The morning schedule remained the same as all Sundays: Rising at 5:30 A.M.; Meditation, 6; Community Mass, 6:30; Breakfast, 7:30; Recreation, until the Solemn Mass at 10.

The afternoon was given over to visits from relatives and friends. St. John's was a provincial institution for the entire state (or province, a Catholic designation). Some students came from the far reaches of Michigan. Most of those could not realistically expect family to come all that way for a mere afternoon.

Vincent Delvecchio's family lived on Detroit's east side. It was a convenient distance; they were sure to come.

The seminary's main building was set back from the highway about one hundred yards. Cars could approach via a large, circular driveway. During short breaks from class or study, black-cassocked seminarians—most of them near chain-smoking—could be seen endlessly walking, in groups of two or three, around and around the drive.

The walking routine was the order of the day on Visiting Sunday. Those receiving visitors greeted their guests as they pulled up and parked in the driveway. There being no telecommunication to rooms or lawns, being at the driveway was the only way of knowing one's guests had arrived.

This, the first Sunday of October, was typically bracing. The color show of turning and falling leaves was spectacular. It was ideal football weather. And had this day not been set aside for visitors, most of the young men in clerical uniform would have been pounding each other's bodies on the playing fields at the rear of the buildings.

Down Sheldon Road a mile or so was the Detroit House of Correction—or, more familiarly, DeHoCo. With some frequency, people looking for DeHoCo would pull into the seminary's drive, come to a stop alongside one or another of the students, and ask, "Where are the prisoners?" More often than not, the student would point to himself and the other walkers.

On this sunny but brisk October day, two such students were strolling together while wrapped in serious discussion.

They were killing two birds with one shot. Tomorrow morning first-year theologians faced a test in Moral Theology. Vincent Delvecchio was tutoring Stan Wonski as they walked and waited for their visitors.

"It's the principle of the double effect, isn't it?" Wonski said.

"Well, yeah," Delvecchio responded, "but it would help if you thought of it as an indirect voluntary."

Wonski grimaced as he dragged on his cigarette. He knew he was smoking far too much. It was just that one tended to take advantage of the more liberal smoking regulations at St. John's. Smoke time had been far more restricted at both Sacred Heart and Orchard Lake—the two main feeding seminaries. Now at St. John's, students who smoked—which was nearly everyone—were still cramming as many cigarettes as possible into longer smoking periods. Serious coughing started here.

"Okay, okay," Wonski said, "the indirect voluntary. But all we ever use is the double effect. Lemmee say double effect."

"Be my guest." Delvecchio was one of the rare nonsmokers. "The essence of this thing is that you're dealing with something that is not directly willed. An effect of something done but not directly willed. Only tolerated. The key word is tolerance."

Wonski scratched his head with the hand not holding the cigarette.

Delvecchio attempted a clarification. "Stan, somebody does something that is either good or indifferent. It can't be intrinsically evil. If it's intrinsically evil, you can stop right there. It's a sin. It has to be good or indifferent.

"Then, say, the action has two effects. The first effect must be good. The secondary effect may be evil. But it is not directly willed, only tolerated. And the good result must outweigh the evil." Delvecchio glanced expectantly at Wonski.

Wonski shifted his cigarette from one hand to the other. With his free hand he again scratched his head. "Lemmee try an example. Suppose a cop is walkin' down a street one night. He sees somebody holdin' a gun on another guy. The cop draws his own gun and yells at the guy to drop his gun. Instead, the crook turns toward the cop and points his gun at the cop. The cop fires, and kills the crook."

"Okay." Delvecchio seemed pleased. "How does that work for the indirect volunt—uh, double effect?"

"What the cop does is fire his gun. I figure in this case that's at least indifferent. The first effect is that the cop saves his own life and on top of that he saves the innocent guy's life.

"The evil effect is he kills somebody. He didn't want to kill anybody—not even the crook. He just tolerates it. And the first effect is more important than the second. That about it?"

"That's about it."

"Hey," Wonski exclaimed, "here come my folks!" A fairly new and brightly polished Ford pulled up behind the two seminarians. The car windows were filled with happy faces. "Thanks a lot," Wonski said as he turned to greet his relatives.

Delvecchio smiled and continued his pacing, now alone.

Wonski, thought Delvecchio, was by no means slow—or dumb. He had come from Orchard Lake Seminary, where most of his classes were conducted in English. At Sacred Heart Seminary, most of the courses, particularly the important Philosophy studies, were in Latin.

Cardinal Edward Mooney wanted Moral, Dogma, and Canon Law taught in Latin at St. John's. Mooney's wish was the faculty's command. As a result, many of the young men from Orchard Lake were handicapped by this heavy immersion in Latin. Latin texts, lectures, verbal responses, tests.

If the Orchard Lake guys could paraphrase Shakespeare's Casca, they would say some such thing as, "The faculty of St. John's did in Latin speak. And those who did understand did nod their heads. But as for me, it was Latin to me."

By far, the majority of St. John's students came from Sacred Heart. But young men choosing to become priests had so much in common that in no time it was difficult to tell who had come from where. Simply, they were students together open to the formation of new friendships.

Delvecchio jumped at the unexpected sound of a horn directly behind him. The serviceable Chevy was grimy; "Wash me" was traced more than a few times in the dust.

The troops got out of the car. There was his mother, Louise. His father had died very prematurely of a heart attack two years earlier. Then there was his younger brother, Anthony, and his sister, Lucy—the baby of the litter. Finally, there was his aunt Martha, Louise's sister, and Martha's husband, Frank. The car belonged to Frank and the caked dirt was emblematic of his lifestyle: laid-back and friendly.

"What say we go down to one of the visitors' parlors," Vince invited. "It'd be nice to stay outside, but with the gang we've got we'd be strung out so far we'd never hear each other."

All nodded as they voiced agreement.

Happily, the parlor was nearly empty, as most of the students and visitors chose to stay out of doors.

No sooner were they seated than everyone began to speak at once. Vincent determined to play interlocutor.

His mother, given the floor, expressed gratitude that everyone was in good health. And was Vincent getting enough to eat? She remembered all too well loading Vincent up with huge jars of peanut butter. At Sacred Heart, though students lived on closely measured rations, they could have all the bread they wanted. That and the peanut butter sustained them.

Vincent assured his family that he was now eating about as well as he had at home; he simply couldn't gain weight. A blessing perhaps, since an overweight body had laid too heavy a burden on his father's heart.

Vince's mother was petite, with olive skin bespeaking her Sicilian ancestry. She wore a dark blue cloth coat, pillbox, and sensible shoes. In short, she looked as if she were headed for church. As far as she was concerned, visiting her adored son in a seminary was about the same as going to Mass.

Her late husband, Sam, from whom Vincent got his height, had left Louise quite well-off, sufficiently so that she didn't need to work outside her home.

Anthony, now a senior at De LaSalle Collegiate High School, was a gifted athlete. He would be offered more than a few athletic scholarships. So far, he had spent much more time exercising his muscles than his brain. This concerned Vincent, who was appalled at the prospect of his brother's wasting talents that could otherwise see him nicely through his later years.

Lucy was in the eighth grade at St. William's. The embodiment of perpetual motion, she showed every prospect of becoming a beautiful woman like her mother.

Martha, at forty-five, was two years older than her sister. Martha and Louise had been close from childhood. Born in Sicily, they were brought to America as infants; thus, neither remembered their country of birth. Their parents had come to Detroit to be with relatives who had preceded them.

The family's first home was a modest duplex in St. Ursula parish, populated then largely by Italian families just beginning to build their lives. In time, as Sam prospered in the construction business, they would move up Gratiot to St. William's parish.

Fifteen years ago, Martha had met Frank Morris. At thirty, she was beyond the customary marrying age. That had something to do with her acceptance of Frank's proposal. But basically, she loved him.

That was not good news to her family. Frank was not Catholic, and was divorced. After one frustrated attempt to be married in the Catholic Church, they found a judge to perform the service.

Of Martha's family, only Louise had attended the simple civil ceremony.

Now, after fifteen years, Martha's relatives were beginning to thaw; at least Frank and Martha were now invited to family gatherings. They were childless. Some of the family saw that as God's punishment.

Martha was Vince's godmother. That selection had been made well before her "pagan" wedding. Vincent had always been close to Martha, even though in more recent years he was troubled by her sinful state.

"So," Frank said, "how ya doin', Vinnie? This place as nice as it seems? It seems new. It even smells new."

"It *is* nice, Uncle Frank. And it's exciting. Our faculty—well, they're Sulpician priests. All they do is teach seminarians. That's what they joined up for. It's not like it was at Sacred Heart. The priests on that faculty never got a chance to do what they signed up for—being priests in a parish. These guys—the Sulps—chose to teach. And it shows. It's challenging.

"Which reminds me, Tony . . ." He turned to his brother. "How're you doing at De LaSalle?"

"Pretty damn good—"

"Tony!" Louise shushed her son. "Don't swear! We're in the seminary."

"Sorry, Ma. We're doin' very well, Vin. We're three and oh. We're lookin' at an unbeaten season. And my arm has never been better."

"How about your studies?"

"Yes!" their mother seconded.

"They're okay . . . well, adequate. They're never gonna put bread on the table. Football will."

"But for how many years?" Vince pointed out.

"Enough," Tony replied. "Enough to salt away a stash. Besides, my plan is to play pro football until my joints won't bend anymore. And then, you know what? I'm gonna do sports broadcasts. I've got more vocabulary than all the guys doin' play-by-play put together."

"Tony . . ." Vince shook his head. "Do you ever look at the statistics? Do you have any idea what the odds are? The odds that you can make it to the pros? Granted, if you get that far, you'd probably be a cinch for broadcasting. But how big a chance do you have to beat out the best of the best?"

"That's what I tell him all the time, Vincent," Louise said. "Listen to your brother, Tony. He knows what he's talking about."

"I'm bored!" Lucy complained loudly. She was close to whining. "Can I go outside?"

"No," her mother said. "Be a nice girl and sit still."

Lucy subsided, but looked as if she might burst into tears at any minute. She wriggled unhappily on her chair, almost in rhythm with her trembling lower lip.

"Why not?" Frank said. "There's nothing out here to hurt her."

"For cryin' out loud," Tony said, "let her go before she drives us all nuts." Tony had seen his sister in action; he knew that she was not about to sit silent and/or still.

"Oh, all right," Louise relented. "But stay out in front where all the cars are parked. And don't bother anyone. Mind now, stay in front."

Freed from the adult world, Lucy went skipping out of the room and up the exit steps.

"Now, if you'll excuse us," Louise said, "I want to talk to my baby for a little while." She grasped one of Vincent's sleeves and tugged on it.

Vincent, laughing, went off with his mother. The others grinned at the sight. Vincent made almost two of her. That she should commandeer her son all the while calling him her "baby" was ludicrous. Only a mother could pull it off.

6

"**Where can we talk?**" Louise asked.

Vincent thought for a moment. "If you don't mind walking, the cloisters."

"Walking is good."

Vincent led the way to the enclosed walkways. Constructed of brick and lots of glass, the cloisters area was H-shaped. Two north-south walkways joined the two residence halls with the main building. An east-west structure joined the aforementioned cloisters. They were used extensively to get from here to there.

The main building contained offices, library, refectory, and classrooms. The residence halls—named Edward and William after two of the founding Michigan bishops—contained student and faculty rooms and large recreation rooms. Students and staff were constantly on the move from one place to another. Cloisters, because they were so light and airy—and heated in winter—were popular places just to walk or, while walking, for conversation or prayer.

Vincent and Louise walked slowly but steadily. Only occasionally did anyone pass them. The area, though wide open, was nonetheless one of the most private areas in the institution.

"Vinnie," his mother began, "pretty soon you're going to be a priest."

"Ma, it's a good four years off."

"Four years goes awful fast."

"Not for me."

"I know. I know, baby. But when you get older, time seems to go faster."

"Ma, you're only forty-three!"

"I know. It wasn't me I wanted to talk to you about. It's your aunt Martha."

Vincent stopped walking. So his mother did too. Then they began again.

"I worry a lot about Martha," Louise said. "It's her marriage. She suffers so much because she can't take Communion. You know she goes to church every Sunday . . . the Holy Days too. Did you know that?"

"No . . . not really. Holy Days too?"

"And Frank goes with her. Of course he's not a Catholic. But he loves her so much. And in four years you're going to be a holy priest of God. Sometimes before I go to sleep at night, I imagine how beautiful it's gonna be when you say your first Solemn High Mass." Louise's smile was beatific. "And then I think of Martha—and Frank too. She's your godmother. She'll be at your Mass. And she won't be able to take Communion." Tears formed, then brimmed.

They walked in silence.

"Can't you do something, Vinnie?"

"Ma, what can I do?"

"Something. Anything."

"We don't even study the marriage laws of the Church until my fourth year. I haven't the slightest idea of all that might be good or bad in their marriage. I'm just at sea, Ma."

"Won't you try? For me?"

He had no idea what if anything he might be able to do. But this was his mother. No one on earth did he love as he loved his mother. "Ma, I promise you, I'll do everything I can to fix things up. Trust me?"

She tilted her chin. He bent closer. She kissed him on both cheeks. "Now," she said, "let's go back to the parlor. Then you can take Aunt Martha and Uncle Frank for a nice walk and tell them you're going to help them."

"But, Ma—"

"Then Aunt Martha will be as happy as me that you're going to help her. Not another word now . . ." She put a finger to his lips to prevent what he intended to be another word.

They returned to the parlor to find Tony doing stretching exercises in one corner and Frank and Martha sitting on the couch contentedly holding hands. At the sight of the couple's bliss, Vincent was confused. He knew from Church law that they were not married in the eyes of that same Church. But . . . living in sin? He wondered.

Louise steered straight for her sister and brother-in-law. "Vinnie wants to take you to see—what was it you were going to show them, baby?"

"The . . . uh . . . the crypt chapels."

"I'll just take Tony outside so we can be with Lucy," Louise said. "You can find us there after your little tour."

Martha smiled conspiratorily. "Come on, Frank . . ."

All the three needed was to turn a corner from the parlor to the prayer hall, which, besides being a place for morning, noon, and evening prayer, tripled as a classroom and an entertainment center.

They entered a series of five impressive small chapels, all portioned off from one large room and separated from one another by nothing more than a small space.

"Each of five faculty members has one of these chapels as his own. And all five celebrate Mass daily and all at the same time."

"Isn't that a little confusing?" Frank asked.

"You'd be surprised, Uncle Frank. Everybody whispers . . . in fact, they're called 'Whisper Masses.'"

Vincent showed them each chapel, though there was little difference among any of them. Finally, he pointed out the large plaque embedded in the floor at the room's center. Beneath this plaque, one day, Cardinal Edward Mooney would be buried. For whatever reason, visitors were most impressed by the future tomb of the Cardinal archbishop of Detroit.

"And now," Martha said as they had quite obviously completed their tour, "what does your mother want you to tell us?"

"What?"

Martha smiled banteringly. "We've been sisters too long not to know what's going on with each other."

Vincent was relieved. He'd had no idea how he would introduce the mission his mother had given him. Somebody had to bring up the subject. His prayer was answered when Martha popped the question. "Come on, Vinnie," she urged, "out with it."

"Well . . ." Vincent did not feel entirely comfortable. ". . . Mother is concerned about your standing in the Church."

Martha reddened. "She shouldn't have involved you. There's nothing you can do. We saw a priest before we got married. He said there wasn't any way we could be married in the Church. I don't think it was her place to involve you—"

"Wait a minute, Marty," Frank broke in. "You never know. Vinnie is smart . . . and he's young. The things he learns here probably are the most up-to-date developments there are in the Church. I know how bad you want to go to Communion. Maybe Vinnie can help. We don't want to turn down an offer like this."

Martha fell silent. Half of her saw the logic of Frank's statement. The other half was upset that Louise had brought the matter up again. Martha went through life trying not to think about it. It was too painful, even after all these years.

"Well," she said at length, "what did you have in mind, Vinnie?"

Vincent thought as intensely as he ever had. Then, an inspiration.

"Look, Aunt Martha, as I explained to Mother, I won't even be studying the Church's marriage laws until I'm in my fourth year here. And by that time I'll be on the verge of ordination and my first Mass—which seems a target date for Ma: She wants to be sure that you'll be able to receive Communion from me . . ." He hesitated.

"So? So what happens now?" Martha demanded.

Vincent brightened markedly. It was as if the Holy Spirit Himself had visited. "I know that you saw a priest before you got married. But maybe the priest you talked to wasn't up on everything. Things in the Church generally don't change very fast . . . but they do change.

"What I'm suggesting is that you see a friend of mine—Father Robert Koesler. As luck would have it, he was assigned to our parish, St. William's, right after his ordination."

Martha recollected. "Yes . . . Louise has mentioned him. He gives good sermons . . . or so she says. When was he ordained?"

"Last June." The words were muffled.

"Last June! Why, he's been a priest only four or five months!"

"Now, Marty," Frank said soothingly, "remember what we just got done talking about—how these younger priests might be up on the latest? What could it hurt if we give this a chance?"

"I don't know . . ." She was skeptical. "I don't have a very good feeling about this. I know how you don't put much trust in my intuition, Frankie. But it proves true more often than not."

"Come on, Marty, what could go wrong? What with where we are now, it could only get better. It's not going to get any worse. I would do anything so you could go to Communion again." Well, Frank thought, just about anything. The one thing he knew neither of them could possibly do would be to separate and get a divorce. But anything else . . .

"I guess . . ." Martha said tentatively, ". . . it would be all right then. Do we know this Father . . ."

"Koesler."

". . . Koesler will see us? We don't live in his parish. We're in the neighboring parish, Nativity. Our pastor is mean and gruff. Maybe he won't let us see your Father Koesler—"

"I don't think he has any choice in the matter," Vincent said firmly. "I think for consultation, you can go to any priest you want."

"Okay, we'll try it. No," Martha said after a moment, "we'll give it all we've got. I've been negative and reluctant about this only because neither of us wants to get hurt again. Really, I'm very grateful to you, Vinnie." She reached up and pulled him down to her height and planted a big kiss on his lips.

Frank shook Vincent's hand vigorously.

"Now," Martha said, "how do we go about this?"

Vincent thought for a moment. "Using the phone here in the seminary is kind of awkward. We have to get permission. And catching Father Bob at just the right moment is problematical in any case.

"I think what I'll do is write him a note and get it in tomorrow's mail. I'll just explain that my aunt and my uncle will be phoning for an appointment. And I'll ask him to see you. I'll just give him a general idea of what this is about. I think it'll be better if I don't get too deeply into the marriage thing. That way you can start fresh. And actually, I don't know that much about it. So if I don't go into it, I won't mess things up."

"Okay, Vinnie." Martha checked her watch. "Visiting time is almost over; we'll have to leave."

"I'll walk you to the car," Vincent said, leading the way.

They all began piling in. Frank, the last to enter, turned and held out his hand. "Really, Vincent, we—me especially—are grateful. If this works out, Marty and me are going to be about the happiest two people on the face of this earth."

As the car pulled away, everyone was waving good-bye.

"How did it go?" Louise asked.

Martha snorted. "You don't know, do you?"

"Know what?"

"Come on, Lou. All you told that boy was to fix things for Frankie and me. You didn't even know what he was going to show us when you suggested that 'tour.'"

"Okay, okay. So I just told him to do everything he could to help so you could receive the sacraments again. How'd he do?"

"We'll see. We're to wait a few days. Vinnie is going to write to his friend, your priest—"

"You mean Father Koesler? Oh, that's good. He's a good priest. He gives such good sermons. And he says Mass so fervently—"

"How is he with miracles?"

"If anybody can do it, he can. And we'll help as much as we can." Louise turned to the others. "C'mon everybody," she said loudly, "we're going to say the Rosary on the way home. It's for the intention of Uncle Frank and Aunt Martha."

Tony began to grumble. Lucy began to whine. But that was all drowned out as Louise began: "'In the name of the Father and of the Son and of the Holy Ghost, Amen . . .'"

Vincent watched them leave. Then he headed back toward the residence hall. It was time for Sunday Vespers.

As he walked, he pondered.

No two ways about it: If Uncle Frank and Aunt Martha wanted an adjustment in their religious status they would have to consult a priest. The only question was: Which priest?

There might well be priests better qualified than Bob Koesler. Oh, he knew his stuff all right; all he lacked was experience.

That could be both good and bad.

If the incidence of success with this sort of marital problem was poor, Bob wouldn't know that. So he could be more confident. But if it involved knowing whom to consult for best and quickest results, Koesler would be behind the eight ball.

Then another thought entered Vincent's head. Lourdes. That repository of astounding miracles. A grotto decorated with crutches and wheelchairs left by the grateful cured.

Yet it was said that the greater miracle was that experienced by those who came and left crippled—crippled but resigned to their fate and filled with inner peace. Another sort of miracle.

It was a good thing that he was headed for the celebration of Vespers, the Church's evening prayer. This enterprise was going to need a lot of prayer.

7

Rumor had it that an Italian priest fresh in America from his mother country was offering ten Masses a day and accepting a five-dollar stipend for each one.

Once the chancery was apprised of this practice, a chancellor called and told the priest in no uncertain terms that he could not offer ten Masses a day.

His response: "Ma, shu' I can. I'm a big-a strong guy."

Father Robert Koesler was a big, strong guy too, and he would have been happy to offer ten Masses a day—sans all those stipends.

Father Koesler had been a priest four months now and he was enjoying every minute of it. In a way, he regretted that his once-a-day Mass (except for Sundays, when, due to the crowds, priests were given permission to offer two Masses) was always scheduled for early morning. Mass was the highlight of his day. He wished he could have all day to anticipate it. He tried to adjust to this minor disappointment.

His days in this first parochial assignment had fallen into a routine. This also pleased the young priest. He loved routine.

On most days, after Mass, he taught in the parochial school. Never mind that he was totally unqualified as a teacher. He was a priest; Father could do anything. Afternoons were usually spent outside the rectory—visiting the sick, or parishioners who, for one reason or another, were homebound. In the evening there were endless instructions for people who wanted to convert to Catholicism. Or he would meet with couples who were making arrangements to be married.

Initially, he had been surprised at the time consumed in clearing the deck for marriage. The simplest procedure—a marriage between two Catholics of independent age, neither previously married—required several visits to fill out all the forms and to be instructed by the priest.

The priest, of course, had never been married. But he was Father: Ex officio, he could do everything.

From his—so far—parochial experience, Koesler had concluded that while it was fairly difficult to enter a Catholic marriage, it was extremely difficult to get out of one.

Canon Law had all the lines—and the questions. Were both parties to this marriage over twenty-one years of age? If not, parental consent was required. Were both Catholic? If not, a dispensation given by the local chancery was required. Were both free to marry, or did either have a previous marriage? If so, the previous marriage had to be annulled. Not infrequently, this process was as easy and successful as jumping the Grand Canyon. Were the parties entering this marriage of their own free will, or were they being coerced by force or fear? If so, the procedure stopped here until the coercion ceased—or, no marriage.

Obviously, once all the questions had been answered and the forms filled in to the Church's satisfaction, it would be next to impossible to claim that due to some circumstance there had been no marriage from the moment of exchange of consent.

Handling marriage cases was not high on Koesler's thrill list.

However, tonight a marriage case was coming at him from left field. The couple were not even his parishioners. Earlier in the week, he'd received a letter from his friend Vincent Delvecchio.

Vincent was not in a position to be very helpful regarding the problem. He had not yet been exposed to marriage law in the Catholic Church. All he was able to contribute was that there may have been a previous marriage on his uncle's part. What Vince knew for certain was that his aunt and uncle had been married by a judge. From the time of that marriage, his aunt had never again received Communion. His uncle was not a Catholic, so Communion was not an issue for him. Not much help there to enable Koesler to anticipate what the problem might be.

On the other hand, even married people would be hard-pressed to explain the canonical status of their marriage. Specific study of Canon Law would be required to understand concepts such as validity and liceity. Canon Law was not kind to the unpracticed eye.

When Mrs. Morris phoned for an appointment, Vincent's letter proved helpful. Without the letter, Koesler would have been most reluctant to see a couple who not only weren't parishioners but who lived beyond his parish boundaries.

The appointment was for 10 P.M. Rather late, but the first slot Koesler had available after instructions. In point of fact, Koesler had a mixed bag this evening. Immediately after dinner, he had scheduled instructions for 6, 7, and 8—followed at 9 by a couple making preliminary arrangements for a wedding.

They were a typical engaged couple. Once they had decided on a wedding, their first move was to reserve a hall for the reception. Only then did they call the rectory to book a time and date that would blend with the hall's availability. It worked; they had no idea how lucky they were.

It was a simple enough marriage. Both were Catholic, of age, free to marry, and were not being forced. Yet each had to fill out "A" forms requiring answers to questions that never would have occurred to them. They were surprised at this—and at the necessity for each to present a copy of the baptismal records showing no notation of marriage. Said record had to have been issued within the past six months—further proof that neither had a previous marriage. Once they were married at St. William's, notice would be sent to the parish of baptism for each of them. Their marriage would be recorded in their baptismal records. And from that time on, whenever either of them was issued a baptismal certificate, notice of their marriage would be included on that certificate.

The chief concerns of this couple, typically, were gowns, invitations, seating arrangements, flowers for the church, food service—buffet or banquet—etc.

Koesler tried to direct them to thoughts of the liturgy and, especially to give them an awareness of the gravity of the step they were about to take.

There was a mere modicum of difficulty in arranging for a canonical Catholic marriage. Challenging the validity of such a marriage would be next to impossible. Koesler wanted them to know that.

For as this carefree young couple left the rectory, an older couple entered with a serious problem that might well face just such an impossibility.

At the door, Martha Morris identified herself and introduced her husband to Father Koesler.

The priest led the way to his small office almost at the end of the hall. The farthest door in this hallway led directly into the church. Rectory, church, and convent were joined. Cozy. That's the way the pastor liked things, and he'd had the buildings constructed to his liking.

Once they were settled in, Koesler commenced. "As I told you on the phone, I got a letter from your nephew. So I was waiting for your call. Vince didn't give me much information . . . I guess he couldn't really. So . . . ?"

"You'll have to excuse us, Father," Martha said. "We're very nervous. We look at you as our last hope. It's . . . well, if this doesn't work, we'll be at the end of the line."

"You shouldn't feel that way." The last thing Koesler wanted was to be "the end of the line." He would, of course, do his best. But he wasn't an ultimate expert. He was shy of experience—very shy. Still, there were all those books on the shelves behind him. He found it encouraging that he could depend on them for whatever he lacked in age and experience.

"But, begging your pardon, Father," Frank said deferentially, "we're more than a little scared. We've told our story to a priest before—or at least we tried to—"

"You tried to? What do you mean, you 'tried to'? Which priest did you see?"

"Our pastor," Martha said. "Or at least the pastor of the parish we live in. He had no patience with us. We barely got started when he practically threw us out of the rectory."

"And your parish is . . . ?"

"Nativity . . . the one next door to this parish."

Nativity, thought Koeser. Father Keller. That bastard again!

Koesler hadn't needed to be ordained to be made aware of Keller's reputation. Keller was the third in a triumvirate of tyrannical east side pastors who were known as virtual autocratic Nazis.

Well, Koesler thought, at least I can start from scratch. The fact that

Keller had treated a couple of well-meaning people like trash had absolutely no bearing on the legitimacy of their case.

"We thought," Frank said, "that it might be very simple. I'm not a Catholic—nor was my first wife a Catholic. Just a couple of people not even married by a minister; we had a justice of the peace. We—Martha and I—figured the Catholic Church wasn't concerned about a marriage that had absolutely nothing to do with the Church."

Koesler shook his head slowly. "That's not the way it works, Frank."

"Well," Frank said, "at least we're making progress. Right about here was where Father Keller threw us out."

They all laughed. It eased some of the tension.

"We go to church regularly," Martha said. "Sundays and Holy Days. When Father Keller sees us, he sort of curls his lip. But at least he doesn't tell us to get out."

"That's because he doesn't tell us anything," Frank added.

Martha seemed suddenly apprehensive. "This won't cause a problem, will it?"

"What sort of problem?"

"Well, a problem for you. Will you get in trouble because you're taking care of us? I'm kind of worried that Father Keller will be upset."

"No, that won't happen," Koesler stated firmly. "It wouldn't happen in any case. But especially since you did see him and he refused to even consider your case."

Privately, Koesler mused about how wonderful it would be to wrap up this package and toss it back to Keller. If this couple's marriage could be convalidated with Koesler's guidance and help, it would be worth the price of admission to see Keller's face when he inevitably found out what had happened.

Koesler pushed aside a mess of papers—notes, mail, and the like— from the center of his small desk. He picked up a pen and pulled a yellow legal pad toward him, looked at Frank and Martha, and said in an upbeat tone, "Well, let's see what we've got . . ."

The Morrises inched their chairs closer to the desk.

"A little while ago," Koesler addressed Frank, "you said you thought that since the Catholic Church was not involved with your first marriage, that the Church would not recognize that marriage. Actually, the opposite is true: The Catholic Church actually recognizes any legal marriage ceremony as being valid."

Frank look amazed. "That's rather open-minded of the Church."

"But it doesn't work to your advantage, Frank."

"How's that?"

"Take your first marriage. The Church accepts that ceremony, no matter how it was performed—as long as whoever performed it was recognized by the state of Michigan—as a valid—real—marriage. That means that, in the eyes of the Church, before you can marry again you must prove that the first marriage is null. That for some specific reason—and there are only a few reasons the Church will consider—an impediment—a block—obstructed the validity of that marriage."

"These 'specific reasons,' Father: What are they?" Martha asked.

"First, Martha: Are you sure you want to sit in on this?" Koesler asked. "It can get a bit . . . personal."

"I want to be here."

"I want her here," Frank affirmed.

"Okay." Koesler nodded. "Now, a lot of these impediments are quite obviously not applicable here. Holy Orders, for instance, is a serious impediment."

"You mean—" Martha began.

"That because I am a priest, I may not marry. But . . ." He thought for a moment. "Okay, maybe I can explain it this way: Suppose I get married. And suppose later on, I get divorced. After which, my ex-wife wants to marry someone else in a Catholic ceremony. The Church starts out by presuming that a marriage exists. Now, my ex-wife has to prove to the Church's satisfaction that our union—well, that it was not a marriage—in other words, that no marriage existed. So she proves that at the time of our marriage ceremony, I was a priest. The Church would immediately grant her an annulment. Because in the eyes of the Church, there was no marriage between me and that woman—because, as a priest validly ordained by the Catholic Church, I am not, in the eyes of that Church, allowed to marry. Therefore, she, in effect, never married, so she is free to marry.

"Now, that's what we want to find in your marriage to—what is her name?"

"Mildred. Do you need her maiden name?"

"No . . ." Koesler smiled. "I was just getting tired of referring to her as 'that woman.'"

Koesler then began to tick off various possible impediments: consanguinity—if she were a close relative; if she refused to have children; if she were previously married; etc.

It reminded Frank of the questions asked before some medical procedure. Have you ever had mumps, measles, whooping cough, etc.?

To both series of questions, Frank's answer would be, No. He'd had—oddly—no childhood diseases, nor had his first marriage involved any of the possible impediments Koesler mentioned. "No," he said aloud.

Questionnaire concluded, Koesler said, "I was afraid of that." Noting their disappointment, he added, "But we're not done.

"Frank, what was there about your marriage to Mildred that didn't work? In your own words, what made the marriage fail?"

"That's a pretty big question, Father." He thought for some time. Finally, he said, "Incompatibility . . . incompatibility that started early on and just got worse. We were great in bed"—his face reddened but he went on—"but after that, in just about everything else, the two of us could have been living on different planets."

"Did you have any children?"

"No. Neither of us wanted kids. The way things turned out it was a lucky break we didn't have any—say, Father: Could that be one of those impediments? I know the Church doesn't look too kindly on birth control . . ."

"'Fraid not, Frank. Now, was there anything the two of you differed on or argued about a lot?"

Frank pondered. "Seems religion came up every so often," he said slowly.

"Religion? What about religion?"

"Mildred was Lutheran. She was pretty strong about it. She was always after me to join her church. She was really sore because I refused to be baptized—"

"Wait a minute . . ." Koesler sat up straight. "She wanted you to be re-baptized in the Lutheran Church?"

"Rebaptized? No. I was never baptized at all."

"How can you be so sure?"

"Because my dad and mother told me more than once. They said they wanted that kind of choice to be all mine. They left the whole thing about religion and baptism up to me." Frank chuckled. "As it turns out, I didn't do anything about either one. I didn't want to join the Lutheran Church. And I couldn't see getting baptized if I wasn't going to join."

"But you go to church all the time now . . ."

"Well, see, as incompatible as I was with Mildred that's how compatible I am with Marty. I would've joined the Catholic Church and gotten baptized long ago, but Father Keller wasn't in much of a receptive attitude."

"To give the devil his due," Koesler said, "Father Keller didn't have much of a choice there. He couldn't receive you into the Catholic Church until or unless you got your present marriage validated."

"You mean this 'living in sin' bit?" Bitterness tinged Frank's voice.

"That's an unfortunate label," Koesler said. "No one can crawl inside you and know what's going on in your conscience. Your life of sin or grace is yours—and yours alone—to know.

"But so much for the internal forum—your soul. What we're talking about is the external forum: whether or not we can baptize you and convalidate your marriage. And I think you have just uncovered maybe the only path to doing just that."

Smiles all around.

"How? How, Father?" Martha asked. "We'll do anything!"

"I've got to tell you right off," Koesler said, "it's a slim chance. I studied it in the seminary—not all that long ago—but I've never used it. Never thought I would."

8

"It's called the Pauline Privilege," Father Koesler informed the rapt couple. He smiled. "I'll try to explain it as briefly as possible," he said, as he turned to search through the volumes on the shelves behind him.

The Bible, the Code of Canon Law, a book on moral theology—he consulted each cursorily, then turned back to his visitors. "This whole notion is based on St. Paul's first letter to the Corinthians—the seventh chapter." He half smiled at some private joke. "For one who never married, Paul had an awful lot to say about marriage and to married people."

Koesler did not reflect that in this he was in the same boat as St. Paul.

"One of the questions for the early Church to settle was how to relate to non-Christians," Koesler explained. "Christians were a tiny minority surrounded by a world where religion was a mixed bag. Polytheists and pantheists could count their gods—and atheists had no god.

"And all the earliest Christians were Jews, of course. So the Apostles had to lead their disciples through the rough waters of controversy.

"While the first Christians were Jewish in nationality, they were no longer Jews as a religious body. So, controversies raged over which Jewish laws should be preserved and which should be abandoned in this new religion. Customs—laws, as far as the Jews were concerned—like circumcision and dietary proscriptions—were wrangled over and, eventually, pretty much abandoned.

"One of the touchiest situations was intermarriage between Christians and non-Christians. And a companion problem was how to treat a mixed religious marriage that ended in divorce.

"Following the dictates of Jesus—and with no time yet for theological development—marriage for Christians was monogamous and lifelong.

"Now: Was there a distinction to be drawn when a non-Christian permanently left his or her Christian partner?

"St. Paul, in his letter to the Corinthians, considers the plight of a Christian whose non-Christian partner leaves. As fate has it, this Christian falls in love again. Oddly, again, the loved one is non-Christian. But this non-Christian wishes to become Christian and marry.

"Paul grants the request as a 'Privilege of the Faith.'

"Here, for the first time, we are not talking about an annulment. This one is called a dissolution."

Frank and Martha were listening—hard. But Father Koesler realized that although they were taking in his words, a good deal of explanation was still necessary, particularly for Frank, the non-Catholic in this affair.

"You see, Frank, as far as the Catholic Church is concerned, you and Mildred had a valid but not sacramental marriage. Now, ordinarily, you'd think of a priest as the minister of sacraments. But not the sacrament of matrimony: The bride gives the sacrament to the groom and vice versa. The priest, in this case, is an official witness.

"Now, in your case there was no sacrament because you were never baptized—and one has to be baptized in order to give or receive a sacrament.

"So, if this case plays out the way we want, you and Martha could be married in the Catholic Church. You would be baptized and then when you give your consent in marriage, your first marriage would be dissolved as a 'Privilege of the Faith.'"

"But . . . but that's wonderful!" Martha was almost breathless and enthused at the same time. "When can we do this—when can we get married in the Church?"

"Not so fast, Marty," Frank cautioned. "There's more to this than meets the eye . . ." He turned back to Koesler. ". . . ain't there, Father?"

"I'm afraid so. Yes."

"What? What?" Martha's enthusiasm plummeted.

"It's in the proof," Koesler said. He looked at Frank. "You've got to prove that you never were baptized."

"How do you prove something never happened?" Frank asked.

"Exactly," Koesler responded. "If you—yes, you, Frank"—Koesler nodded—"if you were to take a baby into a baptistry and baptize that baby, that baby would be validly baptized. Yes . . ." He nodded again, anticipating Frank's question. ". . . in the eyes of the Catholic Church, the baptism would be valid whether the baby was baptized in a Methodist church, a Lutheran church—or a bowl of water in the kitchen. For baptism, the ordinary minister of the sacrament is a priest. But for validity, anyone with the correct intention can baptize.

"So you see the problem when we allege that you never were baptized, Frank. What if when you were a baby, a kindly uncle—aunt, grandfather, whatever—took you to . . . anywhere there was water—"

"When you put it that way, Father," Martha said, "it seems quite impossible to prove that Frank's never been baptized."

"Well, it's not quite that comprehensively difficult." Koesler smiled at Martha, then turned to Frank again. "What we need are witnesses—lots of extremely credible witnesses—to testify that the attitude of just about everyone who touched your young life was that your parents' prohibition of baptism was well known and observed by everyone. Now you yourself can testify about the years after you reached the age of reason. But even then we need witnesses for those years too.

"You see, Frank . . . Martha . . ." he addressed both, "what we must build up is an overwhelming flood of similar testimony that affirms that Frank was most unlikely ever to have been baptized.

"So, actually getting this 'Privilege of the Faith' is most difficult. But not impossible. Such dissolutions have been granted in the past—and, undoubtedly, will be in future. What we don't know is whether we can get it for you."

"Well," Frank said, after a lengthy pause, "how do we get started, Father?"

Koesler rubbed his hands together. "Okay. I'll take you through this chronologically. But remember"—he looked at each of them in turn—"if you find any of this procedure impossible—for any reason—say so now. I'll tell you everything that will be required . . . and I won't pull any punches."

Both his listeners nodded.

"First off, we go through a standard series of instructions in Catholic beliefs and practices."

"How long will that take?" Frank asked.

"Depends. Three or four months, usually—at one appointment a week."

"Can we go at it more often than once a week?"

"If you want to." Koesler could understand Frank's wanting to speed up the process. The sooner the instructions were completed, the sooner they could go on to the next step.

But the priest would have to be careful lest the instructions become merely pro forma. "You must understand," Koesler cautioned, "that at the end of this process—if we get there—you will be baptized. So it'd be a good idea to understand what you are being baptized into. That's the purpose for the instructions."

"Right. That makes sense. Then what?"

"Then we prepare the documentation. There are questionnaires for you both. Then—and you can begin putting this together right away—we identify the witnesses and supply accurate addresses and phone numbers. It won't do to eliminate a very good witness because of an inaccurate number. Oh, and while you're compiling the list: It's a good idea not to contact any of them; otherwise the priest interviewer may suspect some coaching."

"Who picks out the priests who do the interviews?" Frank was intent on taking no chances.

"Depends on where the witness lives. Generally, the local tribunal contacts a priest in the parish nearest to the witness. That priest becomes a notary assigned to take testimony by filling out a questionnaire with the witness's answers. I've already done it a few times in the short while I've been a priest. But I'm getting ahead of myself . . .

"Now, here's something unpleasant . . . but we can get around it: They want you to pay the cost of this procedure. A case like this has to go to Rome for a decision. That involves translating the documents into Latin and hiring a Roman lawyer to present your case. Right off the bat they want three hundred and fifty dollars—with a promise that you'll also pay any additional cost. But," Koesler hastened to add, "all I need do is make a notation in forma pauperum. Which simply means that you cannot afford this much."

Frank chuckled as he looked at Martha. "Well, Marty, I guess there goes the new stove and refrigerator."

"Frank," Koesler protested, "you don't have to do this. We won't be begging; we're simply stating that you can't afford this big a financial commitment."

"Father, I pay my way. Always have. Is that the whole package?"

Koesler hesitated. He knew what final demand would be required. So far, in his young priestly life, he had never had to ask anyone to make such a promise. But, in all candor, he had to clue them into the entire picture. "There's one final promise required of you. And that . . . it's that for however long this case takes to be processed, you and Martha will live as brother and sister."

The atmosphere in Father Koesler's small office became leaden.

Martha reached out and took Frank's hand. "I'm afraid, Father," she said firmly, "that's too much. Too much by far."

She stood up. "I'm sorry we put you to all this trouble, Father. You've been very kind—and for that we're grateful. But"—she shook her head—"that's just too much. How could the Church . . ." She reached for her handkerchief and wiped back tears. "Come on, Frankie, let's—"

"Now, hold on, Marty . . ." Frank patted her hand. "We gotta remember the stakes in this whole thing. We're playing for a big jackpot. Think of all the years we've wanted to be at peace with the Church. I've wanted it almost as much as you do—because you want it so much. I say let's give 'er a crack. At least we can trust the salesman . . ." He smiled at Koesler, then at Martha. "I like this young man. And I say, Let's give it a try."

"Are you sure, Frankie? Are you sure it means this much to you?"

"Aye." He smiled reassuringly at her again. "I am."

He turned back to the priest. "When's our first instruction, Father?"

Koesler checked his desk log. "We're closing out this week. How about Monday . . . Monday evening at, say, nine?"

"Nine it is then," Frank affirmed. As he and Martha stood up, he put his arm around her waist. "Come on, Marty. Be of good cheer. We haven't even begun the process. We can do it. We will do it."

Koesler saw the couple to the door and bade them farewell.

As he prepared for bed, he could not help but think over this evening's final appointment. A young priest, he had just begun a vocation that ruled out marriage. And with that, given the virtue of chastity, his life would be asexual. Some of his seniors assured him that in time it would be easier to live without a woman.

So far he was so enraptured with the newness and thrill of being a priest that he hadn't really given much reflection to the celibate life.

Thus he could not fully measure how life would change for Frank and Martha after the instructions were completed and the process toward dissolution had begun.

The sacrifice was painfully clear to Frank and Martha. But they would give their word. And that, to them, was binding.

9

Based on a two-per-week schedule, the instructions moved right along.

Koesler's concern that this phase of the procedure might be a sham clearly was misplaced. Frank took an active interest in the books Koesler recommended. Nor did Koesler have any opportunity to lecture: Frank did almost as much talking as listening. Indeed, many of Frank's questions taxed mightily those supportive books on Koesler's shelves.

The instructions were completed just after Christmas.

It had been a wonderfully spiritual season for everyone. It was Koesler's first Christmas as a priest. Though utterly exhausted from hearing countless confessions, he was exhilarated by the unique liturgy of the Nativity as well as by the seasonal goodwill of a depth and spirit to capture the heart even of Scrooge.

It was a grand time also for the Morrises. They had taken to attending Mass at St. William's. Since they were not recognized as parishioners at Nativity parish, they felt at ease and were welcomed by Father Koesler at St. William's.

Instructions complete, it was time to enter phases two and three. The first of these was to properly and carefully prepare the petition. Koesler conferred frequently with his Canon Law professor to make certain that everything was being done "by the book" and that no bases were left untouched.

The second part—or phase three—was initiated. Money was sent with the petition. And the Morrises began their new "brother and sister" relationship. It was a time of expectation, hope, and prayer.

Except that the time became endless.

Months passed and no word. No word at all. Sometimes it was difficult for Koesler and the Morrises to remember what life had been before this grand adventure.

More months.

William X. Kienzle

Occasionally and apologetically, one or the other Morris would stop by after Mass or perhaps phone, just to make sure no notification had come in. Invariably Father Koesler would assure them that nothing had happened. He would also assure them that just as soon as any word was received, he would let them know immediately.

After two and a half years, the lives of the Morrises had stretched so taut that Frank and Martha almost began to wish word would never come. As long as they no longer wondered and worried at the start of each day whether they would ever hear from the Curia in Rome, things would be better. The decision—granted or denied—seemed increasingly unreal. The mere act of waiting became the only reality.

Then the call came.

Father Koesler visited them in the evening, having earlier phoned to make sure they would both be in.

Martha was certain from the tone of Father's voice that their waiting was over and, also from his voice, that the petition had been denied.

Frank did not want to speculate on either possibility.

But neither could eat any dinner.

At seven, as promised, Father Koesler arrived. When they were all seated, he delivered the negative verdict with more sympathy and compassion that he would have thought he possessed.

The petition had been denied.

All that work and sacrifice and prayer for literally nothing.

Martha seemed to shrink a bit as she absorbed the finality of Rome's decision.

Father Koesler—who seldom cried—was barely able to hold back tears.

Frank alone kept his head. "Is there anything else we can do, Father?"

"If there is, I don't know what," Koesler said. "And neither does anyone else I consulted earlier today. Without using any names, I checked in with my Canon Law professor and a couple of older priests whose judgment I respect. Nothing."

"How about this 'brother and sister' that we've been doing for the past couple of years?" Frank probed. "The Vatican seems to be terribly interested in our sex lives. How about if we promise no sex for the rest of our lives? Or at least until my former wife dies?"

"Frankie!" Martha was shocked.

"That's okay, Martha," Koesler reassured her. "The same thought occurred to me, Frank. I didn't think you'd be open to that option, but it never hurts to check . . . so I did. It seems the Vatican thinks you're both too young to make such a long-term promise. No . . ." He shook his head. ". . . it won't work. Nothing will."

Koesler did not think it right to drop this bomb of rejection and just walk away. So he settled in for a long visit.

Martha made coffee and the conversation rambled over many subjects. At last, Koesler felt that their churning stomachs had settled and the Morrises were more at ease than they had been.

He reminded them over and over that as they loved God, so God loved them. Their consciences were at peace with God. And that was what mainly counted.

However, even as he spoke, he wondered about the widening dichotomy between their consciences and Church law. According to the "rules," they were "living in sin." But, somehow, he was unable to see this. He had never before felt this way about Church law. He found this disturbing.

It was getting late. After a few more supportive words, Koesler made his exit.

Frank and Martha stood staring out their front window watching the red rear lights of Koesler's car slowly disappear down their narrow residential street. Even after the car turned the corner and the lights were out of sight, they continued to watch, wordlessly.

Frank finally broke the silence. "Well, Marty, my girl, I really think we gave it our best shot."

She did not respond.

"As I always say, there's nothing more to be done once you've done your best."

"That's true," she said finally, "We did all we could, Frankie. So did Father Koesler. He's so young . . . I hope he never gets jaded."

"Aye. Amen to that, Marty. Now, we've had a long, hard evening. Why don't you go climb into bed? I've got just a couple of things that have to be attended to. I'll be right up."

Martha turned to take the stairs, then turned back. "Long as you're at it, you might just check the furnace. It's been acting up lately."

She turned, then once more turned back. "Oh, and by the way: You don't have to use the guest room anymore."

He looked at her and winked.

She went upstairs and as she prepared for bed, she let the tears flow. And freely flow they did. She made no sound; she didn't want Frank to know how deeply hurt she was.

She slipped between the sheets, but try as she might, she couldn't stay awake to welcome Frank. Well, she thought, we've done without each other's intimacy for better than two years now; one more night won't make that much difference.

*   *   *

The explosion almost catapulted her out of bed.

Her first thought was that the furnace had blown up. And she had asked Frank to look at it.

She threw on a robe and dashed down the stairs.

At first she did not comprehend.

Why was Frank on the floor?

Why was his shotgun on the floor?

Why did Frank not have the back of his head? Where was the back of Frank's head?

"Frankie! Frankie! What's happened? Get up! Get up!"

Not really knowing what she was doing, she picked up the phone. The police . . . call the police. After a helpful operator put through the call, Martha, between sobs, got across what had happened.

She hung up the phone, then turned in confusion. Frank . . . She knelt by her husband and straightened his clothing. She did not want him to appear disheveled. Not with company coming.

She didn't have to wait long. The Conner Street station was only a few blocks away. Within minutes the police entered the house and seemed to be everywhere at once.

The first officer through the door saw immediately what had happened. He raised Martha to her feet and helped her to the couch, then sat down next to her. She leaned toward him. He put an arm around her shoulder.

She looked up at him. "Is he hurt badly?"

He knew the question was produced by panic. "Yes, he is. I'm real sorry, ma'am. Can you tell me what happened?"

She looked bewildered at all the activity going on around her. The last thing she could remember was trying to stay awake and failing. Then she thought, Maybe this is a dream. Maybe she would wake up and her darling Frankie would be here and take care of everything as he always did.

Something else told her that nothing would be right ever again.

She tried to answer questions. Yes, they both had had depressing news just this evening. She couldn't explain; it was too complicated.

She continued trying to be helpful.

Was there someone who could come and stay with her? She gave them Louise's number. They phoned, and Louise, shocked, said she'd be right over.

An officer handed a piece of paper to the officer sitting beside Martha. He read it quickly, then handed it to her. "This is for you, ma'am. Is this your husband's writing?"

Martha looked at the note and nodded. Why would Frank write her a letter?

The officer rose from the couch and checked on the progress being made by his team. Things were being wrapped up. Frank's covered body was on a gurney. The officer returned to Martha. "We won't have to ask you any more questions tonight, ma'am. Do you have anything to help you sleep?"

She thought for a moment, then nodded.

"Your sister's here, ma'am. We'll go now. Your husband's body will be at the morgue. I'm sure they'll release it very soon. You can start making funeral arrangements. And, ma'am, I'm very, very sorry."

Louise locked up, then helped Martha up the stairs.

In response to Louise's questions, Martha, between sobs, explained most of what had happened, beginning with Father Koesler's visit and the rejection of their petition. Finally, running out of words, she sat in a stunned daze, eyes open but unseeing. Louise gently assisted her to bed. No sedative was needed; Martha was out the moment her head hit the pillow. She slept, fitfully, until early morning, when she arose and slowly made her way down the stairs.

She didn't understand. Everything was as it should be. But . . . ?

Louise had straightened up everything, even cleaning the blood from the carpet, chairs, and wall. Maybe . . . maybe she had dreamed all this. "Frankie . . ." Then, louder, "Frankie!"

Louise entered from the kitchen, where she had fallen asleep, head on the table. "Oh, my dear," she murmured. "Martha, dear, don't you remember?"

Martha sank to the couch. She remembered. "Get out. Leave," she said, barely audibly.

"What?" Louise heard her, but it didn't register.

"Why couldn't you have left us alone?" Martha said bitterly. "At least we had each other. But no, you had to get us 'fixed up' with the Church. See what happened? My Frankie's gone. Leave. For God's sake, just go!"

Louise wanted to stay but realized that there was no point. She put on her coat. "When you feel better, call me. I'll help any way I can."

"Help?" Martha repeated with dripping sarcasm.

Louise left.

After she told Tony and Lucy what had happened, she phoned first Vincent, then Father Koesler.

The priest was deeply shocked, more so than ever before in his life. Dropping everything, he drove to the Morris home. Martha, dry-eyed, welcomed him distractedly. Koesler sensed there were no tears left.

Wordlessly, she handed him the letter the police had discovered last night—the suicide note. Koesler read it carefully.

My dearest Marty,

You probably will want to blame someone for what I'm about to do. But it isn't anybody's fault. Maybe those guys in Rome. Everybody else has just tried to help.

Without you and our years together, I would have missed everything. I love you more than life itself. Which is exactly why I'm going to do this. You and the Catholic Church go together. Your whole life is built around your Church.

I guess I never have forgiven myself for taking you away from your sacraments. If it weren't for me, you would be in good—top—standing with the Church. Now you'll be able to take Holy Communion. Honest, it makes me feel very good knowing that you will be back in the Church's good graces.

For this, I willingly die.

If God is exceptionally kind, I will be waiting for you.

Thank Father Koesler for—well, for being Father Koesler.

And, darling, remember one thing: I love you more than life itself.

Your own,

Frankie

Father Koesler was fairly sure that nothing that could happen in the future would ever move him more than this. This misbegotten sacrifice.

He looked at Martha. "I am so sorry . . . so very, very sorry."

Martha shrugged. "You're the one—the only one—who is completely blameless. We came to you. You explained everything. You told us how difficult it would be. You were very frank about our chances. And we could tell how embarrassed you were and how bad you felt when you had to tell us we'd have to live as brother and sister . . ." She shook her head. "You're the only one . . ."

"Your sister wanted to help. She knew how much you wanted to live as a Catholic and receive the sacraments—"

"She meddled in our lives. If she hadn't started this, I'd still have my Frankie. I don't want to think of her the rest of my life."

Koesler knew there was no point in pursuing this now. In time, maybe. But not now. "We have some ladies in our parish who are good at helping with funeral details. They volunteer their services. They're really good people. How about if I send them over?"

It occurred to Martha that, having dismissed her sister, she was now alone. She needed help. "Yes," she said quietly, "that would be good. Thank you."

"And," Koesler added, "I'll try to arrange for Christian burial."

Martha looked at him attentively for the first time. "Why would you do that? Frankie committed suicide."

"I know that's what it looks like. But the Church regularly presumes that in such cases the person is not responsible for what he did . . . temporary loss of free will."

"But you read Frankie's note: He seemed to know what he was doing."

"I can try."

"Don't!" she said forcefully. "I can't stand to be crushed by my Church again. The last rejection cost me my husband. I want no more from my Church. Not ever!"

Koesler surmised that Martha's feelings toward both her sister and the Church would soften, given time. Now was not that time.

"I'll ask those women that I mentioned to get in touch with you right away. I'm sure they'll be a big help."

With that, Koesler gave Martha his blessing—which, he thanked God, she did not refuse. Then he left.

He would certainly have to visit and work with Louise and her children. They must be feeling just awful. But at least they had each other.

The one left out on a branch by himself was Vince Delvecchio. He had been informed of his uncle's suicide. But Koesler knew well the macho spirit that was one goal of the seminary training at St. John's. If Koesler's assessment was correct, Vincent had been called into the rector's office and notified. It wouldn't matter whether or not Vince asked permission to go home. He would be advised to "tough it out" and remain working through the seminary's routine.

One thing that could break into that relentless routine and allow Vincent to react emotionally would be a visit from Father—and emphasize the Father—Koesler. The seminary rector had too much respect for the priesthood to refuse him access to the grieving student.

And so Koesler headed for the Provincial Seminary in Plymouth.

In little less than an hour he pulled into the circular drive that he knew so well.

As he had anticipated, he was warmly welcomed by the rector, who immediately sent a secretary to summon Delvecchio.

Koesler and Delvecchio went down to the visiting parlor, where, at this time of day, they could be alone and undisturbed.

Of course Vincent knew of the tragedy; the notification had been as Koesler guessed.

Vince seemed to be holding up well. The rector must have been pleased at Vince's growth in the image of John Wayne.

"Mother didn't say, and the rector wouldn't know, but the cause of this, I presume, was the failure of the Pauline Privilege?"

"Yes. I delivered the news to them last night—just hours before it happened."

Delvecchio shook his head sadly. "What happened . . . I mean, to the case?"

"Too many uncooperative witnesses. Some wouldn't testify. Others were ambiguous about whether Frank could have been baptized."

Koesler didn't mention the petition again. But he filled in some of the details of the conversation he and the Morrises had had last night. He finished by telling Vince he wished he could conduct a Catholic funeral for Frank, but that Martha had turned down the offer. And he scarcely could be hopeful that he could slide that possibility past the pastor of St. William's.

Delvecchio looked surprised. "But why would you want to do that?"

"Because your uncle was a catechumen, by any definition of the word. He had completed instructions. He had agreed to the tenets of Catholicism. The only thing that prevented his baptism was Rome's rejection of his petition."

"But if he had left Aunt Martha . . ."

Knowing their love for each other, Koesler had not considered this possibility. But, technically, Delvecchio was correct. Short of clearing Frank's first marriage, the only way he could have been baptized and become a Catholic would be to live a celibate life. And that had not been in the cards—not in the Morris deck, in any case, because Rome wouldn't go for it and Frank wouldn't leave Martha.

"Besides," Delvecchio continued, "Uncle Frank committed suicide. That demands the denial of Christian burial."

"I think you'll find, Vince, that the Church is rather lenient when it comes to that."

Delvecchio's eyes opened wide. "It is the greatest sin. The greatest evil."

"Yes, yes, I know, Vince. The ultimate act of despair. Denial of even the forgiveness, comfort, and compassion of the Holy Spirit. But who among us can know the mind of a tortured soul in the final moments of life?"

"It is the law."

"It is a law regularly set aside."

"Well," Delvecchio said, "at least Aunt Martha can go to Communion again."

Koesler almost gasped. The only other person who had expressed that sentiment was Frank himself—in his suicide note.

There seemed little point in continuing the conversation. Besides, the purpose of Koesler's visit had been accomplished: Delvecchio was handling what grief was his magnificently. No need to worry about him . . . at least for the present.

Koesler left for the long drive home.

Completely out of character for him, he did not turn on the car radio. He was deep in thought about Vincent and the manner in which he was taking the death of his uncle.

Was this the same kid who'd trashed a liturgical rubric just so campers wouldn't be bored during Communion time?

Now, when it comes to his uncle's suicide, he is appealing to law—Church law—to . . . what? To shield himself from the slightest responsibility for what had happened.

To be brutally fair, there really wasn't much responsibility to be shouldered by young Vince Delvecchio. He'd had a corner of responsibility for a matter of minutes—when his mother asked him to "do something" about the canonically irregular situation of his uncle and aunt.

Then, in the space of just a few minutes, he had shifted the load to others. Suddenly it became someone else's duty to contact a young priest who was busy translating book learning to the school of hard knocks. And from then on, it was the responsibility of Father Koesler.

Finally, there was the business of Communion and the other sacraments. To see death—suicide—as nothing more than making the sacraments available to one who had been denied them, seemed to Koesler to be crass legalism in its shoddiest form.

Where was this boy headed?

10

The Present

At the sound of the phone, Koesler instinctively started to rise from the chair. Just as quickly, he remembered that he was, or very soon would be, a Senior Priest, no longer responsible for the spiritual care of a parish. No longer responsible for answering the phone. With a twinge of regret he eased himself back into his contour-programmed chair.

He looked across at Father Tully, who made no move to pick up the phone. Why not? Koesler wondered.

Maybe it was the seminary of Koesler's day. If it's your job, you clean the floor. If it's your job, you answer the phone.

Koesler's active memory recalled a time when his class was in its final year at Sacred Heart Seminary. His room was in St. Thomas Hall, a residential wing. The individual rooms provided some privacy for the students for the first time in their seminary career. But the rooms were not for claustrophobics. One wag stated that if a student died in his room, the rector would have handles attached to the outside and the room would be the coffin the lad was buried in.

Just outside Koesler's room in the seminary was a phone, used exclusively for intercom calls. However, once, in a unique exception, the phone rang—loudly—at about 3 A.M.

Finally, after about ten rings, it was answered by the student assigned to that task. Groggy, he was understandably confused.

Student: St. Thomas Hall.

Woman: This Mr. Moon's bar?

Student: St. Thomas Hall.

Woman (after a pause): What?

Student: St. Thomas Hall.

Woman: I got a wrong number?

Student: St. Thomas Hall.

Woman: Well, you'd think the least I would get was the right number.

Later they found that the student on switchboard duty, when closing down for the night, had mistakenly programmed all incoming calls to the phone in St. Thomas Hall.

It was the next day's conversation piece. No switchboard operator ever made that mistake again.

However, the compulsion to answer a phone was implanted. In Koesler's case, the compulsion was intensified during his assignment to St. William's, where the three assistant priests took turns being "on" the door and "on" the phone. Callers left to cool their heels at the door or callers on a phone that went unanswered were evidence of sins that cried to heaven for vengeance.

Well, Koesler reminded himself, mundane decisions such as how the congregation would be served were no longer in his bailiwick. Father Tully was in charge . . . or would be, if the two of them could devise a way to treat the double requirement of making the Profession of Faith and taking the Oath of Fidelity.

The phone stopped ringing. Koesler noted that while the light on the dial had ceased flashing, it remained lit: Someone else in the rectory had picked up. Undoubtedly Mary O'Connor.

Sure enough, Mary peeked around the half-opened door. Out of long-standing habit, she looked to Koesler. She quickly corrected herself and addressed Father Tully. "It's Inspector Koznicki on line one—"

Before she was able to go on, Tully was getting to his feet.

"You don't have to take the call, Father," she said. "He just has a question. I can give him your answer."

Tully stopped in mid-rise, then dropped back into the chair, looking up at her expectantly.

"The inspector and Lieutenant Tully are tied up in a meeting. They and their wives can still make the dinner, but they'll be late . . ."

"How late?"

"Nine, he said—maybe a little earlier, but no later. If nine is too late, they'll have to cancel—or postpone the dinner."

Father Tully considered for a brief moment. "How do you and the caterers feel about it?"

Mary smiled broadly. "We're not going anywhere."

"Let's go with nine then. And, thanks, Mary."

As Mary left for the kitchen, Tully turned back to Koesler. "What about the bishop? Should we tell him dinner's going to be late?"

"Let's not," Koesler replied without hesitation. "I have a hunch we may want to talk to Vince before the others arrive."

Tully sipped his tea. "That was some story!" he said after a few moments. "Nothing anyplace close to that's ever happened to me."

"It was a one-time event for me."

"How did you feel? I mean, I can see how you'd want to console Martha and Delvecchio and his mother. But you . . . you must've had some deep reaction yourself."

"I'll say I did. And it happened just as you suggested. I was operating on adrenaline from the first moment I heard what happened. But after I talked with Vince, I had to face up to my part in this . . . a classic time for second-guessing oneself."

"That's happened to all of us," Tully offered.

"Yeah, I suppose it's kind of normal. But this situation with Frank and Martha was well out of the ordinary."

"Are you over it now?" Tully inquired. "I mean, I know it's been a lot of years. But did you ever fully recover?"

Koesler grimaced. "No. Of course, I've come to terms with responsibility. I wasn't even the initiator in that process. And I did everything I could. I was young and inexperienced. But I checked all along the way with older priests. Everybody I talked to was practiced in the Privilege of the Faith cases—including my Canon Law professor.

"I know in my conscience that I'm not responsible in any way for what happened. And yet . . . from time to time I can still see Frank Morris. A good man. A better husband than many comfortable Catholics I've known. Even now, I can hardly think of him as a suicide."

"Do you think you could have provided Christian burial if his widow had wanted it?"

Koesler thought for a few moments. "I don't know. I'll never know. Even back then, when the Church was comparatively strict about granting Christian burial, it might have been possible.

"I can recall one incident involving an Italian family. The family was extremely faithful—pillars of the Church. Uncle Louie died. One of those cases where Uncle Louie had said bye-bye to the Church after confirmation . . . when he was just a kid.

"Mostly for the sake of that faithful family and their desire to bury Louie from the Church, we tried like crazy to find some evidence that Louie might have—even mistakenly—could have wandered into a church at some recent time.

"Finally, the family turned up somebody who remembered Louie tipping his hat as he walked past a Catholic church. The witness wasn't positive that it had been a conscious, voluntary act of devotion on Louie's part. But, in the end, it was—mercifully—judged sufficient: Louie was buried from the Church. They even wound rosary beads in his hands." He smiled. "I'll bet that felt strange to Louie."

They both chuckled. Father Tully had never had that much trouble burying anyone. There'd never been any hostile forces or big brothers peering over his shoulder.

"But"—Koesler grew serious again—"there was that suicide note. It was well thought out and carefully written." Again he reflected for a moment. "I would have tried . . . but I wouldn't have expected much success."

"You think you'd have that much trouble now?" Tully asked.

"That law is on the books. And the note would be hard to deal with. And there surely would be some 'keepers of the faith' who would cause a lot of trouble if they got wind of what I was doing."

Tully shook his head. "It all started with a canonical problem with a marriage. I was going to suggest that you might have gone the route of a 'pastoral solution.' But there couldn't have been many—if any—priests who knew about that relatively painless procedure in those days."

"You mean," Koesler clarified, "when confronted with an impossible marriage case, you let the couple's conscience settle the matter . . .

"Well, for one, as you say, the time had not yet come for that solution . . . though, in recent years, I have used it quite a few times. It's a simple enough concept. Ask a Catholic couple, who've been forced by Church law into a civil wedding, if they honestly before God consider themselves to be truly married . . . or a little married . . . or not married at all.

"It's a loaded question. Of course, nine times out of ten, they consider themselves married. But they also feel that the Church is uncomfortable at their arrangement. So, the priest makes them feel at ease with their conscience and prepares them and advises them to live sacramental lives."

"Actually," Tully observed, "when we were growing up Catholic, we were told we had an obligation to form a correct conscience—and then to follow it."

"Yes. And it's perfectly possible that in forming that conscience, still it may disagree with Church law—in which case a person must be extra cautious about the matter.

"But if, after due deliberation, the disagreement continues, conscience must be supreme.

"I love the story about the First Vatican Council, when the bishops were rather bulldozed into passing part of the doctrine on infallibility. In England, a Catholic college faculty was gathered for drinks before dinner. And Cardinal John Henry Newman raised his glass in a toast. 'Gentlemen,' he said, 'I drink to infallibility—but first, I drink to conscience.'"

"Ah, yes . . ." Tully smiled. "You gotta watch those converts like Newman. They have subtle ways of correcting things.

"But," he said, "getting back to Frank and Martha: I must say I'm surprised that the tribunal would not accept them into full participation even if they were willing to continue living as brother and sister. That would seem to settle the matter for Church law—even if it constituted a nightmare for the couple."

Koesler sighed. "It's weird. I've even known of a tribunal priest who ordered a couple's parish priest to make sure the two were living up to their promise of a brother-sister relationship."

Tully snorted. "Sort of gives a new meaning to 'peeping Tom.'

"I take it," he added, "from the way you told the story, you think these two did keep their promise for the entire two and a half years their case was pending."

"No question," Koesler responded firmly. "Their word was their honor. I believe they lived a monastic life. I believe they did without things they needed so they could pay court costs.

"But"—Koesler shook his head—"even after all these years, I have never gotten over Vinnie's reaction to his uncle's death. Of course, he'd already been told by the seminary rector what had happened . . ."

"And the rector told Delvecchio in just about the manner you anticipated he would?"

Koesler nodded. "It wasn't that the rector didn't have emotions, or that he didn't express them. He could—and did—laugh when something actually funny happened. He could be depressed. And, God knows, he could get angry. He had a special knack when he announced some sort of atrocity one of the students had perpetrated. There he was, sitting up there on a podium in front of us. And he would whip off his glasses and throw them spinning on the desk. The knack was that the glasses would stop moving and spinning just at the edge of the desk. One tossing error and the glasses would be broken on the floor." He chuckled. "That's brinkmanship."

"Marvelous. Do you remember any of the so-called atrocities?"

"One that comes to mind," Koesler responded instantly, "was a white pillowcase that had been turned into a pinto-like black and white. Seems one of our number had been using it to polish his black shoes. That sent the old man into paroxysms.

"Any number of things could get him started. But one thing you can say for him: He never made up any abuses out of whole cloth; ours were actual atrocities.

"He could be very gentle one-on-one. But there was no doubt he was looking to turn out men. Men who could take any blow, face any adversity and forge ahead. I was sure that's what he'd be looking for when he told Vince about his uncle.

"To be very honest, I didn't think Vinnie would do very well with that test."

"How so?"

"A close family member—it had to be one hell of a shock. And Vincent was part of this whole procedure . . . even though all he did was send his aunt and uncle to me. He was a necessary link. I think, honestly, not many could surface from something like that as though nothing had happened."

"And that's how Delvecchio seemed to you?"

"Uh-huh. It was even a bit spooky now that I picture it. I was wishing I had brought some Kleenex or a couple of extra handkerchiefs. I expected Vince to be in a state of shock—come to think of it, maybe he was . . . maybe that's why he seemed so cool and untouched: He must've been in shock!"

"Or," Tully offered, "had one hell of a good defense mechanism."

"Huh?"

"I'm borrowing from a little psych that I took at the University of Dallas. Delvecchio may have been in denial. Maybe the news was so devastating to him that the only way he could deal with it was denial—one of the most basic defense mechanisms."

"You may have a point there, Zack. But he seemed aware of what had happened. We even talked about the funeral. I remember he was amazed that I would consider conducting a Catholic funeral for Frank."

"But there are lots of modes of denial." Tully looked thoughtful. "Maybe not the denial of reality—that's really pretty infantile. But he could deny any responsibility for the matter. And from what you've said, Delvecchio wasn't actually that deeply involved.

"His mother asked him to try and fix an awkward situation. Pressed, and seeking some sort of off-the-cuff solution, he tossed the ball to you.

"True, you were inexperienced. Still, you were fresh from the books . . . and that's not so bad: This procedure had to go 'by the book.' And, when all's said and done, he knew you would at least be gracious to them. And in their situation, any reception would be hit-or-miss—depending on which rectory they wandered into. You mentioned that they had already been treated shabbily by—who was it?"

"Keller at Nativity."

"Ah, yes. I never met the man, but I've met his clone any number of times. I'll bet every diocese and religious order has at least one Keller. Seems like you were expecting one kind of reaction from Delvecchio . . . and you got another one, Bob."

"That's true . . . but Vinnie's reaction to his uncle's suicide was one response. I could think of lots of reasons why he could remain so untouched, so above it all. And I hadn't even thought of a defense mechanism. You put a new light on that, Zack.

"But what really threw me was his attitude toward the possibility of getting Christian burial for Frank. Forget that I probably couldn't have pulled it off. It could've been a great source of comfort for relatives and friends—"

"You thought," Tully broke in, "that Delvecchio's first reaction to Christian burial would be supportive. I agree. And I can't imagine why it wasn't."

"Remember, Zack, we're dealing with a young man who, only a year or so earlier, had that argument with me over fooling with organ music during a Requiem Mass. Now he's surprised that anyone could think of Christian burial for a supposed suicide. One would think there's a hell of a lot more involved in comforting grieving people than in diverting restless kids at a camp Mass."

Tully tapped the arm of the chair with his index finger. "We're just guessing, of course. And it's been—what?—some forty years, so this is hardly Monday-morning quarterbacking. But I guess you could see Delvecchio's entire reaction as within strict legalistic behavior. Frank Morris—and his wife—had a petition that was turned down by a competent Church court. Roma locuta, causa finita. So, Delvecchio wonders, what's the problem? You asked for a decision regarding your freedom to marry, and you got one.

"That's 'A.' And 'B,' your response to this decision is to kill yourself. Okay, if that's the way you want it. But any possibility you had of being given a Christian burial is forfeited."

Koesler nodded slowly. "Quid sit lex? as our Moral prof used to say. But 'What is the law?' is so cold and unfeeling."

"And you couldn't do it, could you?" Tully regarded his confrère with affection.

Koesler looked off into the distance, ready to admit the truth. "No, I couldn't. And I didn't know quite what to do about it. I had paid close attention through four years of study of just about each and every one of the two thousand and four hundred and fourteen laws. The vast majority of my test answers were correct . . . matter of fact, I don't think I did better in any subject than I did in Canon Law. But it was mere law on those pages. Whether it was good or harmful law didn't occur to me—or, for that matter, to any of my classmates . . . or to any other seminarians of that day.

"And then we were ordained. We gave consolation to the afflicted. We handed out chits for emergency food or shelter. We instructed. We did all sorts of things that made sense. And then we interpreted law. And it no longer was the abstract study of law. These were people who, by and large, were wounded. Their marriages had exploded in their hands. They were raw from revelations in a court of law—"

Koesler stopped and shook his head. "Frank Morris confused me, Zack. I was bound and determined to help him. Instead, I destroyed him."

"You didn't do it," Tully insisted.

"I know . . . I know . . . at least I've known it for the past some thirty years. That doesn't much help Frank."

"It was out of due time," Tully said. "Lots of people died because they lived before antibiotics, or chemotherapy, or organ transplants . . . or kidney dialysis."

They fell silent for a lingering period.

"I guess this example doesn't bode well for me in dodging the Profession of Faith and the Oath of Fidelity," Tully said finally. "I can just hear Bishop Delvecchio now: 'What does the law say, Father?'"

"Don't jump to any hasty conclusion, Zack. I'm becoming as concerned as you are about your getting this parish without compromising your conscience. It's just that I've never bothered to analyze Vinnie in such depth. I assure you, we've only scratched the surface."

Tully rocked comfortably in his chair. "We're also getting to know another young man as he goes through his own 'change of life . . .'"

Kosler's eyes widened momentarily. "Me."

"You."

"True, I was developing. That was to be expected after that super-seclusion of the seminary. Twelve very formative years was a long time to be part of a subculture."

Tully tipped his head to one side. "More. It was more than just adjusting to 'the world.'"

"Yes, it was," Koesler said thoughtfully. "For the life of me I couldn't put it all together. It wasn't that I hated Canon Law; all I had done about those laws was to learn about them. But I couldn't resolve the apparent conflict between the law and the rights due a Christian."

"Interesting though, that you and Delvecchio were, apparently, going in opposite directions."

Koesler gnawed on his lip. "I thought it was only a matter of time before Vinnie would join me on wherever the path led. But I figured I'd have to be patient. First he would have to finish his seminary career—and he'd only just begun it. He had almost the full four years before he would get a parochial assignment. Then we would see what was what."

"So? Is that the way it worked out? How did he get on with that first job?"

"It happened before ordination to the priesthood. It was a surprise to everyone. It couldn't have been foreseen. And I'm still not absolutely certain what happened. But something did. It changed his life.

"I'll tell it to you just the way it happened. Then, we'll try to figure out what sort of impact it had on Vince's life."

Tully rocked himself to his feet. "How about some more iced tea?"

11

"The year was . . . let's see . . . nineteen fifty-nine, as I recall. Yes," Koesler nodded, "I was nearing the end of my fifth year as a priest. Vince was in his fourth and final year in the seminary.

"He had received the minor orders of porter, lector, exorcist, and acolyte in turn, and the first major order of subdeacon. Just at the beginning of that year, he was ordained a deacon and, for the first time, he shared in the priesthood: As a deacon, he could play his part in a Solemn Mass, preach, and baptize."

"Strange, isn't it," Tully mused, "that's almost all gone. I took all those steps—but that was before Vatican II."

"Yeah. I miss them."

"So do I."

"'Fifty-nine! We were on the verge of the Council . . . and we had no idea!" Koesler paused, remembering . . .

"It all began during Lent. We were headed for Easter—and then, things and plans had to be changed drastically."

1959

America didn't know it, but we were about to pass from what many were to call the Last Decade of Innocence. Vietnam would tear our country apart. And the Second Vatican Council was about to do the same favor for Catholics worldwide.

The Delvecchio family, however, had more pressing and personal problems to deal with.

To begin with—something that would test his ongoing relationship with the Delvecchio family—Father Koesler had been reassigned from the very urban St. William's parish to the very suburban St. Norbert's in Inkster.

In the Detroit archdiocese there existed a nonbinding understanding that assignments for assistant priests would last approximately five years. Whereas pastors were to work their parishes until either the pastor or the parish dropped.

But after only a year and a half at St. William's, an emergency assignment had to be made. Such an occurrence usually triggered a domino effect: To keep things in working order, X numbers of priests were bumped and moved to new diggings.

So it was with Father Koesler.

It had been especially difficult in this, his second assignment, to adjust to new faces, new names, and lots of excellent people who were beginning their families. They had just started what would be a bumper crop of babies.

Koesler did not completely cut the cord that connected him to many of his special contacts at St. William's. Chief among families he continued to visit were the Delvecchios.

They in turn welcomed him—though the only ones still at home full time were mother and daughter.

Vinnie, of course, lived at St. John's Seminary. After Lent would come Easter and a week's vacation. After Easter, in one's final year, a whole bunch of things were no longer doubtful. You knew all the answers. You knew you would be ordained. Of course there were still classes and important things to learn. And there was the final oral examination just weeks before ordination. A time was assigned when the deacons would face three faculty priests who could ask anything they wished in the fields of Moral, Dogma, and Canon Law.

Vincent had no reason to be concerned with any of that; in fact, he was tutoring.

The senior students practiced offering Mass, although since they'd been attending Mass more or less daily for most of their lives, what did they need with the practice? Surprisingly, some needed a lot of help— particularly with the singing. Again, that was no problem for Vince.

He even had the gold-plated chalice he would use as a priest. He had earned almost nothing at the charity summer camp. But his mother and his two siblings had saved up and bought it for him. His mother's engagement diamond had been set into the cup. It was a dream come true for everyone in the family.

To top it all off, Father Koesler had agreed to preach the homily at Vince's first Mass.

Anthony was a senior at Western Michigan University in Kalamazoo. Having noted the quality of athletes entering the Big Ten universities, Tony figured it would be better for his athletic career to be a very big fish in a relatively small pond than vice versa.

So he had decided against Michigan and Notre Dame and a few others on that exalted level and accepted the free ride at WMU.

It had paid off.

He did extraordinarily well academically as well as athletically, so much so that the area sports writers felt secure in referring to him as the Bomb with the Brain.

But it was his gridiron feats that sent the writers into spasms of superlatives. His arm was "a cannon." His eye was "unerring." He turned the ball into "a bullet with brains." He was "Eddie LeBaron on a ladder." He "drank from the same volcanic cup of fiery competitiveness" as Van Brocklin. His scrambling ability, precursor of the dashes that would later make Fran Tarkenton renowned, "flummoxed" the opposing line. But where Tarkenton would gain more yards running east and west than many pro stars running north and south, Tony Delvecchio never heard of east and west; he "ran for daylight." He "gave 110 percent." Feisty, with a take-charge attitude, he did not accept plays from the sidelines, but kept the opposition on their toes with his imaginative and "bodacious" calls.

In the autumn of his senior year, as the pro draft loomed, the question was: How high up would Tony be selected? A first-round pick, especially for a quarterback, promised gold and glory. Look at Len Dawson, the Purdue powerhouse who was the Steelers' first-round draft pick in 1957: He had made it big. All agreed Tony Delvecchio deserved that ranking. But . . . from *Kalamazoo?*

Some doubts lingered as to how well Tony would do against professionals. But whether or not well founded, hope was high. And then the roof fell in.

The first four rounds of the pro draft came and went without a nibble. Tony, his coach, his teammates, his family, and his friends, were dumbfounded.

Tony put as good a face on it as possible. Okay, so I didn't get picked right off. I guess I should've expected that; I mean, after all, look at the guys they did pick: all from big-name, powerhouse schools. If I had it to do over, I guess I wouldn't't've buried myself in Kalamazoo. But there's still the other rounds . . .

The remaining rounds were held in January. But by the time the thirtieth round had passed by without the name Delvecchio being mentioned, Tony was not only having second thoughts, he was devastated. His entire college career had been predicated on a future in pro football. Now what?

He'd have to make some calls . . . Coach might have some connections . . . maybe some pro club out there needed a backup quarterback . . . and, after all, he *did* have those press clippings . . .

Though down, Tony was far from out. He pulled himself together: He was young, he had talent, he had hopes, he had ideals. Never say die!

Lucy was about to graduate from St. William's high school. Which, due to a pastoral eccentricity, was exclusively for young women.

St. William's elementary school was coed. But when it came to high school, the pastor volunteered parish money to pay half the tuition charged by all-male De LaSalle Collegiate. It was a deal, as he saw it, where the parish saved money in the long run by not having to spring for expensive coaches and sports programs.

Lucy hadn't cottoned to the setup. But after tears and a tantrum or two, she settled down and went along with being part of an all-girls school. And had to admit there were distinct advantages in the uniform, in not having to compete for boys, and in maintaining a long-standing tradition.

Now her thoughts zeroed in on graduation activities: breakfasts, lunches, dinners, caps and gowns, musical and social events, and, as the top priority, the prom.

Lucy had an extra complication that, as far as could be ascertained, no other young lady faced during this graduation hoopla: She had a brother who was going to be a priest. As a matter of fact, her graduation Mass would be his first Solemn Mass. How's that for being eclipsed?

If that were not enough—and it clearly was more than enough—another brother was graduating, not from high school, but from college. Not only that, but his picture was all over the local newspapers—the sports sections anyway.

Nobody was interested in Lucy's grade average: 3.8, thank you very much. Everybody was busy conjecturing about her brother Tony's career.

Agony!

Had any other young woman ever been relegated to so much obscurity on one of the most important days of her entire life?

Lucy's doubts to the contrary notwithstanding, it was a triumphant time for the Delvecchios.

Vinnie would make a central casting priest. So tall that, later, one of the school children referred to him as the "high priest." Pencil-thin and ramrod-straight, he had plenty of room to expand and still be every inch the ascetic—a tall, dark, and handsome ascetic.

By general consensus Vinnie was headed for great things. No one could quite figure out why he had not been sent to Rome for his theological studies. It might have been politics: One of the two seminarians sent to Rome from Vinnie's class was nephew to the bishop of Grand Rapids.

Still, the smart money was on Vinnie's climbing the hierarchical ladder. Not a bad endorsement, considering that he was not particularly close to anyone in his class.

It was almost as if Vincent and Anthony might have had different fathers. Oh, there were similarities, of course, but in physique they were worlds apart.

Tony was listed as a six-footer. A slight exaggeration; he was more like five feet eleven. Where Vinnie appeared to have come fresh from forty days of fasting in the desert, Tony seemed never to have missed a meal.

Lucy was the prize—as close to flawless as a young adult could get.

Several inches taller than her mother, but as fine-boned, Lucy had her late father's surprising strength.

Girls' sports had not yet come of age. But in an all-girl high school, somehow the varsity basketball team became the big game, and the members of that team were the BGOC—Big Girls on Campus.

Besides holding one of the top academic grades in her class, Lucy was also a standout in theater, dance, and on the debating team. In almost any other family, Lucy would have been the noteworthy member. But among the Delvecchios, particularly at this point, she came in a distant third.

It wasn't fair! That she knew. But her day would come. Would it ever!

This was still the era, especially in parochial schools, when young ladies (at least those with no thought whatsoever of entering the convent) were pointed at the vocation of finding a man, having his babies, and answering to the sublime name of homemaker.

Lucy had paid close attention when the nuns spelled all this out— with, nonetheless, of course, a word or two on religious vocations. Realistically, the nuns knew that, of the two life vehicles, wife and mother would draw far more applicants than the religious calling.

Lucy, early on, had set her sights on the medical profession. It mattered not that there were precious few female MDs. Determination was Lucy's middle name. Had the priesthood been her goal, it would not have mattered that her Church did not ordain women. But Lucy didn't crave ordination. One priest in the family seemed enough. Of course, if she were offered an immediate bishopric . . .

Things were rolling for the Delvecchios.

But more and more Louise was able to participate in the fulfillment of her children less and less.

There was a nagging pain that would neither be relieved nor identified. With some frequency, she visited the physician who had treated the family for many years.

Lucy, mostly because she was the only child still living at home, was the only one who knew—or at least had some glimmer, since Louise did her best to mask her condition.

Lucy urged her mother to seek other medical opinions. "After all, Mother, things have changed since scalpels replaced leeches."

"Don't be disrespectful, Lucy. Don't forget: Dr. Schmidt brought you into this world!"

Actually, Dr. Schmidt agreed with Lucy. It was he who sent Louise to a series of specialists. One of whom called Dr. Schmidt. "Werner, I got Mrs. Delvecchio's biopsy."

"And . . . ?"

"It's bad. Doesn't get much worse. Pancreatic cancer."

"I feared as much. I don't suppose we're in time to save her."

"It's inoperable, Werner. Sorry, old man. I don't envy you now—or her."

"Nor do I."

Schmidt phoned Louise, told her he had news that was not so good, and asked if it would be possible to gather the family to discuss the options.

12

Lucy was home, but Tony was in Kalamazoo and Vincent was in Plymouth. Louise would try to gather the tribe. Would tomorrow morning at ten be all right?

Ten would be as good as any other time.

Lucy wasted no time. She got her mother to lie down. Now Louise was fighting whatever was wrong with her and, additionally, the worry over her children. Lucy would contact her brothers. Mother was not to be concerned.

Vincent and Tony were shocked. They knew their mother had not been well. But not being on the scene, they'd had no clue how serious her condition was. To obviate any possible excuses, Lucy painted the situation to be as bleak as her imagination would permit. Even so, she could not match the hopelessness of reality.

Only Vincent encountered resistance to his request to leave immediately for home. In the face of his insistence, however, the rector had to admit that Delvecchio had already proven his "manhood" sufficiently. And if any student could afford to miss classes, it surely was Vincent Delvecchio.

And so, at ten the next morning, all assembled in the Delvecchio living room: Louise, Dr. Schmidt, Vincent, Anthony, and Lucy, as well as Father Koesler, whom Louise had contacted.

To the hushed and increasingly dismayed group, the doctor explained how difficult it was to diagnose cancer of the pancreas. He was not exculpating himself, but merely spoke the truth: As advanced as the diagnostic tools were, as brilliant and capable as the specialist was, the condition was very good at hiding itself.

The diagnosis was bad news, the prognosis even worse: Two to five months. It could be longer . . . but yes, in all frankness, it could be sooner.

Dr. Schmidt explained the only option that current medical science had to offer: radiation therapy. He explained further that it was not much of an option: It would intensify debilitation, while offering practically no possibility of even minimal effectiveness.

Louise, brow furrowed, was thoroughly confused. The decision clearly was hers. But there was no marked path in this maze.

Bewildered, in distress, she looked slowly around the intent circle. "What . . . ? What . . . ?"

Finally, in the absence of any other response, Koesler spoke. "I wonder," he said slowly, "if you shouldn't consider radiation. It seems the only choice to me," he added after a moment. "If we do nothing . . . inevitably it's the end." For the first time in his life he shied from the word "death."

Tony broke the brief silence. "I'm with Father. It's the only shot we've got. I say we take it." Ever the athlete, Tony could not imagine his body betraying him. It didn't matter what injury had been sustained. An hour or more in the whirlpool bath could do wonders. Or a temporary brace. Or a massage. Or something. Sports medicine was forever coming up with novel splints, supports, methods of taping. In the brief experience of this resilient, powerful, young—and emphasize the *young*—man, the body could come back from anything. The body would never fail if you gave it a modicum of care. Tony never thought of death. It was there, of course, but he didn't consider it.

Two votes were in: Koesler and Tony both favored the therapy.

Vince looked as if he were in a decisionary limbo. The news of his mother's seemingly fatal illness had rocked Vinnie to his core. He couldn't think beyond this moment, let alone recommend a course to take.

One voice, though small, sounded loudly. "No!" Lucy insisted. "I've read about radiation therapy. It's worse than the sickness—well, maybe not worse: It doesn't kill you; it just makes you wish you were dead. If you want, I'll tell you what the side effects of this treatment are. Then let's see how you vote!"

Everyone looked at this young woman still in high school. No doubt about it, she would become a force to be reckoned with.

"Doctor"—she turned to Schmidt—"you said it was possible—*possible*—that radiation might help contain or even put a cancer in remission. Does that include pancreatic cancer?"

The doctor slowly shook his head.

Lucy turned to face the others. "Tony . . . Father . . ." Her tone turned apologetic as if she should not dare correct a priest. "Think of what you're recommending. This has hit us like a ton of lead. We can't just pop off. We're grasping at a straw that's not attached to anything. With this therapy we're condemning Mama to months of added sickness and pain while the statistics tell us it's all for nothing."

"I know," Koesler said, "that I'm not a member of this family—"

"You might just as well be," Lucy interjected.

"Thanks." Koesler nodded. "I don't really feel I'm entitled to a vote. But . . . on thinking it over, I have to agree with Lucy. She's focusing on quality of life . . ." He hesitated, then said firmly, "Louise, depending on how important it is to you, this radiation doesn't promise you much of any quality of life."

"Wait a minute!" Tony's tone was challenging. "We can't give up! If Ma doesn't get this treatment, it's . . . curtains. She'll be dead! That's for sure, isn't it, Doc?"

"I'm afraid so," Schmidt said.

"Well, maybe I haven't been around as long as some of you people," Tony said, "but I've learned one thing: If you don't compete you can't win. If Ma doesn't take the treatment, she isn't competing . . . she hasn't got a chance!"

Lucy looked at the doctor. "Please . . . be very realistic. We aren't asking you to play God. But you know more about this than we do. You've had experience with pancreatic cancer when the patient chose radiation. What's it like?"

"Pretty much as you've already said. Especially with cancer of the pancreas, which is inoperable—which is what your mother has. Radiation may retard the disease somewhat. But in the end . . .

"What you and the good father have said is the situation as I have observed it. The effects of the radiation add to the discomfort and pain—so much so that there is not much of any quality of life."

"So where does that leave us?" Tony did not attempt to hide his bitterness. "We're going to give up? Give up without a fight?"

"Tony," the doctor said in as conciliatory a tone as possible, "this may be difficult for you to understand, with your youth and your strong, athletic body. But," he said very deliberately, "there are worse things in life than death."

Tony snorted.

"Unless . . ." Vincent had been silent so long the others had virtually forgotten his presence. "Unless there is a miracle."

Silence.

"I know you're going to get ordained soon," Tony said after a moment, "but that's crazy."

"Miracles don't happen to ordinary people like us," Lucy said, as she looked from face to face. "Do they?"

Dr. Schmidt, now clearly out of his league, become a spectator at an event he had heretofore been directing.

"Vinnie," Koesler said, "isn't what you're proposing a *deus ex machina*?"

"A what?" Lucy asked.

"We can't find a rational acceptable solution to this problem of illness," Koesler explained, "so we drag God in from left field to solve the situation for us."

Vincent bristled. "I'm not suggesting that we pull God out of a hat. I'm suggesting that we dedicate ourselves to prayer for a cure for our mother. And I'm hoping that we'll enlist the prayers of everyone we know. Prayer, Father Koesler, is not a *deus ex machina*!"

For the second time during this meeting, Koesler felt as if he had spoken too hastily. "Of course. It goes without saying that we'll pray. Each of us." Even as he said it, he wondered: What about Tony? Would Tony—who could not envision a body that would not fight for health . . . for life—participate in this group prayer?

"But," Koesler added, "prayer is one thing. A miracle is something else again."

"How can you say that, Bob?" Vincent seemed bewildered that he needed to explain this to a priest—a priest in whom Vinnie had confidence. "The Gospels are packed with the marvels possible through prayer. The mustard seed, teaching the disciples to pray—the examples go on forever. The one necessary ingredient is faith. Faith won cures. Faith won even a return from death to life. Faith won miracles. That's what I'm proposing: prayer backed by faith in a miracle.

"I'm pleading with all of you to pray for a miracle because . . . because it's our only hope." Vincent seemed closed to tears.

"I'm with you, Vinnie," Lucy said. "I'm going to start today, and by tomorrow everybody in St. William's will be praying for our miracle."

"And"—Koesler volunteered his parish—"at St. Norbert's."

Actually, Lucy found the notion well beyond her capacity of faith. But at least outwardly she joined forces with Vincent and the priest because it offered an alternative to radiation or death, which, until the potential miracle, had been the only choice on the table.

"We seem to have left someone out," Dr. Schmidt said softly. He turned, as did everyone else, to look at Louise.

She did not attempt to control her tears, which flowed from a mixture of fear and love. "I am so lucky to have such a family and friends." She tried to smile through her tears. "I want Vincent to have his miracle."

Everyone seemed bolstered by, or at least satisfied with, her decision—with the very clear exception of Tony.

"It's mid-February now," Vincent said, "and Lent has just begun. Easter won't be here until March twenty-ninth. We have a month and a half before Easter. What a marvelous feast to celebrate the miracle of life."

"Now you're putting a deadline on your miracle?" Actually Tony was trying to go along with the invocation, but his heart wasn't in it.

"No deadline, Tony," Vincent said. "Just that we'll be celebrating the epic feast of the Resurrection. It should inspire everyone we enlist to pray for our cause."

"All right now," Dr. Schmidt said after the discussion seemed at an end, "but before I leave, there are some practical matters that must be addressed. For instance, Louise, you can expect to be up and around, though not as comfortable as you're used to being.

"In time, short of the miracle"—the doctor tipped his head toward

Vincent—"you will need more help. If we're talking of a visiting nurse, a practical nurse, someone in the family who has a nursing background . . . ?"

"I'll ask the seminary for a leave of absence," Vincent said immediately. "I'm sure they'll grant it."

"But, baby, what will that do to your ordination?" Louise protested. "It's less than four months from now."

"We can talk about that. If it has to be postponed, well, then, so be it."

"Vinnie, I have lived for that day ever since you went away to the seminary twelve years ago. What if I haven't got a lot of time? I can't take a chance on not being here for your ordination and first Mass. It can't be postponed . . . it can't!"

"All right, Ma, all right. Don't worry," he soothed. "But I'll talk to the rector anyway. I'm sure he'll let me come home at least once a week."

"I'm almost positive that kind of arrangement can be worked out." Koesler was well aware that the seminary faculty appreciated Vincent's talent and gifts. Even though the request would be out of the ordinary Koesler was certain it would be granted.

"I'll try to get home as often as I can," Tony said. "Finals are coming up. They won't be tough, but I've got to work on them. Then, I'll be making the rounds of the clubs, to see if anybody wants to sign me up . . ."

There seemed to be a feeling that Tony was begging off a service he should shoulder. Tony sensed this. "I know, I know: I should try to get out of the whole thing like Vinnie's doing. But it's not the same. Vinnie can get ordained in June, or July . . . or September, for that matter. The thing is, he's gonna get ordained. If I don't follow up now . . . if I don't give it everything I've got right now, while I'm still in the picture, I'll lose out for sure . . . and there goes my life . . ." Tony became aware that his voice had taken on a whiny tone—like a child trying to evade responsibility. He fell silent.

"We understand, Tony," Louise assured with motherly acceptance. "It's just like you say: You've got to take care of your future now, or you won't have a future. C'mere, sweetie . . ." She spread her arms wide. Tony sat down beside her on the couch. They embraced, as Louise lightly stroked his back.

"For what it's worth," Koesler said, "I can juggle my schedule around a bit and come over three, maybe four times a week. I'd be far from skilled nursing care. But at least I could relieve somebody for a while."

"Oh, Father . . ." Louise wanted to thank him; she wanted to tell him that her family could not make such an imposition on someone as busy as a priest.

It was Lucy who interrupted. "Wait a minute, Mama. I'm the one who'll be here for you all the time—and I think I'd like to get relieved once in a while."

"Lucy, darling," Louise protested, "this is a very big time for you. It's graduation. There'll be be so many parties and celebrations, you've just got to be able to enjoy this once-in-a-lifetime thing."

"Mama, I'm not going to miss hardly any of it. Besides, you can take care of yourself . . . and me," she added lightly. "And don't forget: We're looking for a miracle, remember? Just think . . . Vinnie'll be lucky to get out to see us once a week, and Tony's gonna be stressed even more. *I'm* the one who is already home. And I want to do it. Why can't we leave it at that?" She turned to Dr. Schmidt. "Sound okay to you, Doctor?"

Schmidt smiled. "It sounds like an angel planned it." He put his hand on Lucy's head, indicating which angel he was referring to. "Now . . ." Schmidt stood. "I want to talk to you and"—he turned to Koesler— "to you, Father, before I leave."

Lucy and Koesler accompanied him to the vestibule.

"This afternoon," Schmidt said, "I'll send over some prescriptions. They'll be mostly for pain. You'll be impressed by the quantity. Do you know, Lucy, whether or not your insurance covers this sort of thing?"

Lucy shook her head. "I'm pretty sure it doesn't."

"Okay. Drug companies are forever sending me samples. I'll put in as many as I have on hand. But some you're going to have to get at the pharmacy."

"I've got some money," Koesler offered.

Schmidt looked dubious. "A priest? I'll try to keep the cost down. But it'll still be expensive."

Koesler smiled. "We don't make much. But then, we don't need much."

"Well," the doctor concluded, "we'll take it as it comes. One way or another we'll want to protect Mrs. Delvecchio from pain. And in this kind of illness, pain can be a formidable enemy.

"Now," Schmidt emphasized, "I think it very important that Louise be on her own as much as possible."

Lucy looked puzzled. "I'm not sure I understand." Gradually, she was becoming more cognizant of what her role involved. She would be the hands-on "nurse," taking daily care of her mother. The responsibility would grow the longer her mother lived and, sans miracle, her condition worsened.

"What I'm getting at," Schmidt said, "is that the more Louise can take care of herself, the healthier her disposition will be. If we overcare for her, she may retreat into her illness. So, until she is unable to medicate herself, for instance, by all means encourage her to handle as much as possible.

"Do you see what I mean? As much as possible relate to her as you would to someone who is ill but in many ways can care for herself . . . understand?"

Both Koesler and Lucy nodded.

"I am singling out the two of you," Schmidt said, "because, Lucy, you're going to be the primary care person. And you, Father, will be relieving her from time to time. I don't expect much physical presence from either Tony or even Vincent."

"But they'll be here sometimes at least." Lucy's brow tended to furrow much as did her mother's. "What do I do then?"

"Don't worry, Lucy. It'll be easier in practice than it seems in the abstract," the doctor said. "They're big, strong, and young. They may want to carry her up and down the stairs, for instance. Or give her her medication. Discourage that. You can do it. We've got confidence in you." He turned to Koesler. "Haven't we, Father?"

"Absolutely." Koesler smiled at Lucy. "Call anytime you need help . . . or even if you just want to talk."

"Thanks, Father. And you too, Dr. Schmidt." She smiled, though her eyes looked suspiciously misty. "I feel better now."

Schmidt departed. Koesler returned to the living room, where both

Louise's sons, sitting on either side of her on the couch, were comforting and encouraging her.

After a few minutes, Koesler gave the family his blessing, and left.

He started the engine, but hesitated to put the car in gear. He was thinking about parish boundaries. Among the discoveries he had made during his few years in the ministry was the importance placed on parish boundaries. Koesler, who tended to think of a soul as a soul, had quickly learned the Church has rules and regulations regarding souls.

He recalled an experience one of his classmates had had early on. The young priest had stopped in to visit a hospitalized parishioner who happened to be in a canonically invalid marriage—thus "living in sin." The priest was surprised to learn that the parishioner had slipped into critical condition and was not expected to live.

What to do?

Convalidating a marriage was usually a long and difficult procedure. This gentleman obviously did not have the luxury of time.

But he was dying.

Deciding to err on the side of faith, hope, and charity, rather than law, the priest gave his parishioner absolution and the sacrament of Extreme Unction—or the last rites.

By the time the young priest returned to the rectory, he was torturing himself over whether he had done the right thing. To settle his conscience, he phoned the chancery and happened to get that rare creature, a most sympathetic chancery official.

The priest explained what he'd done. The chancery reply was, "Father, you did exactly the right thing. That man was fortunate you happened upon him as he neared the end."

Koesler's classmate was so amazed he spent the rest of that day phoning other priests with the good news, "Hey, the chancery cares about souls!"

Personally, Koesler thought it lucky that the absolved man happened to be a parishioner. Otherwise there would've been a problem, if not with the kindly chancery official then with a pastor whose boundaries had been violated.

Just such a violation loomed in Koesler's near future.

His first assignment had been at St. William's parish. In all his time there, there had been only one technical deviation in protocol in which he was involved: that was when Frank and Martha Morris had slipped out of Nativity parish to try to convalidate their marriage. But Father Keller of Nativity had clearly demonstrated that he was not going to stake a claim on that couple.

This was a different situation.

Koesler no longer was in any sort of assignment to St. William's. Yet he intended to go well out of his way to care for a former parishioner. Without doubt there was a base here that needed touching. And no better time than now to touch it.

13

It took Father Koesler all of five minutes—he hit only one red light—to reach St. William's church and rectory.

He parked on Gunston and stood on the sidewalk remembering his first taste of parochial life as a young priest.

Visions rose before him: There was his suite: sitting room, bedroom, and bath. His chances of duplicating the spaciousness of these facilities in any future assignment seemed remote. There was Father Farmer's suite, with five bottles of beer peacefully cooling on the windowsill—Farmer's silent revenge for the lack of provided alcohol and the locked refrigerator.

The visions receded as Koesler climbed the steps, rang the bell, and dutifully recited the Hail Mary that, the sign said, would bring a priest to the door. It did.

Father Frank Henry was a bit young to be a full-fledged curmudgeon. But he made up for this drawback with a nasty disposition.

"Well, the prodigal son returns." It was neither an original nor a particularly appropriate greeting. But that was Henry's way.

"Hello, Frank. Is the boss receiving?"

"No, I think I heard him say he was going skating." Henry's macabre sense of humor was functioning. Father Walsh, the "boss," had only one leg. Poor circulation had cost him his right leg and threatened his very life. So he might or might not have been up and able to receive visitors just now, but he was *not* skating.

For whatever reasons, Fathers Walsh and Koesler had struck up an instant May-September friendship. Walsh was old-fashioned enough to address all priests—even Robert Koesler, who was but one-third the older man's age—as "Father."

The purpose of Koesler's visit was to inform the priests of this parish of the critical illness of one of their parishioners. The other matter on Koesler's mind was a bit murky. The problem had to do with Koesler's intent to visit Louise Delvecchio with more than passing regularity. Would this involve any territorial law that required pastoral permission? Or was it a courtesy simply to inform the pastor?

Koesler knew of no law forbidding a priest visitation rights, even when he was not assigned to that parish. He was touching this base merely to make sure there would be no problem from any quarter.

"I assume," Koesler said, "the boss has skated as far as the living room."

"That's a fair guess." Henry stepped aside and motioned Koesler in.

A case might be made to explain Henry's brusqueness. Like many another Detroit priest, he was in a holding pattern for a pastorate—waiting for his own parish. Now forty, he'd been a priest for fifteen years. He had more than enough experience to be a pastor, but there were no vacancies. With hardly any priests retiring, he simply had to wait his turn. In effect, he was being squeezed between the older clergy hanging in there and the eager young priests coming up behind him.

Additionally, thanks to his abrasive disposition, he would have to wait still longer while many of his classmates were rewarded with their own fiefdoms preceding him.

As Koesler entered the spacious living area, Father Walsh looked up from the whispered praying of his breviary. Instantly, a smile covered his face.

Koesler glanced through the archway to the dining room. There lining the mantel were legions of medications the pastor consumed with meals.

"What brings good old Father Koesler back to St. William's?" Walsh greeted.

"I've got some bad news that you need to know and I need to talk to you about." Koesler sat down in a chair directly across from the elderly priest. He had hoped that Frank Henry would go on about his business. No such luck; Henry seated himself near the large window overlooking Outer Drive.

Walsh looked deeply concerned. "Well, let's have it." He had coped with his share and more of bad news.

"It's Louise Delvecchio. She's just been diagnosed with pancreatic cancer."

Henry seemed shocked. Walsh groaned. "Can they operate?"

Koesler shook his head. "It's inoperable. They got to it too late."

"That happens . . ." Walsh had known it to happen many times in his sixty years.

"Is she going to have radiation therapy?" Henry asked.

"No. It was sort of a family decision."

"They're making a mistake," Henry said. "A big mistake. That's her one chance."

"It's a crapshoot," Walsh offered. "Damned if you do, damned if you don't. You choose therapy, it doesn't work, the patient just gets sicker. You skip therapy, you wonder forever what would've happened if you'd taken the radiation."

"They considered both options rather thoroughly. Dr. Schmidt was there during the entire debate."

"Hey, wait a minute—" Henry turned full attention to Koesler. "Doc Schmidt was there; I can understand that. But you? What were you doing there?"

"Louise called. The doctor set up this family meeting yesterday. All the kids were there this morning. I was kind of surprised that Vincent got a furlough from the seminary. Even for an event like this . . . especially since neither the rector nor Vincent knew how serious the situation was."

"I see," Walsh murmured.

"Which brings me to the second point," Koesler said, addressing the pastor. "I've grown very close to this family. I think you knew that when I was stationed here. And I've stayed in touch since I left here. That's probably why Louise asked me to be with them this morning." Koesler ignored Henry's glower. "I promised them I would look in regularly and help as much as I can. It was, admittedly, a pretty rash statement. I know that now. I feel I should've asked you first to see how you felt about it.

"I must admit, I don't know what the proper procedure is in a case like this. But I felt that I should at least inform you about what's happened and what I intend to do to help. I don't really know whether there's any kind of permission I need . . ."

"Well"—Henry was sitting on the edge of his chair—"I remember how close you were to that family when you were here. If you'll recall,

I told you not to—I warned you about friendships with parishioners. It leads to poor professional standards. You didn't listen to me . . . and now look what's happened!"

"Father . . ." Walsh said. But Henry blazed away. "What kind of message is this going to send to the people of St. William's parish? That they can't depend on the priests the bishop sent here for the care of souls? That somehow the priests of this parish are incompetent? That if parishioners want the very best, they need to send for you—"

"That'll be enough, Father!" It was as harsh a tone as Koesler had ever heard Walsh use.

Walsh turned his wheelchair to face Koesler. "I don't think any of Father Henry's worries are going to be realized."

"I'm sure you're right, Father," Koesler said. "Because there's one more thing you're going to have dumped in your lap regarding Louise Delvecchio."

"What's that?" Henry's emotional temperature was percolating—increased measurably by Walsh's rebuke.

"You see," Koesler began, "the final decision on how to proceed with Louise's condition was not merely a choice of therapy or death. And this solution was arrived at by Vincent: They are going to have a miracle."

Koesler would not have stated the matter this bluntly had not Henry been close to exploding. "A miracle? A miracle!" Henry was livid. "Just a miracle!" He was almost sneering. "Any particular time?" he asked derisively.

"By Easter," Koesler said as if he were making a casual announcement in church.

Henry stood up, almost suffered a heart attack, and abruptly left the room.

Father Walsh, who understood what Koesler was doing, chuckled. "By Easter, eh?" Walsh, smiling broadly, shook his head.

"I guess you had to be there," Koesler said. "This seemed to me to be Vincent's baby completely. Tony was very strong for radiation."

"Ever the athlete. Mother has to beat cancer."

"Uh-huh. Louise seemed determined to do everything in her power to gain the miracle—not so much for herself as for her son."

"The Italian mother . . . everything for the children."

"Especially for the priest son," Koesler said. "Anyway, Dr. Schmidt was open to whatever the family decided. In the end, he is entrusting Louise's care primarily to Lucy. I'm going to back her up as best I can."

"Ah . . ." Walsh sighed, "Lucy. Got a good head on her shoulders. She's going to make a fine adult. Still, awfully young to lose her mother."

Koesler nodded. "This would be a hard time for all of them: Lucy graduating high school, Tony graduating college and hoping for a pro football career—and, of course, Vincent about to become a priest. Missing her son's ordination would be the greatest tragedy for Louise. But"—Koesler shifted in his chair—"I don't know: What if they got their miracle?"

"Father!" Walsh was surprised at Koesler's willingness to accept that possibility.

"You should have seen Vinnie," Koesler amplified. "His strong faith was so evident. It was almost contagious."

"'Almost'?" Walsh's eyes bespoke wisdom that came from paying attention while growing older.

Koesler reddened. "Everyone eventually seemed to hop on Vinnie's bandwagon," he said after a moment. "But when push came to shove . . . well, Doc Schmidt was humoring the family. Tony didn't buy one share of it. Louise wanted to please her son the priest. Lucy appeared the most sincere, but, I wonder . . ."

"That leaves you, Father."

"Truth is . . . I kind of believe it."

"But . . ." Walsh rubbed his bald pate, a frequent gesture. ". . . a 'kind of belief' is not what you're looking for. Is it?"

"You're right, of course. We'll need a firm, steady faith to gain this favor from Almighty God."

"Indeed . . ." Father Walsh sat back in his wheelchair.

"Something you may soon hear about—that is, if Lucy keeps her part of the bargain—is the request for your parishioners to join the Delvecchio family in their petition for the miracle."

"Lucy's going to ask me for that?"

"So she said."

Walsh patted the arms of his chair with both hands. "Well, we'll pray . . . but not for a miracle."

"*Not?*" Koesler hadn't anticipated this.

"Seen it too many times, Father. People get all worked up—over a very good cause, mind you. But they begin living for that miracle. When it doesn't happen, for lots of them it cripples their faith."

"We'll pray. We'll pray for God's will to be done."

"Lucy will come to you—you can depend on that. You will let her down easily . . ."

"From what you've said, I shouldn't have too difficult a time convincing her."

Koesler didn't argue the point. "You're probably right."

"And, Father, you are perfectly welcome to visit anytime with any of our parishioners. I think it was good and wise of you to tell us your intentions. The only thing you need from me is delegation if you're going to perform a marriage in my parish. You will let me know in that case, won't you?"

It was his small joke. If anything was made perfectly clear to all priests, it was the necessity to be delegated for weddings. Without such delegation, a marriage would be invalid.

"By the way," Koesler said, as he rose to leave, "may I use your phone? I need to call St. John's Seminary."

"You're leaving? So soon?"

If Koesler had not heretofore been aware of it, it was obvious that Father Walsh would welcome some companionable visitations. The younger priest resolved to drop in more frequently.

"Before you go . . ." Walsh wheeled himself closer. ". . . I've been wanting to talk to you for some time . . . something important. Today's subject matter brought it to mind."

"Yes, Father?" Koesler sat down again.

"It's about that couple—Morris, was it?"

"Frank and Martha Morris?"

"Yes. From Nativity."

"Uh-huh."

"Well, I knew what was going on. You told me."

"Yes, I consulted with you. It was my first, and I hope last use of a Privilege of the Faith."

"Yes. Well, there were a couple of things. I didn't get into it before, or even after the incident was closed. But wasn't there some bitterness over that case? Something between Martha and Louise Delvecchio?"

"They're sisters."

"I know. After the trouble, Louise came in to see me. We talked a few times. Didn't really settle anything, as I recall. But . . . Martha: Didn't she blame Louise for what happened?"

The memory of that awful event suffused Koesler's mind. "Yes—even though it was an irrational charge. I thought at the time that Martha was simply striking out emotionally at the handiest target—which happened to be her sister. And Louise was simply trying to help."

"But Martha never changed her opinion, did she?"

"To my knowledge, no."

"She never forgave Louise?"

"No."

"And she's never talked to Louise over all this time?"

"No."

"It's my opinion," Walsh said, "that this might have something to do with Louise's condition."

"The cancer?"

"Haven't you sensed that Louise is very troubled by this whole thing? That in her mind, guilt is not very deep under the surface?"

"Guilt?" Koesler reacted with surprise. "But Louise isn't guilty of anything. She and I have been through that many times . . . though not recently."

"So you think because she hasn't talked to you about this recently, that it's no longer affecting her."

Koesler thought a few moments before responding. "I see what you're driving at. She doesn't talk about it because she knows my opinion—that she has no responsibility, no need to regret anything—and she knows I'm not going to change my mind."

Koesler reflected again. "So she's internalized her feelings and they've been . . ."

"Eating at her."

"You think this caused the cancer?"

Walsh nodded gravely.

"Could that happen?" Koesler asked. "Could an emotional struggle cause something as serious as a terminal illness?"

"I'm convinced of it. In my years I've seen more harm done because of stress than almost any other cause."

Involuntarily Koesler glanced at the empty trouser leg that had once covered a healthy limb. Could stress have—?

Walsh caught the glance and chuckled. "Well, not *every* illness."

"Sorry."

"Forget it."

"Well, then," Koesler pursued the line of thought, "do you think if we were able to patch things up . . ."

"That we'd have our miracle? No; I think the damage has been done. But I also think that reuniting the two sisters would bring a lot of peace to one very troubled soul."

"Maybe even two troubled souls," Koesler added. "But it won't be easy. I've talked to Martha several times. Nothing. Oh, not a great feeling of animosity or hatred—just no feeling at all."

"Ouch, that sounds like a killer. But we can try." The elderly priest looked off into the distance for a moment. "There's one more thing I wanted to mention, Father." Walsh wheeled himself so close that he and Koesler might well have been conspirators. "It's about that suicide—Frank Morris."

"Yes?"

"You and I talked about it at the time—and of course I read everything in the papers. I've never been able to make much sense of it."

Silence. Koesler was puzzled. "I don't understand," he said finally. "It was a tragedy. A terrible waste. But it seemed an open-and-shut case. Frank took his life using his shotgun. Am I missing something?"

"Maybe it's all these years I've piled up. I hesitate to call it intuition; the ladies have that market cornered. But there's always been something wrong with that suicide."

"But the police—"

"I know. I know. It was all very neat. The owner's gun, the suicide note, the motive." He shook his head. "How easily the cops bought the apparent reason—that it was because the Morrises were turned down by a Church court. I mean, that wasn't even close to courts that cops deal with. I was surprised they bought it. And," he added, "I was surprised that I didn't."

Koesler became aware that his mouth was hanging open. He closed it. "You must be the only one remotely involved who doesn't think Frank's death was self-inflicted."

"Not exactly." Walsh smiled. "If my 'intuition' is correct, one other person, in this case, *knows* it wasn't suicide."

"The person who killed him?"

"I wouldn't put it quite that bluntly. More the one responsible for Frank Morris's death."

"But, how . . . ?"

"Among the things I've learned about you, Father, in the year and a half that we worked together was that you have a very healthy imagination. Just think about it, is all I ask. See if someday you come to the same conclusion I have. I think I know what happened. But even *I* can't prove a thing. Maybe *you*'ll come up with the second half of the puzzle—the part I haven't cracked."

Koesler shrugged. A gesture of uncertainty. "I'll give it a shot. But I don't know . . ." He stood up. "For now, I've got to get on my horse. That call . . ."

Walsh nodded toward the main office. "You know where we keep the phone."

Koesler made his call, bade farewell to his host—he could not spot Father Henry, for which he was grateful—and let himself out.

He started on the long drive to St. John's Seminary in Plymouth. On the way, he would give Father Walsh's puzzle a little open-minded consideration.

He stopped at Topinka's on West Seven Mile and Telegraph for a quick lunch. As usual, he ordered hamburger, which here masqueraded as ground round. The portions were generous. As usual, that matched his appetite. While he waited for the entrée, the waitress brought coffee. She was "fathering" him unmercifully, but fortunately made no effort to tap his professional aid. Sometimes a meal out could become an extended counseling session.

He lit a cigarette and watched as the gray plumes left his nostrils, wafted over the tablecloth, then dissipated to contaminate the rest of the dining area.

How in the world could Frank's death not be a suicide?

He himself had brought the bad news to Frank and Martha. As bitterly disappointing as the message was, they seemed to accept the verdict without anger or resentment. If anything, Frank had been the more accepting of the two.

Koesler had to admit that in retrospect, it hadn't seemed that suicide was just around the corner. He had even extended his visit until he was sure the couple was all right.

He crushed the cigarette out in the ashtray. A thin trail of smoke spiraled up as if a genie were going to appear and grant three wishes.

The first wish would not be difficult: Vinnie would get his miracle.

His lunch was served: hamburger just right, crisp french fries, coleslaw, and some carrots. All would be consumed.

As to what had happened after he'd left the Morris house, Koesler would, of course, have to depend on what others had told him.

Apparently, Frank and Martha had talked for some time. Then they'd decided to close up shop. Martha went upstairs after asking Frank to check the furnace and, as she'd put it, inviting him to her bed.

Koesler stopped the replay and reflected on the wife who, after almost three years, invites her loving husband to sleep with her again. He winced. Neither Frank nor Martha had voluntarily chosen a monastic life. Koesler had delivered the demand that they affect a relationship that the Church required. Those few words of Martha's told that they had kept their part of the bargain.

In time the waitress returned. "Would Father like some dessert, Father?"

"No—just more coffee."

"Was everything okay?"

"Yup."

"Well, a gentleman paid for your lunch."

"Really?" Koesler looked around. "Which gentleman?"

"I don't know his name. He left the restaurant about fifteen minutes ago."

Interesting, thought Koesler. I wonder why . . . I'll never know.

The waitress brought more coffee.

"Did the gentlemen leave you an adequate tip?"

"Oh yes, Father. It was very generous, Father. Thank you for asking, Father."

14

Father Koesler put the car in gear and his mind in neutral as he drove out of the restaurant parking lot.

Where was he in this exercise in memory? Oh yes: Martha had just asked Frank to check the furnace before joining her in bed. To consider all this detail, it was necessary to rely on Martha, the only living witness to this event.

Martha had fully intended to stay awake to greet her husband. But with one thing and another, particularly the discouraging news about their petition, she was exhausted. She drifted quickly into a deep sleep.

She was awakened by the window-rattling explosion. She thought it must be the furnace. And she had just sent Frank down to look it over.

She ran down the stairs. That's when she found Frank on the living room floor with the gun.

Sure sounds like suicide to me, thought Koesler, not for the first time. And then there was that poignant note. That pretty well wrapped it up, he concluded.

What sort of loophole had Father Walsh thought he'd discovered?

Wait a minute. If it's just a hole one is looking for, how long had Martha been asleep when she was awakened by the gunshot? She never said. She undoubtedly didn't know; why should she?

You don't fall asleep, then be wakened by an explosion someplace in the house, then check the clock to see how long you've been sleeping.

It was almost ludicrous. Koesler tried to visualize himself in a similar situation. The last thing on his mind would be what time it was or how long he'd been asleep. He would do exactly what Martha had done: As quickly as possible he would go to investigate what had happened.

That must be it . . . that must be the loophole that Father Walsh had found. Koesler couldn't think of a single thing to do about it. But there it was: The time between when Martha actually went to bed and when she was awakened was unknown. And now, years later, that gap would have to remain unknown. What little evidence there had been was gone now. If there was a guilty second person, fingerprints would be blurred by everyone who had touched things. How many people had handled that note, the gun, the body? It had seemed such a clear-cut case of suicide that no one had given an instant's thought to any other possibility.

This single consideration opened the whole matter once again.

What might have happened while Martha slept for God knows how long?

Could someone have rung the doorbell? Would that have wakened Martha? Depends on how deeply she was sleeping. Perhaps someone had knocked at the door. That probably wouldn't have been loud enough to wake her.

Just suppose someone came to the house—rang the doorbell or knocked—why might he or she call at that hour?

Suppose it was one of the kids. Lucy lived only a few blocks away. Tony could easily enough have come in from Kalamazoo. Vinnie would not be the first seminarian to escape from the minimum security of St. John's. Realistically, though, Vinnie would be the least likely of the three to call on Frank. Vinnie would have had one tough time finding transportation. But . . . possible.

Could any of the three have known about the Vatican rejection?

Koesler himself had gotten the verdict in the mail that very day. He had told no one before—or directly after, for that matter—sharing the news with Frank and Martha. How could anyone else have known?

One of the high school girls, in addition to other parochial chores, was assigned to pick up the daily mail from the rectory's main office and deliver it to the various priests' offices. While Lucy did not fill that role, she could've had the mail girl tell her if an envelope from Rome came to Father Koesler.

If the letter came and the verdict was positive, Father Koesler would have delivered the good news immediately. The fact that he received such a letter and put off sharing its contents was a pretty good indication that the news was bad.

Then what?

Say, for sake of argument, that Lucy had somehow learned about the verdict. What if she enlisted the aid of Tony, he being the more mobile of her brothers?

What if they staked out the Morris home? Easy enough to do. Koesler had come early and left relatively early.

They note that Martha goes upstairs, undoubtedly headed to bed. They knock on the door. Frank lets them in without hesitation.

Then what?

They try to talk Frank into leaving Martha so their aunt can finally receive the sacraments again. And just in time for Vinnie's first Mass.

Obviously, Frank will not leave Martha.

Failing that, they appeal to the love that Frank holds for Martha. They urge Frank to commit suicide. It's the only way Martha can be truly happy. Sure she would miss him almost beyond words; but underneath it all, she would be at peace—and so would he.

Finally, he agrees. He writes the note. Confident that he will go through with it, they leave.

Frank gets his gun and kills himself.

This procedure would take a lot of time. How much time did they have? That's just it: Nobody knew. Nobody knows how long Martha slept before the gunshot.

The conclusion: Either scenario could resolve some questions—while raising others.

The burning question: So what? The incident is long settled in just about everyone's mind; nothing can be proved one way or the other.

And yet . . . there is the possibility of the question rising to the surface again. What happens to kids as young as Tony and Lucy if they enter into a conspiracy to, in effect, browbeat someone into taking his own life? Does it scar them forever? And what could a scar such as this cause them to do in the future?

All this because it seemed so foreign to Frank's nature to freely decide on suicide. And because there was no way of telling how long Martha had been asleep that fateful night.

Walsh's doubts found fertile ground in Koesler's imagination.

It was something that would not only haunt Father Koesler but, willy-nilly, would color his relationship with Tony and Lucy for some time. Nothing would be said. But he would look at them in a different light and with some residual doubt.

He swung his car into the familiar circular drive. It was the recreational break between lunch and the afternoon's first class. Cassocked students stood in groups or walked with companions. Some enjoyed the premature springlike weather. Many more smoked cigarettes, cigars, or pipes, any form of combustible tobacco.

Koesler was greeted with a mixture of familiarity and reverence. He was not old enough to be more than one of the boys, yet he had achieved what they all desired.

He headed directly to the rector's suite. Father Finn was in his office with a student. Koesler took a seat in the vestibule.

He had time to reflect on the speculation he'd entertained en route to the seminary. It brought to mind a homily he had recently delivered. He had said that he could make as good a case for atheism as he could for a belief in God. But if he were an atheist, he would have to confront all those questions: Where did all this come from? Who made the laws that nature follows? What was the purpose of all these galaxies? Where is it all going? And on and on.

So, in a much smaller dimension, there were questions on either side of Frank Morris's death. The simple declarative approach: Frank, having left a note for Martha and in order to clear a path for her return to the Catholic sacraments she so missed, had shot himself dead.

Questions: Was it out of character for Frank to take such a fatal action of his own accord? Having endured the sacrifice of a lengthy brother-and-sister relationship, would he not have felt that he had taken every step possible toward the desired goal, and that being the case weren't he and Martha now entitled to resume what for them was a faithful, loving marriage?

Or had Frank thought it all out long before? Had he decided that in the event of a negative judgment from the Church he would take the only other possible step? Had he made the decision out of misguided love to commit suicide so that his beloved Martha could finally receive the sacraments she so desired?

Or: Frank's choice was assisted by outside urging. Question: Isn't this a bit Byzantine? Granted the apparently precipitate decision and immediate terminal act was out of character; still, couldn't Frank have felt his back was to the wall with nowhere to go but from this life?

An argument could be made for either case. And the argument arose out of the unknown time Martha had been asleep before the deed was done.

If Father Walsh's intuition was correct, one had to consider the possibility that two young people had conspired to cause an innocent person to take his own life. No mean charge. Their own lives undoubtedly would have been marked by their action. At the very least, they would bear watching.

At this point, a student exited Father Finn's office. The young man appeared chastened. Father Finn could effect this with little effort. Koesler knew from first-person experience.

The student, obviously embarrassed beyond words, beyond even a glance, walked past Koesler without eye contact.

Koesler wondered idly about the offense. It could have been almost anything. What the young man probably did not comprehend was that if Finn had given him hell, at least the rector was trying to save the lad's vocation. If he were considered dispensable, Finn wouldn't have expended so much emotional firepower on him. Still, as Koesler knew full well, the drill was painful.

Like an abruptly diminishing storm, Finn's demeanor changed.

For the offender, Finn's countenance promised thunder and lightning. But as the door closed behind the student, the rector's face cleared to welcome Koesler.

Father Finn had perhaps two interests in life: one, the priesthood; the other, those who wanted to enter it.

A few years ago, Koesler easily could have been that chastized student. Now he shared a priesthood with Finn; the rector would greet Koesler like a long-lost relative.

And so he did, ushering the young priest into his office.

There was nothing out of the ordinary about the rector's office. Two walls were lined with bookcases filled with works in his fields: moral theology and Canon Law. The oak desk was uncluttered. The wall behind the chair Koesler selected was opaque glass on either side of the entry door. Behind Finn was a picture window overlooking a well-kept courtyard and one of the transverse cloistered walkways.

The rector smiled. "Well, Bob, how are things going with you?"

Bob. In Koesler's four years in these buildings, Finn had called him "Koesler," "Mr. Koesler," or its Latin form—"Domne Koesler." Never anything close to "Bob."

"Pretty good," Koesler replied. "Really, very good."

"Much difference between St. Norbert's and that east side urban parish?"

"Quite a bit. Most of the people in St. Norbert's are my age, roughly, and starting their families. Couple of years ago we built our grade school. Staffed it with Dominican nuns. It really seems to have pulled the parish together. Quite phenomenal."

"Really." Finn seemed to be taking mental notes.

Koesler had come to believe that if Father Finn were vulnerable anywhere, it was in his experience—or rather, lack of it—of life in a parish.

In his day in the seminary in San Francisco, Finn had been invited by the Sulpician faculty to join their society. Finn had accepted the invitation. So, after ordination, off he went to prepare for a life of teaching seminarians.

All Sulpicians were, in reality, diocesan priests, on loan as it were to the Society of St. Sulpice. Finn, for example, belonged to the archdiocese of San Francisco. Should he at any time leave the Sulps, as they were sometimes familiarized, he would revert to his San Francisco diocese.

The point being that he never had: He'd never left the Society. Thus his parochial experience was zilch.

Koesler reasoned that the fact that Finn was preparing young men for a life he had never experienced must be frustrating, embarrassing, and even intimidating.

Koesler could almost see the file drawer in Finn's head slide open for the insertion of "Parochial school: presence tends to pull parish together."

"And how are things here?" Koesler knew he was going to have to introduce the subject very soon. Finn was not one to shoot the breeze interminably. He really worked at his job and even now was spending time that had been allocated for something else.

"Everything appears to be on schedule," Finn replied. "The academic year is ending and we're getting ready for the ordinations."

Every word of that statement could have been previously supplied by Koesler. It was March. Easter was just around the corner. And in a couple of more months, June would see sophomores ordained to the minor orders of porter and lector; juniors would receive the first major order of subdeacon; and of course the seniors would become priests.

"That"—Koesler tapped tobacco into firmness and lit a cigarette—"is, mostly, what I wanted to talk to you about."

Finn had already inserted a cigarette into its silver holder and accepted a light from Koesler's Zippo. Smoke streamed from his nostrils. "Can we be of any help?" Finn opened wide the door to whatever was concerning Koesler.

"Quite frankly . . ." Koesler made firm eye contact. ". . . I'm here about Vincent Delvecchio."

Finn grew a bit more guarded. He was not happy with anyone who might meddle with the students given unto his care. "Delvecchio isn't here just now. I gave him permission to go home for the day . . . something about his mother."

"I know."

Finn cocked an eyebrow.

"His mother hasn't been well for quite some time," Koesler said.

"I know."

"What was different about today," Koesler continued, "was the diagnosis—or rather the verdict."

"That bad!" Not in so many words had Koesler spoken of Mrs. Delvecchio's terminal condition. But Finn had divined the conclusion.

Koesler nodded. "Pancreatic cancer."

Finn exhaled audibly. "Is there any hope? Radiation?"

"Her doctor doesn't hold much hope. No, change that and let's be realistic: no hope."

"And the family?"

"Holding up better than I expected."

"We will, of course, pray."

"That's one of the things I wanted to mention."

"Prayer?" Finn had taken that for granted.

"Vincent has gone a bit beyond a prayer asking for relief of suffering, resignation to God's will, that sort of thing . . ." Koesler paused. "He wants a miracle. No, stronger: He *expects* a miracle. To happen as a result of prayer."

"And his mother?"

"Well, she wouldn't turn down a miracle. Like all the noble mothers I've known, she wants to be preserved so she can care for her children."

"She really expects a miracle?"

"Hopes . . . prays; I don't think she *expects*."

"Vincent's brother and sister?"

It somewhat surprised Koesler that Finn would—off the top of his head—know that Vincent had two siblings. There were so many students here. But that was Finn's way: He knew everything he could about everyone.

Koesler snuffed out his cigarette. "Tony agreed to pray. But as far as enlisting others . . . not much of a chance. It's hard to imagine him making a plea to the faculty and students of Western Michigan to join in prayer for a miraculous healing.

"As for Lucy . . ."

"She's just graduating high school, isn't she?"

If not surprised, Koesler surely was impressed with Finn's familiarity as to his students' families. "Yes," he acknowledged. "She's going to have to be the mainstay of this effort. She'll have the day-to-day responsibility. She was supposed to enlist the special prayers of the parishioners and students at St. William's parish. But I've already talked to the pastor, and it's no dice."

"Surely he would not turn down a request for prayer!"

"No, no. I'm sorry; I didn't phrase that very well. Of course he'll ask the parish for prayer—but not for a miracle."

"Hmmm . . . interesting," Finn mused. "Was there a stated reason?"

"Uh-huh. Father Walsh feared that their faith would be harmed or weakened if and when the miracle was not granted."

"So Father Walsh is convinced there will be no miracle."

"He's been around." It was Koesler's best evaluation of the situation. Probably Walsh had asked for his share of miracles that hadn't been granted. To the point where he believed that a miracle was an extremely rare event—and doubted that he would see one personally.

As it happened, the same line of thought occurred to Father Finn. One more parochial experience for the mental file cabinet. What might have been a smile played about Father Finn's lips. "Well, then, since this petition for a miraculous cure seems to have originated with Mr. Delvecchio, and since he has tried to enlist his brother and sister to start such a crusade in their schools and parish, may I assume a similar proposal will be made to this institution?"

"That is one of the reasons I'm here."

"You are going to make the plea?"

"No, not really. My purpose is to prepare you for Vinnie's request." He figured he might get away with this straight-from-the-shoulder presentation because he was no longer a student but a graduate. Finn was a priest, but no more so than Koesler. And vice versa. Clerically, they were on the same level now: equals.

The rector set his already firm jaw. "I'm afraid we'll have to disappoint Mr. Delvecchio." The statement was emotionless, a simple declaration of fact. While the rector might feel himself on shaky ground when it came to practical hands-on parochial experience, he was more than sure of himself when seminary training was the issue.

"It's just a prayer," Koesler stated.

"Oh, we will pray. Not for a miracle, but that God's holy will be done."

"Then you agree with Father Walsh that if there is no miracle, the faith of the seminarians will be shaken?"

Finn hesitated only a few seconds. Had Koesler been a student, he would have received no explanation. But since Finn was discussing this matter with a fellow priest, he would amplify his statement. "My thinking has something—but very little—to do with Father's Walsh's reason.

But I must admit this is the best of times for a future priest to learn that he cannot—*cannot*—rely in any way on miraculous intervention.

"As a priest, he will have to deal many times over with people who have nothing left to turn to but a miracle. The seminarian learns that God does not multiply miracles. Now— *before* ordination—is the time to learn this. And if it must be learned in the school of hard knocks, all the better. It will save him from supporting the plea for God to change the course of nature."

He paused, then continued, with emphasis. "But I am *much* more concerned with the impact such a singular campaign would have on the student body. We, in these final four years of the theologate, are a community. We cannot permit a student or group of students to fragment this community.

"Do you remember, Bob, when, after you were here a short while, your class wanted to continue your custom from the minor seminary of reciting the Rosary together as a group each Saturday evening?"

At first Koesler recalled the request only vaguely, and that only because Finn had brought it up. Then, memory jogged, he recollected clearly the custom, the request, and the rector's rejection. "Now that you mention it, I do remember: You refused our request. But I'll bet you never heard the rest of the story."

"Oh?"

"Patrick McNiff was the one who acted as spokesman for our class. When you turned him down, he came to the rest of us and announced, 'The old man hates the Blessed Mother.'"

Finn did not find this humorous. "That of course is not true. I gave my reason, and it had nothing to do with rosary devotion. I did not want any one of our four classes to set itself apart from the rest of the student body. And for the same reason: I do not think it wise to set a precedent in singling out one student's petition from the rest. Soon we could be dealing with petitions for miraculous cures from all parts of the prayer hall. I think Father Walsh was wise in not involving his parishioners in a cause that is more or less doomed to frustration. That, as well as not allowing a divisive element in this community, will prompt me to refuse Mr. Delvecchio's request—if and when he presents it."

Koesler could recognize a blind alley when he was trapped in one. "Well . . ." He thought better than to light another cigarette with this visit obviously concluding. ". . . there is one more request that Vinnie will make, I'm pretty sure."

Finn waited without comment.

"Any chance," Koesler said, "that Vincent can be granted extra time at home with his mother?" Koesler sailed on through a possible but premature reply from Finn. "I know that these will be the last couple of months before ordination and they're important. But we both know that Vincent is close to being a genius. He can absorb these courses with no sweat. And it would be such a great comfort to his mother. I would wager that, to a man, everyone—students and faculty—would not begrudge him extra time at home."

No response. Finn was loath to set any sort of precedent. He well knew how students could and usually did take advantage of exceptions to the rule. But what Koesler said carried a lot of truth. Probably no one—at least very few among either faculty or students—would object to a modest latitude in home visitation for Delvecchio. And how many students would have a terminally ill parent . . . especially as ordination approached?

"I think we might be able to reach some sort of accommodation in this matter," Finn said finally. "If Mr. Delvecchio wants to talk to me about it, we'll . . . talk."

The meeting was concluded. Finn would not steer his visitor to the door, but Koesler sensed that this impromptu chat had disrupted the rector's schedule. With a handshake, they parted.

Koesler slid into his black Chevy, rolled down the window, and lit a cigarette.

As he drove away from the seminary, he assessed what, if anything, he had accomplished. It was mid-afternoon, yet it seemed as if he'd been up and about for more than a day. He'd gotten nowhere with Father Walsh. Koesler knew that the pastor's decision on a parishwide prayer crusade for a medical miracle was written in stone. No matter how Lucy might plead the case, there would be no change in the course Walsh had set. And, in his heart, Koesler didn't believe that Lucy was 100 percent in agreement with Vincent's plan of prayer.

Further, Father Finn would disappoint Vinnie in not committing the student body to a radical form of prayer. On the other hand, Koesler felt confident that Finn would cut Vinnie some slack on the matter of home visits. Koesler figured that was one round he'd won. The young man would have to be satisfied with that.

Next, Koesler would see how his present pastor felt about the miracle prayers. Actually, he anticipated a charitable veto. After all, the sick person had no remote connection with St. Norbert's parish.

Funny, this morning, when an enthusiastic Vincent had proposed this program, Koesler had caught the fire and was confident they could pull it together. Now, he felt like a deflated balloon. Things did not look as hopeful as earlier they had.

15

Tony Delvecchio had two things going against him.

One: As a WMU student, he did not represent one of the "biggies." Though Western was not a small college by anyone's standards, neither was it Michigan, Notre Dame, Florida, or Texas. The professionals would take this into account.

Two: He didn't have the height the pros preferred in a quarterback. Granted Eddie LeBaron at only five feet seven in his heyday had managed to reach his receivers with consistency; still the defensive linemen were getting bigger by the year. Nowadays Tony would nearly have to stand on tiptoe to see the pass patterns his receivers ran. Other young men had made it without topping six feet. Still it was definitely a consideration.

Of course, there was the possibility that he might be shifted to another position—cornerback, say, or safety. That was an additional consideration.

The problem with these options was that lots of eager young graduates automatically qualified. There were plenty of big quarterbacks. There were even more young athletes who had played in the defensive backfield from high school through college. Their talent didn't have to be enhanced; they were the proper size and speed with plenty of invaluable experience at their positions.

In his favor, Tony was extremely strong and fast. He could meet almost any physical demand made of him. And, a not inconsiderable bonus, he was highly intelligent.

Surely he was smart enough to know that, as qualified as he might be, there was no certainty that he would be taken on by any pro team, let alone enjoy a reasonably long pro career.

And, should football fail him . . . ? What if the hitherto unthinkable *did* happen?

He would teach. All along, he had favored math. There was something so satisfying about the product of math—absolute answers.

And so, among the courses he carried were trigonometry, calculus II, and statistics. To these he gave minimal attention. He was relatively unconcerned about finals. Had he really applied himself, he would now be flirting with something between 3.4 and 3.8. As it was, he would pass with enough to spare.

At this moment, his mind was launched on a stream-of-consciousness voyage.

"You're not here," Beth Larson, his steady, said. "Where are you?"

"What?" Tony returned to the present.

"Well, there's hope. You haven't heard a word I've said for the past fifteen minutes. I was beginning to think I'd never get you back."

"Uhmm."

"We were going to study together tonight . . . remember?"

"I guess I got distracted."

The two seniors were in Beth's apartment in Kalamazoo. Final examinations loomed.

"I was wondering which team might take me. And what they might pay."

"You're getting ahead of yourself, aren't you, sweetie? First come the exams."

"Not for me. The exams come second. Football comes first."

Beth, legs folded beneath her, was seated on the couch, surrounded by books. "I'm well aware of your plans, Tony. First comes the pro game. Then a long career as a sports announcer. And I know we've talked about this, so pardon me if I'm repeating myself, but tell me again why you can't just skip the playing days and go right to the announcer's booth without passing Go or going to Jail?"

"Yes, we've talked about it, Beth. It's the coming thing. I know it. Sports announcers and commentators used to be hired for their voice. Guys like Red Barber and Van Patrick have sports voices. But put Van Patrick on the field in uniform. Let him try to return a kickoff and watch him have a heart attack.

"No, the coming thing is to get players—guys who've been in the trenches. But—and here's the rub—they'll want guys who are articulate. And, believe me, honey, there ain't too many players can measure up.

"And that"—he rose from his chair and joined her on the couch—"is how come I've got to make it as a player before I can move to the safety of the booth." He kissed her forehead lightly.

Beth's figure was dazzling, though some might argue she was a tad slender. No one would engage Tony in such an argument. In Tony's eyes, Beth was no less than perfect, mind, body, and countenance. Her lively eyes were set off by cheekbones that were the envy of less fortunate females; abundant light brown hair framed a classic profile. At five feet eight, she was tall for a young woman. But not too tall for Tony.

"Why all this concern about my playing career?"

"Because people get hurt playing that game."

"Not everybody."

"It's a violent contact sport."

"As someone said, dancing is a contact sport; football is a collision sport."

"Just what I mean. I don't want to spend our golden years helping you out of a chair or into a bed."

"Honey, you will never have to help me into a bed. You get in and that's all the motivation I'll need."

"Get serious, Tony. I see these stories about players who've been permanently injured. I don't want you to be a statistic."

"I'm studying statistics. That way I won't be one."

"Be serious!"

"I am, lover." Tony swung around, knocking several books off the couch and settling down with his head in her lap. "I know the game cripples some guys. But not all. And I'm one of the guys who's going to come out unscathed."

"What makes you so sure?" Gently, she tousled his hair.

"I'm going to stay healthy. I'm going to keep working out. I'm going to remain strong."

"And what happens if somebody hits you the wrong way, right at your knee joint? Your leg wasn't made to bend that way. Then what?"

As Tony listened to Beth's depiction of the classic knee injury, he almost could hear the dreaded sound of the muscle tearing away from the bone. Inwardly he winced, but was successful in hiding it.

He shrugged, picked up a book at random, and began flipping pages aimlessly. "What if I'm crossing a street and some nut in a car doesn't see me?"

"That's an accident. I'm talking about an injury that goes with the territory."

"I don't want to talk about injuries anymore. I've got a plan and I'm going to follow it. And that's that!"

She dropped it for the moment. There was little she could do. By unspoken agreement, they hadn't mentioned the possibility that despite the plethora of raves, Tony might indeed not play pro ball after all. She read the sports pages, if only because sports was Tony's primary interest. She had agreed with the pundits, especially the locals, who had written that Tony was a sure thing for the draft, with a glorious pro career to follow. And once he had been passed up, and his chances at that pro career seemed suddenly slimmer and slimmer, she had hoped to be able to stop worrying about his being injured. But she played her part: She realized that if she continued to act concerned that would bolster Tony; it would make him feel that there was still a possibility— that he still had a good chance of signing and playing with the pros. He must have a chance, else why would Beth still be worrying about his being injured?

She was keenly aware of the physical dangers in the growingly violent game. Some nights she would wake suddenly from a nightmare, wincing, as Tony had, unbeknownst to her, just done.

She knew how much he'd been planning on this, banking on this. And, as far as she could see, his plan *had* seemed well conceived. *If* it had worked out. And now? *If* a pro team signed him. And *if* he could avoid becoming a cripple.

It was obvious that study was not in the cards this evening. She decided to change the subject. "Speaking of injury and discomfort, how's your mother doing?"

He didn't respond for several moments. "I don't know what to tell you, Beth. I go home usually once a week, maybe more. There's nothing I can do, just be there for a while. I can't relate. Once they decided not to try radiation, I kind of washed my hands of the whole thing. I can't imagine not fighting. She couldn't be much sicker than she seems to be most of the time now. We're just waiting around for death. It gives me the creeps."

"Actually, isn't there something? I mean, something instead of her simply dying of the cancer?"

Tony snorted. "Vinnie's 'miracle.' I don't know what's wrong with the guy! He's smart enough . . . maybe the Church brainwashed him. 'Miracle!'"

Beth was on shaky ground. But then so was Tony. "Miracles happen, honey. Don't you believe in them at all?"

"Oh, I suppose . . . I don't know; I never saw one. Never had one. Why should the Delvecchios have our own little miracle? Because the priest in the family wants one?"

"You'd better go lightly here, Tony," she warned. "You're coming very close to making fun of God."

"What making fun?! I'm excusing God from suddenly turning nature on its ear because some insignificant family on the east side of Detroit wants a fatal illness to be erased. I ain't making fun of God. He's just not going to do it. I'm just telling Him it's all right with me . . . that I'm not counting on it."

"Then what *are* you counting on?"

"Nature. Ma got cancer. I don't know how or why. There was only one thing that might have turned it around—"

"Tony! You know what the odds are even with therapy."

"Outside of a miracle that happens every other century there was only one alternative: therapy or death. They chose death."

"They chose a miracle."

"They chose death!"

His exclamation was so vehement that Beth thought better than to pursue that line of dialogue further.

In truth, she did not expect any miracle. She didn't even know if there was such a thing. But she was concerned about Tony's attitude toward his mother. Particularly at this stage of her life.

Beth firmly believed that Louise was near the end of her days. And that she was suffering. Beth feared that when, inevitably, she would pass, Tony would bitterly regret not giving more of himself to his mother's needs.

But he seemed to have divorced himself from the drama being played out in his home. Resignation was a word not to be found in Tony's lexicon. He felt only contempt for them all—for Dr. Schmidt, Father Koesler, Lucy, and, most of all, his brother, whose idea the miracle was.

It was like Judy Garland and Mickey Rooney in those ancient movie musicals. Always there was some crisis solvable only with a wad of money. So the kids would borrow a barn and suddenly there'd be a wildly expensive set, dozens—hundreds—of Busby Berkeley precision dancers, and an ecstatically successful ending. And the original problem, was, of course, solved.

And so it was with Vinnie and his brainstorm: Lucy would get all of St. William's school and parish praying for this miracle. Likewise Father Koesler's parish. Likewise Western Michigan University. Likewise St. John's Seminary. The result of all this prayer was a miracle to be delivered by Easter. And a happy ending for all.

In either the movie or Vinnie's script this made for a pleasant diversion. But in the real world, a pile of crap.

In any case, after a few more futile attempts at studying, Tony and Beth closed the books and went to bed—together. The Catholic Church of that era reminded sexually active people, especially young people, that steady dating was itself an occasion of sin: It had a nasty habit of leading to "sins of the flesh."

Tony and Beth were horizontal proof of that.

*   *   *

Days turned into weeks.

It was fortunate that Lucy was young. The demands of the situation were extremely stressful.

Under ordinary circumstances, much of the preparation, trappings, and folderol of graduation would have been lovingly handled by her mother.

As it was, not only was Lucy shouldering the demands of final exams and graduation, she was also taking care of her mother.

Nothing was working out the way it had been planned. The help she was to have received was minimal at best. Father Koesler had volunteered what turned out to be a completely unrealistic presence to bail out Lucy. He and Vinnie had been swept up in the exhilaration of the moment when Louise's choice became therapy or a miracle. Doc Schmidt came very close to his promise by dropping in occasionally and keeping the prescriptions coming.

Actually, the one who came closest to fulfilling his promise—or lack of it—was Tony. He had promised nothing. And that pretty much was what he delivered.

Early on, after that pivotal day, Louise got along rather better than anyone could have hoped.

She tired easily. But that had been a symptom even before her illness was diagnosed. She clung to mobility as though it were a sign of health. If she was up and about, she considered herself well; when she lingered in bed, something was wrong. A simple formula.

She attended daily Mass as often as she could—four or five days a week. Everyone in the church these early mornings knew what troubled her. Nearly everyone in the parish—at least the active parishioners—knew. Father Walsh would not sponsor a crusade for a miracle. But he certainly did not discourage prayer. So word got around.

She tried to believe a miracle was in her future. She really tried. And some days she felt so good, so nearly recovering, that she confused small remissions with a miraculous recovery.

Lucy matured dramatically that spring. She was still of an age when death is not quite real. Surely she would never die; she was far too alive. Of course other people died. But not her mother; her mother was still a young woman.

And then Lucy began to see it. It became more and more difficult for Louise to avoid lying down or at least sitting down. Her weight, never much, began to drop. To look in her eyes was to see pain.

Louise bore it all without complaint. She taught her daughter how to pray for and prepare for the miracle. It wouldn't be a miracle if she recovered from a less than terminal condition. In other words, she'd have to be a whole lot sicker than she was for the reality of the miracle to prove itself.

Louise was aware that a significant number of very sincere people were praying for her. The times when the pain was more intense she consciously fell back on all those prayers. And when she did, the pain became quite bearable.

Father Koesler had been unable to convince his pastor to mobilize a prayer campaign. But Koesler enlisted the prayer and concern of many friends and/or parishioners. Together, he and they learned a lot about prayer through this experience.

Koesler, who talked with Tony from time to time, knew that the young man was neither supportive nor productive—or even encouraging, for that matter. The priest knew that Lucy was doing literally all she could. So there was not all the prayer they had anticipated in the beginning. Still, many good people were storming heaven for Louise's sake.

The anchor of all this dedicated prayer was Vincent. No one else had his confidence, his faith. He was in the seminary chapel whenever he was not called to another duty. He spent an unaccustomed amount of time with his Bible. He repeatedly called up passages that spoke to him of requited prayer.

With this in mind, it seemed that the entire Bible was a romance between God and mankind, and that the language of this romance was prayer.

Vincent was encouraged by the frequency of prayer stories in the New Testament. It seemed that Jesus was always assuring His disciples that anything they asked the Father for they would receive if they had faith. Jesus Himself, when performing his miracles, would express His faith. Anything, everything was possible through faith.

And Vincent had faith.

He prayed, "Lord, I believe. Help my unbelief." But there was little unbelief in Vincent's prayer.

He believed. He had faith.

All those marvelous people were a source of encouragement and support.

But this was Vincent's miracle.

Vincent's life of prayer and faith so impressed the rector that he relaxed his previous restriction for a one-day-a-week home visitation. Now Vinnie was home from Friday night to Sunday night each week.

Though Vincent was not notably popular among his fellow students and classmates, a goodly number of them caught his fervor and began praying for his mother's cure.

Each Sunday evening when he returned from home, many, faculty and students alike, asked after his mother. He never tired of explaining that while she seemed to be failing, her faith was strong. The miracle could happen any time now. And the miracle, by definition, could happen no matter how frail she was. Indeed, the more that physical hope declined, the more appropriate would be God's merciful intervention.

So he encouraged them to continue his prayer with him.

But, without doubt, it was Vincent's show.

16

Palm Sunday

The gangbusters church congregations for Holy Week had begun. Attendance at Mass this morning at St. Norbert's was up markedly from what could be expected on an ordinary Sunday. Father Koesler knew the other parishes were experiencing the same phenomenon as his small suburban parish.

He knew also that he could anticipate a full week of virtually nothing but eating, sleeping, conducting liturgies, and hearing confessions.

Confessions would be by far the heaviest burden.

"The Box," as the confessional was called by some, was not designed for comfort. In many cases it was more a torture chamber.

Penitents knelt in murky obscurity on an unyielding board set below a shelf on which one could rest one's elbows—depending on one's size. Short people had better luck resting their chins on the support while tall people could distort their spines trying to lean down. At least the penitents were captive for a relatively short period.

Not so the priest confessor. His center booth shared the musty darkness. His chair, more often than not, was uncomfortable—extremely so. Usually, his hole-in-the-wall cavity was too small for comfort. So there he sat, cramped, conducting business in whispers. He whispered and the penitent whispered, as they blew germs at each other through a tatty, unwashed curtain. He sat in the center compartment of the box for hours. During the Christmas season and during Holy Week, he sat there for days on end. His end.

St. Norbert's added one additional torment. The church was heated through blowers in the ceiling. No matter that heat rises. Some pseudo-architect, probably the founding pastor, thought this method of heating, by having warmth fight against its natural direction, inventive.

As a consequence, the congregation's feet were colder than their heads. Meanwhile, in the Box, heat poured down on the priest confessor from the blower just above his head until the box reached a sauna-like temperature—at which point the blower would automatically quit, allowing the cold air to rush upward from beneath the door.

Such was Father Koesler's prospect for the coming week. And, short of falling grievously ill, there was no escaping it.

All this, of course, paled before the greater pain and fear that held Louise Delvecchio in their grip.

Koesler had mixed feelings as he sat in his car in front of Louise's house. In a way, Louise was an inspiration. Even if she could no longer care for her family, still she fought to at least care for herself. She tried to be a burden to no one, particularly to Lucy, who was by far her most constant companion.

On the other hand, Koesler was angry, so very angry with this disease that seemed to be eating away at Louise from inside. In the face of such ravages, how could he give any thought whatsoever to the minor inconveniences in his own life? They seemed so inconsequential in light of the load Louise carried.

But he hadn't traveled from Inkster to Detroit's east side to sit in his car and give free rein to his stream of consciousness.

In response to the bell, the door was opened by Vincent, done up like a good seminarian: black trousers, black shoes and socks, and a white collarless shirt into which a clerical collar would fit easily.

As he entered the house, Koesler noted fresh palm fronds hung from wall decorations. Nodding at the display, he said, "Who let you guys play in the palm fields? You got enough to plait a South Seas hut."

Vincent smiled. "St. William's is generous when you ask nicely."

Koesler wondered at Vinnie's good humor. Then he remembered the miracle and Vincent's faith. Why not be happy? Vincent's mood was comparable to one standing near Lazarus's tomb while knowing how the story would end.

Lucy appeared from the kitchen. An apron covered most of a pretty spring dress.

"The little homemaker getting supper ready?" Koesler asked.

Lucy nodded. "Can you stay?"

"I don't want to be the Man Who Came to Dinner."

"Don't worry: It's spaghetti and meatballs. That stretches forever."

"Okay then. Is Tony here?"

Neither Vincent nor Lucy responded immediately.

"No," Vincent said, finally. "He won't be here today."

Lucy snorted. "He won't be here *any* day."

"Lucy!" Vincent chided.

"I don't care," she said. "Father's practically one of the family . . . he ought to be plugged in on our dirty laundry."

"Lucy, you shouldn't—"

"Lucy's right, I think," Koesler broke in. "I'm too close to this not to be allowed to know what's going on."

"I can be brief," Lucy said. "I think that Tony thinks Mama's process of dying is going way too slow."

Vincent, about to say something, decided to let the remark pass.

"Tony doesn't come home at all?" Koesler asked.

"Yeah," Lucy said, "he does . . . once in a while. But not for very long. What I really think is that he doesn't know how to handle this. I don't know why. People get sick." She was about to add that not only do they get sick, they die. But in deference to the expected miracle, she didn't.

"You have to keep in mind where Tony's coming from," Vincent said. "His world is built around physical fitness. For him there can be little or no compromise with sickness. He never, not for an instant, bought our decision to reject therapy. Besides, it's hard to watch your mother be so ill. However"—he looked almost beatific—"that will make the miracle all the more joyous."

Rather than have to respond to the possibility of a coming miracle, Lucy quickly said, "By the way, Father, Mama wants to talk to you. We've got a while till supper. Maybe you could see her now . . . before we eat?"

"Of course."

"She's upstairs in her bedroom."

"Is it okay if I just go up?"

"Sure."

Before entering, Koesler peered around the edge of the door. Louise, completely clothed, lay atop the bedclothes. She was so frail she almost blended into the quilt; Koesler didn't find her immediately. She seemed to be napping. He might have let her sleep, but she *had* asked to see him . . .

"Louise . . . ?"

Instantly she was awake and smiling. "Father, come in . . ." She gestured to a rocking chair near the bed.

Koesler pulled the chair closer and sat down. "How are you feeling, Louise?"

Slowly she turned on her side to see him better. "So-so."

"Can I get you anything?"

"No. No, thank you; I'm all right. I was just napping. Father, I want to go to confession."

Why? was his only thought. She had confessed almost every week since her diagnosis. Some of these confessions Koesler had heard. She had nothing to tell. Impatience. A little anger. Questioning God's will.

But if it would make her feel better . . .

Koesler removed a silk cloth from his breast pocket. It was perhaps twenty inches long and two inches wide. Purple on one side for confession or the last rites, white on the other for Communion. Koesler routinely carried the cloth, called a stole, with him. One never knew.

He draped the stole around his neck. "Okay, Louise, go ahead."

"Bless me, Father, for I have sinned. My last confession was a week ago."

So traditional.

"Father, I would like to make a confession of my whole life. What's that called? I forget."

"It's called a general confession, Louise. If you want to do this, it's okay. You can pick up things you may have forgotten to confess. Or you can renew your sorrow for specific sins. The main thing is you want to feel good about your relationship with God."

"Okay. Well, when I was growing up I used to have bad thoughts . . . sort of imagining what it would be like to be with a man. Then when I was engaged we used to neck and pet something fierce."

The good old Catholic conscience, thought Koesler: worried sick about sex.

"And I did a lot of other things, like missing Mass when I wasn't really ill. And, of course, being angry with the kids.

"And—and I'm really sorry for this—when my husband died I was real angry with God. Does God forgive you for that?"

"God forgave you before you even had that thought."

"Now here's something that really bothers me. I can't get it off my conscience that I did something real bad to my sister when I tried to help get her marriage fixed. I didn't know that Frank would kill himself. How could I have known that?"

"You couldn't know that, Louise. You just tried to do a good thing for Frank and Martha. You can't let yourself be disturbed by that. For heaven's sake, I could feel as bad as you. Maybe if I had tried harder to discourage them from trying to get an annulment that was almost doomed from the beginning . . .

"We can't torture ourselves over something we couldn't control."

"Did Martha talk to you after . . . after Frank . . . ?"

"Yes. We've talked."

"That's more than she's done with me."

Koesler clenched his teeth. "I know. I've even talked to her about that. She just won't. But you can't blame yourself for that either. It's simply not your fault."

"She's my sister!"

"But you feel no hatred toward her. You tried to help her. It didn't work out. That she won't talk to you is *her* problem."

"But I thought . . . you know . . . the condition I'm in . . . I thought she'd make peace now."

"So did I. But if it'll make you feel any better, we'll make it part of your confession. If you did anything wrong—and I assure you you didn't—you're sorry and God will forgive you."

Louise was quiet.

"Is that it, Louise?"

"Yes. Mostly I wanted to get that off my mind—that part about Martha."

"Okay. I'll give you absolution now, Louise. And for your penance . . . well, uh . . ." What sort of penance might he add on to her present suffering, he asked himself. Nothing, he concluded.

"For your penance, Louise, offer your suffering to God."

"Oh, I do, Father, I do."

"Good." He absolved her, then tucked the stole back in his pocket.

During Louise's confession, Koesler had gazed absently at the variety of bottles and vials that nearly covered the nightstand.

"Is all this medication?"

"Most of it. There's some vitamin supplements too."

"Mind if I look?"

"Go ahead."

Koesler began to finger the bottles, turning each to read the label. "Hmmm . . . looks like you've got a lot of vitamin C."

"Good for cancer . . . at least that's what I've read."

He picked up a bottle to get a closer look. A very small bottle, he guessed it held fifteen or twenty pills. Even with so few pills the bottle seemed full. And that made it unique among all these medications and bottles. *Morphine*, the label read. "This for pain?"

She nodded.

"You're not taking any? Or you just refilled the prescription?"

"I've taken one or two."

"Don't you need more than that?"

"Father, I haven't told anyone. Will you keep a secret?"

"I'm good at that."

"This may seem kind of silly . . . but all during Lent I've tried to unite my suffering with all that Jesus went through. I'm offering it up."

"For what?"

"The kids, mostly. Lucy is so young and has such talent. She could throw it all away with maybe a bad marriage.

"And Tony's a good boy. I think he's going to get very rich. I pray he doesn't let that go to his head. He could do so much good for others . . . as long as he doesn't get sidetracked.

"And then . . ." She hesitated. ". . . there's Vincent." She hesitated again. "My priest son." She smiled. "When he was little I'd take him to

Mass with us. He took to it like a duck to water. I started way back then to pray for him. He seemed a natural to become a priest. But I didn't want to push him. And I don't think I did; he did it all on his own. I want him to be such a good priest . . ."

She seemed to be making an effort to speak strongly. "And so I'm offering my little illness for the kids."

"That's beautiful, Louise. But if they knew what you were doing I'm sure they'd object. They don't want you to suffer. I can't think that God wants you to suffer."

She smiled weakly and patted Koesler's arm. "Honest, when it gets unbearable, I take one. I've already taken a couple. Besides, the doctor explained some of the side effects that can happen when you take very much. I'm better off without it.

"But you promised," she said insistently. "I don't want the kids to know. You're probably right: They'd be upset. So, you won't tell anybody?"

Koesler shook his head. "No, I won't. But how about Lucy? Doesn't she give you your medication and vitamins?"

"No. I'm determined to take care of myself for as long as I can, for as much as I can—"

"Din . . . ner . . ." Lucy called from downstairs.

Louise swung her legs over the side of the bed and slowly raised herself erect, motioning off Koesler's proffer of assistance.

"Can I help you downstairs?" he asked.

"No . . . thank you. Just be patient, please; I go kind of slow."

She did indeed. But Koesler stayed a step ahead of her just in case she were to fall.

The aroma of spaghetti and meatballs permeated the downstairs, tantalizing to all but Louise. After Koesler had led them in grace she forced herself to eat small portions and then to linger at table for longer than she really wished. Lucy, Vincent, and Koesler exchanged concerned looks as Lucy removed her mother's still nearly full plate after everyone else was finished.

"Dessert, Mother?"

Louise accepted a small portion of Jell-O and listlessly downed it.

Then, explaining that she was very tired, she rose and, accompanied by Vincent, made her way up the stairs.

She stretched out atop the quilt, telling Vincent she just wanted to rest for a little bit before getting ready for bedtime; would he stay with her?

Of course.

She stroked his cheek where a bit of stubble showed. He had been clean-shaven early in the morning. It was getting late in the day and in a little while he would have to return to St. John's.

"Baby . . ."

"I'm twenty-four years old. In a couple of months I'll be a priest. And still she calls me 'Baby.'"

But he didn't really mind. Their love for each other was a mother-son epitome.

"Baby," she repeated, "are you all ready?"

"Ready? For what?"

"To get ordained."

He smiled. "I'm as ready as I'll ever be."

"I mean, this has been really tough on you—me being sick and all. Don't tell me it hasn't been a distraction."

"You didn't choose to get sick now, Ma. We have to roll with the punches." He smiled encouragingly. "But we can do it."

"How are your studies going?"

"What's this all about, Ma? Why are you so concerned about how I'm doing and my studies?"

"It's funny: I'll never be able to make anyone understand. But . . . I can feel your prayers. They seem to take away a lot of the pain."

"No kidding! You feel my prayers?" His eyes lit up. "Maybe it's not just mine. There are lots of people praying for you, you know."

"If it was anybody else, I could tell. That's why no one will believe me. I know it's *your* prayers. But I don't want you to let your schoolwork go. You're so close to the end now."

Vincent smiled broadly. "Don't be concerned about my schoolwork . . ." He nodded assuringly. "That's in the bag."

"Sure?"

"Sure!" he emphasized.

She ran her fingers through his hair. He simply leaned closer to make the gesture easier.

"Baby, I've got one last request for you—"

"What's this 'last' business?"

"Humor me. Someday very soon you're going to be at God's holy altar. You're going to offer the holy sacrifice of the Mass. What I ask you is for you always to have me in your heart. Let me be part of every Mass you offer . . ." She fixed him with her gaze. "Promise me."

Vincent choked back a sob. "Don't talk like this, Ma. Of course you're going to be in my Masses. But you're going to be in the prayers for the living. And you can check me out. You can remind me from time to time. But you won't really need to check: I'll remember."

"Which reminds me: What dress are you going to wear to my ordination? And whichever one you choose, are you going to wear the same one for my first Mass the next day?"

She laughed softly. "Baby, I've lost so much weight, I'll have to buy a new one. And as long as it's new, I think I'll probably wear it for the first Mass too."

"Sounds good, Ma. In another week you're going to wonder what it was like to be sick."

Her smile was like a sunburst. "I can hardly wait, baby." She lay back and licked her lips.

"Can I get you some water, Ma?"

"No . . . no, I'll be fine. But I think I need to get some sleep. This has been a busy day."

He leaned over and kissed her forehead, then his thumb traced the sign of the cross on her brow. She smiled and closed her eyes.

He pulled a comforter over her still form, waited till her breath was deep and even, then tiptoed out of the room and went quietly down the stairs.

He stepped into the kitchen where Lucy was finishing up the dishes. Koesler, after drying the last pot, folded the towel and draped it on its hook. "Maybe I ought to go up and say good-bye."

"She's sleeping."

Koesler nodded. "In that case, I'll just leave. I should at least drop in at home and visit with my folks for a while."

"Tony said he'll definitely be home for Easter," Lucy said, apropos of the word "home."

"Good," Vincent said. "There ought to be a doubting Thomas around at any miracle."

"If custom prevails—and there's no reason it won't," Koesler said, "this will be the busiest week of the year for parish priests. But I'll be here—definitely—right after St. Norbert's last Easter Mass."

"And I," Vincent added, "will be home as soon as the Easter vigil is finished next Saturday morning. And then," he added further, "I'll be home for a full week. To gloat." His chin was firm.

Koesler donned coat and hat. It was late March—spring, which in Michigan could mean bundle-up weather well into April or even May.

After making his good-byes, Koesler, still in the flush of youth, fairly skipped down the steps to his car.

As he drove toward his familial home in southwest Detroit, he played back the memory of today's visit with the Delvecchios.

His experience with the terminally ill was quite limited compared with what it would be when he'd had many pastoral years behind him. He could envision Louise lasting a few more weeks, even a month or two. On the other hand, she could be gone before this week was over; it all depended on the relentless advance of the cancer against her will to live. She did *so* want to be there for Lucy at graduation.

Koesler felt it was not in the cards that she would see even the beginning of any sports career Tony might have. But she did want to see him graduate.

Then there was Vincent. Louise would give anything to attend his ordination. And who knows, maybe she would. It was altogether possible the miracle would save her and extend her life into many fruitful years. But it definitely would be Vincent's miracle.

17

Monday and Tuesday of Holy Week were spent largely shoring up against the special demands of the final four days of that week.

Of course there were the children's confessions. Public school catechism classes were heard in the afternoon and evening. Students of St. Norbert's recently opened grade school were taken care of in the morning.

Instruction sessions and meetings ordinarily held during the last four days of any week had to be capsulized into the first two.

There were the special liturgies of Thursday morning: Chrism Mass at the Cathedral with the blessing of three oils used throughout the coming year, and, in the parish, the evening commemoration of the Last Supper. Friday saw a Communion service as part of the noon-to-three *Tre Ore*. Saturday was the Easter Vigil service.

Tucked tightly around those services were individual confessions. By no means were there as many penitents in Koesler's suburban parish as there were in St. William's. However, St. William's supplied four priest confessors; St. Norbert's, only two.

All in all, Father Koesler was as busy now at St. Norbert's as he had once been at St. William's. And equally exhausted by the close of Holy Week.

At the conclusion of the noon Mass on Easter Sunday, he wanted nothing more than a place to stretch out horizontally and ease the tired muscles used for sitting, listening to endless confessions.

But he had a commitment at the Delvecchio home.

He was surprised to find only Vincent, Tony, and Lucy there. He had expected to see some of the relatives—or at least some of the kids' classmates. He expressed this.

"Oh," Lucy said, "some of our aunts and uncles and cousins plan to stop by later in the day—but just for a short time. Mom's kinda tired. As far as our classmates"—she shrugged—"it's Easter: They're with their families."

Tony nodded. "Yeah, same with my gang: Easter break; most of 'em went South."

"Some of the guys said they'd come to visit during the week," Vincent said quietly.

Vincent looked about as tired and washed out as Louise had the last time Koesler had visited. And thinking of Louise . . .

"How is she?" Koesler asked.

"Weak. But hanging in," Lucy said.

"We've been taking turns being with her," Tony said. "She seems more comfortable without having the whole gang of us at once."

The three kids were right here, in front of Koesler. It seemed no one was with Louise now. "Do you suppose I might go up for a little while?"

"We hoped you would," Lucy said.

Somehow, Louise's condition did not surprise Koesler. In his modest experience, cancer could wreak a devastating punishment. So it was with Louise; Koesler had to look intently to recognize her features clearly.

But she was awake and alert—much more than he'd expected. They greeted each other and Koesler took the rocking chair after pulling it closer to the bed.

"You must be exhausted, Father, after your busy schedule this week. You don't have to visit with me."

"How about I want to?"

Her smile evidenced embarrassment, though her cheeks showed no blush. "But you must be tired," she insisted.

As if triggered by the word "tired," he yawned, segueing into a chuckle. "You mesmerized me. I'm not really all that tired. I'll recover. But you: How are you feeling?"

"To be honest, it's been a tough week. But I'm still able to care for myself, which is a blessing. I don't know how long I'll be able to continue doing that. But I'm grateful."

"Yeah, I guess that is a blessing . . ."

Koesler didn't understand why she was so reluctant to let Lucy do more for her. He knew Lucy was ready and willing to take over.

"To tell you the truth, Father, I think I'll be with Jesus soon."

Koesler shook his head. "No. No. Not if Vincent has his miracle."

Louise's smile was no more than pulling back her lips from her teeth. It was almost ghoulish. "Vincent's miracle," she mused. "It better hurry along."

"Maybe it would help if I prayed," he suggested.

"Yes. I'd like that." She folded her hands over her chest.

Koesler removed from his suit pocket his ritual book of prayers and the small stole, which he draped over his neck. He opened the book and began to read:

"'O God, full of love, forgiveness and compassion, graciously receive our prayer that we and this Thy servant, who are bound with the chain of our sins, may by your kind forgiveness be graciously absolved.

"'O God, the one only help for human infirmity, give to your servant in this hour of her need the power of Thine aid, that by the assistance of Thy loving kindness she may be restored in health to Thy Holy Church.

"'Grant, O Lord God, we beseech Thee, that this Thy ill servant may enjoy continued health of body and soul. And through the glorious intercession of Blessed Mary ever virgin, be freed from her present sorrow and enjoy eternal gladness. Through Christ our Lord. Amen.'"

He traced the sign of the cross over her. "The blessing of God almighty, the Father, and the Son, and the Holy Ghost descend upon you and remain with you always. Amen."

She nodded, and whispered, "Amen."

"I'd better let somebody up here to take my place," Koesler said. "I don't know whose turn it is."

"They're taking turns?"

"Uh-huh. They seem to think that having one visitor at a time is easier on you. I think they picked up this routine from a hospital . . . seems hospitals are always real concerned about the number of visitors. How do you feel about it?"

"Hmmm. I think it's better on them. I'd just as soon have all my kids with me. But don't tell them that, Father: They'll feel better doing it their way. Besides, I am awful tired. It's probably better I don't have a crowd now. Just let whoever's next come up. I'll try to keep track of them."

He smiled and briefly held her hand. "Remember, I'll be down there if you need me. Otherwise, I'll see you when my turn comes around again."

It reminded him of wrestling's Australian tag team matches, where a beleaguered contestant tags his partner, who, in turn, enters the ring a bit fresher for battle.

When Koesler reentered the living room, Lucy stood up. Evidently, she was next to be at her mother's side.

That left Koesler, Vincent, and Tony in awkward silence.

"The Tigers are on TV," Tony announced. He looked from the priest to his brother. "Any objections?"

There were none, at least none stated.

Van Patrick was saying that the score was Chicago White Sox 4, the Tigers 2, in the bottom of the fifth inning.

Somehow, to Father Koesler, watching a game seemed inappropriate with Louise so ill just upstairs. On the other hand—life goes on.

But the first few minutes appeared to have reached Vincent, who retreated into the dining area. He sat at the table and buried his head in his hands. He was praying, Koesler knew. And, while affecting interest in the ball game, Koesler joined, in spirit, the praying Vincent.

His prayerful thoughts were interrupted by Lucy's appearance at the living room door. It seemed to Koesler only moments since she had gone upstairs. He checked his watch: fifteen minutes. Lucy seemed startled at the televised ball game, but seeing how absorbed Tony was, she said only, "Your turn, Vinnie." Her tone carried wonder that he would need to be reminded.

"Oh . . . oh, uh, sure." He rose and headed for the stairs.

"She seems to be taking little naps," Lucy said. "When she comes out of them, she kind of looks around to see if anyone's with her. So, don't go to sleep." Seemingly, the latter remark was intended as humor.

If so, Vincent didn't get it. Somberly, he climbed the stairs.

Koesler glanced at his watch. He would time the upstairs visits.

He was somewhat surprised to see Lucy seat herself on the couch next to Tony and gaze at the television. She must need the distraction, he thought.

Her admonition for Vincent not to doze reminded Koesler of the Good Friday liturgy when, in the Garden of Olives, Jesus is disappointed in His specially selected Apostles when they cannot watch with Him for even an hour.

With nothing better to do, and feeling "prayed out," Koesler became interested, if not absorbed in the ball game.

Someone of the Tiger persuasion hit a home run. Koesler missed the name, but Mr. Kell was waxing poetic about the batter's "extension of his arms" and how he had gotten the ball high into the wind that was blowing toward the right field stands.

Koesler got into a conversation with Lucy about the salaries paid to baseball players, as well as to professional athletes in general.

Suddenly he became aware that Tony appeared distracted; he seemed to be paying no attention to either the conversation or the game. So focused was Koesler on Tony's state that he didn't hear Vincent enter the room; he was startled when Vincent spoke. "She seems a little worse. She's slipping in and out of consciousness. I don't know . . ." His voice trailed off.

Tony rose and without a word climbed the stairs.

Koesler checked his watch. Vincent had been with his mother a little better than fifteen minutes. He wondered if the kids had an understanding on the timing of their visits. He hadn't checked Lucy, but he thought the length of her latest visit mirrored Vincent's.

Vincent took Tony's place on the couch. But it was immediately evident that he would pay even less attention to the TV than Tony had been.

Koesler and Lucy continued their observations on the state of payment for services rendered according to vocation. It was, they agreed, a crime that teachers and nurses were paid so much less than working actors and many athletes.

They were interrupted again, this time by Tony's hurried footsteps descending the stairs. Koesler checked his watch. Fifteen minutes. It had to be an agreed time.

Because Tony had come down the stairs so rapidly, they all stood and turned to him.

"I think . . . I think . . ." His voice betrayed near panic, and he was breathing hard—unusual for a conditioned athlete. "I think you'd better come—all of you."

He and Vincent led the way, followed closely by Lucy and Koesler. None of them would ever forget what they saw.

Louise's eyes were closed. But her mouth was stretched open as if that were the only way she could breathe.

Both her forearms were lifted while her elbows rested on the bed. Her hands were pointed at the ceiling.

"She wants . . . she wants someone to hold her hands. That was the last thing she said before she . . . before she got like that." There was no doubt that Tony was over his head. He had never seen anyone in such a state. And it was his mother. He was not going to be part of her wish to have her hands held.

Quickly, Lucy knelt on one side of the bed, Koesler on the other. Each of them took one of her hands in theirs. Each held it tightly. Her hands were almost icy and she did not return their squeezes.

Tony sank down in the doorway, as far from the bed as he could get and still be in the room. He could not nor did he attempt to hide his bewilderment.

Vincent nearly collapsed at the foot of the bed and grasped both his mother's ankles, to let her know he too was there. He murmured something. It sounded like "Now."

Koesler assumed Vincent was calling for the miracle. It was, Koesler was all too willing to admit, time. This, the brink of mortality, would clearly be recognized as well beyond what could be expected from human nature at its strongest. Koesler had never beheld such a scene. Yet instinctively, he knew Louise was on the threshold of death.

Without taking his eyes from her, Koesler said, "Tony, call the doctor. Ask him to come. If he can't come immediately, tell him forget it. We need him *now*."

No one could be sure what good the doctor might do. This was it: either a miracle or death. And if he were more calm, Koesler would have admitted it. He wanted the doctor there at very least to certify death. If it came to that.

Koesler's gaze was riveted on Louise's face. Her expression was frozen. To him it seemed she was half here and half . . . where? In transit to eternity?

"I think she can hear," Lucy said softly. "I read that someplace. Let's say the Rosary. She always loved the Rosary. You lead, Vinnie."

Silence.

"I said lead us in the Rosary, Vinnie! Come on!" She would be obeyed, even by her elder brother.

Absently, Vincent felt around in his pockets. From one, he pulled a plain black, much used rosary. "In the name of the Father and of the Son and of the Holy Ghost. Amen. I believe in God . . ."

And so the familiar prayers followed one another, with the others joining in. He chose to meditate on the sorrowful mysteries, those events that immediately led to the crucifixion and death of Jesus.

He announced the first mystery: the agony in the Garden of Olives. He began the "Lord's Prayer."

Koesler continued to study Louise's face. Suddenly, there was a subtle change in her expression. Hitherto it was as if she were carved from stone. Now she seemed to wince as if she was struggling for another breath but could not find one.

He thought of the etymological origin of "expire": to breathe out. To breathe one's last breath. To die. Louise had done just that. And he had witnessed this solemn moment. "I think . . . I think she's . . ."

Without rising from her knees, Lucy reached to the night table and pick up a hand mirror. She pressed it to her mother's lips. After several moments, she turned the mirror and studied it. There was no sign of condensation. She looked at Koesler and shook her head.

Vincent, who'd had his eyes closed, started to recite the "Hail Mary." But there was no response. He opened his eyes and looked at his mother. She had not changed in any external way. Tears streamed down Lucy's face and Koesler was draping the stole around his shoulder.

Vincent seemed bewildered.

"The doc is on his—" What Tony saw from the doorway told him the story. He turned on his heel and went back downstairs.

Lucy made no effort to stop him—or her tears. She said only, "Keep going, Vinnie. Maybe she can still hear us."

Now tears were flowing down Vinnie's cheeks as well. He stumbled on. ". . . the Lord is with thee. Blessed art thou among women, and blessed is the fruit of thy womb, Jesus."

"Holy Mary, mother of God. Pray for us sinners now, and at the hour—" Lucy choked. "—of our death, Amen."

Almost in counterpoint with the rosary prayers, Koesler read from his ritual. "'Into Thy hands, O Lord, I commend my spirit. Lord Jesus, receive my spirit. Holy Mary, pray for me. Mary, mother of grace, mother of mercy, protect me from the enemy, and receive me at the hour of my death. St. Joseph, pray for me. St. Joseph, in company with thy spouse, Mary, open to me the bosom of divine mercy.

"'Jesus, Mary and Joseph, I give you my heart and my soul.

"'Jesus, Mary and Joseph, assist me in my last agony.

"'Jesus, Mary and Joseph, may I sleep and rest in peace in your holy company.

"'Depart, Christian soul, out of this sinful world in the name of God the Father Almighty who created you; in the name of Jesus Christ, the Son of the living God, Who suffered and died for you; in the name of the Holy Ghost, who sanctified you; in the name of the glorious and blessed Virgin Mary, mother of God; in the name of blessed Joseph, the illustrious spouse of Mary; in the name of the angels, archangels, Thrones, Dominations, Virtues, Cherubim and Seraphim; in the name of the Patriarchs and Prophets, of the holy Apostles and Evangelists, of the holy Martyrs and Confessors, of the holy monks and hermits, of the holy virgins and of all the saints of God. Let peace come to you this day, and let your abode be in holy Sion. Through the same Christ, our Lord. Amen.'"

18

During the prayers, Lucy gently closed her mother's mouth. The eyes were already closed.

After the prayers, Father Koesler and Lucy stood. Vincent remained kneeling at the foot of the bed, clutching his mother's ankles.

"Do you want to stay with her?" Koesler asked Lucy.

"I think we'd better find Tony," she said.

It occurred to Koesler—and not for the first time—that of the three offspring, Lucy by far was the rock.

Vincent seemed in another land.

"We're going to find Tony and be with him, Vinnie," Koesler said. "Do you want to come?"

No response.

"Vinnie—" Lucy said sharply.

"No," Koesler said. "Let's leave him alone. He wants to be with your mother. Besides, the doctor should be here any minute."

They found Tony standing in front of the darkened TV screen, hands thrust deep in his pockets. Wordless, they stood on either side of him for what seemed a much longer time than actually transpired.

"Damn Vinnie and damn his damn miracle!" Tony said bitterly.

"It's not Vinnie's fault," Lucy said quietly.

"No? Whose idea was it not to try therapy?"

"It doesn't matter whose idea it was originally," Lucy shot back. "The point is once it was proposed, we all agreed to skip a treatment that stood almost no chance of being effective. All of us, that is, with the possible exception of you. You lost that vote. We couldn't ask some hospital to give Ma one fifth of a radiation treatment because you wanted it and I and Vinnie and Father and Doc didn't."

"So, okay: You won." Tony was almost snarling. "The point is, without therapy Ma lasted about a month. With treatments, she could have watched you and me graduate. She could've watched St. Vincent get or-

146

dained. Now she's not going to be here at all. Now," his voice rose, "she'll miss everything."

"This is no good, Tony," Koesler said. "You can Monday-morning quarterback from either side. We agreed it would be better to skip radiation. Even your mother agreed."

"What chance did she have of disagreeing? The vote was four to one before Ma could speak her piece."

"Try and look at it this way, Tony: We tried going without treatment. We know now that had its expected result: She passed away. The only real surprise is that it happened earlier than we anticipated.

"Imagine," Koesler continued, "that we had agreed to have the radiation treatments. We—the doctor, all of us—were quite sure they could not cure her—not with the cancer she had. But suppose we had gone with the radiation. We know she would have been pretty miserable and uncomfortable. Much more so than if she hadn't gotten them. So then, when she inevitably died, we would've been second-guessing ourselves . . . wondering what her quality of life would've been like if she hadn't had to undergo the treatment. Her quality of life was much better without than with.

"What is quite certain is that with or without, she had a terminal illness. But as I said: One could argue either side. No one could claim that each and every one of us didn't want what all considered best for your mother.

"And as for the miracle that Vincent worked and prayed for almost alone, it really was the only possible solution to this tragedy. At times, just based on Vinnie's investment of prayer and sacrifice, I actually expected it to happen.

"The big thing is: It's over. With or without treatment, and without a miracle, it's over. Sooner or later it will be over for all of us. Your mother has gone from here to eternal life. The challenge you two have is to live up to your mother's standards. And one quick way to do that is for you to love each other and forgive each other whenever forgiveness is called for.

"I mean, picture your mother here, now, as well she may be. You wouldn't want her to see you bickering and, in effect, blaming one another for her death.

"With your mother gone, you're all going to have to be closer than ever."

For a minute, there was neither sound nor movement. Then, tentatively, Lucy moved to Tony and embraced him. He returned her hug.

Typical, thought Koesler in his growing admiration for Lucy; typical that she would be the first to make a gesture of reconciliation.

The doorbell broke the silence.

Having been summoned to an emergency call and seeing the three of them in the living room instead of upstairs with Louise, Dr. Schmidt knew immediately. "She's gone." It wasn't a question.

"We think so." As far as Koesler was concerned it wasn't official until the doctor confirmed it.

They followed Dr. Schmidt up the stairs, but remained in the hall while he entered the bedroom.

After some minutes, he called them in.

· He had pulled the sheet over Louise's small body. He was writing on what seemed to be a document and was, in fact, the death certificate. "Do you want me to help make arrangements?" he asked of no one in particular.

"No. Ma and I talked this through," said Lucy. "I know what to do." She left the room and they could hear her firm footsteps going down the stairs.

Tony stood near the doorway, not knowing quite how to react.

"This was fast," Schmidt said. "I certainly didn't expect her to go this quickly." He turned to Koesler. "How long have you been here, Father?"

"I came right after noon Mass." Koesler studied his watch. "About an hour and a half, I'd say."

"Did she seem in any distress?"

"No . . . I don't think so. Mostly she was resting. I talked with her for a while. That was right after I got here. We all took turns"—he looked around at the other two—"of about fifteen or twenty minutes each. It was during Tony's watch that she . . . well, began to die. We prayed for her. Her . . . agony lasted no more than half an hour . . . although," he added, again looking at the other two, "it seemed a lot longer. She seemed to be trying to breathe and finding it more and more difficult. We all were with her when she passed."

"Not all of us," Tony said bitterly.

"I asked you to call Dr. Schmidt," Koesler said, in explanation of Tony's absence at the end.

"I didn't come back."

"This is never easy," Schmidt said. "Don't blame yourself."

"My sister stuck it out!" The statement reflected a chauvinistic spirit; Tony had not lived up to a demand answered by a "mere girl."

The priest and the doctor let Tony's charge stand. Both felt that in time the young man would have a more mature attitude.

Schmidt turned his attention to the medication and supplements on the nightstand. "You said that until near the end she exhibited no apparent pain?"

"No," Koesler responded. "Tired . . . she seemed very tired. But no pain that I could detect."

"Well, this probably is the answer." Schmidt held up the small morphine bottle. It was empty. "For the life of me, I couldn't get her to use a painkiller. I don't know why. Well, evidently, she changed her mind."

"She had joined her suffering to that of Christ," Koesler murmured. He felt that his mind was becoming numb.

Schmidt looked at him sharply. "I don't understand that at all!"

Koesler sighed. "It made sense to her."

When Louise had explained her intention regarding the morphine, Koesler had thought of a sermon given about a hundred years ago by John Henry Cardinal Newman. Newman's homily addressed Mary's presence at the crucifixion of her son. It was an involved theological speculation that began with the hypothesis that Jesus was one person and that was divine. He was God. However, He also possessed two natures: human and divine. Not only was He a human man, He also was God. He lacked, then, a human personality. This absent human personality could not participate in the total suffering that ended in His death. Newman's point was that Jesus' mother contributed—offered— her human personality to complete her son's redemptive act.

It was a most complex concept . . . a theological clutter.

Koesler was certain Louise had never read or even heard of the sermon preached so long ago. And yet that, in effect, was what she had done in joining her suffering with the terminal pain of Jesus Christ.

Now, gazing at the empty bottle, Koesler began to comprehend how intense her pain must have been—so great that she was forced to abandon her resolution.

But he was glad she had done it. It had been the certainty of the painful effects of the radiation, along with the hopelessness of the treatment, that had prompted the decision to forgo therapy.

Without radiation, morphine became the prescribed antidote for the pain of her cancer. Thank God she had finally made use of it.

Schmidt closed his bag, then stopped and looked around the room. "Something's missing."

"What?"

"Vincent. I haven't seen him since I arrived. Surely he's here! He couldn't still be at the seminary, could he?"

"That's strange," Koesler said. "Of course he's here. He's been here since yesterday. After Louise died, Lucy and I left him here with her. He seemed to want to stay near the body. With all that's been happening, I'm afraid I forgot all about him." He turned to Tony, still standing in the doorway. "Do you know where Vinnie is?"

It was as if Tony had suddenly wakened. "No . . . no, I don't. I'll go find him." He disappeared down the hall.

"Can you stay with them for a while at least?" Schmidt asked Koesler.

"I'll stay. They're expecting some relatives and friends later. The original plan was for visitors to come and go without sticking around to tire her. Now, of course . . ." Koesler looked at the outline of Louise's slight form. ". . . there's no reason for them to leave. I'm sure they'll stay to comfort the children and each other. But I'll hang around until the crowd grows a bit."

There was movement at the bedroom door. Tony had returned from somewhere, but Vincent wasn't with him. The boy was ashen.

"What is it?" Koesler asked.

"You'd better come." He turned and led them down the hall to the guest room—the bedroom that Vincent and Tony had shared when they were children.

All Koesler saw was a well-kept room . . . until Tony pointed to the far corner beyond the bed.

Koesler, following Tony's pointing finger, took a few steps around the side of the bed. There, on the floor, curled in a fetal position, was Vincent. He was not moving.

"Oh, my God!" Koesler exclaimed.

The Present

"Oh, my God!" Father Tully breathed.

Neither priest spoke for several moments.

"This is playing out like a Greek tragedy," Tully said finally. "An excommunicated aunt; a failed nullity decree; a suicide; sisterly enmity; terminal cancer at the worst time for the children; and now . . . what? A catatonic young man on the verge of ordination to the priesthood?" He shook his head. "Incredible!"

"It does have a cumulative effect, doesn't it?" Father Koesler agreed. "Although I'm the storyteller, I've never considered the events of the Delvecchio family's tragedy in one continuous chronological line before."

He thought for a moment. "I suppose it's because I'm not dwelling on many of the happy, upbeat, positive things that happened to them. But then, it was this accumulation of really bad fortune that transformed the family—especially Vincent. As I said before, seeing the story this way is giving me a much different perspective." He tilted his head slightly. "Interesting."

During Koesler's lengthy narration, Tully, not consciously, had inched forward until now he was perched on the edge of his chair almost like a bird in a cage.

Aware now that he had become physically involved in the Delvecchio chronicles, he pushed himself back in his seat. "But what happened to Vincent?" he asked. "Obviously, he didn't die. On top of that, he was ordained; my God, he's a bishop!"

Koesler looked grave. "That undoubtedly was a pivotal time in Delvecchio's life. Fate might have taken him in almost any direction. At least for a while, his life's course was not in his hands. Others took on that responsibility for him.

"Looking back on it now, I don't know how those kids got through it.

151

But somehow they did. The funeral for Louise was Easter Wednesday. I gave the eulogy. Ordinarily it would have been one of the St. William's priests. And Frank Henry was *not* happy that Father Walsh actually asked me to do it.

"Easter Sunday evening Vincent was admitted to St. John's Hospital. The day of his mother's funeral, he was transferred to St. Joseph's Retreat."

"St. Joseph's Retreat? What's that?"

"Nothing now. It was a Catholic sanatorium in Dearborn, staffed by the Sisters of Charity—you know, the ones who used to wear the winged bonnets—"

"Like the Flying Nun."

"Pretty close. I was kind of familiar with the place before Vince was committed. For one thing, while I was at St. Norbert's, St. Joe's was only about a ten-minute drive away. When we were shorthanded—usually because the pastor was on vacation—we used to get from St. Joe's one or another of the priests who weren't too far removed from reality to help us with Mass . . ." Koesler smiled, remembering. "One older guy really was memorable. Each time he'd say Mass for us, he'd steal a vestment. When I drove him back to St. Joe's, I'd always try to find a way of retrieving it.

"One day I was driving him back and he started reminiscing about how terribly his bishop had treated him. And, believe me, he had a long litany of complaints. Then he said, 'I just had it with the man. So I went right up to him and told him to go to hell.'

"'Did he go?' I asked him.

"'No,' he answered, 'he sent me.'"

Tully chuckled. "But Vincent . . . what happened to Vincent?"

"I think he was virtually a prisoner in the Retreat. No visitors—not even a priest. I tried to see him and couldn't. That was almost unheard-of . . . I mean, I've been admitted to hospital rooms where the patient is so ill a spouse is denied entry."

"No one knew what was happening to him?"

"Sure. Guys in the chancery knew. The seminary faculty was kept informed. Of course both those groups could be very close-mouthed about things. And in Vinnie's case they were. I was eager to find out what was happening. But I didn't have a clue . . . until the meeting."

Koesler had been sitting too long. He got up and started pacing.

"What meeting? What happened?"

"The meeting was the second Sunday after Easter, at St. John's Seminary. The rector and his faculty; Monsignor Jake Donovan from the Detroit chancery; Father Walsh—as Delvecchio's pastor; Bobby Bear, Vincent's psychiatrist; and I—at Walsh's invitation." Koesler was silent for a moment. "Seems they had been treating Vince with electroshock."

Tully shuddered. "They used that a lot back then, didn't they . . ."

Koesler nodded. "With a lot of therapists it was the treatment of choice. And then, much more than now, being confined in a sanatorium was almost a badge of shame that was difficult to live down. Especially if you were a seminarian. They had awfully tight standards then: Any deformity or questionable health could be cause for dismissal. If this had happened to just about any other seminarian, it would have been curtains for his vocation.

"But Vincent Delvecchio was not your run-of-the-mill candidate. The chancery had plans for Delvecchio. So the top brass had a bad case of mixed emotions. Thus the meeting . . ."

"I know the outcome," Tully broke in. "They kept him in the seminary and ordained him. But I don't exactly know why. I mean, I know it's really rough when someone very close dies. But . . . catatonia? That sure would make me wonder . . ."

"Not so rare. A long time ago Detroit had an auxiliary bishop whose mother died at a very old age. And that bishop's reaction almost set the standard for Vince's. In time, the bishop got over it and functioned again. The difference here was that the precedent incident involved a bishop, whereas Vince was still a seminarian. What can you do with a bishop who's gone haywire? Whatever else happens, he remains a bishop. But a seminarian? He has a breakdown, he can be dumped. Ordain him and you've created a problem that could haunt the diocese for as long as the illness continues . . . maybe for the sick priest's entire life.

"And, I can assure you: If it hadn't been Delvecchio, he would've been dumped even though he had already been ordained a deacon.

They would just have applied for a laicization. He would've been reduced to the lay status and left to get along as best he could.

"But, of course, this wasn't just any ordinary kid who wanted to be a priest. This was the Reverend Mr. Vincent Delvecchio. The archdiocese of Detroit had a lot invested in Vince: not only money but plans for administrative service.

"Thus, the conclave."

"And," Tully asked impatiently, "what happened at the meeting?"

"Oh, I can't recall all of it . . ." Koesler paused to refresh his memory. "Well, first off, Monsignor Donovan identified the state of things. He was present in lieu of Archbishop Boyle. Boyle at this time"—he looked intently at Tully, who could not be expected to remember when the future Cardinal Boyle had succeeded Cardinal Edward Mooney—"had been in Detroit only some three months. He was installed in December 1958 and we're talking about the spring of 1959.

"Donovan wanted to impress everyone that Boyle considered this decision concerning Delvecchio of prime importance—important enough that the archbishop himself would have attended. But since he was new to the diocese and was swamped, he couldn't be there. Nonetheless, all were to understand that Donovan represented Boyle, the chief bishop of the state of Michigan.

"Then, as I recall, Dr. Bob Bear reported that Vince had suffered an extremely severe anxiety attack. He didn't want to be overly technical nor could he reveal any information protected by physician-patient confidentiality, etcetera.

"Bear's prognosis was guarded. With care and intensive therapy, Vince's prospects were quite good. However, at this point, no predictions were ironclad. The doctor's conclusion: One, that Vince not be ordained a priest until recovery was pronounced and solid; two, that during the time of Vince's recuperation he be carefully monitored.

"Then the faculty had at it. It seemed obvious to me that the course the doctor had outlined made sense and that that's what would happen. But I guess each of them felt impelled to contribute something. Father Walsh drew audible lines under some of the faculty's comments. By the time it was my turn, everything that could've been said had been. So, I passed.

"The responsibility for the final word seemed to be shared by Father Finn and Monsignor Donovan. And basically, they pretty much followed the doctor's suggestion.

"Finn said that no matter how quickly Vince might recover, ordination was out of the question this year. He said that no final decision should be made until at least a year from now and maybe longer. But Finn was concerned that Delvecchio not be put upon a shelf somewhere and periodically studied like an insect under a microscope.

"At the same time, it might be counterproductive to take Vince back at St. John's Seminary. Of course he could continue in some sort of graduate work. But he would have to do so on his own. And that would not be feasible in this institution's makeup. With all the other students from the first year of theology to the fourth, Vince would, in effect, be in a fifth year of theology—a class unto himself, as it were.

"Then Monsignor Donovan spoke up. He noted that originally Delvecchio had been scheduled to study theology in Rome. At almost the last instant, another student, who happened to be the nephew of a bishop, had been substituted for Vincent.

"'Why not,' the monsignor said, 'use that appointment now?' So Donovan suggested—with all the clout of the archbishop of Detroit—that Delvecchio be sent off to Rome for . . . the duration, however long that would be. Donovan said he had several personal friends in Rome, who, he was sure, would monitor Vince's progress, behavior, and so forth.

"As a fringe benefit, while he convalesced Vince could be taking some graduate courses in Rome. He could end with a leg up on a master's or a doctoral degree.

"All in all," Koesler concluded, "it seemed like a happy solution to the whole problem."

"So, he went off to Rome?"

"Well, he did have a choice: He could refuse the Rome assignment, he could shop around for another seminary in another diocese, or he could go job hunting.

"He went to Rome."

"We corresponded—irregularly for the most part. Would you believe he spent the next four years studying in Rome?"

"Four years! It took him that long to get well?"

Koesler chuckled. "Not nearly. I could tell from his letters that he was making steady progress.Considering how ill he had been, he recovered remarkably quickly."

"Then how come they didn't ship him home right then?"

"Let's just say—and for some very good reasons—the diocese didn't want to gamble. I, for one, will never forget seeing Vince curled up on the floor, helpless and unconscious. And while nobody from the chancery was there, they couldn't forget what had happened. Vince understood their reluctance to bring him home and ordain him.

"But he did extremely well with his time. Before he left Detroit, he spoke French, Spanish, and, of course, English and Latin. While he was in Rome, he became fluent in Italian. He got a doctorate in theology and a licentiate in Canon Law."

"Wow!" Father Tully was impressed.

"Toward the end of his time in Rome, the guys in our chancery were trying to figure out where to slot him. Word had gotten around about what had happened. Gossip, especially clerical gossip, is a dam that can't hold indefinitely. The brethren couldn't figure what happened to him when he didn't return to St. John's after Easter vacation.

"After Vinnie's endurance effort at prayer, all the guys at St. John's at that time knew about his mother. It was also easy to learn there was no miraculous cure. But he disappeared. Over time, it wasn't that difficult to put it all together. St. Joe's Retreat and then sent off to Rome as if he were wrapped in the secrecy of a spy.

"So, there was that to consider. Vince hadn't really been Mr. Popularity; now he bore the sobriquet of 'crazy.' How would he be greeted when he returned to Detroit as mysteriously as he'd left? Of course he had a couple of degrees from prestigious Vatican colleges. Not only that, he'd been in Rome as the Second Vatican Council began. Unfortunately, his appreciation of the Council was tainted by viewing it through the eyes of some of his more conservative teachers and mentors.

"The Roman Curia was not happy with this plaything of Pope John's. Generally, they were dedicated to doing everything possible to torpedo the Council and return to the good old days—when any Church movement began and ended in Rome. Then, the 'Church' very definitely was the Pope and his administration.

"The Curia put up a determined, but a losing battle.

"And so Vincent Delvecchio returned to his archdiocese. Now his archdiocese had to figure out what to do with this talented misfit."

The phone rang, followed by the sound of Mary O'Connor's footsteps almost running down the hall.

Mary and Koesler had been through some pretty urgent and stressful times. She *never* ran.

"It's the bishop!" she stage-whispered at the door.

"Which one?" Although Koesler would've bet on the answer.

"Delvecchio." She was almost wheezing.

Koesler looked at Tully. "Want me to get it?"

Tully shook his head as he rose from his chair. "I'll get it. Speak of the devil! I'd like to hear how he sounds now that I'm getting a better idea of what makes him tick."

When Tully returned he was smiling.

"What'd he want?" Koesler asked.

"He wanted to get out of tonight's little ceremony."

"Why? What happened?"

"'Unexpected complications'—of such mysterious origin that he couldn't be specific." Tully winked. "He said he couldn't possibly make it before close to nine. That's where he made his mistake. When I told him our other guests wouldn't be here until nine at the earliest and that we were willing to live with that, he didn't have much of an alternative."

"So . . . ?"

"So then he didn't say anything for a moment. I could imagine him cursing his luck in mentioning a time that he thought was out of the question only to find it fit hand in glove. Finally he said he'd be here as early as he could. He said maybe we could get the paperwork out of thc way so hc'd be free to leave before it got too late."

"And you said . . . ?"

"I said that maybe that would work out."

"I wonder," Koesler mused, "what he meant by getting 'the paperwork' out of the way?"

"Your retirement documents, I suppose."

"You don't think . . . ."

". . . that he meant my Oath of Fidelity?" Tully shook his head. "I truly don't think so. I'm pretty sure he wants this Profession of Faith and Oath of Fidelity to be part of a public ceremony. That way some people would have cause to turn me in if ever I strayed from the Pope's course.

"Actually," he said after a moment's reflection, "I'm almost looking forward to going a few rounds with him. Now that—thanks to you—I'm getting to know him better. Bishops can give one the impression that they put their episcopal vestments on in a telephone booth. It's good to be reminded that they put their pants on one leg at a time."

"Or," Koesler noted, "as one of my priest teachers once said of the rather rigid St. Alphonsus Liguori: 'A good man, very saintly. But if you read too much of his stuff, you'll be putting on your pants with a shoe-horn.'"

Tully laughed. "Well, then, tell me more about Bishop Delvecchio. Maybe he's already putting on his trousers with that shoehorn. If he is, I'd sure like to know. I can use all the information I can gather."

"All's fair in psychic games with the hierarchy," Koesler improvised.

"Say . . ." Tully consulted his watch. ". . . we've got a little time on our hands. What say we repair to the basement and shoot some pool?"

"Sounds good."

"And," Tully said, as he led the way downstairs, "you can go on with your briefing."

The basement of St. Joseph's rectory had been divided into several rooms, or more precisely, compartments. The largest of these was huge. Spacious enough to contain an upright piano, lots of metal folding chairs—now stacked against the wall—and, in the center, a slightly smaller-than-official-size pool table.

This room was used by, among others, the parish council and its various committees. When in such use, the plastic cover was drawn over the pool table, turning it into a meeting table. Never mind that the rail made this somewhat awkward.

The table had been added to the rectory's basement by one of Koesler's predecessors. Sometimes, when there was no pressing business—a circumstance occurring less and less—Koesler would wander down and fool with a game of solitaire . . . usually humming the River City pool hall song from Meredith Willson's *The Music Man.*

"How about some eight ball?" Tully invited.

"Sounds good."

"Name the stakes."

"Fun."

"Fun? We don't need to play for much . . . but the pot ought to be there."

"I don't gamble . . ." Koesler felt as if he were going to confession . . . as if gambling were a virtue and he was wrong not to.

"It's not against our religion, you know."

"I'm aware there's no Church law against it—unless it gets out of hand. It's just me. I can't stand to lose. So I don't take that chance."

Tully tilted his head. I'll just pretend we've got something on the game, he thought. He was certain his gambling outings were under his control. He just loved the thrill of chance.

He racked the balls while ceding the break to Koesler. In this, Tully knew not what he was doing. For the break came perilously close to shattering some of the balls. Two solids fell neatly into separate pockets.

Tully was impressed. "Are you sure you don't want a little bet? This is no mean beginning."

"No bets. Just pretend, if you like, that we have a wager."

Just what Tully had silently done. Was Koesler clairvoyant? he wondered.

Koesler's next shot would indicate his wisdom in eschewing a bet.

One of the problems with sinking a number of one's own balls was that one then had to shoot around (in this case) the stripes. Such was now the situation, as striped balls lay in the way of a clear shot. Actually, only one solid was open. It wasn't a difficult shot, but it was a table length away.

Koesler blew it.

Tully knew his pool expertise was no better than Koesler's. This could prove an extended game. Fortunately there was no hurry; all their guests would be late.

Tully walked around the table, gauging possible shots. "So now we've got young Vince Delvecchio back home," he said finally, as he chalked his cue. "What happens next?"

"I was out of the loop—check that: I was never *in* the loop—so I

159

don't know how they settled the question. In any case, everybody was quite sure he'd be in the tribunal or the chancery."

Tully, about to shoot, straighted up in surprise. "The tribunal! After what had happened to his uncle in the marriage court?"

Koesler smiled. "Remember, Vince had a degree in Canon Law."

"Well, yeah, but that could just as easily have qualified him to teach in the seminary."

"Good point. But the thinking was that while Delvecchio would not have harmed the students in any way, the vice might not have been versa. You know how kids can be especially cruel . . . and Vincent's stay at St. Joe's Retreat was an easy target."

"They were really handling this business with kid gloves."

"That's the way it must've seemed to the power group. Anyway, eventually they assigned him to the chancery."

"But first they had to ordain him."

Koesler laughed. "Good point. He was ordained by Archbishop Boyle in the chapel of Sacred Heart Seminary. To tell you the truth, Zack, I think they overdid it. He must've thought of himself as a curiosity.

"Ordinations happen in class groups and, at least at that time, in good numbers. Here was an ordination that Delvecchio had worked for harder than almost any other candidate I ever knew. But he became a priest all alone with a small group of relatives and friends looking on. One nice thing: A fair number of his classmates, who had been priests about five years now, showed up." Koesler, remembering, nodded. "That was nice."

"Did you take part?"

"Vince asked me to preach. I did."

"So you still were close."

"We've never been that far apart. The distance, such as it is, has been established by Delvecchio. But that's okay by me. Whatever he wants our friendship to be is all right."

Tully sank his second stripe. But scratched on the shot. He backed away from the table. "How did he work out in the chancery?"

"In the beginning, not well. Mostly because they were reluctant to give him a lot of contact with the people who composed the chancery's clientele, he was made a member of the team that purchases land for future parishes."

"Land speculation?" Tully's eyebrows knitted. "Doesn't sound like a job for a priest."

"Right. But priests had been doing this for a very long time. Actually, I guess, it started with the growth of the suburbs. The trick was to carefully study the directions in which the developers were expanding and get a central location for a future parish. With enough land for a church, rectory, school, parking, and maybe for an athletic field."

"A big job."

"You bet. And one with little room for error. A mistake could cost hundreds of thousands of dollars. And that's sort of what got Vincent out of that business."

"How so?"

"Archbishop Boyle second-guessed himself and the chancery's brain trust. The boss thought the strain might be too much for Vince."

"They were sort of treating him like a raw egg . . . afraid he would break?"

"Exactly. So then he became the guy in charge of triage."

"Triage?"

"He was the first in the chancery to handle people who were blindly seeking help from the archdiocese. They didn't know whom to see . . . whom to talk to. They had a need . . . or a gripe. So they'd call the chancery. They got Delvecchio."

"How'd he do?"

"Depended on the nature of the call. There were times—not often—that I called the chancery and got Vince. He communicated efficiency, curtness, and not a lot of warmth. After I introduced myself he would relax a little . . . but not much." Koesler circled the table, seeking the best shot.

"There's a story that might help to understand Vince at this point in his life . . ." Koesler rested his cue on the rack. Neither player was in a hurry. "Vince used to relate the story with some frequency. Working in the chancery, he spent weekends helping out in various parishes. Two things flowed from that setup—"

"Let me guess: One, you never get to know people very well because you hop around from parish to parish. Two, you're able to repeat yourself because no one group has heard just about all your stories."

Koesler grinned. "That's it. But as he wandered around retelling anecdotes, one story in particular came up with some frequency. Apparently he seldom uses it anymore. But he surely leaned on it in those days."

Tully placed his cue against the table and sat down to better take in the story that had been a favorite of Father Vincent Delvecchio in his early days as a priest.

19

At the first ring of the alarm clock, Father Thompson swung his left arm in an arc. His hand hit the button, silencing the bell.

He'd been resting on his bed fully dressed. Of course he wasn't wearing his clericals. Gray slacks, a blue jacket, and black loafers.

He brought the clock case close to his face. Just barely could he make out the luminous dial in the darkened room. Eleven o'clock. Just right. He would be there in plenty of time: 11:30 P.M. was the earliest that Mary Lou could get out of the convent without anyone's knowing.

He pulled the car to a stop one block from the convent, killed the lights, and let the engine idle. He lit a cigarette and waited.

This had been going on for the past six months. It had begun innocently enough—didn't all such affairs? Father Thompson had met Sister Gratia during a civil rights march sponsored by the NAACP.

He was young, powerfully built, and handsome. She had an attractive face. That—plus delicate hands—was all that could be seen. The rest was covered by a religious habit.

They had so much in common. Not only were they Catholic and in "religious life," but they were liberal and liberated people involved in social causes. It was only natural for friendship to grow. And that, in turn, again naturally led to affection. And thence, to an affair.

They were young, single, with raging hormones. Without their religious commitment, they probably would've dated for a brief time, then married. Their families would have been proud of them. They would have moved into a small house in the suburbs and had children.

That was not to be. The obstacles were obvious.

So they were reduced to meeting in the most outlandish ways and places. At which times they were transformed from Sister Gratia and Father Thompson to Mary Lou and Greg.

In those days, few people were leaving the priesthood or the religious life. The deluge would come later.

So there was a special sort of disgrace attached to turning away from lifelong if not eternal vows. Leave-taking nuns were known to be smuggled out of the motherhouse completely covered by a blanket in the rear of the family car. Priests who left were pretty much shunned. Not a pleasant prospect in any case.

These thoughts took flight when the passenger door opened and Mary Lou slid in beside him. They kissed with banked passion. She wore a simple dress and a cotton coat. It was all she could do to hide this "lay" clothing in her room, which the nuns called a cell.

Greg had squirreled away enough to pay for a cheap motel room for the night—or most of the night.

They drove down Woodward until, in the vicinity of Highland Park, they came to a series of sleazy motels that catered to the poor, hookers, and one-night stands. As long as the money was delivered up front, the desk clerk didn't care how many Mr. and Mrs. John Smiths registered.

Greg and Mary Lou, though they seldom patronized these flop-houses, took pains not to use any one more than a few times. And then, with long intervals between each visit.

They registered as Mr. and Mrs. Harry Brown. (Greg was feeling creative.) Once inside their room de la nuit, they tore at each other's clothes until they wore none. Then it was into bed where they made wild but quiet love till they were exhausted.

They lay in each other's arms, feeling completely relaxed. They would be able to repeat their performance after a while.

He thought: This is wonderful. This is marvelous. After experiencing erotic passion with Mary Lou, he knew he'd never again be governed by chastity. Maybe the others of his cloth could be without sexual expression until death, but not he. Not now that he was captured by the glories of sex. As far as he was concerned, taking all due precautions against the twin great threats, pregnancy and discovery, he and Mary Lou could go on until death did them part.

She thought: What now? Lying on her side, facing Greg, she fingered the sheet. How many people had ridden this bed? Insecure men attempting to prove their virility. Women seeking escape from a failed life. Hoping to find protection from a stronger person who did not exist. Women willing to become a seminal wastebasket for just a few dollars. Was all this a foundation for what life would become for "Mr. and Mrs. Harry Brown"?

Greg traced an invisible line on her body from her shoulder around her breast to her thigh. It was a signal devised to indicate he was ready again.

She rolled over on her back. But as he was about to cover her, she pushed him away.

He was truly startled. "What's wrong? What's the matter?"

"We've got to talk."

"Later."

"Now."

He pushed himself up and sat on the bed, leaning against the backboard. He lit a cigarette from the pack he'd placed on the nightstand. "Okay. We talk. About what?"

"About us." She pulled the blanket up around her shoulders. The seriousness of what she was about to say seemed compromised as long as her body remained uncovered.

"What about us?" Cigarette smoke streamed from his nostrils.

"How long do you think we can go on like this?"

He grinned. "Till death do us part."

"Really? Face it, Greg: This is terrible. And this is as good as it gets for us."

"What's so bad?"

"You can't see? All we've got in this room is an uncomfortable bed and privacy. And the only reason we've got this much is because you were able to put aside a little money. I don't get to keep any money at all. And you get little more than you absolutely need. Ordinarily, our "date" would be the backseat of your car, where we neck and pet and grope each other in a space that makes this room seem like a honeymoon suite."

Greg snuffed his cigarette. "I know . . . I know. But I've got plans. I can make more money."

Her lip curled ever so slightly. "How?"

"I'm going to apply at our metro paper for a regular column. I can write pretty good. You've said so yourself. That could be a dependable source of extra money."

"So we could . . . what? Spend more time in this hellhole?"

"No, in a better room. In a respectable hotel."

"And increase our chances of being recognized? And then wouldn't the local news media be grateful to us! We would be disgraced and we'd be forced into doing what we ought to do anyway."

"Which is what?"

"Leave! Resign!" She rested on an elbow. The sheet fell away, exposing her breasts. He was always stirred by their resemblance to firm cups.

"We would start a new life. We could make it. I've got a master's degree and teaching experience. You can write. You could get a job on a local paper or with a magazine. We could make it, Greg!" She was stoked by her own enthusiasm.

"I don't know . . ." Fear gnawed at his courage. Deep down he had to agree that their life together, such as it was, was not much. Their relationship was not significantly removed from the early woes of teenagers. Making out in a car. Eagerly occupying any available room of whatever description.

But . . . leave! Each of them might be, in varying degrees, disgusted with their present lifestyle. But both of them enjoyed matchless security. The basics were guaranteed: food, clothing, shelter, even work. In his case, at least, he could do as much or as little as he chose.

All of that would be thrown to the winds by the simple procedure of resigning.

Of course, even resignation would not completely end it all. The security would be gone, totally. But sanctions would be imposed. Her community would undoubtedly disown her. He would be suspended. He would continue to be a priest into eternity, but he would be forbidden to act as a priest unless a life-threatening emergency demanded his ministration.

If they were to be married, they would be excommunicated. Married or not, they would be living in sin.

The cheesy motel room they were occupying began to look better and better.

They did not make love again that night. Nor did they sleep. Each lay shrouded in the questions that Mary Lou had raised.

Long before the dawn's early light, they were dressed and on their way—she to her convent, he to his rectory.

The last words spoken before they parted were Mary Lou's.

"Greg, I was never more serious than I was last night. Either we leave and make a normal life for ourselves, or we stop right now. It's a decision that has to be made. As often as we continue with these trysts, we just put off the inevitable. Call me when you're ready to go. Or . . ." She looked at him firmly. ". . . don't call."

If, over the next several days, parishioners, pastor, and peers thought Father Thompson seemed distracted, they were dead right. He could not get Mary Lou or her ultimatum out of his mind.

No doubt she had a valid point, particularly from her perspective. However, really, he thought he would be capable of continuing their affair, just the way it was, for the foreseeable future and beyond.

But, no, he would be on his own. Several times he had tried to phone her. But each time, after answering her question in the negative, he was left with an eloquent dial tone.

At length, after much anguished thought, prayer, rationalization, and many sleepless nights, he agreed to leave with her.

No point in going through legal or juridical red tape. They compared letters, hers to the Mother General of her order, his to the chancery, mailed them, and left.

Once having arrived at their destination in a neighboring state, they wrote to their families. Those were the really difficult letters. Their loved ones, particularly his, were saddened if not crushed by the abrupt breaking away.

As for the principals, after all this they decided to take their time getting married. They had achieved their state of sin; marriage would only be its canonical imprint.

It didn't take Mary Lou long to find a teaching job in a middle school. Her salary alone made it possible for them to live in a nice apartment and even enjoy a few extras—comfortable furniture, a color TV, and the luxury of eating out occasionally.

Greg got a job with the local newspaper—dividing his time between janitorial services and the switchboard. The managing editor could find nothing in Greg's résumé that would qualify him for anything higher.

Mary Lou was happy. She did miss her religious habit, and the reverence the kids gave "'ster." But not all that much. It was an unwonted thrill to receive a paycheck with her name on it. She could try different teaching methods in her classes without the admonition "This is the way we've always done it." She even found it fun to flirt. The school's male staff knew she was single. They gave her no trouble. All in all, she had never felt more feminine.

Greg's situation was another case entirely. No one called him "Father." No one did things for him. In effect, no one any longer did any part of his job for him. Not a single person would cover for him or excuse a failing.

He had gone from being "another Christ" to the guy who sweeps the floor and answers the phone. On top of it all, Mary Lou was making more money than he. Unbridled sex hardly made up for all that.

Meanwhile, back home, Jake and Mildred Helpern, Mary Lou's parents, were getting used to the idea. Their daughter had been a nun. Now she wasn't.

At first, Jake was angry. He thought he had closed the file on his only daughter. Safely locked in behind inescapable doors. The only practical consequence of her religious life, as far as he was concerned, was that she'd have no kids. He would not have any grandchildren from her. He could live with that. Besides, his only son might produce some legitimate progeny someday. If ever he stopped sowing his wild oats. Like father, like son.

Jake chuckled.

Mrs. Helpern drew a blank. She had tried to make it clear to her daughter that marriage was no bargain. All the silly girl had to do was consider her parents. Jake was one of those walking arguments for the theory of evolution. So much so that Mildred was uneasy about visiting the zoo. There simply was too much resemblance between her husband and the males in the orangutan exhibit.

Years ago, they had packed Mary Lou into the motherhouse on a bright and promising day. Their son hadn't bothered to see his sister off. A heavy date.

Jake wore his blue serge suit. A bit warm for that season. But it was Jake's sole evidence of civility.

Mildred had been so happy. Her daughter had climbed upon a pedestal much like the statuette of the Blessed Mother in their living room.

Where Mary Lou had ever gotten the idea to become a nun Mildred was at a loss to know. But there she was: pristine under yards and yards of religious habit.

And now she'd thrown it all away! To run off with a priest, of all things! What could a priest do to earn a living? In no time, Mildred just knew it, Mary Lou would be back on the Helpern doorstep. Probably bring the priest with her. Two more mouths to feed—or even more, if they had kids. Jake would be furious.

Mildred prayed for her daughter. Mildred prayed that her daughter would find happiness—countless miles from the Helpern family.

On the other hand, there were the Thompsons: mother, father, and sister of the once and—what they determined would be—future Father Thompson.

No sooner did the Thompsons receive Greg's announcement than they made an appointment with a chancery priest. That was the first of many meetings with secretaries, information officers, priests, monsignors, and, at long last, the bishop.

As a result of their perseverance, they reached a tentative agreement with the diocese that (a) If Gregory Thompson had not attempted a civil marriage (b) If it was judged, after careful investigation, that his enterprise had not made him notorious in the diocese (c) If he were ready to blindly, totally, and completely follow the directives of his diocesan authorities, he might be permitted to once again function as a priest.

But, the bishop warned, those "ifs" were very iffy.

Thus armed with a tentative agreement, Harold, Joan, and Rose headed for Greg's and Mary Lou's apartment.

The Thompsons spent the better part of that evening arguing and pleading with Greg and Mary Lou. In the end, considering the small wave he had made in the worldly economy, Greg leaned toward returning to a life he really hadn't wanted to leave in the first place.

It would, of course, be difficult to part from Mary Lou. But . . . she was the only woman with whom he had ever been sexually active. And who knew? With all the good intentions in the world, it might happen again. Except that if there were a next time, he would be much more cautious in his selection.

Mary Lou fought off the Thompsons far more forcefully than Greg did. How dare they meddle in the lives of two consenting adults!

However, as the hours passed that fateful evening, Mary Lou felt her hold on Greg slipping. He was wavering; she knew it. At first she was furious. Then she began to think of all those interesting men at school, as well as in the service station, the supermarket . . . well, just about everywhere.

The only man she knew in a complex, complete manner was Greg Thompson. And he clearly wanted out. More and more she thought she could get on very well without him.

There were so many others out there to meet and experience.

Covering her true feelings carefully, at long last she agreed to the decision that had been reached by everyone but her.

There would be no fuss, no trouble, especially no litigation. Greg was free to leave. Tonight. This very moment, for all she cared.

And so, in the family car—they would arrange for the return of his car later—they headed for home.

At first, Greg took the wheel. But as his father feared, the young man had gone through so much emotional turmoil, his driving was rather erratic. So, just outside the city on the way homeward, Mr. Thompson insisted that he himself drive the rest of the way.

Greg was too exhausted to argue strenuously. With a few pro forma objections, he traded places with his father, leaving his mother and his sister in the backseat.

The passengers quickly drifted off to sleep. For mother and sister there was satisfaction in what they'd accomplished. Much more so than they had anticipated. They had gone after the lost sheep and he had been found. He would be restored to the fold.

Greg, alternating between dreams and wakefulness, slept fitfully. Mary Lou drifted in and out of his dreams.

Mr. Thompson was tired. But he was very much aware of his responsibility to his family. After an exhausting day and most of a night, it was all he could do to stay alert, all the while offering prayers of thanksgiving for his son and for the faith and perseverance that had sustained them and won the battle.

In no way was it Mr. Thompson's fault that the driver of a pickup truck, drowsy and drunk, driving at a recklessly high speed, crossed the median.

Thompson hit the brakes so hard the pedal almost went through the floorboard. The car skidded, fishtailed, and presented its left rear corner to the truck.

The crash was horrendous.

Thompson's car folded like an accordion. Mother and daughter, crushed beyond recognition, died instantly. Father died within minutes.

The driver of the truck lived long enough to be taken to a hospital, where, after lengthy but futile surgery, he was pronounced dead.

Greg had not been wearing a seat belt. Atypically, that proved providential; had he not been thrown clear of the car, he would have been crushed by the large branch that crashed through the front passenger side. Despite multiple internal injuries and broken bones, Greg would live. Perhaps, with faithful physical therapy, he might regain some, if not all of his motion.

A passing motorist encountered the accident and summoned help. Greg knew none of this; all he knew was that he could hear metal groaning as it settled against the pavement, and the drip, drip, drip of liquids.

He could not move. He thought of his life. He thought of Mary Lou. He had sinned. What sudden and overwhelming punishment God could visit on His children when they betrayed His love!

He called out to his father, his mother, his sister. No reply. Did they need help? Were they pinned in the wreckage? *Why didn't they answer?*

Maybe they were unconscious. Please God, let them be unconscious. Not dead. *Not dead!*

He would do anything, be chaste the rest of his days, if only his family could be spared.

Bargaining with God. It had come to that!

There was a distant noise. It sounded like . . . it was a siren. Help was coming.

Thank God. Now he would get some answers.

20

"Some story!" Father Tully had virtually forgotten the pool game. "But isn't it kind of racy to tell in church—or even to church people?"

Koesler smiled. "You got the unexpurgated version. I heard Vince tell the story to a small gathering of priests at a Forty Hours devotion. That was pretty close to what I just told you. And it was the only time I ever heard him tell it. But I have it on good authority that he used it periodically. Lately, with the mass exodus of priests and nuns, he's had to modify some of the details. It's no longer such a cataclysmic event. But the essence of the story remains."

Tully tipped his head to one side. "I'm afraid I don't get the point. If Greg is the focus of that story, then . . . what? He seems to have come out of it smelling like a rose. Here's a fatal car crash. Four people lose their lives. One comes out alive. What's the moral? God spares the sinner and lets at least three innocent people die? Where's the moral lesson in that?"

"You didn't let me finish."

"Oh . . . sorry."

"No problem. This is the way the story ends. Four people die. Two are killed instantly. Two survive for a short period, then they too die.

"Greg survives. But just think how he felt when he came out of surgery and was told he was the sole survivor. It would be perfectly natural to take on a lot of the guilt for all this carnage. If he hadn't run off with Mary Lou, his parents wouldn't have gotten involved in trying to get him back. They never would have made that trip . . . the trip that took their lives.

"Or, given they came to convince him to return, they won. But on the trip home, if he had been more alert, he would have continued driving the car. His dad took over to spell his distraught son.

"If Greg had continued in the driver's seat, he would have died and his father would have lived. It wouldn't have been the fault of anyone in his parents' car. The fault was with the driver of the other vehicle—the pickup truck. It was because Greg was driving erratically that his father had relieved him.

"Imagine carrying that package of guilt around!"

Tully stood and stretched. "I hope I would've had the good sense to get some counseling. It was an accident, pure and simple; it was an accident whoever was driving. It could have been any one of the four of them. Fate. Kismet.

"I can see the temptation for Greg to accept much or even all of the responsibility. It was an open-and-shut case. There were a lot of factors working here. But in the final analysis it just happened to be Greg. But, okay, Greg drove the car and was the only survivor. I still don't get the point."

Koesler laughed. "You still haven't let me finish."

Tully walked away. "Oops, sorry. A problem I have."

"Well, talk about your good news-bad news stories, this one has only one silver lining. And I'll give it to you now.

"When Greg Thompson gave notice to the chancery that he was leaving, his bishop was livid. He stormed through the chancery blowing off steam. The chancery priests had never seen him so angry. He wanted, by damn, his pound of flesh!

"Toward that end, he ordered that, among other sanctions, Greg's medical coverage insurance be cut off.

"The degree of anger and animosity the bishop felt for his priest speaks loudly for the perseverance and persuasion exercised by Thompson's family. That they got the bishop to agree to even consider forgiveness and reinstatement is a minor—or maybe even a major—miracle.

"Anyway—and this is about the only good news—the priest who was supposed to terminate Thompson's medical insurance took his sweet time about it.

"So when Greg was admitted to the hospital, his insurance was in effect; it covered his operations, as well as his subsequent rehabilitation therapy. If that lackadaisical chancery official had been on the ball, Greg would have had no medical coverage at all."

Tully whistled. "The national debt!"

"Indeed. But, as I said, that was the end of the good news."

"Not very much, is it?"

"A drop of water in an ocean. Mary Lou heard about the accident. She tried every which way to get in touch with him. She really—desperately—wanted to help. She thought maybe—against her better judgment—that they might possibly get together again, and somehow make it work. In a macabre moment, she even considered it a blessing of sorts that his family would not be around to interfere in their lives.

"But Greg was having none of it. He would neither see nor talk to her.

"With all the operations he had, it was not difficult to brush aside Mary Lou and, in fact, just about everyone else. His doctors said it would have been easier to identify the parts of his body that hadn't been injured than to catalog his injuries. On top of all that, he was suffering from acute depression. That, of course, was to be expected. What the doctors did not recognize was how threatening this was.

"But eventually, the time came when Greg was able to function on his own—to a degree.

"The car that he'd left with Mary Lou had been returned. He got on the freeway as quickly as he could. It was late morning, and the drive-time traffic had mostly let up. As soon as he saw his way clear, he floored the accelerator.

"He attracted four police cars. It was quite a chase. He was clocked at something in excess of ninety miles an hour when he left the highway."

"Left the . . . ?"

"The expressway veered to the left. Greg kept going straight. He was airborne. This time when he hit a tree, he didn't live to say what he was thinking."

There was silence for several moments.

"I guess," Tully said, "it's pretty clear: He was thinking of suicide."

"That's the point," Koesler said. "Priests, especially today, stress the forgiveness, compassion, and love God has for us. A long time ago, when I was growing up, the emphasis was on sin and punishment.

Back then, eschatology, the study of the last things, embraced death, judgment, heaven, hell, and purgatory. And the only positive part of the study was heaven.

"It's almost as if Greg were back in a preceding era.

"But it's not just the story itself; it's Delvecchio's preoccupation with it—"

"Wait a minute: Is this supposed to be a true story?"

Koesler shrugged. "I don't really know. Vince creates the impression that it's true . . . but he's never flat-out claimed that it actually happened. I don't know," he repeated. "It's such a bizarre tale you'd think more people would know about it—I mean, if it actually took place . . . wouldn't you?"

"I think so," Tully said thoughtfully. "I can't recall having heard about anything like that. It would have to have been in the papers somewhere—wherever it happened—and in any case, a story like that would've made it around the clerical grapevine . . ."

"I think that whether the story actually happened doesn't matter; it's the effect the story has had on Vince that's important. I've tried to go over it lots of times to test its moral. Because, clearly, that's what bugs Vincent.

"And I think it has to do with that old saw: Mortal sin is the greatest evil in the world."

"How could you argue with a premise like that?" Tully said. "Mortal sin is such a big umbrella. It's murder and embezzlement and scandal and on and on. If you figure that hell awaits the serious sinner, and that a serious sinner makes a hell on earth for the victim of serious sin, then you'd have to agree that mortal sin is the greatest evil in the world . . . wouldn't you?"

"Well, there are a lot of distinctions that have to be made. But, yes: Properly defined, it is the great evil. But see what Vincent's story does: Greg, in the story, makes serious sin contagious!

"Contagious?"

"No," Koesler corrected himself, "not contagious; I think more likely Vince sees mortal sin as a contaminating agent. This story is a favorite of his. It means something very important and special to him. So I'm taking a flier that I can analyze Vinnie through analyzing his story.

"The story begins with Greg and Mary Lou having an affair. Mary Lou is ready and willing to call it off if Greg doesn't do the 'honorable' thing and marry her. Greg simply cannot let her go, so he takes her away with him.

"Then his parents and sister come to bring him home—away from 'a life of sin.' He changes his mind and leaves Mary Lou. She's no longer living with anyone. Her life has opened up. She may marry and live a virtuous life.

"But sin still dogs Greg. Even as he drives home with his family, he is open to the possibility of another affair. It is, in Vince's mind, this state of mortal sin that contaminates everything around Greg. And it's that contamination that takes three innocent lives.

"Nor does it spare Greg. Driven by the wretched life he's been living, he commits suicide . . ."

". . . the 'unforgivable sin,' the 'sin against the holy spirit' . . . the 'greatest evil,'" Tully summed up.

"Exactly," Koesler affirmed. "And don't you see: It goes back to Vince's uncle and his suicide."

"The way Delvecchio sees it, his uncle is responsible for his aunt's living in the state of mortal sin," Tully mused. "They are not canonically married. And it's his uncle's fault. *He's* the one who was previously married. So it's 'his fault.' And when he 'contaminates' the condition by not getting an annulment . . ."

"He commits suicide," Koesler concluded. "So Delvecchio has history repeating itself. In fact or in fiction . . . depending, that is, on whether the story is fact or fiction."

"Then . . ." Tully's brow knitted. ". . . how does he twist this so it pertains to me?"

"Hmmm." Koesler pondered. "Well, look at it this way," he said finally. "If you could creep into Delvecchio's mind—"

"I'd rather not."

"If you were to creep into Delvecchio's way of thinking," Koesler plowed on, "this Profession of Faith and Oath of Fidelity is essential to the Catholic faith—"

"How could they be essential? They're not part of the deposit of faith. My God, if that were the case, Paul, arguably the greatest and most influential of the Apostles, would not be part of the infant Church. Far from taking an oath of fidelity to the Pope, Paul corrected Peter, the first Pope!"

"I know, I know, Zachary . . ." Koesler was not happy with the interruption. "But we're dealing with what has become the mind-set of a fundamentalist. And as such, Vince would believe that anyone who would not or could not make that profession or swear that oath could not be Catholic . . . could not be a member of the Catholic Church.

"Then, we move into an *a fortiori.* If a lay Catholic is expected to prove his sincerity through the Profession and Oath, what does a person like Vince expect of a priest?"

There was a pause. Evidently Koesler did not intend this question to be rhetorical.

"Well," Tully said after a moment, "obviously he'd expect a priest to be out in front leading a congregation to live out this fealty to the Pope."

"*And,*" Koesler drove home his point, "if the priest himself would not live out this papal fidelity?"

Tully shook his head. "I suppose to the bishop the priest could not call himself Catholic. He'd be . . . what? . . . a heretic!"

"He'd be in serious sin—at least as far as Delvecchio is concerned. And Vince knows from brutal experience that sin contaminates. His uncle Frank 'lived in sin' and contaminated his relationship with his aunt Martha.

"The same with Greg Thompson. His state of sin contaminated Mary Lou and then spread to include his parents and sister. And look at the price everyone had to pay for that contamination."

"So that . . ." Tully said slowly, "if I refuse to swear, I am in serious sin and I contaminate an entire parish!" He shook his head with a pained expression. "That's ridiculous!"

"Maybe so, but that's the way Delvecchio thinks. That's why he demands that you not only make the Profession and take the Oath but that you do so publicly—in a liturgical setting."

"And if I don't, does the bishop expect me to commit suicide like Frank and Greg?"

Koesler's response was midway between a snort and a chuckle. "I doubt that!"

"Well, this puts me in a tight fix. Having just given me permission to become a Detroit diocesan priest, the Josephites wouldn't look too kindly on my knocking at their door again, I'm sure.

"Of course," Tully reflected, "I don't necessarily have to be the pastor of this parish. I could be an assistant at some other parish. I don't have to live in my brother's backyard. Just about any place in this archdiocese would be handy to get together with my small family . . . and maybe I could escape the Profession and Oath . . ."

"There's plenty of precedent for that," Koesler admitted.

"Because of the Oath?" Tully was incredulous.

Koesler smiled. "No, but the result was about the same even though the reason was different.

"Like so many things that caused upheaval in the Church, this was a consequence of Vatican II. I was only in my mid-thirties then, but especially since I was editor of our paper at the time, it was sort of easy for me to adjust to and even be enthusiastic about the changes the Council brought.

"It wasn't that easy at all for the older guys. A lot of them were overwhelmed by what looked to them like a brand-new Catholic Church. And these guys were mostly pastors. That was a position they had waited for with some impatience. They had achieved all they'd ever dreamed of. They were confident they'd be in charge until death did them part.

"They hadn't counted on the Council. Many of them fell behind on what became current. Disgust and depression ensued. They were supposed to have members of the laity as consultors. But most of the pastors made it clear they wanted consenters rather than consultors.

"Then came the parish councils and for a long time it was up for grabs as to who was really running the parish. That plus all the other changes that swept through the Church. But"—Koesler smiled—"you were aware of what was going on."

"Sure," Tully agreed, "but more as a bystander. The Josephites were working with the poor. Our parishioners were not about to challenge us. But I could see what this was doing to you guys."

Koesler nodded. "That's how come we developed retirement."

"'Achieving Senior Priest status,'" Tully corrected mockingly.

"Whatever. A lot of those who were pastors had been secure and growing even more secure. They had a long precedent of priests working their parishes as pastors until death. Now suddenly that goal no longer seemed attractive to many of them. They looked at the younger clergy imbued with the spirit of the Council. To them the pastors, in effect, said, 'Okay, it's your Church now. You've changed it so much it doesn't look anything like what we grew up in. So, it's yours.' Some seniors backed away from their position and became assistants and/or just floated until retirement time.

"Not everyone, mind you, but some.

"And that," Koesler concluded, "is where the similarity comes in. You are proposing to back down to the role of an assistant rather than take an oath you don't subscribe to. Some priests, after the Council, did step back to being assistants rather than try to continue playing a familiar game whose rules had been changed."

"Well," Tully pondered, "*they* seemed to make a go of it. Why not me?"

"I don't know," Koesler stalled. "I'm not sure how Delvecchio would react to that possibility. But I am concerned about what it might do to you. I'd rather see you make a go of it than retreat."

Tully smiled broadly. "Somehow be installed canonically as pastor of Old St. Joe's without taking the Profession or Oath? The perfect solution! But, Bob, life isn't always like that."

"I know . . . I know. But the longer I reflect on the Vincent Delvecchio I've known, the more I'm convinced there's a chink in his armor."

"You'd think so. After all, bottom line, we're all priests. You'd think the bonding would mean something. But to me, he seems like a well-oiled machine . . . no sense of compassion."

"Oh yes," Koesler responded quickly, "he's got compassion."

"Where? When? I haven't heard any mention of it from anybody."

21

The pool game long since forgotten, Father Koesler still sat on the edge of the table. Father Tully, audience of one, had seated himself on a chair alongside the table. Now Father Koesler would try to demonstrate that Bishop Delvecchio had a heart. Father Tully was eager to be convinced.

"This happened," Koesler began, "about the time the Vatican Council ended. I was editor of the diocesan newspaper and Vince was an assistant chancellor.

"There was a priest, Father Fuller, who was pastor of a suburban parish. He was the founding pastor. Now the parish was about eight years old and there was considerable pressure to build a school. The pressure was coming from young couples in the parish who had a lot of school-age children.

"But the pastor was running into a brick wall—well, actually two brick walls. One, he couldn't raise enough money to commit to the buildings—two buildings at least, the school and a convent. Because starting a parochial school without nuns to staff it was another definition of fat chance; no one could hope to pay lay teachers realistic salaries. And the second problem was getting a commitment from one of the teaching orders. There was an overwhelming need and demand for teaching nuns, especially in the suburbs where so many new parishes had been established basically for young couples starting their families.

"Now it may be hard for you to imagine this, but the pressure got to be too much for Father Fuller. He fell ill . . . very ill."

"Oh, I'm willing to take your word for it," Tully said. "Though it is a bit to swallow. The school wasn't *his* need. All he had to do was step aside and give the people who wanted the school the chance to take the responsibility of raising the money to build it and staff it."

"Dandy idea," Koesler concurred. "But Fuller couldn't see it that way. Most pastors of that era felt it incumbent to do it themselves.

"So, you can argue that it was a useless worry—silly, even. But Fuller stewed himself into an ulcer and lots of other ailments that might well have been psychosomatic, but still had their effect on Fuller's precarious health.

"The chancery—seconded by Fuller's doctor—was convinced that a month's R and R would get the pastor back in the saddle. The problem was getting someone to take over the bare necessities—daily and weekend Masses, confessions, and being available for consultation.

"Well, the ways of the chancery are strange, to say the least."

"Amen!"

"I guess," Koesler said, "they thought two priests part-time equaled one full-time.

"Anyway, neither Delvecchio nor I was assigned to parochial duties at the time. I was at the paper and helped out at various parishes on weekends. Vince had a similar schedule.

"So, we were told to work Fuller's place for a month, minimum. And those were the days when you went where you were sent.

"Delvecchio and I had lived together only during our Camp Ozanam days. And that could scarcely be called living together—not like rectory life. It was Vince and me and the housekeeper. And there was the rub."

"The housekeeper?" Tully hazarded.

Koesler nodded and winked. "Exactly. Sophie cooked."

"That's it?" Tully asked after a pause.

"That was it. Another woman came in once a week and cleaned. There was a secretary during the day—Monday through Friday."

"And Sophie?"

"As I said, she cooked—and none too well. For breakfast the first day, I asked for a couple of poached eggs on toast. What I hadn't counted on was the blistering-hot plate they were served on."

"The eggs kept cooking."

"Exactly. By the time I got to the second egg, it was hard-boiled. Neither Vince nor I was there for lunch. But dinner? Sophie served dinner in common dishes. I quickly learned to take a taste of everything and then start with what had cooled most and work toward what might hold some of its original heat.

"Also I quickly learned to request cold cereal for breakfast. Fortunately, Sophie didn't cook that before serving it. Lunch remained trouble-free because I wasn't there.

"Dinner was nothing but a penance. But I stayed with it.

"However, other things followed from the given that Sophie cooked and nothing more. Sophie neither answered the door nor the phone. She had her own phone and answered that only."

"Meaning that you and Delvecchio got the phone and door even during meals."

Koesler nodded solemnly. "After the secretary left for the day and before she came in the morning, none but a consecrated ear touched the phone. Same thing on weekends.

"Bottom line: Sophie cooked—none too well—and that was it."

"Didn't you wonder why Fuller hired her? Or even more of a puzzle, why he didn't let her go?"

"Absolutely. And at the same time, Vince was exceptionally kind, considerate, and patient with her. Whereas I was barely civil at times."

"Ah . . ." Tully sounded as if he comprehended yet still was a mite doubtful. "So Delvecchio could be compassionate. But why? Especially given his reputation, why would he act that way?"

"That's it!" Koesler said with vigor. "Vince took the time and effort to look into Sophie's history. He took time to talk with her and with people who knew both Fuller and Sophie.

"It's a funny thing, Zack: She was just Sophie to me. In reality, and what Vince discovered, was that she was Sophie Fuller."

For a brief moment, Tully wondered whether this could be a "Mr. and Mrs." Or, perhaps, a "Father and Mrs." Then, intuitively he knew: They were brother and sister.

"Left to my own devices I never would've tumbled to it," Koesler said. "But I should have. I should have realized that there had to be an explanation for Sophie's continued presence in the rectory. The only thing she did—cook—she couldn't do. But, Zack, I wasn't perceptive enough to follow through and dig out the whole story. Vince was the compassionate one, Zack."

Tully pondered that. "Okay, she was the pastor's sister. Just as a matter of curiosity, what was she doing in the rectory? Except getting in the way . . . and, I assume, getting a salary?"

"This was Fuller's third crack at being a pastor," Koesler explained. "His first pastorate was out in the boondocks. That parish could barely pay his salary. So, his mother took her never-married daughter aside and told her it wasn't right for their priest to take care of himself. In effect, Sophie had to give up her own, independent life to serve her brother."

Tully pulled on his lower lip. "To understand is to forgive all," he said finally.

"The thing is that Vince went the distance. He peeled back the layers of misunderstanding. He finally understood what made her the way she was. She was bad at something she didn't want to do. That's not so hard to understand. Vince understood. Then he communicated that understanding to me."

"Hmmmm," Tully mused.

"But, see," Koesler prodded, "all Vince had to do was to appreciate the pressure Sophie was under. Everything was all right then—her deficiencies were accepted without problem."

"And you think that the same thing could happen with me?"

Koesler raised both hands in a gesture of victory. "Why not? If we could make Vince understand what your conscience dictates . . .

"Once he saw the difficulties Sophie had as a housekeeper, and once he understood her sincerity in sacrificing her life for the sake of her brother, everything was more than all right. I don't see why we couldn't expect a similar . . . happy ending."

Tully was wrapped in thought.

Koesler caught himself looking at Tully in much the same way as Kingfish would study Andy in that landmark period piece "Amos and Andy." Regularly, Kingfish would try—and usually succeed—to sell a bill of goods to a gullible Andy. Then Kingfish would give Andy "that look," anticipating whatever Andy's response might be.

Koesler quickly wiped that expression off his face and sat back to await Tully's reaction. He hoped Tully would be encouraged by the Sophie anecdote. On the one hand, it was a true story. And, on the other, it would help Tully's case measurably if they could confidently enter into a dialogue with Delvecchio.

Additionally, he hoped Tully would be motivated by the Sophie anecdote because Koesler didn't have another in his sack; it was the one and only expression of compassionate understanding on Delvecchio's part that Koesler was aware of personally.

Oh, it was bandied about that Vincent was kind and considerate to those in need. The sick and suffering, the troubled, the deserving poor most often received an attentive ear and, where necessary, a generous wallet.

It was said by many that Delvecchio's day off each week began with a visitation to hospitalized parishioners.

But compassion? Especially toward those considered to be challenging the Church or its traditional theology? No Sophie happy endings there!

Indeed, just a few months ago, a much more typical story involving the bishop had gone the rounds. It was not an incident that would have encouraged Father Tully at this moment, so Koesler had no intention of telling him.

Koesler had heard the story—well documented—during a priestly golf foursome.

The story was related by Father Joe McCarthy. He had been a classmate of Bishop Delvecchio and thus, owing to the bishop's five-year delay after his breakdown, was ordained five years earlier than Delvecchio.

McCarthy was one of those who had stepped back from his pastorate to be an assistant. In his case, it was not any theological or canonical problem; it was because his health could not sustain the pressure of pastoral duties. The priest shortage had placed an extra burden to provide services for a growing number of Catholics on a diminishing supply of priests.

So it was that Joseph Patrick McCarthy requested an assignment as an associate pastor. The chancery, as was its wont, had the last laugh in assigning him as an associate to Delvecchio.

The chancery was in no mood to grant McCarthy an early retirement. Thus, to qualify, he would need to hang in there until age seventy. Meanwhile, he had to take orders from a man he did not respect, as well as from a man who had less parochial experience than he.

McCarthy's story was compelling, first-rate clerical gossip. It was one of the rare times Koesler could recall that a golfing foursome was glad to wait on the tee and even ignored the invitation of those ahead to play through.

At this juncture, in the twinkling of an eye that encompassed a pause for Tully's reaction to the Sophia saga, time stood still for Koesler as he recalled McCarthy's tale.

The narration had begun on the practice putting green and continued from green to tee for fully nine holes.

"It was about ten in the morning," McCarthy began, "and *His Excellency,*" the title dripped sarcasm, "was in his upstairs office going over the books. I had just answered the door and let in an old friend, George Hackett—you guys remember Hackett . . ."

George Hackett had been ordained in McCarthy's class. Fifteen years later he left the active priesthood and married.

"When George told me why he was here, I knew he'd have to see Vince. Ordinarily, a request such as George's could be handled by any priest. I could have dealt with it easily. When I was a pastor, any priest working with me would have had a green light to take care of it.

"But Vince is almost the embodiment of a hands-on boss. And especially since George is an ex, I knew that one way or the other Vince would be taking care of it.

"I explained that to George. He wasn't happy about asking Vince for anything, much less something Vince would consider to be a favor. But, in the end, George agreed that he would have to appeal to Caesar.

"So I went upstairs to get Vince. I figured George would stand a better chance if I ran interference . . ."

*   *   *

"George Hackett is downstairs. He wants to see you."

Delvecchio didn't look up from the books, although he did pause for a moment before speaking. "I don't want to see George Hackett."

McCarthy was startled; he knew that Delvecchio was aware that

Hackett was an ex. But McCarthy had never encountered such clerical prejudice toward an ex-priest.

"Vince, George's wife just died."

"So?"

"So he wants us to take the funeral."

"Why?"

"Because they've been coming to Mass here for several years. They live in the parish."

Finally he looked up. "I've never seen the name on our books. Is he registered?"

"No. He anticipated trouble if he did. So they just attended here. George contributed without using a collection envelope."

"I've never seen him here."

"I have." It was typical. Delvecchio knew few of the parishioners.

"I don't want to see him," the bishop said through tight lips. "I've already told you that."

"Why not?"

Delvecchio sighed. "Jesus said it all in Luke's Gospel: *Whoever puts his hand to the plow but keeps looking back is unfit for the reign of God.*"

McCarthy knew this was not the time for exegetical argument. "Vince, you've got to see him. I'm not leaving here till you do."

McCarthy had nothing to lose in launching an ultimatum, and Delvecchio knew it. With another, deeper sigh, he pushed himself back from the desk and headed down the stairs, with McCarthy close behind.

Delvecchio entered his office, where George Hackett sat waiting. McCarthy stopped the door from closing as he followed the bishop into the office.

As Delvecchio lowered himself into his chair, he said to McCarthy—without looking at him—"I can handle this—alone!"

"Did I tell you George wanted to see you? Actually he wants to see both of us," McCarthy said.

Hackett looked confused, smiled briefly, then resumed his grave demeanor.

"I understand," Delvecchio said, "your wife died. Our sympathy."

"Thank you." Hackett had anticipated the lack of recognition on Delvecchio's part. Still, it hurt.

"I am also given to understand that you want the Mass of Resurrection here."

"It was her—"

Delvecchio pulled a notepad toward himself, and picked up a pen. "Have you been laicized?"

"Yes."

"Were you married in the Church?"

"Finally, yes."

"What does that mean?"

"When I left the priesthood, Rome wasn't granting laicizations. We were married by a judge. Later, the request for laicization was granted. Then we were married by a priest. But what's that got to do with—"

"Before we can consider your request for Christian burial from this parish, we've got to know what we're dealing with. Now, Father McCarthy tells me you attended Mass here. But you never registered in the parish?"

"I can't believe you never noticed me. We didn't go out of our way to attend your Mass, but we did from time to time. You never recognized me? We were classmates for years. I remember praying for a miracle for your mother. We were priests together in this archdiocese for years. I just took it for granted that you knew me."

"Whether or not I recognized you is not the question. Whether or not you are a registered parishioner *is*."

"Vince," McCarthy said, "people no longer have to be card-carrying parishioners to be buried—or married, for that matter."

Delvecchio ignored McCarthy's observation. "That you have not registered is not, of itself, a compelling reason to reject your request. But it is a consideration." Delvecchio continued making notes. "Why did you leave the priesthood?" He did not look up as he asked the question.

"Vince," McCarthy interjected, "what's that got to do with Christian burial for his wife?"

Delvecchio's expression was sardonic. "*Mr.* Hackett doesn't have to answer any of my questions."

It seemed evident that George Hackett could indeed refuse. But it would be at the peril of the desired Christian burial.

"It's all right, Joe," Hackett said by way of thanking McCarthy for playing defense attorney, if only briefly. He turned back to Delvecchio, fixing him with a penetrating gaze. "I left to marry Gwenn."

"No trouble with Church doctrine?"

"Some, sure. I didn't wake up one morning after fifteen years as a priest and say, 'Hey, wait a minute: There's girls!' Before Gwenn ever came my way, I began having a lot of trouble—mostly with enforcing some of the Church's pet peeves."

"Such as?"

"Well, the obvious ones: Contraception. Remarriage. Exercising infallibility like a weapon. I don't really have to catalog problem areas; even if you don't agree, you very well know what the problems are."

With lips stretched tightly, Delvecchio said, "I assume then, that you could be called an 'eclectic Catholic.'"

"If I have to be categorized, yeah, I suppose so."

"The present Pope has made it quite clear that Catholics cannot pick and choose among doctrine or moral teachings. The Catholic Church is not a spiritual supermarket."

Hackett perceived that he was virtually playing Frisbee in a minefield. There was silence for a few moments. It was broken by Delvecchio. "Do you have any children?"

"Yes."

"How many?"

In his day as a priest, Hackett had handled many arrangements for funerals. At no time had he quizzed the bereaved like this. "Three."

"Their ages?"

Hackett hesitated in recalling the exact ages. "Twenty-three . . . uh, twenty, and seventeen."

"Odd ages," Delvecchio observed. "Were you using contraception? Was that one of the moral precepts you rejected?"

McCarthy bolted from his post near the door. "Vince, what's the idea!"

Hackett waved him back. "You're way out of line, Bishop. You have no right to ask a question like that. And you know it!"

"All right." Delvecchio's smirk all but disfigured his face. "All right. We're just trying to find out whether we can accept this petition for Christian burial."

"Look, Bishop"—Hackett's face was flushed in anger—"there is nothing wrong with my 'petition for Christian burial.' My wife has just died. It was her wish that she be buried from this parish. She was a Catholic in good standing, despite the manner of her death. She has a *right* to Christian burial!"

Delvecchio leaned forward. He sensed something irregular. Something that could dash George Hackett's hopes. "'Despite the manner of her death'?" Delvecchio repeated. "Just what was the manner of her death?"

Hackett dropped his eyes. "She was a suicide. But no one could have blamed her," he added quickly, "no one who knew her." From the moment he had decided to come to this rectory and ask for what Gwenn wanted, he had dreaded this moment. It was the only remotely legitimate reason to question his wife's right to Christian burial. And the way this interview was being conducted, Delvecchio was sure to climb aboard.

"A suicide!" Delvecchio, countenance noncommittal, leaned back in his chair. "Well, now . . . we finally have all the facts on the table."

"I know the direction you're moving in," Hackett said. "But let me tell you about Gwenn. Let me tell you before you judge her unfairly."

Delvecchio raised the palms of his hands upward—an invitation for Hackett to go ahead with his explanation. The gesture also connoted that the explanation, no matter how telling it might be, almost certainly would not be enough to alter a negative decision.

Neither Father McCarthy nor George Hackett knew that earlier this morning the funeral director had called and talked to Bishop Delvecchio about the Hackett services. A number of details were needed for the newspaper death notice.

Thus the bishop had already known of Gwenn Hackett's death and George Hackett's desire to have her buried from this parish. However, he had not known she was a suicide. Consciously and subconsciously Delvecchio wanted Hackett to pay for looking back after putting his hand to the plow. The denial of Christian burial would be a handy peg on which to hang some well-deserved, albeit vindictive punishment. The bishop had advised the mortician to make no firm plans about the parish details until Mr. Hackett called at the rectory. An event the bishop anticipated this morning.

Delvecchio leaned back in his chair. He fingered his pectoral cross. The crucifix swayed gently against the black cassock with its red buttons and piping.

"Ever hear of neurasthenia . . . or Chronic Fatigue Syndrome?" Hackett asked.

The bishop nodded.

"It hit Gwenn some sixteen or seventeen years ago. Since you're familiar with the disease, I won't go into a lot of detail. But for all these years, she's just traded one symptom for another. She hasn't been what might be described as healthy for more than a few days at a time.

"It's been rough on us, the kids and me. But that's nothing compared with what's it's done to Gwenn. Her depression was so bad that a couple of times she had to be committed to an institution that put her under a suicide watch."

Delvecchio's face remained impassive.

"Anyway, she fooled us this time. She seemed to be making such advances that we were able to relax our vigilance. That's when it happened. But it was because she simply couldn't take it anymore . . ." There was a tremor in his voice. "I don't even know how she made it this far. But the worst symptom was the depression . . ." He shook his head slowly in recollection. "I don't know anyone who suffered from greater depression than Gwenn."

His face tightened again in recollection, then he gazed at Delvecchio almost pleadingly. "I know the Church judges leniently in cases like these. Anybody could recognize the pressure and stress she was under. Taking her life was not a calm, rational decision; it was the final cry of a tortured soul."

Hackett sat back, and looked unflinchingly at Delvecchio. "So, that's it, Bishop. We know that God has judged her with loving understanding. She wanted to be buried from this church. In keeping with that wish, I am asking that you grant this request."

There were a few moments of silence.

"How did she do it?" Delvecchio asked.

"A gun. A handgun. I had one—though I wish to God I hadn't had it. I kept it hidden. She must've found it when she was cleaning." Again, Hackett wondered at this line of questioning.

"A gun." Memories of his uncle flooded the bishop's mind.

Actually, Frank had not been an uncle. He had not been validly married to Vincent's aunt.

Well, Frank was not given Christian burial, though there had been little or no effort to secure the same. Effort or no effort, Frank had not deserved a Church funeral. He was a suicide. And, for several reasons, not the least being that Gwenn also was a suicide and George deserved to be punished for leaving the priesthood for her, she was not going to be granted Christian burial either.

Delvecchio slowly leaned forward until his elbows touched the desk's surface. He placed his hands, palms down, on the desk. "I am sure your wife's bout with Chronic Fatigue Syndrome was a most difficult cross to carry."

"Cross!" Hackett sat upright. "Gwenn didn't carry a cross. She suffered from a supermarket list of illnesses—some physical, some psychosomatic—all of them real and all of them miserable. And underlining all of that was classic clinical depression. Until she couldn't go on. And she ended it."

"I understand, Mr. Hackett. But we Christians are admonished that life can be difficult. We are told when we are confirmed that life can even be a burden. But we are told that the Spirit will be with us, to sustain us. Even St. Paul complains about mysterious thorns in the flesh. They are so troublesome that Paul begs Jesus to relieve him. But the Lord tells him that grace will be sufficient to have him endure.

"That, Mr. Hackett, is what we would have reminded your wife had she come to see us. She was a Catholic. She knew that she would have to bear whatever fate might send. Our crosses may come from observing the laws and moral teachings of our faith. Or our crosses may be physical. Prayer! Prayer is the answer."

"Look, Bishop—!" Hackett was near to exploding. "If I were the one who'd died, I wouldn't want anyone to come to you and beg that I be buried as a Catholic. Not if they had to beg. But I'm trying to be faithful to my wife's wishes. How can you sit there in judgment . . ."

Father McCarthy had heard more than enough. He left the room and entered the adjacent office. He could hear through the thin wall Delvecchio and Hackett arguing heatedly.

When he returned after several minutes, a Cheshire cat grin suffused McCarthy's face. "The Cardinal is on line one, Vince. He wants to talk to you."

Delvecchio glanced sharply at McCarthy. "I didn't hear the phone ring," he said angrily.

McCarthy shook his head. "I placed the call, Vince. I figured you'd have to talk to the Cardinal sooner or later. Might just as well get it over with. And, by the way, Vince, the Cardinal *is* waiting on line one. I'd talk to him if I were you."

Delvecchio punched the button and picked up the receiver. "Eminence?"

"Bishop Delvecchio," the voice responded.

Several Detroit priests did excellent impressions of Cardinal Boyle. So true to life were some of these imitations that more than one clerical victim had been deeply embarrassed to realize that he had just treated the genuine Cardinal with the disdain reserved for one of his mimics.

This voice easily could belong to the genuine Cardinal. No point in taking a chance. "Yes, Eminence."

"I understand that a widower is requesting the Mass of Resurrection and burial rites for his late wife."

"Yes, Eminence, but—"

"I am given to understand that this unfortunate woman took her life."

"Well, Eminence, there are reasons—"

"I am told that her last years have been filled with pain and depression. Is all of this correct?"

"Yes, Eminence." It did indeed sound authentic. Delvecchio had never heard his superior speak in such a tone. The response that sprang to Delvecchio's lips was held in check, but, no mistake, it was there.

"I would remind you," the Cardinal continued, "that the holy Church in general advises compassion in such a situation. And that certainly is the policy of this archdiocese. Do I make myself clear on this matter, Bishop?"

"Yes, Eminence. Perfectly clear. It is your wish, then, that this request be granted?"

"It is the policy of our archdiocese and, yes, it is my wish. I am sure you will settle this in such a manner that I will not be drawn into this liturgical decision again."

"Yes, Eminence."

"Then, good-bye, bishop."

"Good-bye, Eminence—" But the Cardinal had already hung up.

Bishop Delvecchio was both furious and embarrassed. The blood seemed to have drained from his head. He was well aware that theologically he and Boyle were oceans apart. Nonetheless, the Cardinal had always been the soul of civility. A gentleman in the finest sense. This was the first time he had encountered the prelate with his emotions down, as it were.

Delvecchio pinned McCarthy with his gaze. The unspoken message was, I will get you for this. I don't know when or how. But you will pay for this.

The bishop turned to Hackett and cleared his throat. "Your request, Mr. Hackett, for the Mass of Resurrection and the rites of Christian burial for your wife is granted. However, there are some guidelines that I am initiating as of this moment and for the future as well.

"Any priest who officiates at a wedding or a funeral will abide by the liturgical practice of this parish. Which, I add, is in conformity with Holy Mother Church.

"Further, any lay person who wishes to speak in this church on the occasion of a wedding or a funeral will be limited to no more than two minutes. And the remarks that he or she wishes to make within those two minutes must be approved beforehand by me.

"Father McCarthy will handle your wife's funeral. And, Father, you will be careful to enforce these new regulations. Later today, we'll have a staff meeting and the implication of what I have in mind will be made very much more clear."

22

It took only seconds for Father Koesler to recall Father McCarthy's account, which pretty well documented the mind of Bishop Delvecchio.

The incident had taken place only a few months ago. Nothing could have changed much since then. And this was, by far, not an isolated experience. There seemed to be a vicious streak in the bishop—one that manifested itself in an element of vindictiveness, particularly when it came to priests he looked on as sinners.

Whatever had happened to that happy-go-lucky kid with the creative sense of humor who laughed at minor liturgy rules?

That kid seemed to have slipped into reverse at the death of his uncle. From that time on, Vincent grew increasingly rigid, cold, and literal when it came to interpreting and enforcing Church law.

Yet there were "bastard pastors," as they were known by the clergy, who were far more universally autocratic and nasty than Delvecchio. There were those who would neither understand, forgive, nor tolerate a Sophie.

The nonbenevolent clerical tyrant was rare, but not unique. One such notorious soul, after installing comfortable new pews and kneelers in his church, ran short of money. Unable to outfit the entire church, he then issued an edict directing those attending with children to use the old and visibly tired pews. This was the pastor who had his ushers slash the tires of any automobiles in the church lot that were parked over the yellow line.

Vincent Delvecchio was a long way from that sort of despotism and capricious cruelty. Indeed, he could be downright expansive and generous as long as no rules were being broken or bent.

But there was this hangup as far as the behavior of the clergy was concerned, and, in general, a stiff-necked attitude toward those he perceived as sinners, even when any such person was not conscious of any sin.

However, in the light of his response toward the George Hacketts of this world, what reaction could be expected of Vince Delvecchio in the matter of Father Zack Tully?

On the one hand, it could be argued that Tully was breaking no law. To date, he was on record as being unwilling only to take an oath and profess a faith in a *public* ceremony. The canonical command insisted only that the pledges be taken by one—among others—who was becoming a pastor. There was no mention of any ceremony. Could there be, Koesler wondered, some way of squeezing through that hole in the law?

The possibility was worth further exploration.

Somehow, this crusade was growing within Father Koesler. If only he could recall more examples from Delvecchio's past that might cast light on the way the bishop might react to Tully's plight.

At least it was becoming more clear just what Koesler and Tully were searching for: the presentation or approach that might best elicit a favorable response from Delvecchio.

Whatever it was, it would have to be the opposite of a worst-case scenario: a head-on collision between the bishop's insistence on a public liturgical event and a flat-out refusal on Tully's part to have anything to do with such a demand.

But, as in almost any such dispute, the bishop, backed by Church law, held all the cards.

There had to be another way.

Tully's throat-clearing pulled Koesler back from his reverie. "Yeah," Tully mused, "if it happened once, it could happen again . . . couldn't it?"

"Couldn't what?"

"Sophie. The housekeeper!" How could Koesler have forgotten what they'd been talking about? It was Koesler's story after all—and he'd finished it only moments ago.

However, in those moments, Koesler's memory had raced through the incident involving Delvecchio, McCarthy, and George Hackett. Not only had Koesler replayed the story in fast-forward, he had determined not to cite it as an example of the care and feeding of this auxiliary bishop.

But that was all right. In determining a course of action, it helped to know what one wasn't going to use because it wouldn't work. "Oh yes," Koesler said, "Sophie . . ."

"I mean," Tully said, "the thing we could try to get over to the bishop is that this is a part of my background as a Josephite. We weren't schooled to play out all our cards at once and in public. We had to be flexible for the sake of our parishioners.

"And, as a matter of fact, if parishioners have problems relating to the Pope in the way those documents demand, if my stand is not on public record, I'll be able to respond to their view. I mean, if I take the Oath and Profession in a public ceremony, people with problems will shy away from me. They'll assume that my mind is already made up. There'll be no room for discussion.

"That's *some*thing like Sophie, isn't it? Delvecchio could understand that . . . couldn't he?"

Koesler tilted his head in thought. "I guess so," he said finally. Then he looked at Tully brightly. "We certainly could try it. But if we can find some other arguments—strong ones—it would help."

Actually, Koesler doubted that Delvecchio would appreciate a comparison between Sophie's background-plus-mandate-from-Mama and Tully's Josephite indoctrination. But it was *something*. Koesler had introduced Sophie with the intention of indicating that Delvecchio did possess a sympathetic side.

"What time is it getting to be?" Tully asked, as they both glanced at their watches.

"Almost eight o'clock"—Tully answered his own question—"just about an hour till our guests start arriving. I think I'll look in on the cooks—let 'em know we haven't forgotten them."

He headed for the stairs, then turned back. "You know, one of the problems I've got with Delvecchio is that he comes across like a knight in shining armor. As far as I can tell, he's never done anything wrong. You certainly can't fault him for enlisting your help with his aunt's marriage problem. He has no responsibility for his uncle's suicide.

"He had a breakdown when his mother died. Far as I know, there's no morality in a nervous breakdown. You said a previous auxiliary did pretty much the same thing when *his* mother died.

"And in all the stories about Bishop Delvecchio, he's forever conforming to the wishes of Mother Church. He just seems to never do anything wrong . . ." Tully paused a moment. "God forgive me, but I wish he would slip and be mortal. Just once. Then he might know what it's like to be human and fail once in a while—like the rest of us."

Koesler made no response. "Don't get me wrong, Bob," Tully said after a moment. "I wouldn't want to be like him. But," he said, as he turned back toward the stairs, "I wish he could be a little like me."

And off he went to bolster the spirits of the cooks.

Alone, Koesler mused. I would have thought that things like the way Vince had treated George Hackett were 'wrong.' The compassion, understanding, and forgiveness that Vince was able to extend to a poor soul like Sophie were seemingly lacking in his other relationships. *That* I would have thought was 'wrong.'

But I know what Zack had in mind: Wrong equals sin equals sex. For so many, illicit sex was *the* sin that carried a strong burden of shame.

It also awakened the prurient in others.

There was the funeral of France's President Mitterrand. Among the mourners in procession and photographed at his casket were his wife, his mistress, and his illegitimate daughter. Could any such public figure in the United States have pulled that off?

Back to Zack and his whimsical wish that Delvecchio would join the rest of the human race and do something that would cause him embarrassment—read have a sexual encounter with somebody . . . *any*body.

That and the resultant shame might bring him down to earth.

It just so happened that Father Koesler could speak to that question. But he would not do so.

23

1966

It was late November. Michigan's trees had flaunted their colors and now were pretty much bare. A strong, frigid wind raced over the Detroit River. It whistled through the nearly deserted canyons of downtown Detroit. One could fire cannons down Jefferson, Gratiot, Woodward, or Fort Street with impunity.

Though a short avenue, Washington Boulevard was not sheltered from this preview of winter. Actually, with its angle to the river, it was one of the colder thoroughfares.

The boulevard boasted one of downtown's more noteworthy addresses: 1234 housed St. Aloysius Church and rectory and, possibly even more important, the archbishop's office, the chancery, the tribunal, and other headquarters of ecclesial business.

Today, everyone had shown up for work except the priest-secretary to Archbishop Mark Boyle. Monsignor Shanahan had come down with an early and virulent cold.

Perhaps it was fate.

Shanahan had no backup. And since this archdiocese was—with an occasional exception—wed to seniority, it was a simple case of finding the low man on the totem pole.

Enter Father Vincent Delvecchio.

An outsider would have been amazed at how positions were filled in the Church. The answer was seniority, or, more exactly, chronology.

Another standard method of filling priestly positions was the educated guess. Since this option had little to do with qualification, the Peter Principle ran rampant.

In the seminary there seemed no rhyme or reason in designating an infirmarian; it was pure accident if the student-infirmarian knew anything at all about maladies, medication, or therapy. Such a situation could be dangerous.

With less fraught possibilities were other assignments made. Take, for instance, the appointment of teachers in the diocesan seminary. Students who got good grades were tapped for teaching. Of course if they had wanted to teach, they could have joined a teaching order such as the Basilians, Sulpicians, or Jesuits. It mattered not that they had chosen a school that graduated parish priests; they earned high grades, therefore they became teachers. By fiat of the bishop.

Father Vince Delvecchio had barely learned his way around the chancery when Monsignor Shanahan called in sick. Lacking the seniority to remain fixed in his fledgling position, Delvecchio was up for grabs.

He had been at work less than an hour today when he was called to the chancellor's office.

"Vince," Monsignor Jake Donovan said in his typically brisk manner, "Shanahan threw a shoe. Laid up. We're short on the boss's floor. Think you can handle it? Fine!" Donovan never waited for an answer when issuing a rhetorical command. "Go on down there and do a shallow dive. You'll catch on before you know what's happening." Oblivious of the Irish bull, Donovan pressed on. "Anyway, Shanahan should be back in no time; how long does it take to beat a cold anyway?" He didn't wait for answers to rhetorical questions either. "There's a good man."

Thus was Delvecchio dismissed to learn another trade.

He took no tools with him as he left the fifth floor. He had no idea what he'd need. As he entered the elevator, he noticed his name on the list of those the operator was allowed to deposit on the second floor. He reflected that he had received this assignment only seconds ago and already his name was in the Book of Life. Sometimes the mills of the Church did grind swiftly.

The foyer of "the boss's floor" was a long rectangle with some doubtful art on the walls. At the far end of the foyer, in a partially enclosed work space, was the receptionist. Delvecchio knew her name. Jan Olivier. That was about the extent of his familiarity with the sacred second floor.

Beyond Jan's station was an office. Mine, he thought. Temporarily, he hoped.

At the left of his office, the foyer turned a ninety-degree angle leading to the archbishop's office. He couldn't see that portion of the foyer, but he'd visited Boyle in his office more than once.

Hands jammed in trouser pockets, Delvecchio made his way along the carpeted floor. Reaching the receptionist's station he turned to face her.

She smiled. "We've been expecting you, Father."

His expression was grim. "I didn't expect to see me down here."

She laughed lightly. "We don't bite. The archbishop wanted to see you when you arrived. I'll tell him you're here. Go right in."

As he turned to enter Boyle's office, Delvecchio heard Jan, in a low tone, announce his arrival.

He knocked; a firm voice with soft brogue overtones invited him in.

Delvecchio entered the spacious office with its broad windows overlooking Washington Boulevard. Boyle rose and extended his hand as he circled his desk.

Delvecchio took the proffered hand and began to genuflect as he leaned forward to kiss the episcopal ring. Gently, Boyle pulled him erect.

That's right, thought Delvecchio, Boyle represented the new breed that was changing the changeless Church, even down to innocent conventions such as reverencing the ring.

Delvecchio didn't learn much from Boyle about the duties of secretary to the archbishop. Except that the receptionist would help him. But not to depend on her too much; she had her own duties to attend to.

So, Delvecchio concluded as he left the archbishop's office, it was he, a simple priest, and Jan Olivier against the world. He didn't like the odds.

In fact, if anyone wanted to know—but apparently no one did—he was not happy about this entire adventure. It was grossly unfair to thrust him into this new position with no briefing, let alone training.

It didn't matter. When Delvecchio was ordained, the bishop had enclosed the young priest's hands in his own and said solemnly, *Promitis mihi et successoribus meis reverentiam et obedientiam?* ("Do you promise to me and my successors reverence and obedience?") And the new priest had replied, *Promito.*

This was going to test that promise.

He returned to the foyer. There seemed little point in going into his office; he didn't know what to do there.

Jan was on the phone. She raised a finger, indicating she would be with him in a moment. And she was. "I'm supposed to teach you everything you need to do this job"—she smiled understandingly—". . . right?"

He nodded.

"The problem with that," she said, "is time: I haven't got the time you need. And you're wondering what to do right now, aren't you?"

Again he nodded.

"Well, here's what I think may be a help . . ." She led the way into his office, where she picked up a small pile of phone messages from his desk. "This," she said, "is the most urgent business. These are requests for . . . varying things. Most of them are calls from priests. Most of them want an appointment with the archbishop. Some of them have scheduled confirmation services at their parishes. Of course each pastor wants the archbishop himself to conduct *his* service at *his* parish—"

"That's impossible, right?" Even though Delvecchio had never been a pastor, it was patently obvious that if Boyle personally conducted confirmations at all the parishes that wanted him, that would take up just about all his evenings throughout the year.

Also, Delvecchio had been exposed to enough parish politics to know that it was not reverence, respect, or love of Boyle that motivated nearly everyone to want him for confirmation. No, they all just wanted to be known as important enough to rate the supreme archdiocesan boss.

"Yes, that's impossible," Jan agreed. "So, when you return this type of call, you need to assure the pastors that late next month the schedule of which bishops go where for confirmations will be drawn up. 'Every effort will be made at that time'"—her delivery made it obvious that this was the appropriate jargon—"'to have the archbishop come to your parish.'"

"What," he asked, "will that accomplish?"

"Buy time. It's the best we can do now. The bit about drawing up the schedule in late December is for real."

Delvecchio fingered through the phone messages. By no means were all or even most messages concerning who would come to confirm. "What about all the rest of these?"

Jan shook her head. "I've gone over them with Archbishop Boyle. I have little marks next to the phone numbers. All of those little marks mean something . . ." She shook her head as he started to ask. ". . . but it's too complicated to go into right now." She looked at him pointedly. "You may not think so, but just returning the confirmation queries will pretty much fill the rest of the day."

"Really?" He found that hard to believe.

"You don't know how tenacious some of these pastors can be. Some of them feel that having an auxiliary bishop is a negative commentary on their parochial work. They'll chew your ear off to get some sort of special consideration."

Maybe, thought Delvecchio. But I don't think they'll get much chance to chew these ears. "When do I learn what your shorthand stands for on the other messages?"

Jan bit her lower lip. "That's a good question. There just isn't time during office hours. How about this evening?"

"I've got a couple of appointments. But I can postpone them. How about if we meet at my residence? I have an office in the rectory."

"You could be interrupted by phone calls," Jan reminded.

He winced and nodded.

"How about dinner out?" she suggested.

"I've never been able to stick to business in a restaurant. Taking notes while eating seems incompatible."

Jan shrugged. "Then it's got to be my place. I've got a first-floor apartment in a large complex in Warren."

Delvecchio hesitated. This was *solus cum sola*—one on one. The only time thus far he'd been alone with a woman was in a safe situation . . . under correct, even if not chaperoned, circumstances. Except when he was bringing Communion to a shut-in he'd never been alone with a woman in her apartment.

But this seemed safe enough. Strictly business.

He agreed; he would pick up Chinese takeout on the way over. She gave him the address and directions.

*　　*　　*

Bundled up against the cold, he arrived at her door a couple of minutes before seven. As she took his coat, hat, and scarf to hang up, she was mildly surprised to see that he wore not clericals, but a flannel shirt, chinos, and a sweater.

He noted her puzzlement. "Anyone sees me come or go, they won't think I'm a priest."

"Just a date." She was sorry the moment the words left her mouth. This was to be business; there should be no hint, no overtone of anything else.

She had set out a series of papers on the coffee table. They sat together on the couch and ate as she explained the cryptic symbols—her shorthand transcribing the reactions of His Excellency to each message.

Along the way, they discovered that they both knew how to use chopsticks.

From time to time, her nearness distracted him. She really was a most attractive young woman. Her dress was so "Marylike" he could only guess at her figure. Though she was slender, he presumed she was curvy.

There was a delicate scent of just the right perfume. Her dark hair fell well below her shoulders. The corners of her extremely expressive eyes crinkled with humor.

Occasionally, she brushed against him as she reached for food or to turn a page. He found that somewhat stimulating.

*　　*　　*

Jan had long been aware of Vincent Delvecchio.

His name, of course, had become well known when he'd suffered the breakdown, recovered, and then been sent to Rome. What to do with this talented yet perhaps flawed young man had been a periodic topic in the chancery for sometime. As a secretary in the archbishop's office, Jan was privy to much of the gossip.

Eventually, he had arrived at the chancery, his appointment after ordination.

While he did not seem to notice her, she was acutely aware of him. He was tall, dark, and handsome. She fantasized about him.

*   *   *

And now, here he was. In her apartment. Alone. Without making it seem intentional, she brushed up against him. She was aroused. But she did not let on.

They finished the Chinese dinner. She made coffee, chattering on about the symbols she'd devised to capture the thoughts and disposition of the archbishop.

They drank a lot of coffee while Delvecchio committed her hieroglyphics . . . or at least most of them . . . to memory.

By the time Delvecchio glanced at his watch, it was almost eleven. "Holy cow! Look at the time! And I've got early Mass tomorrow morning." He stood. "I'd better get going."

She handed him his scarf and stood holding his coat. "You're a quick study," she observed. After all she'd heard about him, she'd expected him to be sharp; still, his acumen surprised her.

"But not quite quick enough. There's still a lot for me to absorb before I can be confident that I'm really filling in for Shanahan. Would you do what you did this morning? I mean, bring in the messages and record the archbishop's reaction to them? Then I'll go over them with you and see if I've got this all down. One more day will probably do it— that is, as long as we can put in another evening on this crash course."

"Sure. I think I can swing that." She helped him on with his coat. "Just remember that lots of people want to see the archbishop. But only a few will make it. The thing is that most of this business can be handled by lower-echelon personnel. We—well, *you*—have to steer these people to an auxiliary, or a monsignor, or a priest—or even someone like me. Mostly you'll be a filter protecting the archbishop from having to deal with problems and questions that others can take care of.

"That sounds simple enough," he said as she handed him his hat.

"Maybe because I'm oversimplifying it."

"Maybe." Ready to face November's cold, he reached for the doorknob.

"Oh—"

"Yes?"

"You don't have to bring dinner. I'll make it. Tomorrow's Friday. You want to eat meat?"

Earlier in the month, the Vatican had announced that there would no longer be a law obliging Catholics to abstain from meat on Fridays. The announcement had triggered some simplistic humor. Such as, What is God going to do with all those people who are in hell because they ate meat on Friday?

It also caused a furor among traditional Catholics who looked on as yet another ancient tradition went down the drain.

Delvecchio glanced at her sharply. "Certainly not! Besides, the decree doesn't become effective until December second."

She tried to cover a blush. "Just kidding."

"Okay. Well, see you at the office tomorrow, and here tomorrow evening."

There was little traffic; it took him only half an hour to drive home.

She cleaned up in record time. They had spooned out portions from the cardboard cartons, so there were only the coffee cups to be washed. And since they had used chopsticks, aside of the serving pieces, there was no flatware to be washed.

*   *   *

Neither got much sleep that night.

He felt much like a teenager after his first awkward date. By contemporary standards it was extremely odd that this *was* his first date. He found his reaction curious.

He lay in bed thinking of her. He imagined he could still smell her delicate perfume. He figured her to be roughly his age, perhaps a little older. He found her beautiful and intelligent. He remembered his reaction each time she'd touched him . . . inadvertently, of course, but touch him she had. And he had reacted . . . involuntarily, of course, but react he had.

He wondered about her.

That he'd had no sexual experience was one thing. What with parochial school, the seminary, summer camp, his priesthood, sexual expression had been a forbidden fruit from early childhood on. Not many men in their early thirties were virginly intact.

But what about her?

She was an attractive, available young woman. She must be experienced in sex. The way he'd acted and reacted to her tonight must have seemed foolish and adolescent—if she was aware of it.

What was he supposed to do? How was he supposed to behave when he was alone with a beautiful woman?

Well, he knew the answer to that!

The Church demanded that he never marry. And morality demanded that any sexual expression whatsoever be confined within marriage. Chaste! That's how he was supposed to behave when alone with a beautiful woman—any woman.

He expected tomorrow evening would present the most difficult temptation he had ever faced.

*   *   *

She lay in bed thinking of him. He was so talented, so brilliant, so interesting—and handsome, to boot. She had heard the expression made regarding certain priests, though she herself had never had occasion to use it. Now was that occasion. She thought of his celibate life and said to herself: What a waste!

Then she felt guilty.

She could sense that he had been aroused when she brushed against him.

The first time it was accidental. Thereafter, she certainly had not gone out of her way to avoid touching him.

Was there chemistry between them? She had been interested in this young man when she first heard of him. When he began work in the chancery, she would see him from time to time. For instance, in the elevator. She would smile at him, at least in the beginning. He rarely returned the smile—or even acknowledged her presence.

But that remote, standoffish man was not the same as the overwhelmed priest who needed help with a new job. He was not the same as the young man who had reacted to her innocent touches this evening.

He would be at the office tomorrow, still needing her help. They would work together—at least as much as she was able and time allowed.

Then . . . he would be back here tomorrow evening.

There was not really all that much work to do. Surely she had little more to teach him. That business about shielding the archbishop from unnecessary appointments by finding others who could handle the various sorts of demands, advice, etc.; that really was at the heart of the position that Vince Delvecchio was filling for the duration of Shanahan's illness.

Jan Olivier had grown up sheltered by parents who treasured their one and only child. Parochial schools led to Marygrove, a Catholic womens' college. And that led to a job in the offices of the archdiocese of Detroit.

She had dated. But her dating and her dates had had to pass her parents' muster—the upshot being that she was still a virgin. Even though she was living through the turbulent sixties. Even though she had her own apartment.

Maybe, just maybe, after tomorrow night, she would no longer be a maiden lady.

It's a good thing Mother couldn't know what her fine Catholic daughter was thinking; she would be mortified!

*   *   *

Shortly after assuming jurisdiction over the Detroit archdiocese, Mark Boyle set the tone for diocesan bureaus. Everyone would be as-

William X. Kienzle

sembled and ready for work by 9 A.M. In the beginning he made it his practice to drop in on the various offices—unannounced and seemingly haphazardly—a few minutes before 9.

It did not take long for the bureaucrats to catch on. Boyle set the style and expected everyone else to follow suit. Rather quickly, everyone did.

Among those who followed faithfully were Father Vincent Delvecchio and Miss Jan Olivier. They both arrived within minutes of each other at approximately 8:30.

Delvecchio began by boning up on the rating system Jan had devised. He'd had no time either last night or this morning to study it.

Jan gathered the messages that had accumulated late yesterday afternoon and the few that had trickled in earlier this morning. She brought them in to the archbishop. She began reading them and, where she had some insight, commenting. Boyle gave directions for their distribution. That meant that either he would handle the matter himself or find someone to take care of it.

Actually, the archbishop had expected Father Delvecchio to be handling this by now. Realistically, he knew that was expecting a bit much. So he made no comment. In another day or so the bright young man would master the job.

Jan brought the messages to Delvecchio and looked over his shoulder as he read and interpreted them. He misread only a couple.

He was alert to her scent. He thought he had read somewhere that perfume takes on a different fragrance as it is applied to different skin. He expected he would never forget what Jan's perfume did for her. Or what she did for it.

As she leaned over, he felt something touch the back of his neck, just above his clerical collar. It must, he thought, be her breast. That set him off on another fantasy. He certainly did not attempt to escape from her touch, or to push her—or himself—away.

Enough of that. He had work to do.

He began his second day of phoning, or, rather, returning calls that had been directed at Archbishop Boyle.

He was getting into the swing of it. It was a kick phoning pastors, men much older than he, and, in effect, telling them where to go.

209

For their part, the pastors hung on his every word, trying to interpret the message within the message—between the lines, as it were.

After talking to Delvecchio, some of them thought: The Arch isn't going to see me, but I must still be in his good graces—after all, now I've got his permission to talk to his senior auxiliary. Maybe that's enough . . . maybe I won't even call that brown-noser after all. Keep 'em guessing. Yeah!

Others thought: Oh, my God! The old man agreed to see me. What the hell, I didn't expect him to give me an interview. Why is he going to see me personally? What does he know? He can't know that the guys and I are going to Florida during Advent! Who would have told him! Who would have given us away? I'll bet it was O'Malley. Sure; that's why he canceled out on the trip.

In each case, from his listener's tone, Delvecchio could measure the effect his message was having. He began deliberately changing his speech patterns to create differing pastoral modes.

He enjoyed having and exercising power. It was one of the things he was learning about himself lately.

Around 11:30 he strolled out to Jan's desk. "Almost lunchtime. Want to go? My treat." He was smiling, something he seldom did.

She looked up brightly. "Any other day of any other year. I've got some catching up to do."

"My fault, eh? I took your time to teach me my job. Sorry about that. But without your help, I wouldn't have the foggiest idea of what I'm supposed to be doing."

"It's all right. A raincheck . . . okay?"

"Okay."

Instead of taking a normal lunch hour, Jan got a carry-out from a nearby drugstore. She also did some judicious shopping in a Woodward Avenue apparel shop. She had no plans for tonight, nor any idea of what would happen. This "date" could lead anywhere; she wanted to be ready for whatever.

It was almost five. The workday was winding down.

Once again, Delvecchio popped up in front of Jan. "Listen, I've just got to see someone at the rectory at six-thirty. I figure we'll be done by seven-thirty. So how 'bout I get to your place about eight?"

The incipient frown that broke out when she'd thought he was canceling their get-together quickly dissipated. "Actually, that'll be perfect: I need a little time to put dinner together."

On the way home she stopped at her favorite fish place for some swordfish and at a small bakery for French bread. At home were potatoes, vegetables, and the makings for a tossed salad.

What was it they said in the tribunal? *Omnia parata.* Everything is ready.

✳   ✳   ✳

By the time he arrived a minute or two after 8, everything indeed was ready. The table was set, the candles were lit. He handed her a bottle of light Chardonnay.

As she was putting food on the table, he asked to wash up. Through the door to the bedroom and past the walk-in closet, he was instructed.

He glanced around the bedroom. Typical woman's room. Lots of frilly things. Lots of white. The bed—queen-size, he conjectured—became the focus of his interest. A bed, in this pagan age, had become the symbol not of sleep and rest, but sex. For just a moment, he imagined himself and Jan together on that bed, naked. It was such a strong image that he had to force his mind to let it go.

He washed his hands and, steadfastly looking away from the bed, returned to the dining room.

The table wasn't large enough to hold all the serving platters. She kept popping up and down, offering dishes to him, and from time to time dropping dollops on her own plate.

Small talk surrounded how good everything tasted, how easy it had been to make, what had happened at the office today, and the like.

How much this resembled married life, Jan thought. Working couples coming together in the early evening to share the highlights of their day. Even though their conversation was a bit strained, she liked the experience. After all, they had known each other only a couple of days; there was plenty of room to develop.

From the moment he entered her apartment this evening, he had been acutely aware that something was different. That fetching fragrance was the same. The hair was the same. She was wearing a tad more makeup. But her dress: No Marylike creation this.

It was black or possibly a very dark blue. And there wasn't an extra inch of cloth to it. It met and caressed each and every curve. The neckline was cut so that each time she bent over to serve him, he could see—he couldn't miss!—more than a hint of full, molded breasts.

Vaguely he had been aware of all this at first glance this evening, but the passing minutes developed the details.

Entrée finished, Jan suggested they repair to the living area for coffee and dessert.

She put the tray on the coffee table. She sat where she had last night—on the couch. He could easily have taken the chair across the table from her. But he too sat on the couch. As he sat next to her he recalled her touches last night.

They had dessert and two cups of coffee each. Finally, he passed, claiming he would float if he had any more.

An awkward silence followed.

"Would you like to watch some TV?" she asked tentatively.

He shook his head. "I can watch TV any night."

"You don't really need teacher anymore, do you?" she said playfully.

He shook his head again. "That's what you get for being such a good instructor."

She was aware that during dessert and coffee, he had inched over; their bodies were lightly touching.

"What do you think of the job?" she asked.

"Which job?"

"The archbishop's secretary."

He thought for a minute. "It has its moments."

She smiled. "I heard you today on the phone a few times. You sounded like you were enjoying yourself . . . sort of throwing your weight around."

He snorted. "I haven't got any weight—particularly where those pastors are concerned. It's the archbishop's weight that can get thrown about." As he let his arm fall to his side, his hand landed on hers.

She waited for him to take his hand away. When he made no move to do so, she opened her hand and held his. Both their hands trembled slightly.

After a few moments, she said, "It's just possible that that job might be opening up."

"Huh?"

"It's been noised about in the chancery . . . Monsignor Shanahan has mentioned it to me. He's getting tired of the job. He may ask for a change . . . back to parish work. From the position he's in now as secretary to the archbishop, he probably could get just about any parish he wanted—provided it was open."

"No kidding! It never entered my head—I mean, continuing after Shanahan recovers." He looked thoughtful. "That's interesting. But"— he shrugged—"I'm there only as a temporary substitute—very short-term. And even that's only because I'm low man on the totem pole. If they wanted a permanent replacement, they'd look for someone way higher on the ladder . . ." He looked at her. ". . . don't you think?"

"You're going to have quite a bit of experience by the time Monsignor Shanahan gets back. It's just as possible that they would favor your experience over chronology." She smiled. "I have it on good authority that when Monsignor Shanahan gets his annual cold, it usually takes him a good two to three weeks to get over it and go back to work."

She lifted her hand from his so she could gesture. "What if the rumor that Monsignor Shanahan wants to retire from the chancery is true? And what if *someone*"—she emphasized the noun—"were to get word to Monsignor that *you* wouldn't mind taking over his job?" She smiled again. "I could imagine that Monsignor might extend his sick leave as long as possible to let you get really familiar with the work . . ."

"Maybe," she added, "along with Monsignor's request for a transfer, he could recommend you for the job."

They both allowed a few moments for that thought to take root.

"We could work together . . . every day!"

"That would be nice," he mused. "Real nice."

His thought took a flight of fancy.

It was by no means uncommon that a priest who became a bishop's secretary eventually became a bishop himself. Not always, but it *was* one possible path to the office.

A full-time secretary lived in the same mansion with the archbishop. The secretary was also the customary chauffeur. The secretary met with other bishops, regularly. The secretary usually accompanied his bishop on trips, particularly to Rome.

Having studied in Rome was also a consideration in the candidacy for a bishopric. He, Delvecchio, had touched that base already. Not during his basic theology training, but postgrad—after his damned breakdown.

Based on his years of study there, he already had a familiar name in Rome. Being the archbishop's secretary would only enhance that familiarity.

Then he wouldn't have to borrow the archbishop's clout to toss his weight around. Then, Delvecchio would be a force with which to reckon.

He felt the power of the episcopacy. It was just beyond his grasp. As long as he kept his nose clean. He couldn't afford a stupid mistake. Not with his breakdown being one strike.

Jan leaned forward to stack the dessert and coffee dishes.

Without thinking, he laid his hand on her back. Through the thin dress he felt her bra strap. It was an intimate item of apparel. He felt the intimacy.

So did she. She froze.

Instantly, he realized what he had done. He jerked his hand away.

She left the dishes on the table and sat straight up. She turned slightly to face him. She didn't know what to say. His face was flushed.

"Did you . . . do you . . ." She was stammering. ". . . want to . . . to . . . kiss me?"

He looked deeply into her eyes. "Very much so."

She put her arms around his neck. He put his around her back.

After a few seconds, he released her. She did not release him. So he put his arms back around her.

He felt her tongue against his lips.

She was lost in the kiss.

He was thinking.

French kissing. He'd first heard of it in moral theology. When entered into willingly and when prolonged, it was a mortal sin. *Oh, my God: a mortal sin!* Now that he was experiencing it for the first time, he didn't think it was worth being a mortal sin.

But he was firmly wrapped up in it.

Her arms remained locked around his neck. They had no place else to go.

His arms and hands were free to roam. And they did.

Consumed by the passion of the moment, his hand touched her knee, then slipped beneath the hem of her dress. Soon his hand fondled a firm, smooth thigh.

Suddenly, she stood up. She straightened her dress. She looked at him, inhaled deeply, and said, "I'll be right back."

Bewildered, he remained seated.

Immediately after thinking that he must at all costs avoid any stupid errors on his road to becoming a bishop, he had blundered.

Thank God it had gone no further.

He stood. He prepared to leave.

His trousers were wrinkled. He had been seriously aroused. But that was gone now.

She reentered.

She had bought two items during her brief shopping expedition. One was the dress she was no longer wearing. The other was the diaphanous robe she *was* wearing.

In but a few moments, he drank into his memory bank her every bodily feature. She was offering him her very self.

Part of him urged a shout of ecstasy and welcome. Part of him wanted to burn her at the stake. What triumphed was the outraged, Victorian Vincent Delvecchio.

"How—dare—you!" He shouted every drawn-out syllable.

Her shock and embarrassment was such that she grabbed a chair covering and quickly drew it around herself.

"But . . ."

"We were building what could have been . . ."

"You kissed me . . ."

"A platonic . . ."

They were shouting over one another. Their voices carried into adjacent apartments.

"And your hand . . ."

"Our friendship could have grown . . ."

"You were feeling me . . ."

"Into something beautiful . . ."

"You made me believe . . ."

"All of this could have been . . ."

"You wanted me . . ."

"You ruined everything . . ." He slipped into his coat, grabbed his hat, and made for the door.

"What was I to think . . . ?"

"And it's all your fault!" With that shouted crusher he slammed the door behind him.

She stood sobbing and trembling, then, with a howl, she threw herself on the couch. Tears flowed hot and copious. She couldn't come close to calm consideration.

How could I have been so wrong? I tried to let things happen naturally. I didn't try to force anything.

We've known each other just two days. And it's over now?

The archbishop told me to help him. He asked for my help. I gave it to him. No strings attached. I really did help him. He learned quickly. The way he reacted when I was near him. I thought he was hungry for a woman. Did I think that because I was hungry for a man?

That dress, that robe . . . I bought them today. Was I trying to force things? Subconsciously?

That kiss! I was the one who started that. I was the one who started the French kiss. I don't think he even knew what it was.

No! Dammit! It wasn't the kiss. We could have kept control if it had just been the kiss.

But not when he put his hand on my thigh and started to caress it. That was the message. It was unmistakable. We had to get out of our clothes then. It was our only direction then.

My fault! That's a laugh.

This was an angry thought that turned almost immediately defensive.

What am I going to do now?

Can I go back to work at the chancery? Just like nothing happened?

He'll be there! Only one wall between us. One constructed wall. The emotional wall will be much more powerful than one of plaster.

What if he tells the others? Men do that. I'll be laughed out of the building.

I can't go back. I simply can't.

I'll call in sick tomorrow. Later I'll send them a noncommittal letter of resignation.

Where will I go?

To another city. Smaller.

I can get a letter of recommendation from Archbishop Boyle.

This part of my life is over. If I'm not careful, I may just wrap my car around a tree. Then all of my life will be over.

*   *   *

He thought:

Damn! I've got to get control of myself. I just ran a red light.

What an evening!

Now I know. Now I know why seminarians and priests must separate themselves from females—girls, women.

Suddenly it's clear that only marriage can contain the lust between men and women. Women are the great temptation.

Admit it! Face it! I came this close to making love to her. Going to bed with her. Sleeping with her. And any other euphemisms they use for sex.

Tonight I came this close to throwing away my entire career. And for what? A moment of pleasure. Intense pleasure—I admit it. But momentary.

That kiss! I was flooded with desire.

Maybe there's some good in this. I've got a much better appreciation of St. Paul. He wished everyone could live in the celibate state like him. But he realized not everyone could resist the seductive wiles of women. He hit it on the head when he wrote that it was better to marry than to burn in hell.

Such was the power of women. Without half trying, they could and did pull men into hell.

Even now, as I drive away from that woman, I can still feel the urge to throw good sense away and plunge into her.

Again, like St. Paul, I can almost hear Jesus tell me that His grace was sufficient for me.

Thank God!

But there's still something that has to be made right. I'm in mortal sin and I've got to say Mass tomorrow morning. I've got to get to confession.

What time is it?

Almost ten-thirty.

Who can I go to at this hour? Who would understand?

24

"That's it?"

"Why, yes, that's it."

The philosophical if not theological approach to confession was tricky, Father Koesler had long thought.

The rule of thumb was clear enough: The confessor—the priest who hears the confession—is instructed to believe the penitent whether he or she speaks for or against him- or herself. That's simple enough.

But the confessor is not supposed to dispense absolution like an automaton. He is expected to help the penitent, be understanding, clarify things for the penitent if such is necessary, and, finally, make a judgment as to whether or not the penitent is truly sorry for sins committed.

It had been almost 11 P.M. when the doorbell rang. That definitely was not a run-of-the-mill time to be calling at a rectory. Which someone had once defined as a home for unmarried Fathers.

It was with some apprehension that Koesler went to the door. Who knew what dire emergency needed a priest?

Koesler was surprised the caller was another priest—Vince Delvecchio, of all people.

When Vince announced that he wanted to go to confession, Koesler drew the natural conclusion that there was some sort of mortal sin that stood between Delvecchio and the celebration of Mass tomorrow morning.

In any case, Koesler was willing to do whatever he could to help his longtime friend.

As they climbed the stairs to Koesler's room, he recalled the classic story—probably apocryphal—of priests on vacation together. One asks the other to hear his confession. He kneels at the chair of his friend and, before beginning his confession, admonishes the other to "just give me absolution, Fred; no *pia stercora*." Which can be translated, "No pious shit." Just absolution, no spiritual pep talk.

In similar situations, confession among priests, Koesler was amenable to skipping the nosegays.

But Delvecchio's was an odd confession. For one, he had gone into far greater detail than necessary. Koesler did not need to know the woman's name. He was only barely acquainted with Jan. He'd had some chancery dealings with her, getting information and the like. But her identity was extraneous to the confession.

Secondly, Koesler had difficulty finding the mortal sin. "Excuse me, Vince, but I figure you're here because you think you're guilty of serious sin."

"Yes, of course."

"What?"

"Well, all that French kissing. And then my touching her leg."

"The last time I read up on the theology of serious sin, there had to be some considerable deliberation there. Not anything done on the spur of the moment. As far as I can see, the two of you entered into this innocently and got carried away."

"She didn't! She seduced me!"

"I don't think so. But, of course, that doesn't matter. We're talking about your confession exclusively. And, besides, my reading indicates that a woman's thigh is not any part of her genitalia. Not even an erogenous zone.

"Much more serious, I think, is the way you treated her before you stormed out. But, then, again, you were swept away by spontaneous emotion.

"I think it would be good for everyone if you would help her feel better—or at least less bad—about what happened. It being nobody's fault. Of course it would be wise for the two of you not to be together like you were this evening."

"That part about helping her feel better—you're not making that a condition for granting me absolution! Are you?"

"Of course not. For one, I don't think you've got a mortal sin here in the first place. You don't have to do this. But I think it would be good of you. She probably feels terrible."

"I'll give it some thought."

As little thought as possible, Koesler suspected. There were loads of questions rattling around in his mind—the product of idle curiosity having nothing to do with the sacrament.

So he gave Delvecchio a small penance of prayer. Then Koesler absolved him. No *pia stercora*.

As he showed Delvecchio to the door, Koesler thought he detected a sense of arrogance in the younger priest. If he had to guess, Koesler would bet that Delvecchio was guilty of the sin of pride.

In fact, of all the things bandied about as sins this evening, this—pride—easily could be the most damaging and dangerous.

The scenario was so clear now that Koesler was able to piece together this evening's events.

While it was difficult to picture the controlled Delvecchio in the throes of sexual passion, according to the penitent himself, that's where he'd been. When Jan appeared wearing practically nothing, sending out green "Go" rays, it must have been literally all he could do not to succumb. It must have taken almost superhuman control to walk away from an offer, a temptation like that.

But Delvecchio did it!

He walked away.

Koesler thought at the time that this pride could lead to a sense of moral superiority in Delvecchio: If he could survive the "ultimate test," he could demand the same from every priest. And should a priest show any weakness in this or any other matter, such priest would be harshly dealt with.

Koesler tucked his well-founded speculation on the rear burner of his memory.

No one else would ever know. Unless Vince or Jan revealed the secret. And there was little chance of that.

The Present

So, Father Tully wishes Delvecchio had sometime in his life proved himself weak—even merely human would have been acceptable. Little did Tully know how close Vince had come to proving himself extremely human. And, consequently, having won out over that critical temptation, he was more stiff-necked than ever.

Whatever happened to Jan Olivier? A mystery.

Koesler had made no attempt to ascertain whether she was at her post the day after the "event." But, in time, it was common knowledge that Jan had moved on, destination neither disclosed nor known.

Most everyone, if giving it any thought at all, probably surmised that she had left for a better-paying job. Generally, the various archdiocesan offices did not pay competitively. One did God a favor in working for the Church.

Others, while missing her cheerful voice and helpfulness, were vaguely happy she had found something better. But Koesler was saddened that nothing could have been done to heal her wounds.

Admittedly, "awkward" was not strong enough to describe what it would have been like for Jan and Vince to work together after what they'd put each other through. Still, Koesler believed that with a sincere concerted effort something could have been done. He supposed that Delvecchio had not had the opportunity to take the initiative in making peace. He also had his doubts as to whether Vince had any intention of trying.

However, as fate had it, Shanahan got the word that Delvecchio coveted the job of secretary. And Delvecchio got the job. A definite step on the road to the episcopacy.

The background of Delvecchio's harsh treatment of priests in almost any problem or trouble would never be revealed to Father Tully or anyone else. It was protected by the king of all secrets, the Seal of Confession.

Just as well. It wasn't the sort of example that Tully would find encouraging in his confrontation with the bishop.

Father Tully entered the room, shaking his head and smiling. "God bless 'em, the women are in the kitchen playing cards."

"Cool," Koesler observed.

"They say they're ready whether or not Bishop Delvecchio stays for dinner. They have contingency plans.

"Personally"—Tully grimaced—"I'd just as soon he didn't stay. I'd be happy if he just presented you with the papers, the documents . . . whatever, that make you a Senior Priest. If he leaves after that, he and

I can argue this thing out later by ourselves. Better that way; this isn't your fight."

"No, no," Koesler disagreed. "This parish is like my child. It's got great potential. I doubt I'd be leaving it if I weren't leaving it in your care. You've got the ability, experience, and talent to lead these people to a growingly Christian ideal.

"I want you to have this parish. There's no reason, outside of Vinnie's stubbornness, that you shouldn't be pastor of St. Joe's.

"Besides, it's time someone talked some sense into him. He doesn't have to be so by-the-book. Sometimes the book slams down hard on legitimate human freedom.

"And I think I'm the person who should reason with him. And now's the time to do it. I'm retiring and I'm his friend. And, sad to say, there aren't many who would call themselves his friend."

"Well, that seems to be true," Tully commented. "I guess he doesn't even have many friends in the hierarchy or he'd be an Ordinary—have his own diocese by now."

"I don't know about that." Koesler moved to the pool table and racked the balls for another game. "I don't think friendship has all that much to do with moving onward and upward in the hierarchy. Although," he added after a moment's thought, "I suppose the popular concept is that all auxiliary bishops eventually get their own dioceses."

"Well, that's certainly not true." Tully examined each cue stick in turn, hoping a change would bring better luck. "Lord, there are so many auxiliaries in these large metropolitan dioceses that they all couldn't live long enough to become Ordinaries."

"I don't really know all that much about Church politics," Koesler confessed. "But I would put my last dollar on Delvecchio's breakdown as the impediment that's blocking his advancement. He's certainly conservative enough. The Vatican probably just won't gamble on that breakdown."

"Like he's in limbo . . ." Tully offered to break. Koesler did not object. Tully's break shot spread balls all over the table, but nothing fell.

Koesler sank a stripe and the game was on.

"Let's see," Tully said, "a brother, a sister, an aunt; his parents dead: That's not much to count on for friendship."

Distracted, Koesler missed an easy shot. "If you're looking for Delvecchio's friends, don't start with his family."

"No? You're kidding?"

"Definitely not!"

"Well, okay, according to what you told me earlier, he wasn't particularly close to his brother. But the sister: He got along fine with her . . . no?"

"To a point. The last thing I told you about their relationship was when their mother died."

"Something happen to mess things up after that?"

"I'll say! It was a big news story here . . . although probably not where you were." Koesler reflected, then smiled. "I have a tendency to assume that news that's big locally gets some play nationally—or, at least regionally. Of course realistically that's not so."

"Well, what happened to them?" Tully began to line up a shot.

"Lucy was about to graduate from high school when her mother died . . ."

"I remember. Of all of them, she seemed to keep a good head on her shoulders."

"Well, after Mrs. Delvecchio died, the focus was pretty much on Vince and his condition. But life went on. Lucy graduated. So did Tony.

"Lucy transferred in college to premed. She was a terrific athlete. Unfortunately for her—and maybe for everyone then—she was a female and women's sports were not taken seriously. Otherwise, she could have had a free ride. As it was, she won an academic scholarship that helped a lot.

"She graduated summa cum laude, went on to medical school, and became a doctor."

Tully whistled softly. He missed a shot and leaned back against the wall. "Good for her."

"After her internship, she got a lot of offers. But she chose the Emergency Room at Detroit's Receiving Hospital. She wanted action and plenty of experience at healing just about everything. And she certainly got it at Receiving.

25

"**This story goes back** . . . what? . . . about twenty-five years—
Lord, how time flies when you reach Senior Priest status." Koesler
chuckled. "A quarter of a century! It seems like last month. And part of
this story is well known and remembered by anyone who was following local news around that time.

"I got some of the details later . . . and only because of my special
contact with the Delvecchio family."

1973

Monsignor Vincent Delvecchio was several minutes early for his
luncheon date with Merl Goldbaum, who also was early. The two met
four or five times a year. It was habitual for each to be early for appointments.

The two men could not be described as friends; more on the order
of good acquaintances. They had met originally under the auspices of
Father Robert Koesler.

At the time Koesler was editor of the *Detroit Catholic*, Goldbaum was
a crack reporter for one of Detroit's metropolitan newspapers. Their
position at their respective papers, one Catholic, the other secular, had
brought them together.

Goldbaum was no longer with the newspaper. Building on his jour-
nalism experience and contacts, he had launched his own firm and
now headed one of the most respected public relations companies in
the Detroit area.

The threesome had first come together during the mid-sixties. Goldbaum had phoned Koesler with an invitation to lunch on a day when
Koesler and Delvecchio already had lunch scheduled. Koesler cleared
the water with the two—neither of whom objected to the other. So it
became a movable ménage à trois.

It worked out this way: The ball remained in Goldbaum's court. He did the calling—and picked up the tab. He counted Koesler a friend; Delvecchio was a resource. From time to time he wanted from both priests insights, clarifications, explanations, and the like regarding Church teachings and customs.

From Koesler, Goldbaum expected reliable replies tempered by an innate kindness. But there were times when he sought the "authentic word" undiluted by a humane reaction. For the *vera doctrina*, Goldbaum turned to the monsignor.

And so this day, Goldbaum and Delvecchio met at a few minutes before noon in the foyer of Meriwether's on Telegraph Road. They were familiar patrons of this popular eatery and were greeted as such by personable manager Jim McIntyre.

They were immediately seated in a secluded booth. Decades-old volumes lined—and were glued to—time-eaten shelves. Both books and shelves were cleaned periodically, but their antiquarian nature gave the impression that they bore the dust of Caesar. From time to time Father Koesler wondered how much a decorator had charged the Muer chain to achieve this Old English effect—an effect heightened by the framed Victorian prints and the witty quotations in old-time script that adorned the walls.

But Koesler wasn't here today, so no one wondered about those things.

Neither Goldbaum nor Delvecchio ordered drinks; both ordered fish.

As they enjoyed the restaurant's signature teacup bread, they engaged in small talk. The dreariness of a Michigan winter. (It was February, the meanest month of the year, unrelieved by any celebratory occasion—unless one counted Presidents' Day.) The PR firm was doing quite well, thank you. PR was such a competitive business that one had to constantly be on one's toes and on the ball. Phyllis and the girls were well, thank you.

That took them through the salad course.

With the arrival of the pièce de résistance, Delvecchio expected to learn the purpose of this luncheon meeting. He knew from experience that in good time, Merl would get around to it, but in his own inimitable circuitous fashion.

"So," Goldbaum said, "how's your sister doing?"

"As well as can be expected," replied Delvecchio, borrowing the hospital catchphrase.

Goldbaum grinned. "I mean, it must be something to have a medical doctor in the family—a close relative, I mean."

"There are perks." Delvecchio hadn't the slightest idea where this conversation was going.

"I mean, what do you do if you get sick? Does your sister take care of you?"

Delvecchio shrugged. "I guess I haven't been sick . . . at least not since she finished her internship. I suppose she'd step in: What are sisters for?"

"What if you—or your brother, for that matter—had something that was out of her field. She's in ER, isn't she?"

"Uh-huh."

"Well, s'posin' you needed something that called for a specialist . . . say, a bypass operation: What then?"

"Hmmm. I suppose I'd ask her whom she'd have operate on her. One thing about doctors: They get to know one another, and each other's strengths and weaknesses."

Goldbaum chewed on that for a while.

Finally, having finished the main course, Delvecchio leaned back, smiled, and said, "Merl, I'm very proud of Lucy. She's not only a physician, she's terrific in her field. I've got a feeling that everything she touches will be gold. If I got sick or was carried into the Emergency Room, Lucy would be there for me.

"That pretty well takes care of Dr. Lucy Delvecchio.

"Now, Merl, you may think that I pay no mind to the fact that every time we meet for lunch or whatever, you always have something 'Catholic' that you need or want explained . . ." Delvecchio glanced at his watch. "Both of us are going to have to get back to work soon. What, I pray thee, is the problem area?"

Goldbaum did not meet Delvecchio's gaze. He carefully compressed his napkin and laid it beside his plate. "Diaphragms, condoms, contraceptives."

Delvecchio was taken aback. "Well, that's sort of off-the-beaten-path from where you began. So, what about them?"

"Your Church is against their use . . . right?"

"Yes."

"No exceptions?"

Delvecchio tilted his head. "You mean, could Father Koesler find an exception? Probably. Well . . ." He almost smiled. "Maybe."

"But the straight word: No exceptions?"

"None."

"Wasn't there an attempt to change the rule sometime back?"

Delvecchio's eyes narrowed. "You mean the commission that Pope Paul VI appointed to study the matter?"

Goldbaum nodded.

"You got that from Bob before you set up this lunch."

Again Goldbaum nodded.

The monsignor shifted in his seat. "It's true Pope Paul set up the commission and it did recommend some changes in the law. But the Pope said, 'No,' and wrote an encyclical on it—*Humanae Vitae*. And that was the end of that. We have an expression: *Roma locuta, causa finita*."

"Yeah, I know that one: 'Rome has spoken, the matter is closed.'"

"So?" Delvecchio spread his hands wide. "What is there to say when the matter is closed?"

The waiter appeared. They would have coffee, regular.

"See, Monsignor, I tend to look at things from a PR point of view. And that decision was very poor PR, if you'll pardon my saying so."

Delvecchio obviously was not amused. He did not take Goldbaum's remark personally. Long ago, the monsignor had concluded Goldbaum was not "convertible." Nevertheless, Delvecchio didn't enjoy having Church teaching questioned . . . no matter by whom.

"Well, Merl, the Catholic Church is not in the public relations business. Nor is the Church a democracy. In another—secular—society, you might expect an organization to follow the directives of a commission that the organization itself created. Not all the time, but most of the time. Now, the Vatican can consult with whomever it wishes. But the last word is still the Pope's—"

"Even when poll after poll shows that the majority of Catholics in effect have rejected the Pope's stand on this? Even when studies show there's practically no difference between the percentages of Catholics and non-Catholics practicing contraception?"

"Merl, you're not listening. It makes no difference. *Roma locuta, causa finita.* **Finita**." Delvecchio leaned back again. "Now, maybe you'll tell me why we're talking about this"—he glanced at his watch—"interminably."

The waiter brought coffee and the bill. As usual, Goldbaum picked up the check. He waited till the waiter left. Then he said, "Monsignor, there's this guy in our office who has eight kids—"

"That's a good-size family for these times. Let me guess: He's Catholic."

"Right!" Goldbaum nodded decisively. "It's been a sort of joke in the office. At first, the guy went along with the ribbing. But lately it's seemed to reach him.

"Well, to make a long story short, a couple of weeks ago, he went in for a vasectomy. It was like a last resort for him. His wife got tired of being the one who tried to prevent conception . . . and failing! So, he did it.

"Now, that doesn't square with the Church, does it?"

"No. He'd have to be sorry he had that done. And he'd have to go to confession to have that serious sin—the sin of the mutilation of a sex organ—forgiven. But what's that got to do with me? Do you want me to talk with him?"

"No."

"Then . . . ?"

"The guy's wife has a favorite doctor. Even though this doctor does not have a private practice, his wife still goes to this doctor in a family clinic. The wife pushed her husband to go to this doctor for the vasectomy. And he did."

Delvecchio was beginning to have an inkling. "And this doctor is . . . ?"

"Lucy Delvecchio."

"Oh!" The monsignor was afraid his fish luncheon would reappear.

"Like I said before, Monsignor, I tend to look at things from a PR standpoint. It's not going to look good PR-wise that the sister of a monsignor performs vasectomies."

Delvecchio did not reply.

"But there's something more, Monsignor. Last month, the U.S. Supreme Court did away with state laws restricting abortions during the first six months of pregnancy."

"I know that."

Goldbaum leaned across the table and spoke as softly as possible while still able to be heard over the crowd's noise. "Well, this clinic that I mentioned earlier—its main business is pregnancy counseling."

"You mean . . ."

"Your sister handles abortions, although she restricts her practice to the first three months of pregnancy."

Goldbaum was not sure Delvecchio was still listening. The monsignor's face was ashen and his eyes appeared to have glazed over.

"Listen, Monsignor, I'm not telling you this for spite or like gossip, or to hurt you. First, I wanted to make sure that these things . . . procedures . . . contraception, vasectomy, were still against your Church's teaching. I knew abortion was. You just confirmed what I suspected. This guy in my office, once he dropped the name of the doctor, I knew you were in a lot of trouble."

"I? In trouble?"

"As the saying goes, in 'deep do-do' . . . from a PR standpoint. I would guess—and, believe me, this is an educated guess—that no one in the media is aware that you have a sister who counsels contraception and performs abortions. If any reporter was on to this, you wouldn't be sitting here hearing it from me. We'd be reading it in the papers and watching it on TV and hearing it on radio."

"You think so?" For Delvecchio, this was a learning situation. Goldbaum had caught his attention.

"Believe me," Goldbaum said, "these clinics are no longer news by themselves. They just sit there doing their jobs. Even pickets are no longer news. But if a pro-lifer stinks the place up, or if they dynamite it, or shoot a doctor . . . or"—his meaningful gaze almost impaled Delvecchio—"if the sister of a Catholic priest—a monsignor—is performing abortions, believe me, that is big news."

Although it was obvious that Delvecchio's mental wheels were turning furiously, when he finally spoke, it was with aplomb. "Well, I'm grateful to you, Merl. Of course I'll talk with my sister about this. It's intolerable!" he concluded firmly.

"Monsignor, you'd better do more than just talk."

"Then *what?*" Delvecchio spread his hands in query.

"We should sit down and work out a statement for the media. It would have to be very carefully worded. For instance, it would say that you just discovered your sister's involvement. That you can in no way condone this. But she remains your sister. You love her, but repudiate what she's doing. You will pray for her and you enlist the prayers of all in the pro-life movement.

"We might also get a statement from Lucy. The point is, bring this out in the open—before the news media gets hold of it—and tie up all the loose ends. That way, it'll be news for only a short while. But if the media breaks this story, it'll be *their* story. They'll push it for days. They'll be hounding you, Lucy, the medical establishment—and most of all your archbishop." Goldbaum looked at the monsignor expectantly.

"As I say, I will talk to Lucy. I prefer to think we can keep this from going public. But I thank you for telling me." He thought for a moment, then said, almost as if to himself, "Maybe I can save Lucy from herself."

Goldbaum paid the bill, leaving a generous tip. "Monsignor, think about what I said . . . or you're going to be up to your ears in what we in the business call public damage control."

26

Though brother and sister, Vincent and Lucy Delvecchio seldom got together. Each was proud of what the other had accomplished. Each wished a closer bond with their brother Tony. All three of them were busy. And the glue that once held them together—their mother— had dissolved with her death.

With infrequency marking their relationship, when Vince phoned, Lucy was pretty sure what it was about: He had to have learned of her pro-choice activity. If that was indeed the case, this evening would not be pleasant.

Actually, Lucy did not consider herself pro or con anything. She simply followed where the trouble traveled. The recent vasectomy, for example. She handled few such procedures. Partly because few men opted for that resolution, partly because most men preferred a male physician for that "man's" operation.

She would not have counseled the procedure for this healthy man. But when she learned to what extremes he and his wife had gone to plan their family, and their failure with every method but abstinence, and his determination to have the operation, she went ahead with it.

Lucy was not part of any movement for or against abortion. She was just as apt to counsel carrying to full term with possible adoption thereafter as she was to counsel abortion.

However, she knew the odds of convincing her brother of the validity of her position fell between no way and never.

When the doorbell rang, her back stiffened. The inevitable moment she had most dreaded was here.

They hugged. She took his hat and coat. Dinner was ready. He'd brought a bottle of domestic wine.

It did not occur to Vincent that this was only the second woman with whom he had dined alone. So deep in his subconscious had he buried Jan Olivier that it was as if she had never entered his life. All that stood in that space was an imaginary monument to his victory over concupiscence.

The atmosphere through dinner affected to be convivial, friendly, and old-shoe—much more so than was warranted. Somehow, they made it to the dessert course.

Lucy, unable to stand the tension any longer, broke the ice. "Well, big brother, this has been nice, but there's no evident reason we should enjoy dining together. No birthday, no holiday—come to think of it, we don't get together even on those occasions. You called me. So, what's on your mind?"

Vincent was eager to be the first to dive in; once again, he was on the side of the angels. The problem would be Lucy's should she not respond properly to his admonition.

"I had lunch yesterday with a gentleman who has a business colleague who recently saw you professionally."

"Oh?"

"This colleague, your patient, has—or rather, had—a problem with family planning. You solved the problem by giving him a vasectomy!"

"He wanted it," she said calmly.

"If one of your patients wanted something that was foolish, would you give it to him?"

"It's not the same."

"You're right there: A vasectomy is a sin—a serious sin."

Lucy sighed deeply. "Vince, either one of us could write the rest of this script. I know what family planning procedures you object to. I know what my patients need. Sometimes there's a conflict between your morality and my medicine. We know all this. Why go through the agony of arguing about it?"

"You went to a parochial school. You came from a good Catholic home. How dare you question these matters! This is not *my* morality we're talking about; it's the moral stance of our Catholic Church!"

"I was a kid. Sure I learned—and believed—what the nuns and priests taught us. I'm an adult now. I can think for myself. And I can read about a Cardinal who thinks it's wrong for a man to wear a condom to prevent communicable diseases—even if it's a gay man. As if a condom has some sort of morality in and of itself!"

This was going nowhere, just as Lucy had anticipated. Vincent decided to drop the bomb.

"Lucy, we can get back to these 'procedures,' as you call them, later. Let's talk about something we can at least agree on: abortion."

"If we must."

"I hope—and I pray—that you can deny this. I've heard that you perform abortions in a clinic that deals in such things."

"Did your informant tell you I have a policy of not performing the procedure after the first trimester?"

"What difference does that make?"

"A lot . . . to me . . . and to lots of people in the medical community—"

"That's not a wart that's growing in a pregnant woman!"

"It's a zygote."

"It's a human being."

"Come on . . . it's two cells, for God's sake!"

"For God's sake, indeed! You're killing a person."

"Vince, with the union of a sperm and an egg there's something that, left alone and with no trauma, will develop into a fully human being. I believe that happens during pregnancy. When? I'm not so sure. From the beginning, the multiplying cells will develop into a person. So, from fertilization to some point in the pregnancy only the most compelling reason can justify terminating. I believe it would be wrong to induce an abortion after that point unless there was some medical necessity . . . such as an ectopic pregnancy."

"And you can terminate up to three months. Why not six? Eight?"

"After very long and serious study and consideration, three months seems right. Besides, Vince, the Church wants it both ways: You won't prevent a pregnancy and you can't terminate one."

"Of course pregnancy can be prevented: rhythm and abstinence."

"One is by no means foolproof and the other is unrealistic. Add to that, mistakes happen."

Silence. Vincent studied his sister. She did not turn away.

"You won't change, will you?" he said finally.

She shook her head, firmly.

"I don't know whether you're aware of it, but you are excommunicated."

"What?"

"Anyone who performs an abortion, causes one, or provides needed assistance for one is automatically excommunicated."

"What a terrible thing to say!" Lucy stood. "You may leave!"

"I can't—"

"You . . . may . . . leave!"

Vincent stood. "I'll pray for you."

He didn't need to don his clerical collar and vest; he hadn't taken them off. Without further word, he left.

Tears flowed freely. Lucy loved her Church. She had turned down marriage proposals from two men. Not because she was not compatible with either of them, but because they were antagonistic to everything her Church meant to her.

She could not believe her Church would turn against her because of a prayerful and painful decision she had made—a decision that represented the best effort of her conscience.

She did not know where to turn.

Shaken, after some thought, she dialed a number.

＊　　＊　　＊

"Father, this is Lucy Delvecchio. I hope I'm not interrupting anything. I've got to talk to you."

Koesler detected the distress in her voice. "No, go ahead. What's the problem?"

She gave a detailed account of her just completed discussion with her brother. "I think he's wrong, Father," she concluded. "But I've got to know . . . and I trust you. Am I . . . am I excommunicated?"

Lucy did not hurry the pause that followed her very personal question.

It was well that she didn't. Koesler needed to think about this one.

Vince, as usual, had given a textbook decision based on institutional legalism. It was the Vatican line. But the Vatican generally is tardy when it comes to keeping up with the ever more rapid developments in theology as they are nurtured by theologians, priests, and laity. The most recent exception was when Pope John XXIII called for an ecumenical council and the reform of Canon Law. In this directive, a Pope was way ahead of everyone else in charting a new course for the Church.

But that was a singular event.

The present Church law was clear: In the 1917 Code, under which the Vatican currently operated, the Church held that any and all involved in the deliberate and successful effort to eject a nonviable fetus from the mother's womb incur automatic excommunication.

But what Vince had forgotten—or decided not to include—was a strange paradox in Church doctrine, to wit: That, on the one hand, Catholics must respect the teaching authority of the Church, yet, on the other hand, Catholics must follow their well-formed consciences.

After weighing the pros and cons, Koesler decided to level with his young friend. But he would do so in gradual steps. There were a couple of relevant questions he was pretty sure Vincent hadn't asked.

"Okay, Lucy, did you know there was a special penalty attached to the sin of abortion?"

Silence. "I guess I felt some guilt," she said slowly. "But that was because I knew the Church condemned it."

"You went through twelve years of parochial school and never heard of automatic excommunication for abortion?"

"If they taught that, it must've gone in one ear and out the other. I guess I just never considered that I would be involved with an abortion."

"That takes care of one phase. If the Church attaches a penalty to a sin, the person has to know about the penalty—in this case excommunication—before he or she can incur the penalty. So, you're not excommunicated. That would be a very ancient interpretation of Church law," he explained parenthetically, "way back before my time in the seminary. Actually, excommunication is not as bad as it sounds; usually it requires only a slightly different way of confessing a sin to be absolved."

"Okay." She felt more relieved than she should have.

"Now, let's consider whether or not you've actually been committing a sin. You told Vince that you studied and prayed over this matter . . . right?"

"Yes."

"So you knew that the Church's 'official' position was that from the moment of conception a fertilized egg is considered a person. Right?"

"Then . . . ?"

"I just wasn't convinced that the Church was realistically facing the problem."

"What problem?"

"As to when distinctively human life begins."

"So . . . ?"

"So I read everything I could get my hands on. Talked to everyone I could—pro-life and pro-choice. Considered what I saw under my microscope. I was convinced that human life begins long before normal delivery. But when? Certainly not in those early cells dividing and multiplying.

"I think what finally threw me into the end of the first trimester was St. Thomas Aquinas."

"Aquinas?"

"He taught that a fetus was invested with a human soul at the time of 'quickening'—the end of the first trimester.

"Then I prayed like mad over it. It was as if I were tortured. Not about the conclusion I reached . . . but whether I would act on that conclusion.

"Finally, I decided I had to act."

"So, after study and prayer, you found your conscience differed from Church teaching. You followed your conscience. Which, oddly, is also what the Church teaches: that one must follow one's carefully formed conscience. Is that what happened?"

"Yes!" He could not see her vigorous nod.

"Let me pose a hypothetical question, Lucy. If you were dying now, and you were making your final confession, would you confess to having carried out any abortion procedures?"

She paused, thinking. "I don't think I would . . ." she said finally,

". . . unless I was scared and wanted to touch all bases. But . . ." She considered further. ". . . really, no," she said firmly. "Confession is for absolution from sin . . . and having gone over it in my mind, and after all the thought, prayer, and consideration I've given it, I don't believe I'm committing a sin in this regard."

"Then I'd have to agree with you: You are following a carefully prepared conscience.

"But you must be extremely cautious about performing an abortion—even in the first trimester. Only the most compelling reason can be sufficient for such an intervention." Koesler paused for a moment. "I think your use of the clinic should be most rare. After all, a zygote's sole purpose is to be human. So only the most compelling possible concern should be allowed to interrupt its development."

"You're right, Father. I will watch that carefully." It was said in a measured tone, as if taking a vow.

"But"—her voice lightened—"you don't know how good you've made me feel. Now, what do I do with Vinnie?"

"Leave it. Maybe someday we'll get a chance to talk it over, just he and I. I know where he's coming from. But in this case the question is the supremacy of conscience."

Still, Koesler hesitated. He was loath to leave it at that. It was not all that simple. "But," he said, after a moment, "we can't afford to get smug about this. At this stage we're muddling through at best. Every abortion is sad. Most of them are tragic . . . and every one of them is the end of a living thing. You know that and I know that. And someplace in this procedure, there is sin. Serious sin. Our Church is not teaching infallibly here. But, it is teaching. Add to that, we—you and I—are not infallible. We're trying to reach a tolerable compromise. Because we need to.

"For now, I can tell you two things: You're not excommunicated. And you listened to our Church reverently and you prayerfully formed your conscience. And now you're following your conscience. You— we—may be wrong. But you are not committing a sin."

"Thank you!" Never were these words more sincerely meant.

*   *   *

After he hung up, Koesler continued to think.

Not all that long ago, defining an actual time of death was of little practical value. There are, of course, incontrovertible signs that death has occurred. But there was no general agreement as to the exact moment of death. Then medicine and religion combined to agree that the cessation of brain function—as evidenced by the flat line—marked the moment of death. Then came organ transplants, and with them the need to know the exact instant the donor organ was available for "harvesting."

In the opinion of Koesler—and many others—a similar criterion was needed to identify and agree upon the time that human life begins. The need was unquestionably there. But the problem polarized the concerned parties. One must be pro-choice—holding that human life begins at birth—or pro-life, holding that human life begins at the first moment of conception.

Neither side had so far been able to prove its point convincingly enough to reach any sort of agreement with the other.

Conscience, he pondered, what a tricky concept.

Dissenters from the supremacy-of-conscience theory frequently point triumphantly to the occasional murderer, thief, or traitor, and mockingly cite such wrongdoers' claims that they were only following their conscience. But the people committing such acts are plainly sick people with sick consciences.

The conscience that must be followed is the "well-formed" conscience.

Such as Lucy's.

Whimsically, Koesler turned to his filing cabinet and pulled the file on "Conscience." It held treatises on abstract theological applications and definitions. There were normal or abnormal consciences, lax or scrupulous, tender or burned out . . . and so on.

Then came the conscience blockbuster.

Pope Paul VI wrote his encyclical "Humanae Vitae." In it, he stated that every act of intercourse must be open to the possibility of conception. And lots of the faithful—including the Pope's own appointed committee—for the first time in their lives disagreed with the ordinary teaching of the Church.

In response to this encyclical, the French bishops wrote, "If these persons [who dissent from "Humanae Vitae"] have tried sincerely but without success to conform to the given directives, they may be assured that by following the course which seems right to them they do so in good conscience."

Of course, thought Koesler, as Henry Higgins of "My Fair Lady" observed, "The French don't care what they do, actually, as long as they pronounce it correctly."

But if the French bishops were not convincing, there is the testimony of far more conservative American bishops: "There exists in the Church a lawful freedom of inquiry and of thought, and also general norms of licit dissent. . . . In the final analysis, conscience is inviolable and no person is to be forced to act in a manner contrary to his or her conscience, as the moral tradition of the Church attests."

The final document in Koesler's file was, as far as he was concerned, the clincher. It was from Vatican II's Pastoral Constitution:

"Conscience is the most secret core and sanctuary of the person. . . . Where one is alone with God, and there in one's innermost self perceives God's voice."

"Alone with God" says it all.

Lucy Delvecchio studied, queried, then prayed, before dissenting from official Church teaching. Now she is alone with God. She perceives no sin. She sleeps tranquilly.

*　　*　　*

The Koesler conscience is not that untroubled. For him, contraception is one thing, abortion another. But he has not seen nor studied what Lucy has.

He fixed himself a gin and tonic.

He would drink to conscience.

27

It did not take long for Merl Goldbaum's prediction to become fact.

It was a slower than usual news day. The city desk was floating in a sea of lazy tranquility. Things did seem to be moving right along. But, as W. S. Gilbert once wrote, "Things are seldom what they seem."

In late morning, the city editor beckoned to one of his reporters who was not in the running for an Oscar for his portrayal of a busy newsman.

"There's a pro-choice rally at Cobo Hall this weekend. We've got that covered, but we need some sidebars. Go dig up some abortion clients and get their comments on how they were treated—their reaction to the whole thing. Be sure to get the date of the procedure so we can do a graph on whether things are getting better or worse." Such a setup was hardly a scientific approach—but, what the hell . . .

"You want me to do a customer survey on abortion clinics?" The reporter tried to make the assignment sound ridiculous. He didn't want to do the story.

"Yeah."

"Where am I supposed to find these broads . . . at least the ones who'll talk for the record?"

"That's why we pay you such a lavish salary: so you can put together simple stories like this." The reporter was dismissed with a get-outta-here gesture.

How the hell was he supposed to find somebody who used an abortion clin— Wait: His wife's friend had a cleaning woman who'd had an abortion . . .

A few phone calls nailed it down. He would interview Loretta.

*   *   *

"So what was the worst part of the procedure?"

"There wasn't no wors' part. They treated me good. Course, I was only six weeks along."

"Okay . . ." That sort of quote would not interest the reader or, more important, please the editor. "What was the best part of the procedure?"

Loretta brightened. "Oh, the doctor. She was so nice. She stayed with me all the way through. She kept telling me what was gonna happen and that I wasn't gonna suffer none. And I didn't!" she finished triumphantly.

"What was this doctor's name?"

"It was Dr. Delvecchio. Bless her."

Delvecchio . . . Delvecchio. Why was that name familiar? There was a Delvecchio way back in the original six-team pro hockey league. For Detroit. For the Red Wings. In the Detroit Red Wings' dynasty years. Gordie Howe, Ted Lindsay, Sid Abel, and Alex Delvecchio. Could this doctor possibly be a relative of Alex?

Wait . . . there was another Delvecchio who was famous for something or other. Yeah, a football player. A pro. Some years back. Let's see . . . he had a brother, didn't he? A Father—no, a monsignor. A Catholic priest whose brother was a pro football player.

And they had . . . a sister . . . yeah, a sister who was . . . a doctor! A Catholic priest and his sister the abortion doctor—oh, please, God, make Dr. Delvecchio be the sister of Monsignor Delvecchio!

His prayer, of course, had been answered retroactively.

Then, the good times rolled.

The editor was ecstatic. Forget the pro-choice rally. Forget Russia and nuclear bombs. Go get the priest and his sister.

The archdiocesan director of communications held news conferences. The archbishop referred questions to the director of communications. Monsignor Delvecchio returned barely two of every ten calls. Lucy Delvecchio used the language of her conversation with Koesler to respond to questions. Monsignor Delvecchio, putting two and two together, guessed that Lucy had spoken to Father Koesler. Delvecchio promised himself that he would even that score one day.

Meanwhile, PR expert Merl Goldbaum sat back, read the papers, watched TV, listened to the radio, and shook his head. He should've taken the lead—cut them off at the pass.

The story played itself out over a five-day period. But the media made the most of it while it lasted.

The Present

"That's why I have a hard time imagining that you didn't hear about this at the time," Father Koesler said.

Father Tully shook his head. "It does sort of ring a bell now that you mention it. But if I heard about it at all, I probably passed it off with something approaching relief—sort of, There but for the grace of God go I."

"Well, it was no picnic for the brass of this archdiocese. I wouldn't be at all surprised if that 'scandal,' if I may call it that, might have further delayed Delvecchio's promotion to bishop. And it could be what's keeping him from becoming an Ordinary."

Tully, having called the shot, sank the eight ball. He won. "Another game?"

"Why not?"

Tully racked the balls and motioned Koesler in for the break. Once more, balls were spread all over the table, but nothing fell.

Tully sank a solid and another game was under way.

"I'm in the same position as that reporter who broke the story about the monsignor and the abortion doctor," Tully said. "I know Delvecchio has a brother. I remember Tony as a player—but he's more familiar as a sports commentator. But I didn't know about his sister. What's happened to her?"

"Oh, she's still in town. Still working in the ER at Receiving Hospital."

"How about the clinic?"

"She had to give that up. Before the story broke, no one paid much attention to the little building. It helped the anonymity of the place that it was located in a nondescript neighborhood near downtown.

"But after the news got out, a whole team of protesters and pickets descended on the clinic. It wasn't safe for Lucy to go down there.

"But Lucy and I are still friends. Maybe sometime we can have lunch," Koesler suggested, "just the three of us."

"That would be nice." Tully chalked his cue. "We could have it here at St. Joe's . . . that is, if I can get by her brother and take over this parish officially."

"Oh, I'm sure you will."

Actually, after dissecting Vince's personality and MO this evening, Koesler was not all that sure of a happy outcome.

Tully, on a run, was now studying his shots more carefully. "I was wondering"—he straightened up—"as you were telling that story: Do you think Delvecchio knew his sister had talked to you?"

"I don't know. Not for sure. He's never brought it up. And there have been occasions when he could have. But he's never mentioned it."

"You'd think he'd have tumbled to it. I mean, you've been so close to that family; it would have been natural for her to turn to you."

"I guess."

Tully laughed. "Maybe he's taking it out on me instead of you."

Koesler did not laugh. On the contrary, he grew more thoughtful.

"That," Tully continued, "leaves only Delvecchio's brother to be accounted for."

"And his aunt Martha."

"Oh, yeah, the aunt. But the brother . . . that relationship fascinates me. I mean, I get the impression that they were never very close . . . were they?"

"Not to my knowledge. But compared with the space between them now, they could have been the best of buddies as kids."

"Deteriorated, has it?"

"Disintegrated," Koesler said emphatically. "It's really a shame what's happened between those two. And it's almost totally Vince's fault."

"Really?" It was Tully's turn to shoot. Instead, he sat on the arm of one of the chairs. Evidently, he would rather hear the story of the brothers Delvecchio than shoot pool.

Koesler laid down his cue. But instead of being seated, he began to pace. "We've already talked about Tony's big plans. A pro football player, retiring from that into broadcasting.

"Then came reality. No team took him in 1959. So he followed the example of a few other players and joined the Canadian Football League. He was sensational in his first year. His performance grabbed the interest of the NFL. He went to the Chicago Bears. He and another quarterback alternated, and while Tony didn't set any records, he held up his end.

"Eventually, he was traded to Detroit, where in his waning years he was the backup quarterback.

"With the Lions, the big thing was he was the hometown kid come home. He was a native Detroiter and the fans loved him for it.

"By the time Tony retired from the field, the number of teams had mushroomed. Television was using more and more former players for either play-by-play or as color announcers. That's when Tony got his big chance. First the networks and then the sponsors discovered how articulate and funny he could be. One thing led to another and Tony also became a high-priced pitchman for a whole bunch of products advertised on TV.

"It was as if Tony's ship had come in: Everything seemed to be going his way."

"Sounds good to me," Tully said.

"Yeah, it does. But when it came to Vince and Tony, fate played some funny tricks. This, I think, was the most tragic relationship of them all."

"I remember Tony's playing days," Tully said. "And I see him on TV during the season, but I don't really know anything else about him. You mentioned a young woman—when he was about to graduate from college. Did they marry?"

Koesler almost winced. "No. And that's what gave Vinnie his opening."

1985

"'Samatter, babe?"

Beth Larson looked about her. "What could possibly be wrong surrounded by the ambience of the Lindell A.C., with Wayne Walker's jockstrap on the wall?"

"It's bronzed."

"Oh, that makes it all the more aesthetic."

"C'mon now," Tony Delvecchio pleaded. "Don't go and ruin my night."

Tony and Beth were seated at a table in the Lindell A.C., downtown Detroit's quintessential jock beefeatery and watering hole—one of whose claims to fame was the now bronzed athletic supporter presented by Detroit Lions linebacker Wayne Walker upon his retirement from football.

Tonight there was another celebration. Tony Delvecchio's jersey, "Old Number 28," was going to be hung in the bar. Tony would never be elected to the Pro Football Hall of Fame. Nor would his number be retired by either the Bears or the Lions. But, for a time at least, it would be on exhibit in the Lindell A.C.

This was Tony's crowd. Probably there was little reason for anyone to patronize the Lindell A.C. if one were not wildly in love with sports. It served its clientele well.

It held little attraction for Beth. She was here solely for Tony's sake and the honor being paid him.

The presentation had been made minutes ago. Things were returning to normal: arguments over statistics, bets on sports trivia, recollections of yesteryear's heroics.

"Can't we go yet?" Clearly, Beth was bored.

"In a little bit." Tony's brow knitted. "I'd think this place was beginning to reach you except that you've been like this for . . . what?— three, four weeks? What's the problem?"

She picked up the sweating glass that held her gin and tonic and began making wet circles on the table. "You know the punchline, 'It's the whole damn thing'?"

"Yeah . . . ?"

"Well, that's what's wrong: the whole damn thing."

"That doesn't give me much to go on."

She put the glass down and caught his eyes in her gaze. "We've been together for twenty-six years. Over a quarter of a century. And aside from setting some sort of record for living together without benefit of clergy, what have we got to show for it?"

"Lotsa good times. Lotsa good memories. And . . ." He shook his head. ". . . some that weren't so good."

"Couldn't just about anybody say that?"

"So what's so bad about it?"

"Tony, we should be grandparents by now. And we've never even had a kid. We could've had some really close friends. Where are they?"

"What do you call the people we chum around with? How 'bout"—his gaze swept around the room, then back to her—"the folks here tonight?"

"Jocks . . . and jocks' wives. Look at the configuration: We're the only couple sitting together. The men are hanging around the bar. The women are off by themselves. I know this happens at most gatherings, but at the parties we give—and go to—the separation of the sexes happens immediately—almost the minute they walk in. I know you know that there's a world out there. But the rest of these guys—their world stops at the locker room door."

"Honey, *I'm* a jock! It's just natural that we hang together. But it doesn't have to be like this. If you want to, we can pal around with some of the folks from your law firm . . . although," he joked, "I got the impression you see enough of them during the week." He realized she wasn't sharing the joke. "Look, hon, at this stage in our lives, we can be with anyone we want. I'm just not at all sure a lot of the people in our tax bracket would be all that interesting."

"That's not it!" Her voice took on a tone of annoyance. "It's . . ."

"I know: the whole damn thing. Well," he said, after a moment, "there must be something we can do to get things off Square One."

She toyed with her glass again. "Well, I have been thinking of something . . ."

"What?" *Tell-me-what-it-is-and-I'll-get-it-for-you,* his tone said.

"Religion."

He laughed so heartily that the level of conversational noise in the bar dropped abruptly. When the others noted that Beth was not laughing, but rather was flushed, they returned to their chatter. But not as loudly as before.

"What field did that come out of?"

"I've been thinking about your heritage. All your people are—were—

Catholic. You attended parochial school. Your sister goes to Mass. My God, your brother's just been made a bishop. But you haven't gone to church since your mother's funeral. Why?"

"Hypocrites."

"Hypocrites? I beg your pardon?"

"The once-a-week churchgoers. They stab everyone in the back, pull the carpet out from under everyone. Lie, cheat, steal. Then they get pious on Sunday. They think that makes them holy . . . that it makes the lousy tricks they pulled between church visits okay. And Catholics are maybe the worst. I don't know why . . . maybe 'cause they've got confession to really clean things up."

"You're talking 'they' and 'them.' You're not a Catholic anymore?"

He slid down in his chair. "Once a Catholic, always a Catholic—that's what the nuns and priests drummed into our little heads. And"—he pushed himself upright again—"I wouldn't argue: I'm a Catholic, I guess. But I'd hardly say I was practicing it."

"Would you object to my looking into it?"

"What? Catholicism? If it'll make you happy—whatever you want, babe. How're you gonna do this?"

"I thought I'd get in touch with our pastor."

"'Our' pastor! We got a pastor?"

"I've done a little investigating."

"Oh, so this bit about religion didn't come right off the top of your pretty head!"

She ignored his gibe. "We live in St. Waldo of the Hills parish . . . that is, we live within its boundaries."

"And our pastor?"

"You aren't going to believe this . . ."

"I won't believe it? Then I'd guess it would be my old buddy Father Koesler."

"Close. But much closer than that."

He looked at her expectantly.

"Our pastor is Bishop Delvecchio." Disregarding his startled expression, she went on. "I think it says a lot about your interest in your faith that you don't even know where your brother went after he became a bishop."

"This is spooky." Clearly, Tony was impressed.

"I thought so too. But spooky or not, what do you think?"

"There's something about this that rings all the wrong bells."

"I really feel strongly about it, Tony."

She was drumming her fingers on the tabletop—always a sign that she was about to become emotional. Her emotional outbursts confused him. He had never learned how to deal with them.

"Well," he said at length, "I guess it couldn't hurt to look into it."

She brightened. "Great! I really think this will do wonders for us. I feel I want to get involved in a church group. We need more meaning in our lives."

"Yeah. Sure."

∗   ∗   ∗

It was ten days since Tony's jersey had been hung in the Lindell A.C. Not another word about this religion business had been uttered.

Tony was quite satisfied with the status quo. He did not need another word. Beth had another word, but was waiting for the appropriate time.

Dinner tonight featured lamb chops, Tony's favorite.

It was coffee and dessert time.

Now.

"Honey, I saw your brother, the bishop, the other day." Actually, she had made an appointment and called on him the day after their talk at the A.C.

Tony's brow knitted. "If you saw Vinnie, 'the other day' and you've waited this long to tell me about it, the news can't be all that good."

"It's good news and bad news."

"And you're going to start with the good news, like you always do."

She smiled. "I can respect the bishop. I think I can trust him too. And it looks like this religious experience is what I've been looking for."

He toyed nervously with his spoon. His coffee sat half drunk, his dessert half eaten. "Seeing that all the good news happened to you, I'd guess the bad news is mine."

She began drumming on the tabletop. "Well, what the bishop said about us seemed to make a lot of sense—"

"How come you keep addressing him as 'bishop'?"

"That's what I started out calling him, and he never suggested that I use any other title or name."

"Okay, so what about us?"

"The bishop said that we couldn't overlook the obvious: We've never been married."

"I'm not Frank Gifford and you're not Kathy Lee. Our private lives are private. Did you volunteer our marital status?"

"The bishop asked if we had been married in a civil or a religious ceremony. I told him neither."

"Okay. So then?" Tony was picking up threatening vibes.

"The bishop said he didn't think he was anticipating anything that wouldn't be covered later in the instructions, but the fact that we never married in any legal manner meant we were living in sin."

Tony's furrows grew deeper.

"The bishop said it didn't make any sense that I would be taking instructions—and thus agreeing that you and I are living in sin—without doing something about our situation."

"Oh? What's he want us to do: Get a divorce when we've never been married?"

"This is the tough part, Tony. Please . . . just remember how much I want to at least find out about this. And the bishop is trying to make this Church rule as easy on us as he can—"

"I can hardly wait to find out what comes next."

Beth swallowed what seemed to be an indigestible plea. "The bishop wants us to promise not to have intercourse during the time I'm taking the instructions." She figuratively ducked.

The fork Tony had been handling bent in half.

"Now, please, wait a minute, honey," she pleaded. "They have a regular convert class that runs all through Lent and ends at Easter. The bishop offered to give me private instructions. He said he'll do it himself because you're special to him."

Tony snorted.

"The bishop promised he would hurry things along. Your agreement—consent—is all that stands between me and my finding out if this is what I'm looking for."

Silence.

"How long for the instructions?" Tony asked finally.

"Three, four months at the most."

"Brother and sister . . ." Tony almost laughed.

"What?"

"That's at least what they used to call this crazy arrangement: brother-and-sister relationship. That's what Aunt Martha and Uncle Frank had to promise while the Church fooled around with their lives."

"Frank? Your uncle who committed suicide?"

Tony nodded.

She was silent for several moments. "Four months at the maximum," she said finally. ". . . maybe it'll be more like three."

Tony moved his chair and leaned forward so his face was inches from hers. She had tears in her eyes that refused to run down her cheeks.

"Sweetheart, I don't know what all professional jocks did about sex. But there was a lot of pressure . . . and a lot of opportunity. We were on the road so much. And there were groupies and desirable women in every city . . . at every stop. Having sex for a jock was the easiest thing in the world.

"But I can tell you straight to your face: I never fell. I never cheated on you. Part of that was because I respect you so much. And part was because you are always here for me. You seem to enjoy sex as much as I do."

She nodded vigorously.

"And we've just never had a problem with that. For that, I'm grateful . . . and I guess you are too.

"But I've got to tell you at the outset that I don't know if I can make it that long."

She was certain this abstinence would hurt her as much as it would him. But it was she who had the motivation. The carrot at the end of the stick was for the lady.

"Honey . . ."—she laid her hand on his arm—"I'm sure the bishop meant that we should give this arrangement our best effort. I'm sure the Church allows for a slip . . ."

"And," he replied, "I'm sure your friend the bishop doesn't have room in his meticulous life for messups."

Tony thought for a few moments. "Okay," he said finally. "Okay, I'll agree for one reason and one reason only: because you want so badly to give Catholicism a try. But I warn you: When I agree to a contract, I intend to keep it."

Ignoring her grateful expression, he asked, "So, now what? Is there some sort of form I've got to sign?"

She smiled. "The bishop trusts me. He said if I showed up for instructions it would mean that you had agreed to those conditions."

He smiled mirthlessly. "So, big brother trusts me. There's a switch!"

"What is there between you two? Is it because you went into athletics and he went into religion? You yourself told me he was brilliant—I think you said he was a genius . . . is that it?"

"It's the whole damn thing."

They both smiled.

"There have been studies," Tony said reflectively, "of siblings who don't get along. That was Vinnie and me. He set the scene in school by achieving—setting standards I could only approach, but never equal— well, at least not often. We competed constantly—in school and out. The only thing I could beat him at consistently was sports.

"It didn't help our relationship that *he* was the one who was fulfilling Mama's dearest wish: that one of her sons would become a priest. I think, at the end, she knew he would be a bishop some day . . .

"And then, when she was dying . . ." He seemed to look into the distance, then shook himself, as if throwing off the past. "Just remember as we go through this, hon, I said old Vinnie was brilliant; I didn't say he was human."

Starting that evening, Tony slept in the guest room. He did not reflect that his uncle Frank had followed the same course many years before.

28

Murphy's Law prevailed. If four months of abstinence was the worst possible scenario, that's how it would play out: Three months segued into four as the instruction lessons dragged on.

Tony's lifestyle for the past three months had been monastic. It had not been a rose garden. But at least the pro season hadn't yet begun, so he didn't have to accompany the teams on the circuit.

He had plenty of time—too much time—on his hands. Under normal circumstances he would have solved this problem by reading, or visiting with friends, or with exercise.

But he grew so fixated on his nonsexual state that it became impossible to concentrate on any book. He grew increasingly fidgety and quarrelsome in the company of friends. With no other outlet, more and more he fell back on exercise—lots of exercise. But there was a limit even to that. There he was, in the full vigor of healthy virility . . .

He was now close to peak condition physically—to the extent that he was nearly in shape to join the players. But he was not foolish enough to try.

Increasingly during the past three months, Tony had stayed away from home as much as possible. Particularly on those nights he was "out with the boys," he tried to return after Beth's normal bedtime. He had given his word, and he would keep it. But he didn't have to make it any more difficult than it already was.

Particularly on those evenings when they dined together, he got a refresher course in basic Catholic teaching.

For one thing, he was being "bishoped" to death. Apparently, Beth seemed incapable of pronouncing Vince's name without prefixing his title. And, apparently, the bishop did nothing to dissuade her from what had become ingrained.

Tony was somewhat surprised at what Vinnie was teaching Beth.

Tony was a voracious reader. And although he was not much interested in religious news, he was aware of the Second Vatican Council and some of its effects on Catholics.

As far as he could tell, a liberal wing had formed as a result of the Council. He had no idea of its numbers nor of its strength. But it seemed to be waging a blitzkrieg on an entrenched conservative force.

Tony had no intention of enlisting in either camp. But if he were forced to choose, from what little he knew of each, he found himself leaning toward the left.

And there the question would undoubtedly have stood—with no participation on his part—had not Beth committed herself to these instructions.

As these sessions continued, and as Beth reported what she was learning, he found himself more and more paying attention. It seemed that he had heard these things before. Could these doctrines, these moral laws, be the ones he'd learned in parochial school? Indeed, they could be.

As Beth recounted what she was learning, she might as well have been one of the nuns, brothers, or priests who had drummed these teachings into Anthony Delvecchio's young head.

Satan held sway in the world. Thus the world was a threat, a threat to our immortal souls. We had to have a guide to lead us in safe passage through the world, the flesh, and the devil.

That guide is Holy Mother Church. The Church had guaranteed indefectibility as well as, occasionally, infallibility. From this came laws and rules. There was a distinct comfort in abiding by these laws and rules in that this would give us a safe journey through temptations and blandishments.

That was about the way Tony remembered it from school. The law said Catholics must not eat meat on Fridays. When Catholics observed that law, they were justified. The law said Catholics must attend Mass on Sundays. When Catholics did this, they were justified. The law said Catholics must support their parish. When they did this, they were justified.

It was all very comforting and reassuring. Did you wish to go to heaven? The Church, in the person of the Pope, the bishop, and/or the priest, told you exactly how to get there.

To borrow again from W. S. Gilbert, you did not have to think for yourself at all—just obey.

It all came back to Tony quite clearly. From what little interest he'd had in what was going on currently, he believed this is what the altercation was about.

The other side held that the Pope was the tour guide, not the captain, of the Bark of Peter. The Church, in the person of Pope, bishop, priest, theologians, etc., could be a unique aid in helping each Catholic form his or her individual conscience. But the ultimate responsibility for conscience formation and conscience following rested with the individual Catholic.

There was much more to what was going on . . . that Tony sensed. He regretted that he hadn't paid more and closer attention to the evolution of his Church over the decades he'd been "away."

What was obvious—and exceedingly clear—was that Vinnie was giving unadulterated pre-Council instructions to Beth and she was conforming to this school of thought like a compliant student to a persuasive instructor. For Beth, it was like becoming aware of Beethoven, Mozart, or Gershwin late in life and wondering where they'd been hiding all along.

To have someone other than herself making rules and decisions seemed to Beth to be the perfect way to go through life en route to heaven.

Tony had just come to the realization of what was happening to Beth when, at the end of the fourth month, she dropped the bomb.

*　　*　　*

She had prepared lamb chops and secured his promise that he would be home for dinner. He knew Something Was Up. Exactly what would have to await her good pleasure.

Once again, over coffee and dessert, Beth made an announcement.

She had completed the instruction phase of this program. The four-month period was over.

Tony thought this great news. Perhaps this meal was a celebration. But if so, it was not Beth's usual MO.

She said that having finished the instructions, she had decided to become Catholic. This, after having heard her running commentary of the instructions, came as no surprise to Tony.

She would not need to be baptized. She had been baptized Lutheran but the Catholic Church recognized the baptism of other Christian denominations.

That was a surprise to Tony. That had not been part of his parochial classes. In his day, converts were rebaptized "just in case" the prior effort lacked something for validity.

So there would be a simple ceremony and Beth would become Catholic.

Tony could tell from the slight tremor in her voice that Beth was about to put this evening in perspective.

Having carefully prepared to become Catholic, now she was about to enter a new phase. She—and Tony for that matter—were going to prepare for marriage.

"Prepare for marriage!" Tony laughed heartily. "Don't our twenty-six years of living together count for anything?"

"Not as far as the sacrament of matrimony is concerned," Beth explained.

"Okay, okay . . ." Tony got control of himself. "What next?"

"We have to make a preparation for marriage. It's a prayerful time when we talk with people who are trained to guide us through this preparation."

"Crazy! We could probably help *them*."

"We've got to do it, Tony. It's a Church regulation. I'm about to become a Catholic now. And I have to go through with this. And so do you."

Tony stood up and leaned against the chair. "I know you. I know you like a book I've read over and over. There's more. You're just coming to the heart of this thing. Go ahead: Drop the other shoe."

She wet her lips with her tongue. "We've got to live apart for six months."

His mouth dropped open. "You mean they expect us to extend this brother-sister crap for six more months?! Making a total of ten months for me to be wanting you!"

Beth's face showed that her spirit was wincing. But she went gamely on. "Tony, the way the bishop explained it, the problem is the number of marriages that break up. It used to be that Catholics stayed together. Now as many Catholic marriages end in divorce as those of any other religious denomination."

Tony's face was stony.

"The Church is trying to stem the tide," Beth plowed on. "The Church in the United States grants a phenomenal number of annulments. These steps—the preparation—and the living apart, if the couple is already living together—are intended to help the couple, calmly and sensibly, unemotionally consider what they can expect and bring to their life together." She looked at him imploringly.

"Don't"—Tony was almost sputtering—"don't you see how ridiculous this is? We didn't have a clown around to give us a paper. That's all we lacked; other than that, we've been married for twenty-six years. *Twenty-six years!* Now we're supposed to get instructions from people who would be lucky to stay married as long as we have. And I'm supposed to find a place to flop for six months! Honey, our marriage has been as good as marriage gets—up until this very moment!"

He turned and stood, back to her, shaking his head as if it were leaden.

"Tony . . . I'm halfway across the bridge." Beth was pleading abjectly. "Help me get all the way! Please." Her voice sank. "Please . . ."

He turned back and stared at her as if seeing her for the first time. "I'll be out for a while," he said finally. He wheeled about and left. He didn't even slam the door.

From that moment on, she knew, though she tried to deny, that what had been a lifetime commitment was no more. Tony would not budge—she knew he wouldn't. She would have to choose between Tony and her newfound faith.

*　　*　　*

Tony drove aimlessly, not knowing where to turn. Then, in an inspired moment, he pulled off the road and placed a phone call.

257

*   *   *

I'm batting a thousand, thought Father Koesler. First—years ago—it had been Vincent Delvecchio asking to go to confession. Then, years later, Lucy had phoned to get some help in conscience formation. Now it was Anthony who wanted to see him. That took care of the last Delvecchio sibling. Something had to be pretty important for a non-churchgoer like Tony to want to talk to a priest.

Koesler answered the door. Tony seemed to be all right. But when the two were seated in the rectory living room, it became apparent that the younger man was deeply shaken.

Koesler listened as Tony told the complete story. Meeting and falling in love with Beth. Their setting up housekeeping. His mother's death. His loss of faith; his abandoned church attendance. The good years of football, celebrity, an announcing course. And always Beth and their deepening love. Then her need for "something more" and her attraction to Catholicism. And then, in great detail, the instructions given her by his brother. The four-month brother-sister relationship. Now the demand of six more months.

"Those are the essentials, Father. To be honest"—he looked at Koesler steadily—"I don't think you priests understand what being married is all about. To expect a married man—well, almost any man except a priest—to go ten months without sex is . . . well . . . unrealistic, to say the least."

When Tony had reached the point in his story spelling out the final six-month abstinence and separation, Koesler's mouth dropped open and stayed open. He now closed his mouth only in order to speak.

"Tony . . ." Koesler stopped and, as if overcome with the enormity of it all, shook his head. After a deep sigh, he continued. "It's true about the statistics involving divorce among Catholics and the skyrocketing of annulments granted. The latest Code of Canon Law orders a better, more complete, more realistic, more thorough preparation for marriage. In this archdiocese, if a couple, usually a young couple, are already living together, there is a directive to, if possible, live separately for six months.

"You see," he explained to Tony's uncomprehending gaze, "the thinking is that young people become infatuated and passionate. Now there's nothing wrong with that. But it seems very clear, and experience supports the view, that this is not sufficient to sustain marriage through the long haul. So when difficulties mount, the young couple with nothing more than mere fascination and passion as a foundation can't hold things together. And so follows divorce, and annulment, and a second marriage that has no better foundation than the first."

Koesler paused for a moment. When he spoke again, his voice, though still firm, had softened.

"But, Tony, the priest has a lot of discretion in this matter. I can't think of a single priest I know who would require separation of you and Beth. In fact, I can't think of a priest who wouldn't convalidate your marriage with no waiting period."

"I can," Tony said dejectedly.

Koesler wanted to be helpful in some practical way. "You can tell Beth what I've told you about the separation requirement. She may be agreeable to talking to me—or just about any prie— no, hold that: If you go to see another priest, better check it out with me first. I can't think of anyone who would be so rigorous, but I don't know everybody. Besides, you might find someone who, while agreeing with what I've told you, wouldn't want to confront a bishop."

Tony assured Koesler he had been a great help. And, as Tony left, Koesler promised to pray for him.

As Tony drove home, he rehearsed what he could say that would move Beth away from his brother and toward sanity. This had better be a moving, convincing argument: His future teetered in the balance.

He let himself in and walked to the dining room. Everything, like a freeze-frame, was exactly as he had left it. Dishes on the table; dessert half eaten; coffee half drunk—and Beth seated just as she had been. Tony was impressed.

He told her he'd been to see Father Koesler and recounted what the priest had said. ". . . so, will you go with me to talk to Father?"

Beth looked at him wearily. "The bishop warned me this might happen . . . even to your going to appeal to Father Koesler." She shook her head. "I can't go to anyone else, Tony. I'm convinced that the bishop is right. There isn't any chance that you . . . ?" She left the sentence unfinished.

Could he? He had to give it one more time around his brain. Was it worth it? Moving out for six months? The alternative was to move out for good. Life without Beth. They would be dead to each other without being buried. Was it worth all that?

He looked long and longingly at his love. She was gone already. The real Beth had disappeared into Vince's peculiar world. Tony had already lost her. All that remained was for him to leave.

"I'll be here tomorrow to pick up my stuff. I'll have our lawyer get in touch with you. Anything you want from our life together, you can have. I won't be back."

Tony turned and left and never looked back.

As the front door closed, Beth collapsed in wrenching sobs.

Tears flowed freely from Tony's eyes as he drove away. Vision obscured, he pulled off the road and wept.

The Present

"Wow!" It was Father Tully's turn to have his mouth drop open. "Delvecchio has his own Church going out at St. Waldo's. I can understand you may prefer people to live apart while they're preparing for marriage . . . *if it is not too inconvenient,*" he added with special emphasis. "But I can't imagine demanding that somebody leave home for six months—only to move back, presumably after those six months.

"And that business of requiring a brother-sister arrangement for the duration of instructions is just plain crazy!"

"Not to Vincent. These policies of his are neither broadcast nor secretive. When a couple shows up at St. Waldo's to arrange for a wedding, they're screened by one of the other priests. If it's not a 'problem' wedding—if it's a straight Catholic marriage with no complications—the associate priest handles it.

"But if there's a hook, like cohabitation, Delvecchio takes it. If they refuse to live apart, they may get married somewhere else— but not at St. Waldo's.

"And," Koesler added, "since it's Vinnie's law, he can—and occasionally does—dispense with it."

Tully's brow raised in wonderment. "But not for his own brother?"

"Not for his own brother!"

"But why not?"

"I have no idea . . ." Koesler began to pace. "You know, Zack, in the course of giving you at least a partial biography of Vincent Delvecchio, I have begun to see him in a different light. Something's knocking at my brain . . . it's like a badly formed mist that's trying to clear up so I can perceive Vincent with a clarity I didn't have before."

"What about Martha?" Tully asked, "the last peg in this story?"

Koesler stopped pacing. "Martha . . ." He shook his head. "Bullheadedness I think, on both their parts. Delvecchio got it into his mind that his aunt caused his mother's cancer by shunning her. And the cancer became fatal when Martha refused reconciliation. Martha, for her part, divorced herself from a Catholic Church that she felt had caused her husband's suici—uh, death." Father Walsh's long-ago doubts again crept in. Koesler shook his head as if to rid his mind of cobwebs.

"Later, Martha married again," he continued. "There were no 'surprises' in this wedding. Depending on who was judging it, Martha was either a widow, or a woman who hadn't had a valid marriage. The man she was marrying was a Catholic and a widower, who, like Martha, was free to marry. But due to Martha's private war with Catholicism, they married before a judge. They moved away and I lost touch with them. I wouldn't be surprised if they had died by now.

"In any case," he concluded, "I don't know anything more about them." He shrugged. "Not a very happy tale, is it?"

"No. And Vince Delvecchio seems to be at the heart of each event in this tragedy."

"Yeah."

The doorbell couldn't be heard in the basement. So the two priests were startled when Mary O'Connor appeared at the door of the meeting room. "Fathers, Bishop Delvecchio is here."

The two men looked at each other. "Well, Zack," Koesler said, "let's go fight the dragon."

"Easy for you to say," Tully replied. "You know," he said, after a moment, "I'm actually trembling."

They climbed the stairs and made their way to the living room, where the bishop awaited.

Bishop Delvecchio was not seated. Instead, he stood in approximately the center of the room.

He was thin to the point of gauntness, with a fragility that brought to mind Pope Pius XII, though Delvecchio was much taller than the late Pontiff. His black suit seemed of modest material, but the creases could cut paper. A small patch of episcopal red was visible in front, where the clerical collar met the clerical vest. Stretched across his chest was the silver chain of his pectoral cross. His shoes were shiny enough to credit that black patent leather really could reflect up. Neither nature, age, nor use had contributed laugh lines around his mouth or eyes.

The bishop held a large manila envelope. Presumably it contained the papers that would make Father Koesler a Senior Priest.

Suddenly, Koesler's eyes widened, as if the figurative bulb of discovery had lit above his head. "Look, pardon me," he said without preamble to the bishop. "I've got to make a couple of phone calls. I won't be long. Zack will entertain you till I get back."

Father Tully, looking as dumbstruck as if he'd been poleaxed, almost glared at Koesler. "You wouldn't do this to me!" he muttered through clenched teeth. But Koesler was already headed for the door.

As he started down the hall, he heard Tully offering Delvecchio a drink. The bishop declined.

Koesler had no time to commiserate with Tully. He had to make some calls. He prayed he would be able to reach those who were on his mental list. If so, and if the responses were what he expected, this matter might well be wrapped up this very night.

29

As he came up from the basement, Koesler heard angry voices. Concerned, he hastened toward the living room.

The conversation ceased as both men turned toward him.

"Bob," Delvecchio said, "I've had a really ugly day. And"—he glowered at Tully—"this evening has worsened a migraine. I pray you hold me excused. There really isn't any ceremony called for; all I need is to give you this envelope. All the necessary papers are in here. This takes care of everything; all you'll have to do is go talk to the boss. You may arrange that at your mutual convenience."

"Wait," Koesler said. He made no move to accept the proffered envelope. "You and I have to talk. We have to talk tonight. You don't have to stay for the party . . . but, believe me: *We have to talk.*" He put special emphasis on the final four words.

Delvecchio stared at him for several moments. A knowing expression grew into a confrontational gaze. "Okay, Bob. Maybe you're right. Maybe in the middle of a horrendous headache would be a good time for a showdown we've put off too long."

"Let's go to the basement," Koesler said as he gestured toward the door. "We won't be disturbed there." He stood aside to allow the bishop to precede him. As he left the room, Koesler stage-whispered to Tully that they were not to be interrupted.

Tully nodded, but mouthed to Koesler, "This has *not* gone well!"

Koesler nodded understanding and followed Delvecchio downstairs.

They stood on opposite sides of the pool table. Koesler assumed that Delvecchio would fire the first round, if only to get everything off his chest and start to work on losing his headache.

But the bishop, silent, only stood and stared at Koesler malevolently.

"Vince," Koesler said finally, "whatever happened to the kid who had to play the organ during Requiem Masses . . . the kid with the devil-may-care personality . . . the kid who was *fun*?"

"He grew up. He learned that rules are important. And that life is serious business."

"Long as we're talking about rules, how about the Golden Rule?"

"You're a fine one to invoke the rule of doing to others as you'd have them do to you! How would you like it if *your* sister debated you in public on moral theology?"

"I suppose you're referring to Lucy and the abortion question—"

"'Question'? There's no question. Not among Catholics. It's a serious sin. And carries the penalty of excommunication!"

"Of course abortion is a serious matter. But that depends on how one defines abortion. And excommunication? You know as well as I that a person must know beforehand that an ecclesial penalty is attached to a sin before one can incur the penalty."

"And you believe that Lucy didn't know?"

"That's what she said. You just didn't ask her. And you should have."

"You believe she was telling you the truth?"

"Of course I do! I believe she was telling me the truth about not knowing about the penalty *and* about believing that a person, for an adequate reason, could terminate a pregnancy within the first trimester —without sin."

Delvecchio, arm raised, finger pointing at Koesler, said, "You know very well the Church's official stand on abortion!"

"Of course I do. But we're not talking about me; we're dealing with what I believe is *Lucy*'s well-formed conscience."

"Should we have gone along with Hitler's 'well-formed conscience'?"

"Hitler was a homicidal maniac. We're talking about a sane, serious, and conscientious young woman. We're talking about the supremacy of conscience."

"Supremacy of conscience!" Delvecchio spat out the words.

"It is as John Henry Cardinal Newman said . . ." Koesler again invoked one of his favorite epigrams. "'I will drink to infallibility. But first I will drink to conscience.'"

"You're just playing with words!"

"And you were trying to intimidate your sister so she would be on the defensive if and when the media tumbled to the story of the Monsignor and his Sister the Abortion Doctor. But"—Koesler raised his hand in a stop-traffic gesture—"we'll get back to Lucy later.

"Earlier this evening, Zack Tully asked me what made you tick. This as a prelude to taking you on about this Oath and Profession thing.

"In telling him what I knew about you, some questions came to mind. I found some answers in my own experience, as well as from a few phone calls I made here tonight."

At any other time, or to anyone else, the bishop's fish-eye might have been daunting. But Koesler, like a locomotive picking up steam, was not to be sidetracked.

"This steady march of yours to the conservative right wing began with Frank Morris's suicide. You were in complete agreement that he should have no Church funeral, even though he had attended Mass regularly and tried his best to get his marriage 'fixed up.' The denial of Christian burial dumped all the guilt of suicide on Frank. You were involved in this, even if in an innocent way. But you found a rule that absolved you. Rules could be helpful."

Delvecchio looked as if smugly safe in his bunker barricaded by rules.

"But by far the most serious question I had concerned your mother's death."

For the briefest instant, Delvecchio's eyes lost their focus. Then they snapped to attention with a snakelike fixedness.

"Specifically, I wondered about her medication for pain," Koesler said. "The morphine bottle remained untouched even into the midstage of her cancer when she was in considerable pain.

"I asked her about that. She explained that she intended to join her suffering to that of Jesus on the cross. It was a heroic decision. I'm sure I couldn't have carried it off," he added reflectively.

"But after she explained this, I paid no further attention to the bottles at her bedside. You'll recall the doctor wanted her to medicate herself. And so she did."

Delvecchio gazed at Koesler unwaveringly, but wordlessly.

"When she died and the medications were being removed, I noticed the morphine bottle was empty. I assumed the pain had become so unbearable that she had begun taking the morphine. It didn't occur to me what a coincidence it had to be that she had run out of the pills just as she had died. For surely if she had run out of them, she would've asked one of us to get her some more."

Though it was cool in the rectory, especially in the basement, a thin line of perspiration had formed on the bishop's upper lip.

"Then," Koesler continued, "I ran back in my memory the sequence of events as your mother died.

"It was early afternoon and we were taking turns sitting with your mother. I remember you went upstairs. You stayed about twenty minutes. You were followed by your brother. Then he came down and told us he thought she was going. We all went upstairs. She was, indeed, breathing her last. She seemed to be having a most difficult time getting a breath. And then she died.

"One of the calls I just made was to Dr. Moellmann, the medical examiner."

Delvecchio started, then seemed to regain his composure. But so attentive was he that it was as if an electrical current had switched on inside him.

"I presented it as a hypothetical question," Koesler clarified. "I described the bottle containing the morphine and asked if a person took all the pills at one time in a suicide attempt, how long would it take for this person, already near death from cancer, to die?

"He said about twenty minutes—just the length of your visit. Allowing for you to dissolve the tablets and have your mother drink the lethal amount, and for Tony's brief visit, that would pretty much use up the time between your visit to your mother and precipitate her death throes while Tony was with her. "

Then there was her special difficulty breathing. The doctor said that death in such cases is caused by asphyxiation."

Koesler paused. The bishop stood statue-silent, his gaze penetrating.

"Dr. Moellman added," Koesler went on after a moment, "that after all these years there would be no trace left of the morphine in the body."

He paused again. This time he gave no indication that he would continue for the moment.

"That's not the way it was . . ." Delvecchio seemed to have regained total composure. "That's not the way it was at all," he said more firmly.

"How was it?"

"Mother was planning suicide. She wasn't taking her pain pills. She was squirreling away the morphine so that if the pain got to be too much, she could end it. That was obvious."

"Did you ask her about it . . . or talk to her about the morphine?"

"Of course not. It was obvious. She wouldn't have told me the truth if I had asked; she'd be afraid I'd take them away from her."

Koesler shook his head. "You just assumed all that. I talked to her about the pills and, as I told you, she didn't take the pills because she wanted to join her suffering with that of Jesus on the cross."

"What are you saying, Bob?" Delvecchio was now obviously on the verge of losing control.

"What I'm saying is that with a very badly mistaken intention . . . you killed your mother." Koesler made the accusation reluctantly.

"That's where you're wrong," Delvecchio shot back. "It was the indirect voluntary—the double effect. I gave Mother some pills. The immediate effect was to prevent her suicide and save her from hellfire. The secondary effect was her death—which I did not directly want," he added quickly. "My God, I tried to organize a prayer campaign for a miracle that would save her!"

Koesler shook his head again. "Vince, even if you could introduce the double effect principle—which I refute from the outset, since she told me why she wasn't taking the medication, and it was *not* for suicide—it wouldn't qualify. You're torturing the concept. You didn't give her 'pills'; you gave her a lethal overdose of morphine. The first consequence would be her death. Only secondarily would it save her from hell.

"And anyway, she was not headed for hell. She was going to join her Savior, with whom she had already joined her suffering."

"Believe what you want," Delvecchio said disgustedly, as if lecturing an uncomprehending student. "I know I did the right thing."

How can you be so blind? thought Koesler. What an impenetrable set of defense mechanisms you've erected!

"I suppose you've poisoned the mind of Father Tully toward me with your lies. What other calumnies have you invented?"

Koesler was pained that Delvecchio would accuse him of lying.

"First," Koesler said, "this business"—he could not bring himself to call it by its proper name, murder—"with your mother is between us and no one else. For the rest of what I've learned tonight, all I can say is that you have usurped one of God's functions."

"What—!"

"In the Bible it says, 'Vengeance is mine, I will repay, saith the Lord.' But you have proven *yourself* a most vindictive person."

In the examples he was about to offer, Koesler knew he would have to skip over Delvecchio's harsh, cruel treatment of Jan Olivier, late of the Detroit chancery. That event was protected by the Seal of Confession. It could not be discussed even with the penitent unless the penitent gave permission.

But Koesler felt he had more than enough examples of Delvecchio's vengeful bent.

"You, to my knowledge," Koesler said, "never took even the smallest step of reconciliation toward your aunt Martha. She has been estranged from you and the Church for all these years. You thought she was responsible for your mother's fatal illness."

"How many 'small steps' did she take to apologize for what she did?"

"But you're a priest!"

"So?"

Koesler began to sense the probable futility of his hope that Delvecchio would wake up to his own meanness of character. Still, now committed, he plowed on.

"Your brother long ago discarded you. It probably would have worked out better if the separation had been mutual. But Tony hurt you. Your mother's funeral Mass was the last Catholic service Tony participated in. He didn't even attend your ordination as a bishop.

"Making matters even worse for you, Tony was a popular celebrity, especially locally. He was a sports and TV personality. In occasional interviews it came out that he had nothing to do with any organized religion. And you, his brother, a priest, a monsignor, a *bishop*!

"I know that hurt you. And you do not endure hurt stoically; the person who wounded you must suffer too. But you really had little opportunity to strike back until Beth, Tony's significant other, came to you for instructions.

"She couldn't know it at the time, but she was presenting Tony to you on a silver platter.

"On paper, you could justify requiring sexual abstinence of Tony and Beth for the instruction period. On paper you could tack on six more months of not only abstinence but living apart.

"You knew with the knowledge of a close relative that Tony would never stand for a separation that long, especially one requiring him to move out of his home.

"And this with a couple who had lived together a quarter of a century! Even you would not have done this except out of sheer vindictiveness.

"You got at Tony through Beth, and in the process destroyed their relationship—their life together. All you had to do was convince Beth that you had the words of eternal life. And, I must admit, you're pretty good at that—"

"You know, Robert, it's peculiar how we start with similar premises and end with vastly different conclusions. Mother dies at my hand. You think it's murder. I know I saved her from hell.

"And now, as far as our Catholic Church is concerned, Tony and Beth were living in mortal sin. Each time they copulate it's another sin. How can she learn of our moral teaching and continue sinning? How can she prepare for marriage, especially, without showing the good faith of living apart?" Delvecchio spread his hands, indicating the argument was self-evident. *"Res ipsa loquitur."*

"Vince, it was within your power to dispense. How could you have been so rigid, so uncompromising, so lacking in understanding? How could you demand that a man move out of his own home? Especially when you knew the couple had lived together so long? If they committed a sin—and when will you stop being other people's conscience?—it would have happened when they launched their original relationship. They were headed in no other direction than into the arms of Mother Church. Until you drove them away and ruined their lives.

"I wondered about that until it occurred to me that you wanted to punish Tony for having embarrassed and disgraced you—by making it awkward for you as a priest and a bishop to have a fallen-away brother."

"All you've proven," Delvecchio said, "is that you and I treat people differently. And you are, at the very least, an erring bleeding heart. Now, if we can end this—"

"One more thing, Vince. It came to me just this evening. It's practically your signature."

"Well?" Delvecchio, eyes now closed in pain, rubbed his head, as he had off and on during this entire interchange.

"About Lucy and the abortion question. While you had no way of knowing whether she had incurred a penalty, still you accused her of being automatically excommunicated. I believe you did this to scare her, to intimidate her. That would have made it difficult for her to state her case under media scrutiny. Then I came along and let her conscience speak, thus crippling your plan. And so, just as you did with Tony, so did you do to me. All these years, you couldn't get even with Tony because there was no way to reach him. That must have been extremely frustrating. And then eventually you were able to use Beth to get to him.

"I helped your sister in derailing your plan to make her helpless in defending herself. At the time, I didn't know I was upsetting your apple-cart, but I was. So you had to get even with me. But you couldn't; there wasn't anything you could do to me.

"However, as you used Beth to reach Tony, you are trying to use Father Tully to have your revenge on me."

"That's preposterous!"

"Is it? I don't want anything for myself. But I wanted Zack to have St. Joe's parish. You knew you could get to me by making it difficult, or better yet, impossible for Zack to become pastor here. And you easily sensed that Zack had a real problem with the Oath and Profession. All you had to do was demand he swear his fealty in a public ceremony.

"Well, you were right about one thing: He'll never do it. So, you can block his appointment as pastor here. It hasn't been officially announced yet. You'll take a good pastor away from this parish. But you figure you'll have gotten to me. You'll have your revenge."

Delvecchio shrugged. "It's his choice. If he doesn't want to follow the rules, so be it. But he'll never be pastor here, or in any parish in this archdiocese." Then, remembering that he scarcely could speak for all of Detroit's auxiliaries in charge of territories, he added, "At least none of *my* parishes!"

"'The rules,'" Koesler repeated scornfully. "Yes, the rules. Besides speaking with Dr. Moellmann this evening, I also called Pete Jackson and Fred Haun."

Delvecchio, instantly recognizing the names of two priests recently transferred into his bailiwick and named pastors, winced as he realized where Koesler was headed.

"I asked them specifically," Koesler said, "about the Oath and Profession. Haun wondered why I asked. He was in complete agreement with both documents. He had even suggested that the two of you make the taking of these statements a paraliturgical ceremony, inviting the parishioners to attend. You assured him that was not necessary. And in the privacy of the rectory you listened as Haun read the documents.

"I didn't expect such docility from Jackson. And I was right. He's the one, the only one, I believe, who's on record as thinking there's no priest shortage. He said there are already too many. He also told me this evening that if ever he read those documents in your presence, he would follow that with going to confession to you. During which he would confess that it was all a lie. And you couldn't act on it or tell anyone because of the Seal of Confession.

"Now I'm sure he was kidding. But the fact is that he has withstood you. His appointment as pastor is official; he is installed. And he is not going to take the Oath or make the Profession."

"So?"

"So you have on record one pastor who plainly refused to read those documents, even in a private setting. And another pastor who was ready, willing, and eager to read them during a public ceremony. And in Zack Tully you have a priest who cannot in good conscience do this. While you, for your part, are insisting on the public ceremony for Father Tully that you dismissed in the case of Father Jackson."

"So?"

"So, remember when you were trying to deny Christian burial to the deceased wife of George Hackett? You were making up your own rules—demanding more in that case than the Church required. And you were shot down by Cardinal Boyle.

"What if the Cardinal were to be informed that you're at it again? Making up your own rules? Telling one priest to forget an unnecessary ceremony, then demanding the same ceremony of another priest? And what if I let the Cardinal know why you were doing this?"

This open threat was very unlike Father Koesler. And Delvecchio well knew it.

"You . . . you would do that?" the bishop said in a near whisper.

"If you do not promise to back down from insisting that Zack take the Oath and make the Profession, yes. I'm willing to go to the mat on this!"

"What could Boyle do to me?" Delvecchio demanded in a mixture of desperation and bravado. "I'm a bishop!"

"An auxiliary, not an Ordinary. It's simple enough to relieve you of all your functions. You would be bishop of nothing, going nowhere. It's been done. Much tougher to do that to an Ordinary, pretty easy when dealing with an auxiliary."

There was a pause that seemed longer than it actually was.

"Well?" Koesler pressed.

"I . . . I'll think about it."

But Koesler knew he had won the day. He hadn't actually convinced Delvecchio that he ever had failed, that he'd been wrong. That he'd ever sinned. But he had persuaded the bishop that getting even with Koesler through Tully was simply not worth the consequences.

"And now," Delvecchio massaged his forehead with a great deal of pressure, "I'll be going. Here are the documents you want." He tossed the envelope onto the pool table and wordlessly left the basement.

As he stepped out the front door, he came face to face with the two couples just arriving for the retirement party.

Why, they asked, was the bishop leaving? He pleaded a bad headache. The Koznickis and Tullys expressed their concern. The encounter was over in minutes. Delvecchio was gone. The other guests were in the rectory, being greeted by the two priests.

Due to the comparative lateness of the hour, they all went directly to the dining room.

As he took up the rear of this procession, Father Koesler at least knew that this entire matter was finished . . . ended.

Even the theory—unproven and undocumented—that there had been some sort of conspiracy on the part of somebody—one or more of the Delvecchio kids?—either to kill Frank Morris or cause him to take his own life . . . that scenario, Koesler had long since concluded, was nothing more than the pipe dream of an elderly pastor with an extremely active imagination.

All the i's were dotted. All the t's were crossed. There couldn't be anymore to this story.

Could there?

30

Father Koesler hoped the party and light conversation would lift his spirits. After what had gone on in the basement, he needed this convivial gathering.

He knew he had won. But he wished there didn't have to be a loser. He abhorred confrontation and avoided it whenever possible.

This evening it simply hadn't been feasible. He was resolved that Zack Tully be pastor of St. Joe's. All the more so when he'd realized that Zack had become Delvecchio's sacrificial lamb as the means to get back at Koesler.

And Koesler deeply regretted having to dredge up all the unpleasantness of the past. But there was no avoiding it; it was a continuum.

He promised himself that once settled in retirement, he would try to mend his shredded relationship with Vince Delvecchio.

"This is excellent soup, Mary," Anne Marie Tully said.

"Indeed, yes," echoed Wanda Koznicki. "You've got to give us the recipe."

Mary O'Connor chuckled. "Better yet, I'll give you the address of the caterers who made it."

The two officers' wives looked at each other and laughed. "You not only could, you *did* fool us," Anne Marie said.

"Say," Zoo Tully said to his brother, "that bishop we met on our way in: Is he the one you told us was giving you a hard time about something?"

"Uh-huh," Father Tully affirmed.

"Well," the lieutenant pressed, "did it work out okay? You gonna be pastor here, and our neighbor as well?"

Father Tully had no clue how the meeting between Koesler and Delvecchio had gone. The bishop's departure had coincided with the arrival of the guests. Tully hadn't had any opportunity to quiz Koesler.

274

Now, with the question on the table, as it were, Tully looked inquiringly at Koesler, who smiled and nodded reassuringly.

"I guess," Tully said to his brother, "it all worked out. I'm going to be your neighbor. And," he added quickly, "your pastor. Somehow I've got to get you in the fold."

"Good luck," Anne Marie said.

Soup course finished, Mary O'Connor was clearing away the bowls.

"And how about yourself, Father," Inspector Koznicki asked Koesler, "have you firmed up your retirement plans? You will continue living here, I assume."

"No." Koesler shook his head. "No in answer to both questions. Much as I would like to stay here—inertia being so basic a part of my life—the diocese prefers that a Senior Priest move on. It makes sense to clear the old guard out and let the new pastor do things his way without some parishioner appealing a decision to one or the other. No whipsawing.

"But," he continued, "I don't have any firm plans for after retirement. Not even where I'm going to live. So"—he turned to Zack—"I hope our new pastor will tolerate me a little while longer."

The two priests, smiling, inclined their heads in a mutual bow.

"The future for me," Koesler said, after a moment's thought, "is kind of exciting, I think. There's just all sorts of things opening up. I could go back to school, travel, baby-sit parishes, see if they want me to teach in the seminary, take in some theater—I haven't done much of that lately . . . Or," he added, "all of the above."

"Or," Lieutenant Tully suggested, "you might continue solving crimes." He turned to the inspector as if for affirmation, then back to Koesler. "We can use all the help we can get.

"And," he added, "though I didn't think so when we first met, I've got to admit: You've got a knack for it."

Everyone laughed.

"This is funny," Inspector Koznicki said, "but the other evening we were watching a rerun of that detective series, "Diagnosis Murder," where Dick Van Dyke plays a physician who is a consultant to the local police department. And"—he smiled at Koesler—"I thought of you."

Koesler's brow knitted; he looked at his longtime friend. "That thought never entered my mind. But"—he grinned—"as James Bond says, Never say never."

The party was doing the trick. Father Koesler was feeling increasingly relaxed.

* * *

Bishop Vincent Delvecchio was feeling increasingly distressed as he drove north on Woodward Avenue toward his parish.

He never should have agreed to tonight's meeting with Bob Koesler. To all appearances, Bob was feeling fine; whereas he himself was under the weather, to say the very least.

Vince could not recall a headache ever afflicting him as agonizingly as this one was. Undoubtedly, that argument with Bob had worsened his condition.

Even compromised as he was by that horrible pain, he'd done pretty well in the thrust and parry with Bob—until it came to the matter of Tully's taking the Oath and Profession.

Vincent knew that Cardinal Boyle did not much like him. That was evidenced when he was about to deny Church burial to Hackett's wife. Boyle had come down on him pretty hard.

Clever of Bob to bring up that incident! Vince's demand that Tully take the Oath publicly would look silly in the context of Vince's having turned down Fred Haun's proposal for a similar public ceremony. Added to which was Pete Jackson's flat-out refusal to swear—an unfortunate precedent. Boyle would never support his bishop when he heard all that.

How had Bob found out about Hackett?

It must've been Joe McCarthy.

McCarthy and Jackson! True, the Church needed priests, but if Vince were an ordinary, his priests would know they would be disciplined. Priest shortage or not!

Bob was wrong in citing Beth and Tully as means to get even with

Tony and him. That was because Bob didn't trust in providence as Vince did. Beth and Tully had been sent to Vincent by God to make His will done on earth as it is in heaven. It was cruel of Bob to think otherwise.

Ohhh! The pain in Vince's head forced a moan from his lips. After all, why shouldn't God provide Vince a special measure of Divine Providence? He had passed the test with that Olivier woman. And besides the woman, Bob was the only one who knew about Vince's major temptation.

The pain was becoming close to unbearable. It brought to mind his mother. Perhaps he should join his suffering with that of Christ, as Bob claimed his mother had.

She couldn't have done that . . . not without confiding in Vince. No, it was crystal clear what she'd intended to use the morphine for. God may not have granted the miracle cure he'd prayed for, but God surely was not going to let Mother condemn herself to hell as a result of the greatest evil.

If anyone on earth, anyone in all of history, understood what Vincent had to do, it was Mother.

He was driving a steady fifty mph, the official speed limit on this section of Woodward's boulevard. He would keep the law even though he yearned to be home in bed coping with all this pain.

He thought again of Bob Koesler. He may have won this confrontation, but there would be others. Vince would even the score. He would triumph for God.

Bob probably was enjoying himself tonight. But even though he was retiring, there would be a way to get at him. If nothing else, Vince could depend on Divine Providence.

A pain like nothing he had ever experienced washed over him like an angry wave.

He ducked involuntarily as if he could somehow elude this overpowering throbbing. When he raised his head he realized he was about to hit the left-hand curb. He tried to swerve, but it was too late; he and his car were hurtling across the median strip.

The Greatest Evil

Flashing before his eyes was the image from his favorite morality tale: the disgraced priest flying off the freeway hell-bent on suicide. The greatest evil. But Vince wasn't attempting suicide. This was an . . .

The car was almost wrapped around a huge tree.

Vince was above the car now. Everything seemed quite peaceful. He looked down and saw two wheels spinning in place.

Then he seemed to be somewhere else. It was dark—very dark. There was a light in the distance. It was moving toward him. It was . . . his mother. Her arms were open to him. Then she faded. It was dark again.

For some reason he dreaded what was to come.

*　　*　　*